A Druid
Rises

A Druid Rises
Copyright © 2023 by L.R. Kreutzinger

Additional copies may be ordered from the publisher for educational,
business, promotional or premium use.
For information, contact ALIVE Book Publishing at:
alivebookpublishing.com

Edited by Ashlyn Daniels and Chad Kreutzinger
Cover art by Jessica Warren
Map art by Evan Kreutzinger
Book design by Alex P. Johnson

ISBN 13
978-1-63132-217-4

Library of Congress Control Number: 2023919482

Library of Congress Cataloging-in-Publication Data
is available upon request.

First Edition

Published in the United States of America by ALIVE Book Publishing
an imprint of Advanced Publishing LLC
3200 A Danville Blvd., Suite 204, Alamo, California 94507
alivebookpublishing.com

PRINTED IN THE UNITED STATES OF AMERICA

10 9 8 7 6 5 4 3 2 1

A Druid Rises

L.R. Kreutzinger

ABOOKS
Alive Book Publishing

CHAPTER 1

The autumn breeze shook the remaining leaves from the branches of the tall trees. Scattering them from where they had started as small nubs. Gliding through the air without control, they drifted further from where they once were. Giving signs that seasons were changing and winter would soon be arriving. Secluded in a valley surrounded by hills and mountains rested the village of Orinton. Nestled in a forest with a river to the north and one far to the east, no major trade routes passed through. It was a village built by those trying to escape the conflicts between rival lords generations ago. They were simple people who lived off the land and their surroundings, with an average population of nearly two hundred. No walls or evident borders marked where the village started or ended, just the seemingly endless forest and the bank of the northern river. Many lived only a short walking distance to the center of Orinton, marked by a grand hall of the Bastin family. Some had built homes and trade shops within sight of the hall. While others lived further into the woods, hunting, fishing, and gathering from what the forest provided. A few families had small farms on the patches of cleared land among the trees, but they needed to be more significant to support many villagers.

A boy, age fourteen, ran between the trees on the outskirts of Orinton. His dark green wool jacket flowed in the air like a cape since it was too large for his small frame. He was swinging his hatchet at the trunks of trees.

Imagining himself a great warrior, defeating faceless foes. "You are not welcome here, elf!" The boy yelled, gripping the hatchet's handle tight. His eyes fixed on a knot in a tree where a branch had broken off, resembling a face. "Ahhhh!" He shrieked as he charged. With a heavy swing, the hatchet blade dug deep into the tree. The boy took a few steps back and smiled at his precision. The hatchet head was deep in the center of the knot. He grabbed the handle and yanked, but the hatchet did not budge. He tried tugging it out with both hands, but the head did not come free.

"Shouldn't you be helping instead of out here, attacking defenseless trees, Owen?" A voice called out.

Owen quickly turned to see his older friend Hendric walking towards him with four rabbits hanging by strings in his left hand. He was covered in his sheepskin hunting outfit to ward the cold away. It had been a successful morning of hunting deep in the woods, but a deer would have been much better.

"I did help," Owen said as he tried to tug the hatchet free once more.

"There are many more things to be done before the storms come," Hendric said as he reached over Owen's shoulder and pulled the hatchet from the tree with one hand.

"I helped!" Owen shrieked. "I cut firewood. I fed Herrah's goats. I even helped your mother fix the loose step to your house," Owen said pridefully as Hendric handed him his hatchet.

Hendric looked down with a grin towards Owen. "Thank you for coming to the aid of my mother." He said as he ruffled Owen's blonde hair with his hand. "You know there is much more to do instead of you out here fighting trees."

"Fine," Owen said as his shoulders slacked, and he slid his hatchet back into his belt. He then started walking with Hendric toward the center of Orinton. Taking one last glance at the slit in the knot of the tree. *I'll be back to finish you off.* He thought in his head.

Hendric was tall for seventeen, taller than most of the men in Orinton, particularly since he would always stand up straight. He was in peak physical condition with broad shoulders and not overly muscular arms. His brown hair was long, hanging down to his shoulders, an average hairstyle among the men of Orinton. He was rugged-looking by the short brown beard he had finally been able to grow. Making his dark green eyes stand out even more.

Owen was of average height for his age and thin. His dark blonde hair was cut short on the sides and back. The hair on the top of his head was parted on the right side and hung down to his eyebrows, so his blue eyes were still visible. It was the same haircut his mother always gave him since childhood. Convincing him that it was the most handsome look on his face since he wanted to grow his hair out to match Hendric's. His thick wool jacket, once Hendric's, was worn thin and oversized for him. With holes that had been stitched together by his mother since the two did not have enough to buy him a new one. He stood straight while walking beside Hendric as if trying to imitate him. He had looked up to Hendric like an older brother since his father abandoned him and his mother before he could remember.

"So. What monsters were you fighting today?" Hendric asked as they made their way past a few outlying houses.

"I was fighting elves,"

"Does the hero in your mom's stories ever fight elves?"

"No... but since most of the other men went to fight in the war against elves... I thought...." Owen said nervously as he glanced up and saw Hendric's face grow sorrowful at the mention of fighting elves.

Owen knew that just the mere mentioning of elves was tough for Hendric. Four months ago, his father and two older brothers left with most of the men of Orinton to fight the Ellious Empire, an empire of elves. It was a war that Owen did not entirely understand. He heard rumors the Ellious Empire had been expanding into Miterra for many decades. The Empire took food, supplies, and even some people from noble families in other towns and villages. However, the Ellious Empire had never come to Orinton. Nor had Owen ever seen an elf, for that matter. It all seemed like another of his mother's fanciful stories to him. That was until Duke Chalin called on all the fighting men of his fiefdom to go to war. Then, the stories became suddenly real to him.

"There are still many things you can help with instead of being out in the woods playing," Hendric sternly added, snapping Owen out of his reverie.

"Alright, Hendric," Owen said, not wanting to aggravate him.

"Here, take these." Hendric separated two rabbits from the bunch and handed the strings to Owen. "At least make it so it looks like you have been helping instead of playing,"

"Are we taking these to Kenet, the butcher?" Owen asked as he looked at the two hanging rabbits.

"We're taking them to Gustoll. He asked for a few rabbits yesterday and wanted the first pick," Hendric answered as they turned toward the Hall of Orinton.

"Wouldn't he want them cleaned before cooking them?"

Owen asked, thinking how messy it was to clean rabbits for cooking. An experience he would rather not repeat, but his mother insisted he learned.

"Gustoll is nothing like his son Lord Willhem. Gustoll does things himself. Including cleaning and cooking his own rabbits." Hendric added. "He would probably be out there hunting them with me if his knee didn't hurt after walking a mile," The large Hall of Orinton came into view between the trees and the other buildings that made the village center.

The hall was the largest and oldest building in the small village. The Bastin family built it generations ago, one of the first families to settle in the valley. The long hall's exterior walls were constructed of logs on top of each other, with some windows along the sides. The roof was high and vaulted with two tiers to allow the smoke from fires within to escape and covered with long clay tiles to prevent embers from igniting the top. The wooden steps in front led to thick wooden double doors that made the main entrance to the hall. It was constructed large enough to house the six founding families during the first winter when the other houses were being built. Later, the hall became the village's meeting place until its population grew more extensive than the hall could fit.

The two large doors were ornamented with twenty sets of deer antlers. Many of the antlers were brittle from the sun, only being allowed to be replaced when the ruling lord brought a buck down. Something Lord Willhelm did not have the talent for, like his father Gustoll or his father before him. Leaving many of the antlers grey for too many summers.

Five smaller houses and one granary formed an uneven

circle in front of the hall. Each was made of thick-hewn planks with mud covering them and triangular thatch roofs that later became the village center as it grew. Each was initially built as a home, except one designed to store food. Over the years, some families built houses outside the village center. They repurposed a few central buildings for trades like woodworking, butcher, and seamstressing. A seventh building was built years after for blacksmithing that wedged itself into one of the large gaps between the original buildings.

As Owen and Hendric grew closer to the village center, they noticed some women gathered. Many of them whispering to each other, glancing at the hall's two enormous wooden front doors. A look of worry was on all their faces. A few of them were even crying quietly.

"What is going on?" Owen asked Hendric, thinking it was strange.

"I am not sure," Hendric responded as he spotted a riding horse with full saddlebags tied to a post. Horses were rarely seen in the village center, as the stables were a short distance away. He scanned the crowd and spotted his mother, Cassan, standing with a small group of women. Hendric stopped after a few steps as Tavia came into his view from the seamstress's shop. Tavia's light blue eyes met Hendric's. Quickly, she swept aside some strands of her wavy blonde hair with her free hand as she started to walk towards the two boys, carrying a basket of blankets.

Tavia was a year older than Hendric. He had found her beautiful since he was a young boy, and so had many others, making her out of Hendric's reach. The last four months since most of the men had left allowed them the chance to grow closer, much closer than Hendric had ever thought he would have the opportunity to be with her.

"Hello, Tavia," Hendric said eagerly as she neared. A large grin grew on his face at just the sight of her. "Do you know what's happening?"

"A rider arrived with news of the war. Lord Gustoll took him into the hall before anyone else could hear what he had to say." Owen's eyes shifted to the large doors to the hall, and he began to walk towards them, leaving Hendric and Tavia to talk to each other.

Owen's eyes fixed on the double doors to the hall as he approached the wooden steps. He half-expected someone to stop him, but no one said a word. The right door slightly ajar, Owen squeezed his body through the opening as he heard Gustoll's deep voice far from within.

The hall was full of shadows from the several dying flames in the large, rectangular fire pit. There were some tables and benches, dimly lit, towards the front. A single shaft of sunlight through a gap in the tiered roof was the only significant light in the back of the room where Gustoll and another man stood over a table. Owen quickly moved out of the door and shuffled behind one of the nearby wood pillars holding the roof.

Owen peered around to better look at Gustoll and the man standing in the sunlight. The sun shone brightly on Gustoll's bald head as he read a piece of yellow parchment rolling up at the sides. The bright sunlight made his short grey beard white color. He stood straight, under his cloak made from the skin of a brown bear that left three long scars going down the left side of his weathered face. His bare arms were scared from years of fighting against bears, orcs, elves, humans, and monsters. The most recent scare was from an elven arrow that pierced him in the knee a few years ago. Making it so he could no longer walk long distances and had knee pain every cold day.

The other man was tan, even sunburnt. He was of average height and had long black hair pulled back, hanging between his shoulders. His torso, shoulders, and upper arms were covered in dirty, worn leather armor held together by small rings.

Owen noticed a sword on the left side of the man's belt, hanging under a large leather bag full of rolled-up parchments of different shades of yellow. The sword looked different from other swords he had seen. This sword had a thin blade that was curved towards the tip. The hilt was small and rounded like a golden clam shell. There were no straight lines, only curves as if it were... *elven*. Owen thought to himself.

"How long ago did my son write this letter, Balthis?" Gustoll said to the man as his brows scrunched while reading what was written on the parchment.

"Three weeks ago," Balthis responded.

Gustoll looked at Balthis. "It says that Horden and Min were injured during a raid on supply wagons. What can you tell me about their injuries?"

Owen continued to inch deeper into the room to listen better. He was so excited that he did not think about the two rabbits he carried with him. Moving from pillar to table, he froze mid-step when he heard the names Horden and Min. *Why would Horden be fighting? He makes pots and clay sculptures. He doesn't even know how to use a bow.*

"I do not. I only received the letter from Lord Willhelm to deliver here since he knew I was riding this way to tell people the war's progress and to request more supplies." Balthis responded.

Gustoll looked back at the letter, his hand caressing his beard. "And how is the war progressing?"

"We pushed back the Ellious legions to Fort Gwenil and Fort Eldis," Balthis said and cracked a grin. "Forced them, pointy-eared bastards, south faster than we expected. They should be off Miterra lands and into the Alphis mountains in a month."

Gustoll scoffed at what Balthis had said. "It will not be as easy as you think."

"They are running away." Balthis retorted.

"They are now in defensive positions behind high walls of stone," Gustoll said in a severe tone. "This is not some squabble between Dukes about a piece of land or a lord's manhood being mocked; these are elves. Led by commanders who have been fighting and studying war for over a hundred years."

"We outnumber them three to one," Balthis said with confidence.

"A dragon does not care that the wolves outnumber it," Gustoll said as his gaze met Balthis's eyes.

"Then why…" Balthis began to retort from having what he stated questioned. But was interrupted as the large door to the hall opened slowly.

Owen tried to squeeze himself and the two rabbits he held under a table and behind a bench so he could not easily be seen from the open door. Catching a glimpse of Cinda walk in.

Cinda Bastin was Lord Willhem's only daughter and Gustoll's granddaughter. She was viewed as a figure of pure beauty by Owen and many in the village. Her thick hair was dark red with copper-colored highlights, a hair color only shared with her mother, who had passed away years ago.

She usually wore her hair in a ponytail, but this time, her hair was damp, hanging over her shoulders. The natural waves curved around her face as if crafted by the god Forus himself. It was obvious she had just returned from her daily swim in a secluded pool fed from the river to the north when the weather permitted. Unlike many other women in the village, her skin was soft, without scars or blemishes. A sign of the life of privilege her father had given her. Her eyes were unique as well. Indoors, they were a light brown, but they had a shimmer like a dark yellow topaz in the sunlight. It made her eyes almost otherworldly to behold.

Seeing her made Balthis stop his arguing as he could not help but stare at Cinda while she walked through the hall toward him and Gustoll. Her thin white dress swayed with each step she took.

"Is it just the two of you in here?" Cinda asked in confusion and slight fear from not knowing who Balthis was or what news he carried.

"Just us and Owen," Gustoll answered.

Owen's eyes opened wide at the sound of his name being said. He froze where he was, afraid to move.

"Where is Owen?" Cinda asked as she looked around from where she was, only a few strides away from where Gustoll and Bastin stood.

"He is hiding behind that table," Gustoll said as he motioned with his chin toward the area Owen was in. "You can come out, Owen."

As Owen climbed out from under the table, Balthis quickly spoke. "I thought you wanted to have this conversation in private."

"Owen does not have a father or brothers fighting in this war. So he would not overreact at the mention of a family member." Gustoll said as Owen came into view.

"How long have you known I was here?" Owen asked quietly as he fidgeted with the strings holding the rabbits. His eyes looked at the ground and not directly at anyone out of embarrassment.

"Since you slid through the doors," Gustoll answered. "You are not as sneaky as you might think." He added with a grin on his face.

"I brought the rabbits you wanted," Owen murmured sheepishly as he presented the two rabbits to Gustoll. His head still looking down.

"Thank you for that," Gustoll replied with a slight nod before turning to face Balthis. "You have told me all I need to know, Balthis. You should go on your way. Tell the other villages the news about the war."

"What of the supplies?" Balthis asked as he closed and buckled the flap to the leather bag he carried on his hip.

"We can spare the full amount of arrows but only half the amount of food you ask for,"

"Only half!" Balthis responded in a sharp tone.

"Any more, and the people here would starve," Gustoll answered calmly. "No point in our men fighting if there is no village to return to." Gustoll could see Belthis's jaw clenching with anger. "Was this war not started because the Ellious Empire took more from people than they could spare?" Gustoll added as he shifted his body to face Balthis, solid and unwavering. "We should not trade an elven slipper on our throat for the boot of Duke Chalin."

Owen watched as the quiet tension between Gustoll and Balthis grew briefly until Balthis stepped back. "When can we expect your supplies to be sent?" Balthis asked as he calmed his tone.

Gustoll relaxed as well, feeling the tension dissipating between them. "I shall send Korgan with all we can spare in a few days."

Balthis begrudgingly bowed. "Thank you. I shall inform Duke Chalin of your support, Lord Gustoll." He said with a spiteful tone. He then turned and walked past Cinda and out of the hall.

Cinda looked up at Gustoll as Owen walked around the tables to get closer. "Is father returning from the war soon, grandpa?" She asked kindly.

Gustoll struggled to step towards a chair and quickly sat in it. He looked up at Cinda and Owen as they stood close to him, his eyes full of worry. "With only Duke Chalin willing to go to war against the Ellious Empire, and the other four Dukes not sending aid... I am afraid they won't be returning soon."

* * *

Hendric stood alone in his dimly lit room from the candles he had around. He placed a skin of water, a large pouch of dried berries, and some dried meat slices into his pack for his hunting trip, preparing for the cold nights ahead. It was an easy plan; Gustoll asked him to venture into the mountains to the northwest for a few days to see if the deer were soon migrating near Orinton. A source of food and hides that Gustoll was hoping would come earlier since so many hunters were gone fighting. Hendric did not mind the trip, feeling perfectly at home in the woods. As he finished packing, he heard a soft knock at the closed shutters of his window.

"It's me," Tavia whispered from the other side of the

wooden panel.

Hendric quickly opened the shutters, seeing Tavia's beautiful face, his heart pumping quicker as she smiled at him seductively. "Hi," he whispered back, knowing his mother was just now going to sleep only two walls away in her room.

"Can I come in?" Tavia asked quietly as she smiled at Hendric and bit her lower lip slowly.

Hendric swallowed hard and glanced at his closed bedroom door. *If we are quiet, I'm sure Mother won't notice.* He turned and looked back at Tavia, "Of course," he whispered excitedly as his breath quickened. He loved these moments of being alone with Tavia. Typically, it was in the forest or when his mother was not home.

Tavia raised her arms and leaned into the window as Hendric quickly hugged her and lifted her into his room. She slowly ran her fingernail down the side of his neck and shirt as he lowered her down. "I was hoping to give you some memories to keep you warm while you are out there," Tavia whispered, her fingers traveling slowly down Hendric's chest and stomach.

Hendric quickly removed his shirt, giving Tavia pause before she leaned up and kissed him passionately. The sweetness of her lips made Hendric's mind blank. All he could think about was touching her. As they kissed, Tavia slowly pushed Hendric backward to his bed and pushed him over. She looked down at him with a devilish smile as she crawled over him. Hendric pulled his blanket over them to share each other's warmth.

"Try not to be too loud this time," Tavia whispered into Hendric's ear.

"I'll try not to," Hendric whispered with a smile and

turned his head to kiss her again. He held her against him as they shifted in the bed together. They felt nothing but each other in those moments, no war, no coming winter, just the two of them; nothing else existed. That is until Hendric let out a loud, involuntary moan.

Tavia held still, looking down at Hendric as they recovered. "Think you woke your mother with that?" trying hard not to giggle from the nervous tension.

They both lay in silence, listening for movement on the other side of the bedroom door. Hendric couldn't help but think about Tavia as she sat above him.

After a few moments of silence, Tavia asked, "What would you do if your mom did walk in and see me here?" as she slowly ran her nails over Hendric's bare chest.

"Cover you with the sheet, I guess," Hendric responded uncertainly. They both quietly laughed at the thought, neither knowing what to do in such a situation.

They had only done anything like this a few times before, but those few times were enough for Hendric to know he never wanted this feeling to end. He thought about Tavia constantly and tried to spend as much time as possible with her, but she often seemed busy, except at night when they could be together.

"My father will be taking the supplies for Duck Chalin South tomorrow or the day after," Tavia whispered as her head rested on hendric's shoulder. "Maybe we can fall asleep in each other's arms for once."

"Will Korgan be gone long?"

"A few weeks at least. Even more, if he stops at every tavern between here and there."

"It would be nice to wake up next to you," Hendric whispered as he moved so his eyes could meet Tavia's. He looked at them deeply as he slowly moved his hand to lightly touch her cheek. "Tavia… I love you." Even though he whispered it, he was unsure if he truly loved her. He had strong feelings for Tavia, much like the ones older couples described when talking about love, and he just let it out without genuinely thinking. The words, however, felt right as they left his mouth.

Tavia's eyes widened with surprise. She smiled, looked at him peacefully, and leaned to kiss him. *I love you.* Tavia repeated the words in her head, not out of feelings for Hendric but out of hate. Those words haunted her. Memories from childhood. Always heard her father, Korgan, saying them to her mother when he finished hurting her out of drunken anger. As if those three words made everything he did to her and her mother alright. *Love. Such a silly thing. Does Hendric know what that means or how close it is to hate?* She finished kissing Hendric and looked at him reassuringly, unsure how else to react. It was not that she did not like Hendric, but she knew she did not have deep feelings for him. Being wanted. Being seen. Those were the moments. Moments where she could forget her life. That was what she craved. Nothing more. He was sweet to her, much more precious than any other man she had been with. For that, she did not want to hurt him. So she smiled and avoided the truth of her feelings.

"I should be on my way, " Tavia said as she got up from the bed, quickly fixing her dress so it was not bunched around her thighs. "Have a safe trip, Hendric. I'll see you when you get back." She then climbed out the window and blew him a kiss before running into the moonlit night, leaving Hendric standing at the window alone, thinking of her.

* * *

A gloomy rain passed over Orinton in the morning as if to match the sorrow and worry the villagers had for loved ones who weren't there. The harshness of the war touched many of them after hearing the news of Horden and Min being injured the day before. The first of their village to be hurt bad enough to be mentioned in one of Wilhelm's letters. The people of Orinton were quiet as they gathered food, arrows, bowstrings, bandages, ointments for healing, and personal letters to loved ones for Korgan to take to their families. He loaded it all into his unhitched wagon in the village center.

Gustoll found the short-lived rainstorm a blessing, brief enough to show holes in the roof of the food storage building, and they could fix them without the burden of working in the rain. After leaving instructions on what was needed to be packed into the wagon, he quickly gathered a few of the boys to the center of the village. Hoping to teach them how to repair the thatch roofs of the building.

"There is a leak on the lower section," Gustoll yelled at Conner as he watched the boy trying to move around on the thatch roof. Pointing out with his finger where Conner needed to go. Gustoll chose him to be on the roof since he was the oldest and strongest of the group. Kervin and Seby tied bundles of water reeds and other dried grasses they could use while the younger twins, Frin and Derin, gathered more materials.

Conner quickly moved to the section Gustoll pointed to, finding that a rat had made its home in the roof. "I am probably going to need a few bundles for this section,"

Conner called back to Gustoll as he started pulling up sections of the roof to find the extent to which the rat had made its home.

"Have you seen Owen, Gustoll?" Tavia's voice rang out from behind Gustoll as he watched Conner.

Gustoll turned and saw Tavia struggling with a goat, holding it by the horns. "I have not."

"Herrah's goats are wandering around, and I need Owen's help," Tavia said with clenched teeth as the goat struggled to escape her grasp.

Gustoll rushed to her side, grabbing one of the goat's horns in his hand. He then noticed a few more goats. "Where is Herrah?" He asked, surprised she would have let the goats wander so far from Harrah's small farm.

"I am not sure. No one has seen her," Tavia answered.

"You go and find Owen. I will send Kervin and Seby to help take the goats back to Herrah." Gustoll said as he struggled to gain control of the goat. "Kervin, Seby," He called out, getting their attention. "You two gather those goats over there, and any other goats you find, take them back to Herrah's," Gustoll ordered, and both boys complied quickly.

"Thank you. I'll be back as soon as I find him. He is probably off fighting trees again."

"When you find him and get the goats back to Herrah, tell Owen to come and find me," Gustoll said, and then Tavia turned and walked away.

He didn't discipline Owen harshly for falling short of his responsibilities. He liked Owen's sense of adventure and carefree spirit. Owen reminded him of himself at that age. His own son, Willhelm, preferred talking, planning, and delegating. Which made him a much better leader than

Gustoll could be. This caused Gustoll to gladly step down from being the leader of Orinton and Willhelm to take his role. Those thoughts quickly left when he spotted Cinda walking out of the hall.

"Cinda, come help me with this goat," Gustoll yelled to his granddaughter.

Cinda quickly turned and looked at her grandfather, seeing him with the horn of the goat in his hand and an expression that he had when about to instruct her. She had seen it many times these past few months since her father left. "What is it now?" Cinda asked reluctantly, knowing her grandfather was about to make her do something that would have a lesson.

"You are going to take this goat to Herrah," Gustoll said kindly, emphasizing for Cinda to do it while the goat struggled against his strength.

Cinda walked closer to Gustoll, feeling much like the goat, caught in his grasp and unable to free herself of the task. "You know my father doesn't want me doing such things," she said, feeling sympathy for the animal since neither wanted to be in their current position.

"If Willhelm had it his way, you would not even be allowed out of your room," Gustoll said with his eyebrow raised. "I showed you how to control a goat last week. I want to see if you remember."

Cinda let out a breath of defeat as her shoulders went slack.

"Just come here and take the goat," Gustoll said as a look of intolerance grew.

He was not angry but more discouraged. He knew Willhelm had become overprotective of Cinda after her mother died a few years ago from a fever. Treating the young woman more like a living doll to be seen and not a person who needs to know how to be a part of the village. Helping the others and surviving in the world, something he hoped to remedy since Willhelm left to fight four months ago.

Cinda walked reluctantly to the goat and slowly stretched out her hand, reaching for the goat's horn, her soft fingers barely touching the rough ridges. The goat suddenly flailed about. Its head twisted, and its body swung around, slamming its back hip into Cinda's thigh. The impact was quicker than Cinda could react, knocking her down. Her bottom landed in the cold, soft mud with a thud while Gustoll grasped the goat and pulled it away from Cinda to prevent it from kicking her with its hind legs.

"I told you my father didn't want me doing this!" Cinda snapped at Gustoll as she lifted her now mud-covered palms. Looking at her dirty hands, she heard the snicker of a child nearby. Quickly, she turned and saw not only a little girl watching her but many other villagers, all with looks of doubt or grins as they whispered to each other. *Now they are all laughing at me.* She stood up, feeling embarrassed and disgraced.

"Are you alright?" Gustoll asked kindly as he let go of the goat and pushed it away.

Cinda looked at the back of the blue dress she had spent so much time preparing and ensuring was perfect earlier that morning. Now, the back of the skirt was covered in mud and wet to her skin. "I'm fine," she growled as she shook her hands, flinging the large clumps of soil from them.

"Sorry, the goat..." Gustoll said hesitantly, unsure what to say to Cinda, trying to be sympathetic but worried this might have closed her off to learning new things more than she already was.

"My father did not want me doing this kind of work for a reason. There is no point in me herding goats when I am supposed to be married to a lord in a grand castle, not here in the mud," Cinda angrily said to Gustoll. She looked down at herself, thinking about how she must look at that moment. "I'm going to get changed," Cinda said as she turned and started to walk away, not only upset with Gustoll for making her do things her father would never ask of her but also at the people around who just laughed at her. Her shame began to rise, part of her hating that she was useless in the eyes of many in the village, but she knew she had to do as her father asked to stay graceful in the eyes of lords and ladies. Because after she turned seventeen, she would be expected to marry.

* * *

Tavia searched for Owen, asking everyone she came across if they had seen him. She was told Owen had walked deeper into the woods not long ago. Tavia was quick to pursue, striding through the forest. Her anger only grew more with each step. She disliked searching for Owen as she still had to help prepare her father's wagon.

"Psst," Tavia heard coming from some bushes after walking for a distance.

"Owen, is that you?"

Owen quietly emerged from the bush with his finger over his mouth. "Shhh." He then moved his finger and whispered, "Be quiet."

"What are you doing out here?" Tavia whispered back

angrily. She then noticed the slight look of fear in Owen's eyes and crouched down. "What is it?"

Owen looked around a tree and then back at Tavia. "I saw something...in the woods."

"What did you see?" Tavia whispered as her mind started to panic, thinking Owen had spotted a pack of wolves and knew they were far from the closest house to find help.

Owen grabbed her hand and pulled her to the bushes to look around the other side. "I'm not sure. It was strange, like a floating torch," he said quietly.

"You saw people carrying torches?"

"No, it was like the fire from a torch, but it was floating," Owen whispered with conviction.

Tavia looked at him questionably. "Did you eat any of those mushrooms that Kenet likes?" Tavia asked, concerned, knowing Kenet would make outlandish claims after suffering the effects of the mushrooms.

Owen looked at her with a stern face. "No, I haven't."

"Owen, I think it's time we went back to the village," Tavia said, not believing what Owen said.

"No, there is something out there," Owen said. "We need to find it."

Tavia stood up and took Owen's hand firmly, pulling him out of the bushes. "We need to get back to the village,"

Owen struggled to free himself, but Tavia's grip was too tight. "We need to find it."

"We need to go back," Tavia said in a frustrated tone as she continued to pull, Owen still fighting every step.

"There it is!" Owen gasped.

Tavia quickly turned her head, her eyes opening wide with amazement.

It was not a torch but a glowing red ball about the size of her fist. She watched in disbelief as the glowing orb slowly drifted through the air about a stone's throw away from them. Moving among the trees, raising and lowering like a giant bug slowly flying around. Different shades of red moved within the ball, making it look as if it was alive. Yet, the light of it would brighten and fade. It faded so much that it would disappear for a few moments and reappear.

"What is it?" Tavia asked, mostly thinking out loud. But that still didn't stop Owen from answering.

"I'm not sure," Owen said quietly as if his voice might scare it away. "I saw it near the village and followed it out here."

"Has it done anything else?" Tavia asked.

"No, it's just been floating around."

"Have you gotten a good look at it?"

"No, it stays away from me, like it's watching me and doesn't want to talk."

"What makes you think it can talk?" Tavia asked as she took a slow step towards it. The orb continued to float in a small area.

"I thought maybe it was a fairy, like in the stories we were told," Owen answered as he took a few steps closer.

Tavia was about to ask more questions but was interrupted by screams in the distance towards the village.

CHAPTER 2

Gustoll watched as Conner lowered himself down the ladder from the roof. "You did a good job, Conner," Gustoll said with encouragement. He then handed Conner his old, elven, silver coin he held on to so it would not fall from the boy's pocket while on the roof. It was a strange keepsake to Gustoll, but the coin was given to Conner by his father before he left to fight the elves. Conner never went anywhere without it, believing he would lose his father if he lost the coin.

"Thank you for keeping it safe," Conner said as he took the coin and placed it in his pocket.

Gustoll did not reply as he looked around for other boys supposed to be helping them. Thinking it was strange that they had not returned.

"What's wrong?" Conner asked Gustoll, seeing the look of concern in his eyes.

"Derin and Frin never came back with more water reeds from the river," Gustoll said. "Also, Kervin and Seby have not returned from taking the goats back to Herrah's,"

"Maybe Herrah cooked them some food," Conner suggested.

"Mmmm," Gustoll mumbled as he looked around, noticing two goats were still wandering about. "Something is wrong. Herrah would not have fed them if goats were still missing." He looked around from where he stood. Noticing that Korgan's wagon was only half full. He quickly strode to the wagon, leaving Conner behind confused. He looked at what food was packed. *There is no flower, barley, eggs, or anything from the small farms on the outskirts of the village.*

"What is it?" Conner asked as he walked up to Gustoll and peered into the wagon.

Gustoll looked at the tree line around the village center. He hoped to see a glimpse of movement but saw none. No squirrels or birds were in view like they usually were. The goats were wandering among the buildings, far from the fresh green grass, closer to the trees. It seemed quiet out in the forest.

"They are coming!" Cassan yelled while running towards the village center from the single road leading south.

Gustoll quickly moved to Cassan as others stopped what they were doing and walked into the interior of the village center to see what was happening. As he got to her, he grabbed her by the shoulders. "Who is coming?" he asked in a panic, his mind flaring with fear. Cassan looked into Gustoll's eyes with panic on her face. Struggling to get air in her lungs. "They're coming... on... horses... Ten of them."

"Who!?" Gustoll shouted.

"Elves," Cassan said to Gustoll in between breaths. The other people gathering around them began to panic with fear.

Gustoll felt his heart sink at the mention of the word. *Impossible. The elves are far south from here. Why would they even come to Orinton? There is no reason for them to travel here. I didn't even think they knew about this village.*

Gustoll looked down the road and spotted the horses and their riders trotting towards them from around the bend. His eyes fixed on them, thinking about what to do. He knew out of the entire village, only a few could fight. There was no possibility the villagers could defend themselves if events took a turn for the worse.

"There are others over there!" a woman's voice shrieked. Gustoll quickly turned and saw a group of women running between buildings from two elves on foot in the tree line.

"Grandpa!" Cinda yelled as she and a few other women with their kids ran into the village center from near the hall, wearing a loose dress, unlike the formal one she had on before. "There are elves in the trees to the north of the village," she said when she got near Gustoll.

Gustoll looked at the column of elves riding towards them. They were dressed in different armor than he had seen on soldiers of the Ellious Empire. These elves wore leather armor, not fully covering their bodies but only their torsos and sections of arms and legs. None had helmets, whereas the soldiers of the Ellious army wore metal armor and helmets. These elves looked more like a scouting party.

As they drew closer, Gustoll noticed they had silver animal blazons on the chest of their armor. There were dragons on six, a bird with spread wings on another, the side profile of a vertical lion on two, and another one with the profile of a wolf head.

Other villagers were being forced into the center of the village as the elves around them seemed to close in just beyond Gustoll's view. *The goats were not wandering around but moving away from them.* He quickly looked at the women's faces, not seeing Herrah or any other people from outlying homes. As the crowd around him grew to nearly sixty women, children, and a few elderly men, Gustoll felt trapped. His mind began to spin. *They have us surrounded like cattle, none of us with weapons or ways to defend ourselves. This isn't a typical group stopping by to gather tribute. Could this be in retaliation for us sending our warriors to fight them? No, they have never done something like this. Maybe execute a few people to demonstrate their power, but not like this.* He then spotted a wagon coming at the very end of the column. It was thinner than any wagon he had seen and long. Only a little wider than the large horse that pulled it. It carried a single large cage. Seeing it made him even more worried about why they had come.

Gustoll looked at Cinda, faking a smile to show her everything would be okay, but he could not hide the fear in his eyes. "If you have to run, make sure all of you run in the same direction. You have to break through the circle to get away."

"What do you mean?" Cinda asked in a panic.

"Just listen to me, Cinda. Make sure you run with a group. You have to push through them and keep running. Don't stop no matter what," Gustoll said sternly and hugged her. "I love you, Cinda." Then he let go of her and walked towards the elven column between the defenseless villagers and the elves.

The column commander signaled everyone to stop about twenty feet from Gustoll. He dismounted along with half of the others. Gustoll's right hand began to shake from nervousness. He wished he had his sword with him right then, but all he had was the knife held on the back of his belt for cutting reeds.

The commander was tall for an elf, almost coming up to Gustoll's eyes. His blond hair was long and firmly tied into a ponytail, showing his long, pointed ears. Gustoll looked at the silver dragon on the chest of his armor, never seeing such a sigil before. He walked towards Gustoll slowly and with purpose, looking around at the villagers and hardly at Gustoll as if he did not fear him. His eyes were cold as he stopped short, only a quick lunge from him, looking over the villagers while the other elves with him began to walk closer to the mass of scared people. Then he started to yell in Elvish, a long sentence in a commanding tone. The eloquent language sounded harsh and brutal from his mouth. Gustoll only recognized one word from the order. "Take."

Gustoll turned towards the crowd as three elves went into the group of villagers, pushing one and then another to the side as they searched for something or someone. The sound of a wailing mother pierced the crowd. Then another and another soon followed with shouting. Gustoll quickly reached for the knife behind his back out of instinct to fight, but as his hand touched the handle, the elf in front of him also gripped the handle of the sword on his hip. He did not draw the knife, knowing it would only escalate things if he did.

Gustoll's eyes locked with the elven commander's dark green eyes. They stared back into his, unwavering as his lips pressed together with an emotionless expression. Not the slightest sign of anger, remorse, or pleasure was on the elf's face. It was as if the wails of the crying mothers had no effect on him.

The three elves emerged from the crowd and walked toward the other soldiers. One held Conner around the chest as the boy struggled to get free. Conner cursed the elf with all the profanities he knew as other women held his mother back from trying to get to her son.

Conner refused to go without a fight and leaned forward in the elf's grip. Quickly twisting in the opening, he spun and drove the back of his elbow into his captor's face. The elbow connected with a thud, making the elf lose his grip. Conner started to run back to his mother, but before he could take a second step, another elf drove his fist into Conner's gut. The punch's force knocked the wind out of him and made him struggle to breathe. The elf slammed his other fist into Conner's jaw, knocking him out.

"You can not do this!" Gustoll yelled at the elf commander. His blood began to boil with rage as he watched two elves drag Conner's body away. Then, walking out from behind a building, he spotted Derin, Frin, and Seby being led by two elves. Each of the boys with their hands bound and ropes around their necks in a short rope chain. Another elf came into view with Kervin over his shoulder, carrying the boy as his arms and legs flopped loosely with each step. The villagers in the crowd shouted and screamed as they saw the boys. Other elves from the column edged in between them to protect their comrades. They lined the boys up next to Conner's unconscious body. As if to display them to the villagers.

"Is this all of the males around thirteen years of age?" the commander asked in Terrish, the common language among humans in Effrin. The continent that Miterra rested near the middle of.

Gustoll looked at the children. He saw each of their faces. It took a moment to realize Owen was not among them. *If I say yes, they may leave with them as long as Owen stays away. But it might be worse for us if they find Owen and know I lied.*

"Please don't take them. I'll do anything," Gustoll pleaded. Letting go of his knife handle so he could present his hands openly.

"Is this all of them?" The commander asked harshly as

his face began to show anger. His hand moved, holding the handle to his sword as if to threaten force.

Gustoll nodded his head in agreement and then cried out. "We will give you all our food, anything you want. Just please don't take them."

"They are all that I want," the commander said coldly, his voice sending shivers down Gustoll's spine.

Gustoll's instincts took over, and he drew the knife from his back. But before He could even attack, the commander reacted. The commander's sword cut through the air in one solid swipe before Gustoll's neck.

The slash was precise. The blade's sharp, thin tip sliced cleanly through Gustoll's throat. The crowd of villagers looked on in horror while Gustoll began to choke on his own blood. He fell to his knees, his lungs spasming for air as they filled with fluid. The elven commander shouted another order. Gustoll recognized the words from what little Elvish he knew. "Kill them all."

Cinda watched in terror as her grandfather's body fell to the ground. Her hands raised in front of her mouth as if to scream, but no sound came out, as she froze with fear. The other elves that were with the commander began to advance toward the group of villagers. Each of them pulled, not their swords, but hand axes from their belts. Unique axes that had a blade on one side of the head and a hammer on the other. A design unique only to the nomadic Torsnam tribes that traveled the continent.

The mob of villagers grew tighter and tighter. Cassan pressed into Cinda, breaking her from her grip of fear as all the elves encircling them stepped closer. People's bodies pressed against Cinda. She struggled to push back but felt like she was being forced deeper into the mass of people as many screamed in terror around her. Cinda couldn't see except for the few people around her as she felt them press tighter and tighter. The chaos made her want to curl into a ball and await death, but she could not even bend down. Feeling like she was being squeezed into a giant's grip, she struggled just to breathe.

"Make sure you run with a group through them," Cinda said to herself out loud as she remembered the last words her grandfather had told her. She struggled to get higher, to get a better view around her. Forcing her arm between two people, fighting to raise it above her head, she placed it on the shoulder of Cassan and pulled herself up. Her legs dangled off the ground as the crowd held her in place.

The elves were taking their time, not rushing in but holding an ever-closing perimeter around the remaining villagers. A few women tried to strike or claw at them or break through but were quickly put down. The crowd shifted away from the elves that had just killed their friends, forcing Cinda to panic as she was moved uncontrollably. *Make sure you run with a group through them.* She thought in her head as she looked around at the elves. She spotted a section to the right of the hall where only two elves held the perimeter. She knew the river was further away in that direction.

Cinda then took a deep breath and yelled with all her might, "Everyone, run to the river!!" her voice rang out with a sense of command. Many people before her heard every word as the mass began to move. Others heard only the shout to run among the screams of fear and pain. The villagers became a stampede. As they spread, Cinda's body fell. She landed on her feet and went straight into a sprint with the others running towards the river. Many villagers ran in front of Cinda while some scattered in other directions. The two elves drew their swords in desperation against the advancing horde. They swung wide, curved steel blades cutting deep into flesh, but too many people came at them to swing more than twice. Cinda watched as others ahead of her pushed them to the ground, trampling them under their feet. Cinda kept going even as she felt a crunch beneath her foot. Glancing down, she could see by the clothes that it was one of the elderly men from the village, trampled underfoot.

As the people passed the hall, they began to scatter further apart. Cinda saw an opening among them and pulled her skirt higher to allow her legs to run faster. She ran with all her might, as did everyone around her, repeating in her head what her grandfather said: *Don't stop no matter what.* Then, suddenly, she heard an arrow fly past her ear. The arrow went deep into the back of a woman running in front of her. The woman screamed in pain and fell to the ground as Cinda ran past her. She glanced back as she ran, seeing several elves pursuing with their bows, releasing arrows at women and children as they fled.

Cinda continued to run and dodge, keeping her eyes ahead of her. Trying to get more distance and trees between her and the elves. Her legs burned from running. Never had she run so fast before, repeating in her head as she heard the screams of others behind her. *Don't stop no matter what.*

* * *

Owen and Tavia ran to the sounds of screaming. As they got closer, Tavia spotted a figure in the distance, standing at the tree line of the village center. She grabbed Owen's hand

and pulled him behind a tree. She slowly peered out to see an unknown figure. It looked like a thin, short man. He was dressed differently than any of the people of Orinton, and he was holding a bow.

Owen looked around the tree. "We have to help them."

"No," Tavia said as she pushed Owen behind the tree they were hiding behind. "We would be seen long before we got to him."

The screams in the village grew louder as they both watched the figure draw his bow and start releasing arrows into a group of people pouring out from the village center. Tavia slowly stepped around the tree in horror, knowing it was too far of a distance to run and help.

"The red orb is back," Owen said in a panic.

Tavia turned and saw the floating red orb heading straight at them. She grabbed Owen and pulled him behind her to protect him. Suddenly, only a few feet away, the sphere turned and circled them a few times.

They watched in amazement as it flew, not dimming or disappearing. The different shades of red swirled and rapidly shifted much faster than before. The red orb drifted around them and then returned to the direction it came. Tavia turned and looked back at the figure with the bow, hoping he would not see the orb's glow. Breathing easier as the figure seemed to be looking in the other direction.

"I think it wants us to follow it," Owen said, trembling as the screams filled his ears.

Tavia did not turn to look at Owen, as she was too occupied seeing his mother running through the forest along with others. Tavia could only watch as an arrow hit Owen's mother in the back. Her body jolted and fell to the ground as the others ran past her. Tavia grabbed Owen's hand and pulled him away, shielding his view from his mother's body lying in the dirt.

"Follow the light," Tavia said to Owen as she began running with him deeper into the forest, following the red-glowing orb, not fully knowing what to do. She did not want to be spotted by the figure.

The two of them followed the floating orb for a distance. It led them on and always stayed the same distance from them. Tavia noticed it was not taking them back to where they had spotted it before. It was almost like the orb was looking for something, going side to side as it went. She kept looking behind her, not seeing anyone. The screams coming from the direction of Orinton became quieter and less frequent.

The red orb started flying around in circles next to a large tree. Tavia and Owen slowed down and walked to the tree cautiously. As they approached, the orb faded and disappeared. She looked down and saw a deep crevasse between the large tree roots. The dirt was dug out like a burrow for a fox or dog. Tavia glanced at their surroundings and didn't see anyone else.

"Should we hide here?" Owen asked as he peered into the crevasse. It even curved under the tree, providing cover for the two of them. Their heads whipped around as they heard a woman scream nearby, begging for her life.

"Who was that?" Owen said in a frightened panic. Abruptly, the pleading stopped, and an eerie silence fell over the forest. "We should go and save her," he said as he lunged forward to start running in the direction the scream came from.

Tavia grabbed Owen by the chest, pulling him close to her before he could make his first stride. She pulled him into the crevasse between the roots, forcing Owen to the ground. "We have to stay here," she whispered to him. "We need to stay safe."

Owen struggled to get back up, ignoring Tavia's advice, but she held him tightly. Holding him down between the roots until, finally, he stopped. Tavia curled up with Owen in her arms as they tried to become as small as they could, shuddering in fear for their lives as the sounds of distant screams filled the forest once more.

* * *

Cinda gasped for air as she finally stopped behind a large tree. Her friend Hilda stopped next to her. Finding her in the chaos while fleeing the village through the forest. They could hear the sound of the river up ahead.

"We...should...get across...the...river," Cinda said in between breaths as she hunched over with her hands on her knees.

Hilda rested her forehead against the large tree's trunk. "Why did they want to kill us?" she cried.

"I don't know," Cinda said as she looked at the ground before her feet, trying to catch her breath. "We should keep going."

"I don't think they are following us,"

Then Cinda heard a strange noise, a deadened thud. Her eyes turned to the left and saw Hilda's body fall to the ground next to her. An arrow stuck out of her forehead above her right eye. Cinda stared at the face of her dead friend, the hollow look in her eyes staring blankly back. Cinda's body was so shocked from fear that every muscle tightened. She struggled to breathe as her heart began to beat so hard it felt like it might burst in her chest.

Her mind began to scream at her: *RUN!* But she could not move from her spot. All she could do was look at her friend's lifeless face.

Another woman screaming in the distance snapped her out of her reverie. Suddenly, her legs began sprinting again before her mind could even think. She dared not look back, not knowing if someone was right on the other side of the tree or a distance away. It did not matter; she just needed to run.

Cinda ran as hard as she could, spotting the river through the trees. She saw the thin line of flat rocks to cross to get to the other side before it flowed downhill into treacherous rapids. She hoped to get across, to safety.

The rocks were slick, and there wasn't enough time for caution. Cinda knew she had to run. She reached the bank and jumped, aiming for the rocks she could use to quickly walk across the river. The river's current was stronger from the morning rainstorm. The water only came up to her ankles, but she fought the current with each step to stay upright.

A sudden, sharp, searing pain bit her left thigh as she looked down to see a metal-tipped elven arrow pierced through it. Her leg gave out from under her, unable to continue. She screamed in pain as she fell on the rocks, her body being pushed by the current into more treacherous waters.

The arrow stuck through her thigh and hit against rocks repeatedly. She screamed in pain as the violent current tossed her around. She glanced above the water and saw one of the elves standing on the bank where she had jumped. He stood still, watching her, no longer chasing her, as if the elf knew she would die in the river's rapids.

* * *

The screams in the distance seemed to be at an end as Owen began to quietly cry into Tavia's chest. She held him tight to comfort him. He would whisper to her, asking if she thought everyone was okay. Tavia always said that she thought they were fine. Unable to tell Owen that she watched his mother fall with an arrow in her back. She began to think of her mother and wonder if she was still alive.

Tavia's concentration broke as she picked out the sound of two people quietly talking in the distance. Unable to make out what they were saying. Tavia felt Owen's heart racing, matching her own, as she pulled him tighter. The voices grew closer, and they talked strangely, in a language she had never heard. Tavia's chin began to tremble as she prayed to her god. *Please, Forus, guardian of humans and our one true god. Let them pass. Make us invisible to them so we may live.*

Tavia's heart began to pound as she watched a short, thin man carrying a bow with a notched arrow come into view. Her eyes opened wide in the shock of seeing an elf, recognizing him by the pointed ears. She squeezed Owen's head close to her so that he did not see as the elf walked without making a single noise. She knew they were in the open between the large roots from her position; all the elf needed to do was turn his head, and they would easily be spotted. Tavia glanced around her, thinking about how hard it would be for them to get up and run if they were seen. She felt trapped with no way out. *That light sent us to our deaths.*

Owen peeked from under Tavia's arm, seeing the elf. His pointed ears and short brown hair. Then suddenly, Owen felt something tickling the back of his neck. He squirmed from the feeling, but Tavia tightened her grip to hold him in place. The sensation began moving down his back, over his left shoulder blade. It was long, feeling the many feet touching his skin. Owen bit into his lower lip to keep himself from screaming. He closed his eyes tight as he felt it moving down his lower back. He could tell it was an insect, like a centipede, by how it felt. Wanting so badly to knock it off him or roll over to squish it. Tavia still held him tight so they did not make a sound. The centipede finally crawled out of the bottom of his shirt, and he could breathe again.

The elf stopped and turned his head, looking away from the two of them. Tavia held her breath in hopes of not making a single sound. The elf started walking again. She waited and watched as the elf left her view. She let out a relieving sigh and began to relax a little. She looked down at Owen and nodded, letting him know they were okay, but Owen began to fidget. His skin still crawled where the bug had walked down his back.

Suddenly, Tavia spotted a figure in the corner of her eye. She quickly looked and saw a male elf standing near the opening of the roots, his bow in hand with an arrow at the ready, staring right at her. Tavia panicked and started to shift, almost about to cry out as she knew her life was over in the next few moments. She looked up at the elf's face, looking straight at her, but he seemed almost sad.

The elf glanced to his left as if looking for the other elf and then back at Tavia. He swallowed hard as if nervous and pressed his finger to his lips, signaling Tavia and Owen to be quiet.

They both looked at the elf and were silent. They could see the elf's green eyes. The whites of them were red as if the elf had been upset, even crying. The elf looked around carefully and crouched before them, putting his bow and arrow on the ground.

The elf looked at them as if concerned and held up his fist, slowly shaking it. "Sone," he whispered. Then he held his other hand flat, sideways below the fist, lowered his fist slowly below his hand, and nodded a few times. Then he held up his hand, motioned with his two fingers pointing down in a back-and-forth motion, and pointed toward the village.

Tavia nodded in understanding, and the elf nodded back in relief. He looked around again, got up, gave them one last nod, and walked away.

Tavia closed her eyes and started to cry, thankful to still be alive.

"What did he say?" Owen whispered.

"I think he wants us to wait until after the sun sets before we head back to the village," Tavia whispered back, her grip on Owen tightening. This time, however, it was not for his comfort but for hers.

CHAPTER 3

Cinda floated down the river. Her arms wrapped around a thick branch she had dislodged from some rocks she had bashed into. The current had steadied and was pushing her further downstream. She looked at the river banks longingly, no longer having the strength to fight the current. It took all her power to hold onto the branch and stay above water. She grew afraid with each moment, not knowing where she was anymore, just that the river flowed east. Never had she gone this far down the river. Never had she felt so alone.

Every breath she took hurt. Her right side was bruised from hitting so many rocks as she descended the rapids. Every time she moved her left leg, the pain would shoot throughout her body. The left side of her head throbbed. She touched her left temple, her palm covered in blood and water. Every muscle ached with pain as she was bruised all over.

She could see ahead that the river flowed into a wider river. She began to kick her legs to swim to the river's bank. As she moved her left leg, the sharp pain in her thigh spiked, making her scream. Cinda strove to lift her head to glimpse her thigh to see what was wrong. As her leg struggled to reach the surface, she saw the glint of the arrowhead in the water. *An arrow!* She screamed in her mind. *That elf loosed an arrow into my leg!* The back of her head relaxed back into the water as she felt the current begin to grow faster. Cinda struggled to kick with her right leg, hoping to reach the left river bank before being forced into the much wider Grentel River. It felt like her leg weighed a thousand pounds. She was exhausted with each push until she reached the water's edge just before flowing into the much wider river. Finally, she felt a reprieve as she pulled herself onto the shore.

Cinda rolled over onto her back and lifted her head. Seeing the arrow protruding from her skin. The broken arrow shaft still stuck out a few fingers width from the back of her thigh. Her blood still came from the wounds and mixed with the water underneath her. She let her head rest in the mud, feeling the current of the water rushing over her feet. She felt lost. Not knowing where she was or what to do. Her mind swirled, wondering if she was even safe. She was too weakened to resist anything that would mean her harm. She saw a boat coming in her direction in the broad river. "Help," she whispered, unable to raise her voice as she lifted her hand towards the ship. Then her arm went limp and fell to the ground, no longer strong enough to move. Her eyes began to close as she fell asleep on the river bank.

* * *

Hendric ran through the forest, spotting a large amount of smoke from Orinton a few hours earlier. Adrenaline was the only thing keeping his legs moving as he ran. Knowing he had to get back. As he approached, he saw a woman's body lying on its side and quickly stopped. He pulled an arrow from his quiver and notched it in his bow. Cautiously, he looked around as he approached the body.

He recognized the pale face, Saleen. She used to take care of his brothers and him when they were younger. One of the nicest people he had known, and now she lay lifeless, her once warm glow faded to cold. He noticed only one puncture wound in her back amongst the blood-soaked cloths. It looked like an arrow had killed her, but someone had pulled it out. Gently, he closed her eyes and spotted boot tracks near the body. He knew he was still some distance from the village center. His mind shifted to his mother and Tavia, hoping they were all alright. He started walking again, his eyes constantly sweeping the forest around him.

As Hendric came closer to his home, he smelled the smoke. He saw the wall and window to his bedroom between the trees. It was the only part of his house that didn't burn down.

"Mother!" Hendric yelled, throwing all caution away if those who had done this heinous act were still around. Some small fires still burned among the fallen timbers. The smoke burned his eyes as he looked through the window into what remained of his room. He hoped to find his mother hiding there, but no one was there. Just the charred remains of half the room's walls and floor.

Hendric looked around him, hoping to glimpse his mother, until he spotted three more dead bodies a distance away. They were slightly in a sparse line as if they were running away. He walked to them slowly, seeing that they, too, were killed by arrows. Again, they were removed. *Who were they running from?* He looked at the ground near them and saw similar boot impressions that he had before. Inspecting them closer in the mud, he could tell whoever walked through did not rush. Nor did they weigh much. *Small boots, lightweight, maybe a woman's shoe size. Were they attacked by women?* He asked himself as he followed the bootprints from where they came from until he spotted fires through the trees a distance away. All thought about the bootprints left his mind as he saw the hall of the village center burnt asunder. With just the crumbling, scorched walls still ablaze.

Hendric stopped when he reached the tree line around the village center. All of the buildings of Orinton were engulfed in flames. Bodies of adults and children riddled the ground. It was just too much for him to bear. He turned away, not wanting to see so many he knew in such a way. Then he noticed a small child, Evert, only a toddler, lying under a bush as if he was hiding. His body was lifeless. *Not even the young were spared from the slaughter.* He felt his heart shatter and his stomach turn as he fell to his knees and began to cry. Everything and everyone he knew was here, and they all lay dead in front of him. "Mother!" he shouted as his tears streamed down his face. "Anyone!" he called again. But all he heard were the fires burning as he sat and cried to himself until his tears had gone dry.

The fires had died down, but Hendric could still feel the heat on his face as he walked into the center of the village. He noticed many were cut down, some with fatal wounds and others dead from bleeding out. A large number of bodies littered the ground near the hall. All of them seemed to be heading north towards the river. Then he spotted an axe lodged into a young girl's chest near the burned-out granary and Kenet's half-full wagon, which looked to have been singed by falling embers. He leaned down next to her, the last of his tears dripping down his face and onto her dress as he gently pulled the axe head free.

His hand tightened with rage on the axe handle as he recognized its style. The back of the axe head was a hammer. *Why would the Torsnam tribe attack us? Why would they slaughter everyone like this?* He stood up and looked at Korgan's wagon, seeing that a few of the burlap sacks had caught fire along with most of the arrows, but there were still bandages, ointments, and some food left. *They did not even take everything.*

He looked around at the bodies. A few were too close to the buildings and burned beyond recognition. As he wandered the carnage looking for his mother or Tavia, he spotted Gustoll. His body was lying flat on the ground. His arms were raised above his head from being dragged by the ankles. The trail of blood from where he was killed was not long. Being left in the middle of the road for anyone coming to Orinton to see. A Torsnam axe was firmly planted into his head. Hendric, however, could tell that it was his slit throat that had killed him. No significant blood was around the axe blade on his forehead and hair. *It's a warning. As if the Torsnam tribe wanted people to know that they had done this.*

Something glinted on the ground to the side of Hendric, reflecting the light from a burning building. He walked over. It was a silver coin, mashed into the dirt from one of the female boots stepping on it. He bent down and picked it up. It was a coin from the Ellious Empire, circled with Elvish writing. On the face was a profile of an Elven Emperor with an ex scared into it by a knife. He recognized it right away as Conner's coin.

Hendric gripped the coin as he stood, looking around for Conner's body. He did not see it and then realized he did not see Owen, Derin, Frin, Kervin, or Seby. He looked at the ground and noticed drag marks in the dirt, drag marks left from pulling someone kicking and fighting, and some of the small boot tracks that seemed much deeper from carrying extra weight.

The drag marks were easy to follow like multiple people were being pulled against their will. He followed them until they came to horse tracks and wagon marks. *They took prisoners.* He looked up at the sun, knowing he still had about an hour of good light before the sunset.

Hendric turned to face the village and all those dead on the ground, knowing every one of them would instead save those alive rather than take time to bury the dead. He quickly walked to Korgan's wagon. He searched and pulled out an extra blanket, dried meats, and a few good arrows. Not knowing when he would be returning.

"I'm sorry I wasn't here to help you," Hendric said somberly, talking to the villagers' spirits as he walked among them to follow the wagon tracks. "May Forus protect and guide you to him. So you may know peace with our god."

* * *

"Wake up, Tavia," Owen whispered as he shook her shoulder.

Tavia's eyes opened to see the night sky through the trees. She tried to stay awake after Owen had cried himself to sleep in her arms, but the day's exhaustion had set in, and she passed out.

"Come on, Tavia. I think the elves are gone," Owen whispered as he stood up.

"We should still be careful, just in case they are still around," Tavia said as she slowly peeked over the roots, looking for anything in the darkness.

They could hardly see, but there was enough light from the moon to walk around the trees as they made their way through the forest. Every rustle of branches made the two of them jump with fear. Never letting go of each other's hands as they went.

"Do you think everyone is alright?" Owen whispered in fear.

"I hope so," Tavia whispered back. She tried her hardest not to step on noisy branches or leaves as she walked in case the elves were still around.

Owen stepped on a branch that cracked loudly, echoing through the quiet forest. They both froze where they were, holding their breaths, trying not to make a sound. They listened to the forest around them.

"Do you think anyone heard that?"

Tavia turned and gave him a strict look but kept herself from shushing him. Owen understood the look and stayed frozen until Tavia started slowly walking again.

"Do you think the glowing orb will come back?" Owen whispered after a long time of silence.

"Hush," Tavia said to quiet Owen. "I'm not even sure what that was," Tavia whispered, thinking it would be nice for the orb to come back to light the way for them.

"But it saved us. Do you think it saved everyone else?"

Tavia stopped moving, her mind remembering Owen's mother, the look in her eyes, how her body jolted from the arrow hitting her. *Do I tell him his mom is dead? We can easily walk back another way in the dark, and he won't see her body.*

"Did you see something?" Owen whispered when he noticed Tavia had stopped in front of him.

Tavia looked at Owen. She could barely see the streaks of tears down his dirty face from crying most of the day in the moonlight. He looked tired and weak like he might drop from grief and worry at any moment. "No, it was nothing," she whispered back. "Let's go this way." She pulled Owen, leading him away from where she saw his mother fall. *I can't let him know she is gone right now. It would kill him to see her.*

As they both walked, they came across two bodies in the darkness. Tavia swallowed her sorrow, trying to appear strong for Owen but afraid to get closer to them. Owen was silent, however. He had seen dead people before at a younger age, but seeing it like this was different. Owen sighed in relief when he stepped closer to them, realizing neither was his mother. Both stood motionless, looking at the dead, afraid to find out who they were. Then, they spotted a reddish-orange glow through the trees.

"Did the glowing light come back?" Owen asked. The hope of seeing it made his sorrow diminish.

Tavia looked harder and realized it was a smoldering fire. "No, it's just a fire," she said, slightly depressed. A part of her also hoped it was the glowing orb. "Come on," Tavia whispered as she lightly pulled Owen to follow, wanting to escape the sight of the two dead bodies.

The village center came into view as they quietly walked closer. The small fire they spotted was one of many among the charred remains of the buildings. The ground was riddled with the dead as they looked at the destruction the elves had brought. Tavia held Owen's hand tightly as they stood still, looking at everything they knew now gone.

"Do you think anyone else survived?" Owen whispered as his eyes filled with tears and wandered over the bodies, hoping to see his mom but too scared to check their faces to know the truth.

Tavia clenched her teeth, wanting to fall to the ground and cry until she could feel nothing. She could not even look at the people around them and pushed their deaths out of her mind to remain strong for her and Owen's sake. *We need to survive. We need to survive. We need to survive.* She repeated in her head, trying to gather the strength to move her legs.

Tavia started walking deeper into the village, stepping over bodies and trying not to look at them as she walked. "Hello!" she yelled.

"Shhh. What if the elves are still around?" Owen whispered, pulling Tavia's hand to get her attention as he spoke.

"Elves can see in the dark as well as cats. If they were still around, they would have spotted us already," Tavia answered. Part of her did not care if the elves spotted them; at least their deaths would be quick, and her pain would be gone. "Is anyone out there?" she yelled again.

There was no reply as they both continued to yell for anyone while they walked through the remains of Orinton's center. Tavia walked to Korgan's wagon to gather some much-needed food and blankets that had been packed earlier that day.

"It looks like they went through the wagon but only took some meat and arrows," Tavia said as they went through the pile. Shuffling through the pile, Tavia found a few blankets that had been lightly singed, some dried meat, and some full waterskins. She handed them to Owen as she found them.

"Why wouldn't they take all of it?"

"I am not sure," Tavia answered as she wrapped herself in a thick blanket.

"Do you think your father is okay?" Owen asked since it was his wagon they were going through.

"I hope he isn't," Tavia whispered spitefully to herself. Thinking her father being gone would be the one good thing out of all of this.

The remark made Owen uncomfortable, and he tried to push it out of his mind. He unfolded a blanket and slung it over his shoulders. Tavia lit a torch so they could see clearly as they started to walk again. They shouted into the forest occasionally but still were afraid to let go of each other's hands. Together, they walked to Owen's house, which had most of it burned to charred timbers.

Owen quickly ran to where his front door once stood. "Mother!" He shouted towards the remains of his home. "Mother, are you there?" Owen fell to his knees as he began to cry. Quietly calling for his mother once more between his sobs.

Tavia slowly walked the path leading to the house. Unsure of how to console Owen, she watched his shoulders shake under the blanket. She looked around them, not looking for Owen's mother but for any help with the situation they found themselves in. Then she noticed Owen's hatchet, its blade sticking into an old stump a few feet from her. Tavia retrieved the hatchet and brought it to Owen.

"We should go," Tavia said as she held the hatchet out for Owen to take.

Owen's eyes widened as he saw the hatchet and quickly grabbed it from Tavia. Holding it in his hands, looking at it fondly. "My mother gave me this hatchet." He said and then snorted to clear his nose. "She worked so hard to get this for me. She gave it to me on my thirteenth birthday."

"Why would she get you a hatchet?" Tavia asked as she knelt down next to Owen.

Owen slowly shook his head as he frowned. "Because Hendric had one..." Owen's eyes widened with a glimmer of hope. "Hendric! Hendric will be coming back from his trip north."

"I hope he will, but for now, we need to take care of ourselves," Tavia said. She then placed her hand over Owen's to get him to look at her. "Right now, we should get moving. We need to find someplace to sleep and rest." Both of them walked away, Owen only looking back once at what was left of his house.

They spotted other homes burned to the ground as they walked. Not even a shed was left unscathed. Tavia stopped walking as her house came into view. Looking at the charred remains, she lowered her head without saying a word.

"What do we do now?" Owen asked as it was getting close to midnight and the cold was setting in through their thick blankets.

"There is that old stone house to the east of here that is hard to spot. Hopefully, it's still there." Tavia thought out loud.

"Isn't that house haunted by the spirit of the Seer?" Owen asked, in fear of actually entering the forbidden place.

Tavia knew the same stories Owen did about the house, how a Seer had lived there for over a hundred years, and that when she died, her spirit stayed, protecting the home and keeping others out. Owen, however, did not know that Tavia had slept in the house many times over the last several years on the nights that her father would drink too much. It was her own private place to hide. She even fixed the roof and shutters and put in a makeshift bed during her time there.

"It will be okay, Owen," Tavia said in a kind voice as they started to walk toward the old stone house.

* * *

The wagon trail went down the road for a distance before it turned into the forest. Hendric followed the wheel ruts as they weaved between trees. The setting sun slowed his pace significantly as he did not have much light to see the tracks.

He hoped to spot a torch or a fire in the distance, some sign he had caught up to them. The hour had become late, and his exhaustion began to catch up with him. He argued with himself as he walked. *If you are so tired, you will be no good at saving them. If you stop now, they might get too far away. If you're tired, they'd be tired too. If you sleep now, you'll be faster tomorrow. You can't stop. You're the only one that can save them.* Then Hendric tripped on a root and fell to the ground.

He rolled onto his back and looked at the sky through the canopy of the trees, gazing at the stars and thinking of home, his mother, and Tavia. He dreaded the worst in his mind but hoped for the best in his heart. *Maybe they got out of the village. Maybe they are looking for me right now. Maybe they are just dead, lying on the ground in the dirt.* His eyes began to well up, and he felt tears flowing down his face. *They are dead.* His eyelids grew heavy as he lay there, fighting sleep. He looked at the tree that had just tripped him. The branches were thick and nicely shaped, a good place to sleep. He stood up and climbed, finding a nice spot to relax and fall asleep. Knowing tomorrow would be an even longer day.

* * *

The old stone house was easy for Tavia to find. She had made her way there many times in the dark. She knew it would be challenging to find for most, for half the house was built into the side of a steep hill, leaving only part of the structure visible. Over the decades, grass and weeds had grown over the roof while bushes had grown and covered most of the walls. Though the door was wide open, the house was still intact.

"Do you think the elves found it?" Owen asked as they got closer to the open door.

"If they did, I'm sure they just looked around and left,"

Owen stood a distance from the open door and the darkness within. "Are you sure this is safe? Won't the Seer's ghost curse us or something?"

"It's okay, Owen. I've been inside before," Tavia said as she held the torch to look Owen in the eyes.

"Yeah, but we are about to sleep in there," Owen whispered as if to avoid the ghost hearing him.

Tavia slightly forced a smile as best she could, trying to keep Owen calm. "I've slept here many times. There is no ghost. It's just a story parents tell their children so that they won't play in there."

Owen nodded in agreement and took Tavia's hand, squeezing it harder and harder as he followed her into the stone house.

The inside of the house was not as frightening as Owen had thought. He had heard stories about the ceiling having the bones of people and birds hanging everywhere. Blood stained the floor and walls from the sacrifices of children to the old gods to see the future. Even one ghostly story about an altar built from the skulls of babies. Owen was surprised to see none of that as he walked through the door, and the room was lit up by Tavia's torch.

The house was simple. One large room made up the interior, about ten feet wide and twenty feet deep. A raised stone fire pit was built into the center, with an iron frame to hold a pot over the fire. Only roots hung down from the thatch ceiling, with some sections patched with mud. Many of the roots had been cut so they did not hang down too low, but no bones among them. The floor was made of stones with hard dirt packed between them, clean of blood stains. The walls had faded runes written with white paint and thick roots weaving between the rocks. Then Owen noticed a bed near the back of the room, new shutters on the windows, dry wood and kindling already in the fire pit, and a chair. He sighed in relief that there was no alter made from the skulls of babies.

"See, Owen, it's not that bad," Tavia said as she watched him look around.

"Do you sleep here often?" Owen asked in confusion.

"Only when I need to," Tavia answered as she closed and barred the front door and the shutters.

"Who helped you fix all of this?" Owen asked as he looked at the patches in the roof and new window shutters.

"I did it all myself two summers ago," Tavia said with a hint of pride in her tone. "Gathered everything that was needed. Fixed the roof, cut the shutters, and put them in all on my own. The bed and chair belonged to Kenet, who helped me bring them here." Tavia quickly realized she might have said too much, mentioning Kenet's name, and hoped Owen would not ask about what she did for that help. "We should get some sleep." She rushed to say in hopes of changing the subject. Putting the torch into the fire pit, lighting the kindling and a few split logs to warm and illuminate the room.

Owen sat on the small bed that held only one person comfortably. "Do you sleep here often?"

"Only when I need to," Tavia responded as she sat beside him.

"Why would you need to sleep in here?"

"My father," Tavia said as she looked at the ground. Her face grew sorrowful. "When he was home... He was not a kind man to my mother and me. Always drinking and angry. Made me wish he would never return from his trading runs to other towns." Owen slowly placed his hand on Tavia's to comfort her.

They both lay under the thick blanket, too frightened to be apart. Not a word was shared between them as they both thought about the past day and how afraid they felt. There was only silence as they both fell asleep.

* * *

Owen's eyes slowly opened. The cold of the night woke him. He looked at the smoldering fire. He felt so cold; even being under the blanket with Tavia was not warm enough. He slowly got up from the bed, trying hard not to wake Tavia as he shifted from her arms. Quietly, he walked to the pile of dried wood against the wall and grabbed some small cut kindling and a log.

A shiver went down his spine as he exhaled, seeing his breath illuminated by the dim light of the embers. His body began to feel cold. Like the chill pierced his muscles and froze his bones within. Only felt a similar cold when he fell into the iced-over river. He placed the wood into the fire and knelt next to it, steadily blowing through his shivers on the embers, trying to get the fire to relight.

After a few labored puffs, the kindling caught, and the flame lit up the room before his eyes. He then spotted a tall, dark figure facing away from him in the corner of the room. The sudden sight startled him, and he fell back on the floor.

"Owen," hissed a slow whisper.

The figure's thin body was hunched over, keeping its head from hitting the roof rafters. It slowly turned, showing part of its gray face in the shadows.

"Son of Olsen," an aggressive voice hissed from behind him.

Owen quickly turned his head but saw no one there. He then looked back at the figure of darkness, which was gone. *What did it mean, son of Olsen?* He had never heard that name before. Quickly getting to his feet, he ran over to the bed. "Tavia, Tavia!" he shouted in a panic, shaking her shoulder under the blanket. "Tavia, wake up!" Owen yelled as he pulled the blanket off of her. His eyes opened wide in shock as he looked down at the bed and saw it was empty.

"Death follows you," the voice hissed quietly behind his ear.

Owen flailed his arm wide to hit whatever was behind him, but his arm only passed through the figure of darkness as if it were smoke. "Tavia!" He screamed.

The figure flung its head back and began to cackle. Owen covered his ears as the chaotic noise echoed around him. It sounded like thousands of people were laughing at him from the shadows.

Then the figure leaned in towards him faster than he could step away. Its face stopped, only inches away from Owen's. It was the face of an old woman, ancient even. Her skin was light gray with wrinkles throughout. The withered skin of her cheeks made her cheekbones prominent. Her large nose was crooked. Dark eyes peered deeply with a red glow deep inside them. Owen recognized her from the description of the old Seer who once lived in the house.

"Good, you will need that spirit ... Druid," the old face hissed. Her pale lips parted while she spoke, with a breath reeking of rot.

Owen quickly lunged for his hatchet and gripped the handle. He turned back and charged at the figure. But before he could get close, a pair of large black crow-like wings erupted from the figure's back. He felt a wave of force from her like a strong wind as the wings spread. The force hit Owen hard, pushing him back, but not hard enough to knock him off his feet. It did, however, blow apart everything around him. The wood supports and thatch roof broke away with a multitude of cracking sounds. The stone walls of the room shattered into rocks. Everything in the house was broken and destroyed. Even the handle of Owen's hatchet shattered in his hands, and the metal axe head flew behind him, leaving just himself and the house floor intact.

Owen looked around at the destruction and realized he was standing in a grass field that stretched as far as he could see. The sky was lit like it was the early hours before dawn. It was filled with bright stars of different colors of the likes he had never seen. Billions of stars from horizon to horizon. The air smelled sweet, like lavender, yet only grass surrounded them.

"Tavia!" Owen called out in a panic.

"She is safe." The Seer hissed. Her gaze shifted from Owen to something behind him.

Owen slowly turned, hesitant to look away from the dark

figure, but he had to see what was there. His eyes widened with surprise as he saw a large, lone tree about fifty feet away.

There was no forest like the one that surrounded Orinton. Just this lone tree, grander than any tree he had ever seen, the top of it hundreds of feet above him. Blocking out the shimmering stars behind it. The thick canopy and gnarled branches reminded him of an oak tree, but the bark was white with gray underneath. The trunk in the ground was massively thick, much larger than the stone house he was just in. Four other figures encircled the large tree with Owen. These figures were not figures of darkness like the ancient woman behind him. Each was a different height and width, and each glowed a different color: blue, green, white, and dark purple.

A rumbling sound began to come from the tree as Owen watched the bark on the trunk shift and move. The bark separated, making lines that started to glow red, the same color as the floating orb. The glowing red lines formed shapes: one large triangle with four smaller and thinner triangles above it, two on each side, the outside ones being lower than the middle two, with all five pointing upwards. Different shades of red-shifted among the lines that were formed at a steady pace.

"He is but a child!" the Seer yelled behind Owen.

The tree shook its branches like a strong wind flowing through them, but Owen felt no wind. The lighter shades of red within the tree sped up and brightened. He could hear the old woman growl with disapproval from behind him as the branches stopped shaking and the shifting shades calmed.

Owen felt the ground beneath his feet shifting. He looked

down and saw the floor of the house was no longer there, and he was standing in ankle-high grass. The grass began to shake violently in a line from the tree, heading straight for him. Owen quickly turned and started to run, but four roots shot out of the ground as he took a second step to get away. They wrapped themselves around his limbs like ivy tendrils. Two wrapped around his legs, going from his ankles to his thighs. The other two snaked around his wrists over and over. They lifted him off the ground and turned him to again face the tree.

"Don't resist," The Seer said as Owen struggled to escape. The roots pulled his arms wide and kept his legs straight. He continued to attempt to flail, but the roots tightened their grip.

"Help!" Owen screamed. "Help me!"

Another root emerged from the ground slowly. The tip of it pointed towards Owen like it was watching him. It swayed side to side like a cobra about to strike.

Owen clenched his teeth and pulled against the restraints. The roots tightened around his wrists as he fought against the constricting pain. His arms shook as he tried with all his might to break free. The tip of the swaying root began to glow orange, shining like a hot coal. Then, it struck him in the right side of his chest. It burned a hole in his shirt as it changed shape and flattened against his skin, spreading out over most of his torso from under the cloth.

Owen felt a burning sensation on his chest as it grew hotter. He started to scream as the heat became painful. "Stop it!" His back and head arched back as the pain became excruciating. "Leave me alone!" He could feel his right chest's skin searing under the root. He screamed and flailed as much as he could, begging anyone to stop the pain.

Then, the glow of the root on his skin began to dissipate. The burning seemed to slow, and Owen's chin fell to his chest, barely conscious from the pain.

"Help me..." Owen said quietly. He could not raise his voice as he felt himself drift into unconsciousness.

"Remember, death follows you, Owen, son of Olsen," the Seer hissed into his ear from behind him. She then moved and spoke into the other ear. "They ... hunt you ... Druid."

CHAPTER 4

The late morning sun shone through a shutter, casting light into the room as Owen's eyes opened. Looking at the stones in the wall next to his bed, he touched them with his hand. Their surface was smooth and cold, but it was real. He raised his head, seeing he was still in the bed he had laid down to sleep in, but Tavia was not beside him.

His groggy mind did not fully understand what had happened last night, nor did he fully remember. *Was I dreaming about the Seer?* Owen then sat up on the edge of the bed. He felt pain in his chest as the shirt shifted over his skin. He quickly pulled the shirt collar away from his front and saw his skin blistered and burned as if he had been branded on the right side of his chest. He then noticed his wrists were darkly bruised as he held the shirt. His mind began to race. Owen stood up, holding his shirt away from his chest. He started to take a step; each joint ached where the roots had restrained him. *Was it a dream? How is this possible?* He reached the door, opened it, and stepped outside.

Owen's eyes took a minute to adjust to the brightness as he looked around. Tavia sat a short distance away from him, going through the few things she had gathered from the remains of the village earlier that morning.

"Nice to see you finally woke up," Tavia said as she put some vegetables into a sack, not looking up at Owen.

"Tavia," Owen said in a soft, somewhat panicked voice as he stood staring at her. His heart was pounding in his chest.

Tavia turned her head, her face shifting from exhaustion to terror as she saw Owen standing there. His face was pale as if he had just seen a ghost. His wrists were dark purple with shades of green bruised skin leading halfway to his elbow as his hands pulled the collar of his shirt. Part of the scorched skin could be seen with reddish hues around it.

"Help," Owen softly said.

"What happened?" Tavia shrieked as she stood up, dropping everything in her hands to rush to Owen and quickly help him take his shirt off to get a better look at his chest. "What did you do?"

"It wasn't me," Owen said. Tavia lifted the shirt over his head.

Tavia froze while she looked at Owen's skin. On his right chest was the large, even-sided triangle with four triangles above it, two on either side. To Tavia, it looked almost like a dog's paw print. Owen strained to look down at it, recognizing that it was the same glowing symbol on the white oak tree.

"It was the tree," Owen said, not even believing himself when he said the words. "I had a nightmare and woke up like this."

"Does it hurt?" Tavia asked with an unsure expression.

Owen nodded his head. "A lot." Even the slight breeze against this chest made the burning sting worse.

Tavia looked at the gathered pile, knowing she had gotten bandages and ointments from her father's wagon. "Go back inside, and I'll dress it."

Owen turned and looked at the open door to the stone house. "I don't want to go back in there."

"It's okay to go in. I need you to sit in the chair so I can clean your burn," Tavia said as she stood beside him.

Owen didn't move; his eyes were fixed on the doorway. Unsure if his eyes were truthful or deceiving him, he saw a shadow shifting around on the room's back wall. His breath began to quicken as the shadow seemed to form into a figure. "I can't, Tavia." He looked up at her with tears of fear as he shook his head. "Don't make me go back in there."

Tavia looked down at him with concern. "Okay, Owen," she said softly. "You stay here. I'll go get a chair."

"No, don't!" Owen interjected as Tavia took the first step toward the doorway. Tavia looked back at Owen. "She's in there," he said whimperingly.

"Who?" Tavia asked and looked back into the doorway.

"The Seer," he whispered, almost like saying it too loud might summon her.

Tavia could tell that something was wrong. Usually, she would blow off such talk of ghosts, but this was different. Owen was truly afraid, and with his mysterious injuries, the glowing red orb that saved their lives, and everything that had happened, her mind did not know what to believe anymore.

"Okay," Tavia said calmly as she turned toward him. She only wanted to scream with frustration. Nothing made sense to her anymore; she only wanted to hide in a hole. She knew she needed to stay strong, not just for Owen but for herself as well. With no one alive in the village, she felt utterly alone. She had always been able to go to someone for help. That had once been a nice, comforting feeling, but it was gone now. She was caring for herself and Owen, a responsibility she was unprepared for.

She looked around and spotted a rock for Owen to sit on. "How about we go to that rock? You can tell me about this… nightmare while I clean you up and get it bandaged."

Owen sat and described what had happened, remembering it more like a memory than a dream. He tried to tell Tavia every detail, but as he got to the end of his description, he could not bring himself to tell Tavia the warnings from the Seer. Death following him or that someone or something was hunting him made him afraid just to think about it.

Tavia did not interrupt him while he told her the story. She wouldn't have believed such a tale were it not for the brand and the bruises. Even with that, it was still hard to accept. Wondering how she had slept while all that happened to him. She had so many questions, and so did Owen.

As Tavia wrapped a long cloth around Owen's chest and shoulder to secure the ointment under the bandage, Owen asked, "Umm…Do you know what a Druid is?"

"I've heard of one in an old story. Something to do with fay," Tavia answered.

"The fay?" Owen asked. He had heard a few stories about fay, how most are fairy-like people, but there was a variety of them beyond just fairies. None of the stories he had heard about them were good, though. They were known for kidnapping children, destroying entire fields of crops, or driving people crazy with their magic.

"I'm not completely sure about the story. I heard it before you were born, but I think someone talked about a powerful Druid who fought against fay. I'm not sure about the rest,"

Owen looked at the ground, thinking about the other figures around the tree. *Could they all have been Druids?* He wondered and looked back at Tavia. "Have you ever met someone named Olsen?" he asked, Olsen being the name the Seer used. Owen remembered his father's name was

Borin. He had never heard of someone named Olsen.

"I'm not sure. Maybe it was your grandfather from when the Seer was still alive," Tavia said while she stared at the open door to the stone house. "I think I've seen that mark on your chest before…" Tavia got up and walked to the stone house.

"You can't go in there!" Owen yelled.

Tavia turned and looked back at Owen with a stern face. "I need to see it."

Owen quickly got up and followed her to the doorway as Tavia stopped at the threshold, looking in as if expecting something to happen. She did not see anything unusual, but she was hesitant and unsure.

"What is it?" Owen asked, peering into the large room around her.

"Do you see anything strange?"

"No… I don't."

Tavia took a deep breath as she slowly put her foot across the doorway. As her foot landed firmly, she exhaled a sigh of relief. Then she took another step in and stood. "Is there anyone here?"

"I don't see anyone," Owen answered, thinking the question was for him.

Tavia then tip-toed to the wall as if trying not to disturb anything. Examining the faded symbols, she walked along the border, inspecting each symbol she saw. Then, near the back of the house, she finally found what she was looking for.

"It's right here!" Tavia waved Owen over. Her finger pointed at the symbol as she squatted in front of it. The white paint was easier to make out than the skin of Owen's chest, but there was no mistake. A large triangle with four other triangles. The large triangle was faded more than the others and difficult to see. "It looks like a paw print," Tavia said to Owen as she looked at him.

Owen had not budged from where he stood, his feet firmly planted outside the doorway. He stood and thought about the symbol on the tree and was now seeing it also as a dog's paw print. "I think you are right. Is there anything else?"

Tavia looked around. Seeing that many other symbols had faded, but then she noticed branches. She got on her knees, looking at where the leak in the roof caused water to run down the wall, removing most of the paint but leaving tiny specs in the crevasses of the rocks. "I think there was a painting here," she said as she stood. She walked to the fire pit, grabbed a piece of charcoal, and returned to the waist-high depiction.

Tavia started drawing on the stones with the charcoal, trying to use what white paint remained as a guide. As she drew, it began to take shape. The trunk, the branches, the roots. It all went together. "It's the tree," Tavia said in excitement. "There was a white tree painted here!"

Owen's face still looked afraid, even just standing near the doorway. "Can you come out now?" Owen asked in a concerned tone.

"Hold on, there is something else," Tavia said as she shifted to get a better look at the symbols to the left of the tree. "You said there were others around the tree with you?"

"Yes, four others that were glowing different colors."

Tavia saw two more symbols that were not faded by the water leaking over them. "There is a symbol here. It looks like a three-pointed leaf, like a maple leaf." She then inspected the other symbol. "This one has four lines starting together, but each one branches off and swirls by itself. Did you see any of those symbols in your dream?"

"No, just the one on my chest. Maybe they are from something else?"

"There are two others that I can't make out, but all five symbols are spaced around the tree evenly. Like you described."

Owen felt uneasy as he watched Tavia squatting in front of the wall deep in the stone house. "Are you finished looking around?"

"Yes, for now," Tavia answered. Walking towards the door, she grabbed Owen's hatchet while looking at the other symbols on the walls. *If those mean something, then maybe the other ones do as well.*

"I don't want to stay here tonight," Owen told Tavia as she walked out of the stone house and handed him his hatchet. He quickly slid it back into his belt.

"There isn't anywhere else to sleep. Every house I have seen has been burnt down. Even the sheds were not left alone,"

"What should we do then?" Owen asked with a worried tone.

Tavia looked at what supplies she had gathered, knowing she had enough food to last them a few days, hoping to use that time to bury the dead. Knowing that it would be hard for her to do with just Owen. "We can walk to Keerike. It is only half a day from here, I believe. We can go and get some of the goats I saw wandering around and leave after that. We should make it before the sun sets."

"What if the other survivors return and we aren't here?" Owen asked.

"I will leave Hendric a note on the bed."

"Will he be able to find the Seer's house?"

"Hendric had followed me here once. He knows that I sleep here some nights. We also can't take everything I gathered, so he has some things when he comes."

"What about the other survivors, though?"

Tavia's jaw clenched as she shook her head slowly at her frustration with Owen, but she was primarily angry about their situation. "You are too afraid to sleep in our only shelter," she said angrily and then looked at Owen. Her expression showed the rage she felt. "I am not going to sleep on the dirt in the open for the wolves with a perfect bed right there. But if you don't want to sleep there, we go somewhere with a bed and protection. That would be Keerike."

"But what if our families come looking for us?" Owen pleaded as he felt a shiver of fear from Tavia, who grew visibly angrier at what he said.

Tavia could no longer contain her emotion. "Our families are dead!" Tavia screamed in rage. "Your mom died trying to run away! My mom and dad were cut down!" Tavia's eyes began to fill with tears as her angry tone turned to sobs. She fell to her knees. "Everyone is dead. The elves killed them all. It's just… It's just us… all alone." She cried into her hands as Owen stood in shock, his heart shattering with each beat as Tavia's words settled into his mind. He could not help but kneel down and embrace Tavia as they began to weep. Owen finally saw and felt Tavia let go of her strength and succumb to the harsh reality in which they both found themselves.

* * *

The Fortress of Theris was old and outdated, built almost a hundred years ago when the Ellious Empire first tried to tame the lands of Miterra by bringing elven civility and laws to the inhabitants. It was built large enough to house two hundred soldiers comfortably, just enough to keep a presence in the area, but made far from any trade routes or large towns to help keep its existence out of the way. Its outer wall was a ring of rocks mortared together, only standing a mere twelve feet tall on the outside, with rough steps leading to the top on the inside. A large, two-story tower stood in the center of the fort with stone walls with arrow slits, each only a few steps apart from the next, and battlements lining the upper level, making it easy to spot anyone approaching within the large clearing to the tree line.

The ground around Fort Theris was once flat, with nothing large enough to hide behind. The grass was never allowed to grow higher than someone's knees, being cut low by the cows that keep the grass down and feed the soldiers inside, making it almost impossible to sneak up to the walls except for the stream that cut through the field. All of that, however, was when Arminiul was stationed there. Now, it was abandoned, and the grass was allowed to grow tall. The stone walls, beaten by time and weather, were lined with moss and weeds growing in the cracks.

"Is it the same as you remember, Arminiul?" Maltius asked in Elvish.

The overcast clouds blocking out the late sun made everything appear darker, more dreaded, like a haunted keep in a desolate place. The slight breeze whisked around the clearing, like invisible spirits running through the grass.

"I remember it being more ... cheerful, and the grass was

not so tall," Arminiul said to his commander.

"Well, it has been almost twenty years since it was abandoned," Maltius stated.

"Seventeen years this winter solstice,"

"That is right. Those snobby senators decided to recall you all in the middle of winter." Maltius said and then started laughing. "All because your commander was approached by Senator Veritin's wife."

"That was the rumor."

"Guess it was luck for me. Otherwise, you would have never asked to join us hunter groups."

"It was nice not to have my orders dictated by greedy, jealous politicians for a change,"

"Yet here we are… doing the work required by a greedy, jealous Senator," Maltius said with spite in his tone.

"Required by a Senator," Arminiul mumbled as he turned in his saddle, looking at the wagon holding the five boys in the cage as it cleared the trees.

"We will be free of them soon," Maltius said, noting the grimace on Arminiul's face.

But will we be free of what we did? Arminiul thought to himself. One of the children looked up at him. He quickly turned away, unable to look him in the eyes. He hated what he had done and tried to push it out of his mind, but the children were a constant reminder.

"When we get inside, we will take some much-needed rest for us and the horses," Maltius said as he pushed his horse toward Fort Theris.

Two riders emerged from the gates as the column of horses approached. The elves coming towards them had symbols of a dragon on their chests, unlike Arminiul and Maltius, who had falcons on theirs.

"The fort seems empty," one of the riders said as he drew closer.

"So, the Senator is not there," Maltius responded. He was assigned commander of all four units of hunters for this mission but longed to be back to commanding just his fellow falcons.

"No, she has yet to arrive," the rider said.

Maltius signaled to all the units to continue into the fort's walls. Arminiul followed, and he could feel his horse getting tired under him as it walked. None had slept for two days and only took short rests since they left Orinton.

He could breathe as he rode through the wrought-iron gates of the walls, knowing he was safe.

"Rest the horses and rest yourselves. We wait for Senator Galadin to arrive," Maltius ordered.

Arminiul took his horse near the back of the fort, further than most traveled, so that his horse didn't have to fight with others for the patches of grass that had grown around the central tower. He quickly removed the saddle from the horse and let her roam freely as he sat on the steps of the wall. He looked up at the top of the tower and spotted some elves taking position there. *Good, I wasn't called for guard duty,* he thought to himself as he let his head rest and closed his eyes, falling asleep.

* * *

Tavia and Owen had been walking for hours when they finally came to the large stone bridge crossing the Grentel River. The river marked the boundary between Duke Chalin's territory and Duke Revnar's territories of influence. Tavia held her breath as she looked at the bridge, doubt creeping in about whether to go to Keerike. She turned to look at Owen, who was struggling with the five goats they had with them. She wanted to keep them both safe and knew Keerike was the largest town close enough to travel too easily. She wanted to go to a large town, thinking it was safer from the elves since Duke Revnar was a friend of the Ellious Empire.

"Are you sure you know the way to Keerike?" Owen said as he pulled the goats with the ropes tied around their necks.

Tavia nodded her head. "My father would bring me with him to Keerike from time to time." She grew silent at the memory of her father but also felt relieved she would never feel the brunt of his anger again. She then turned to look at Owen. "We should get going, though. It will be dark soon, and we have a few hours of walking after sunset."

"Are you sure Hendric will be able to find us?"

"I left that note for Hendric on the bed, telling him you and I were okay, and we left for Keerike. He Should be able to find us there,"

"I hope he looks there for us," Owen said but grew quiet. "What if the elves come back and find it?"

"They already…" Tavia trailed off with her statement, unable to mention the horrific slaughter. "I hope there is no reason they would go back."

"What if they came for me?" Owen whispered as his hand lightly touched the bandages on his chest.

Tavia looked down at Owen, unable to answer that question. "We should get going," Tavia said as she grabbed their two sacks of provisions and walked across the empty bridge.

CHAPTER 5

"Wake up, Arminiul. The senator is here," Maltius said as he kicked Arminiul's foot.

Arminiul's eyes opened wide, but he was still tired after only two hours of sleep. He quickly gathered his weapons and strapped them to himself as he walked. He noticed Sepher, another Falcon member, sitting on the wall. "Sepher!" Arminiul shouted to get his attention. But Sepher didn't move.

"He hasn't been talking much. Seems distant," Maltius said to Arminiul as he looked at Sepher. "I told him he can keep watch on the wall and talk to me when he is ready." They continued walking towards the front gates, standing in formation with many other elves as they watched the Senator and her escort approach.

Maltius leaned towards Arminiul, waving his hands elegantly in the air. "Now, don't forget to smile. Bow to the senator, show your respects." He said in an overexaggerated formal voice. Arminiul and others around them began to laugh, releasing the tension many felt.

Senator Galadin was at the head of her entourage, sitting up with her shoulders back on her horse like a victorious conqueror. Her straight blond hair hung down past her shoulders. Wearing gold-trimmed, bright red robes that looked like they were freshly washed. Her face was stern, lips thin, and anger taut through her jaw. Galadin's ice-blue eyes were cold and emotionless as she drew closer. Riding with no fear, as if knowing she was perfectly safe, being so far ahead from the guards that trailed her. The sixteen guards that followed were dressed for war. Fully armored in black leather and steel with light red cloaks. Their helmets covered their face entirely except for the eyeholes. The cover was blank as if to make them all look the same. They were the best-proven soldiers on the battlefield to be Senator Guards. The only evident difference between them was their weapons. Each carries their favorite, be it a sword, spear, axe, or bow, or even one of each. Behind them was a wagon full of barrels and provisions.

"Is she insane being dressed like that this far into Miterra?" Arminiul asked Maltius, knowing that no one of her level of authority would ever dress in formal attire while traveling these lands. All it did was draw attention and risk.

Maltius turned and looked at Arminiul with a smile. "You are free to tell her your thoughts if you like," he said jokingly. Arminiul shook his head, knowing he should just stay quiet. "Thought so," Maltius laughed.

As Galadin entered through the gates, her eyes fixed on the children in the lone wagon, so much so that she did not look or greet any of the soldiers. The elves parted before her as she had no intention of waiting for them to move.

Maltius, Arminiul, and the other three commanders of their units walked through the shifting elves to gather around Galadin.

"Have they caused any problems?" Galadin asked in Elvish, continuing to watch the five boys who sat in the cage. The twins and Seby were asleep, while Conner and Kervin were too tired to move.

"No, Senator, they have not caused any problems," Maltius answered as he inched into Galadin's view, trying to gain her attention.

Senator Galadin swiftly dismounted from her horse and walked to the caged children. Conner and Kervin shifted in fear as she looked at them coldly, like a butcher inspecting cattle to slaughter.

"This is all of them?" Galadin asked while her eyes fixed on Conner. He shrank back against the bars, unable to meet her eyes.

"All the ones in the village of Orinton that fit your description. As you ordered," Maltius answered.

Galadin looked at each child, inspecting them from head to foot, trying to get the ones awake to look her in the eyes, but none of the children would. "And the rest of the villagers?" she asked sternly as she turned and looked Maltius in the eyes.

Her cold gaze sent shivers down Maltuis's spine. "I followed your orders. There were no witnesses left. We made it look like the Torsnam tribe attacked Orinton. Even searched the area before and after we attacked the village." Maltius's voice lowered, ashamed of what he had done. "Everyone in the village and around was slain."

Galadin's face slightly turned from stern to inquisitive as she heard the tone in Maltius's voice shift. "Thank you, commander," Galadin then turned towards her guards. "Hook the wagon to one of our horses and prepare to return," she commanded, gesturing towards the wagon with the imprisoned children. Three guards dismounted and began tying the wagon to one of their horses.

"Will you not be staying here during the night?" Maltius asked, knowing only an hour of sunlight was left.

"I must return to the capital. I have more business to attend to there," Galadin responded. She leaned in towards the guard commander and whispered into his ear, too quiet for anyone else to hear. The commander nodded and walked to the back of the wagon they brought. She then turned and faced Maltius. "I know it is in the tradition of you hunters to have a toast after each successful hunt, so I brought you some of the finest wine from the Romagus Valley. Enjoy this night; tomorrow morning, you are all to head out and return to your former commands," she said as her guard passed two of the four wine barrels and a box of clay cups to the soldiers.

"Our thanks, Senator Galadin," Maltius said with a bow, Arminiul and the others bowing slightly.

Galadin walked back to her horse. Maltius walked behind her. He waited as she climbed back onto the saddle.

"Senator Galadin," Maltius said, trying to get her attention. She turned and looked down at him. "Why... Why was all this necessary?" he asked quietly.

She looked down at him with that cold, emotionless look of hers. "For the glory of the Ellious Empire." She turned her horse around abruptly, causing Maltius to back out of the way to avoid being hit by the beast's flank.

Maltius stood and watched as the wagon with the children was finished being secured to a horse. Then the Senator, her guards, and the now two wagons rode away from the fort.

"So the rumors are true about how cold Senator Galadin has become," Arminiul told Maltius as they watched the wagon with the children recede farther and farther away.

"Seems so," Maltius said, his thoughts wandering. *For the glory of the Ellious Empire.* An excuse he had heard many times before. *What glory would be had from this, and what was so important about those human children?*

"At least she left us wine," Fernil, the commander of the Dragon unit, said. "I think we should drink, celebrate a good hunt, and take some much-needed rest."

Arminiul clenched his teeth, not wanting to lash out at Fernil. He noticed how the Dragon and Lion units almost enjoyed the sport of what they did to the people of Orinton. He even heard Fernil brag about how he had killed the village leader while Maltius was commanding the hunters circling the village.

The wine barrels were opened, and the elven hunters began to drink. Some out of celebration for a hunt well done, others to numb the sorrow from what they had done.

"What is with that one?" Fernil asked Arminiul while he was standing in line to get his cup and wine. Arminiul looked at Fernil and followed his finger, pointing at Sepher sitting on the wall, his back towards the celebration. "Why is he not drinking with us?"

"Maltius assigned him to guard while we enjoy ourselves," Arminiul answered.

"Well, get him a cup of wine as well. Maltius is too strict on you, Falcons."

Arminiul filled two cups with wine and started walking over to Sepher. He could sense something was wrong by how he was sitting, slouched over and quiet. Usually, Sepher would be the first to get to the wine. He was the youngest in the Falcon unit and behaved immaturely quite often. This quiet, however, was nothing like him.

"Mind if I sit?" Arminiul asked Sepher as he climbed the steps of the wall. Sepher didn't say a word or even move. "Sepher?" Arminiul said louder.

Sepher's head quickly turned from being startled. His green eyes seemed hollow and distant to Arminiul, far from the joyful eyes of the young elf he was used to.

Arminiul didn't wait for another response and stepped to the top of the wall, handing Sepher one of the cups and sitting down next to him, both legs dangling off the side as they looked out over the grass field.

Arminiul looked at Sepher and raised his cup. "To a hunt well done," he said steadily, the toast the hunters said when celebrating the completion of a mission.

Sepher's head didn't even turn towards Arminiul, his hollow eyes looking down at the cup in his hands. He stuck out the cup before him and poured it onto the grass far below. "There is nothing to celebrate about what we did," he said sorrowfully.

Arminiul lowered his cup, not taking a single sip, and stared at it in his hands. "I didn't like it either." He then took a deep breath and exhaled. "We were following orders; it is our duty."

"Is that what you will tell the gods … when they weigh your soul?" Sepher quietly said. "I was only doing my duty."

Arminiul knew this philosophical question well. He often asked it himself when he was still a new recruit and had his first engagement with the humans. Over the years, it had faded into the back of his mind, telling himself that he was doing what he had to do.

Arminiul looked up. The sun was fading, and a parting of the clouds showed a dark blue sky. "I'm not sure what the gods will think, Sepher. But I hope they do not judge us too harshly."

Sepher shook his head lightly. "Our *duty*," he said, emphasizing the word, "is to hunt monsters and deserters. Maybe help out hunting food for people in need. Nowhere does it say kidnapping and massacring women and children."

"I know," Arminiul said somberly.

Sepher took a deep breath. "I'm not like you or the others. I wasn't in the military or had to fight in any battles. I was just a good tracker and decent with a bow. I never even fired an arrow at a human or elf until...."

"Arminiul!" a voice yelled from behind them. Arminiul and Sepher looked back and saw their friend Ramous shouting at them, already slightly drunk. "You owe me five coin."

Arminiul knew why. Among the Falcon unit, they had a running bet. Whenever one of them would miss a shot, they would have to pay five gold pieces, a week of pay, to whoever witnessed the attempt. The price was steep, but the tradition made the hunters strive harder to never miss.

"I didn't miss," Arminiul answered back.

"Like hell, you didn't." Ramous looked at Sepher with a drunken smile. "It was a perfect shot. Arminiul was sure-footed; the human girl was running a straight line across the river," Ramous held his hands up like he was shooting a bow and let go of an imaginary arrow, "and hit her in the thigh." He then propped his foot up on a step and rested his elbows on his knee. "You ... missed."

Arminiul looked at Ramous and smiled slightly. "How about this. I'll give you two pieces since I still hit the girl." Ramous nodded in agreement while Arminiul reached into his pouch and tossed two pieces of gold. Ramous struggled to catch them both.

"Thank you," Ramous said with a grin and stumbled away.

Arminiul went back to look out over the field of grass.

Sepher sat still, staring at him.

"What?" Arminiul asked, feeling Sepher's gaze on him.

"You don't miss. Maybe while riding a horse or running but not sure-footed," Sepher said in a questioning tone.

"You're right. I don't," Arminiul said.

"Then why did you shoot the human in the thigh and not kill her?" Sepher asked in disbelief at what he was hearing.

Arminiul fidgeted with his fingers out of nervousness, not because he did not trust Sepher. Their bond was strong, and they would never report on one another. It was just his making the admission out loud that made him nervous. "She was running too slow," he said quietly, looking down at the cup of wine. "The current in the river was strong and would get her away faster than she could run."

"Did she get away?" Sepher asked, concerned.

"The river was rocky, and I lost sight of her," Arminiul answered. He then extended his cup and poured the wine onto the grass below. "I'm not proud of what happened either."

They both sat silently, watching the wind pass through the grass, Arminiul thinking about the girl and hoping she had survived.

"Not all the young boys were in the wagon," Sepher said quietly, yet the severity of the words shattered their shared silence.

Arminiul slowly turned his head towards Sepher in shock. "What?" he asked breathlessly.

"I found a woman and a young boy hiding in the roots of a tree," Sepher said, his hands and voice shaking. "I told them to stay there until the sunset."

"How? You don't even speak Terrish," Arminiul asked. His mind was spinning about this revelation, and he surprised himself with that being the first question coming out of his mouth.

"Hand signals, like talking to a child, I suppose," Sepher said.

"And they understood?" Arminiul asked, surprised.

"No one found them, so I guess they did,"

Arminiul sat for a minute, thinking in his mind before talking once again. "Do you know what will happen if someone finds out you let them go?"

Sepher nodded his head. "Throw me in a dungeon, cut off my head, string me up to die as an example." They sat quietly for a few moments. "I just couldn't do it. I just couldn't kill the woman and throw the boy into a cage like an animal to suffer whatever fate awaited the other children we took."

Arminiul put his hand on Sepher's shoulder. "I won't tell anyone," he said, then retracted his hand to his lap.

Sepher sat silently. A few tears slowly dripped from his chin. "I can't do this."

"I don't think we will ever be ordered to do something like that again," Arminiul said somberly. "At least… I hope."

"I keep seeing their faces, thinking about them, wondering if they are all right," Sepher said. He seemed to be talking to himself more than Arminiul as he looked over the grass.

"I'm sure they are fine. Humans…" Arminiul paused, thinking of the correct phrase. "Humans, even though they only live a short time, are quite resilient." He then smiled a little, remembering some of his interactions with them. "They can also be surprisingly clever."

"You sound like you respect them," Sepher said in slight surprise that Arminiul was complimenting the human race.

This was the first time they had openly talked about the humans since they were ordinarily deep in elven territory.

"I can appreciate them. In truth, they are not that different from us elves, I have found." Arminiul said.

"Would you leave a young woman and child alone in a forest if they were elves?" Sepher asked.

No. Arminiul answered with his thoughts but couldn't bring himself to say it aloud. He knew what Sepher was saying, how what they did was wrong.

Sepher waited in silence for the answer, but none came. "If I leave tonight...will you stop me?" he asked in a whisper.

"Why would you go?"

"What we did was wrong. I must seek forgiveness and ensure the women and child don't die because of us."

Arminiul could feel this subject coming but had hoped it wouldn't come to this. He noticed the change in Sepher since they rode out of Orinton, how he was not handling killing others well, but Arminiul could not blame him. Sepher was full of life and far from a killer. In the years since Sepher joined their group and Arminiul took him under his wing much like a brother, Sepher had difficulty hitting the deserters they captured when they fought back. He had no proper military training to help desensitize him, no one to teach him the cruelty in the world. His family was kind to him growing up. He was an honest person, a good person. Then, he was in the middle of the massacre of defenseless people, which made Arminiul shudder at the thought.

Arminiul turned to Sepher and spoke quietly. "I won't stop you." He then turned back to face the open field. "You will be labeled a deserter once others realize you are gone. Then we will be forced to hunt you...I will be hunting you."

"I know," Sepher answered, exhaling a deep nervous breath.

Arminiul leaned forward, looking at the stream on the other side of Sepher, and then looked straight again. "At least you won't be hard to follow." Arminiul then smiled a little. "You'll take the stream south, won't leave tracks for us to follow. But it turns East in a few miles, and you will want to head west. Get yourself further from the Empire's borders. So you'll exit the river there," Arminiul explained quietly. Though in his mind, he knew Sepher would be heading northeast to Orinton to help the young woman and child. "But there are three other hunter units here. One of them might travel north to look for you. I can't control that."

Sepher swallowed hard and nodded. "I know."

Arminiul looked behind him. Seeing the celebration had died down, and many of the hunters were beginning to prepare to sleep. He stood up and looked down at Sepher, holding his hand out. "Well, Sepher, thank you for volunteering to take the first watch," he said in a little more than average volume, so others around heard him clearly.

Sepher stood up and shook Arminiul's hand. "Of course."

"Just remember that there are also men on the top of the tower who are observing. So you aren't alone in staying awake," Arminiul said. He wanted to give Sepher one last hug, a brotherly affection, but couldn't, given the fellow soldiers around them. "Good night and good luck, Sepher."

"Good night, Arminiul,"

* * *

Hendric told himself to keep going with every stride as

he jogged through the forest, knowing he had to catch up to the wagon eventually. Exhaustion had crept deeply into his muscles, laboring to stay at his current pace. His tired mind did not even notice that he was no longer quiet. He was only thinking about getting to Conner and the other boys.

Hendric came to an abrupt halt. Seeing a tall stone tower in the distance through the trees. This was further south than he had ever been. Cautiously, he approached, seeing figures on the top of the tower and the wall surrounding it. The clearing of trees around the walls made him want to avoid getting too close. The hoof prints and wagon ruts trail went straight from the trees to the wall gates. But he could not see into the fortress from where he stood.

Hendric skirted the edge of the forest as he moved around the fort. His hunting clothes blended in with the forest as he went. Coming to the road leading straight to the gates in the wall, he crept closer, wanting a better view through the wrought-iron gates to see what was inside. He would have to move with just the cover from the grass to get any closer.

The sound of horses approaching from the road behind him startled Hendric. He quickly moved into the cover of the trees, hiding but maintaining some visibility of the road. He watched as someone in a red outfit riding a horse came into view. Her ears stuck out through her straight blonde hair. *I must be in elven-controlled lands. But there is no way I have traveled that far south.* Hendric thought to himself. More elves wearing armor, along with a wagon, came into view behind her. He shifted in his spot, watching as the group approached the fort. The gates opened, and he spotted a thin wagon holding people within. *They are here. But why would elves take the kids and slaughter everyone? There are so many closer villages. Do they want the kids for ransom?* His mind continued to churn as he stayed unmoving, taking note of the guard's rotation on the walls.

After some time, the gates opened again. Hendric watched as the elf woman led the same group out of the fort. The short amount of time caught him off guard. Quickly, he moved into a better position to see who was in the wagon as the elves rode back along the road. As they passed before him, his heart began to race, unsure if he might be seen, but it was too late to move. All worry vanished as the wagon with the cage came into view. There was the prison with his friends, the boys he knew. He watched them, seeing their faces, memories of each one filling his mind, but then, he noticed Owen was not with them. His heart began to sink. He had hoped to see Owen still alive as he had searched for him back in Orinton but couldn't find him, and now he wasn't in the cage with the others.

Feeling the crushing blow in his heart, Hendric took a moment. His grief finally caught up to him. His stomach twisted, his limbs fell slack, and the tears he could no longer keep in began sprinkling the ground. He gave all his thoughts to his mother, Gustoll, Tavia, and Owen. He covered his mouth to hold back a wail of despair. He looked down the road, the dust still in the air from the horses. *I must save them.*

CHAPTER 6

Cinda slowly cracked open her eyes. The left only opens slightly from being so swollen. The world moved under her. Looking around, she was confused, seeing some light at her feet and above her head. *Where am I?* Yet, it was still too dark to understand her surroundings. Lifting her left hand, she felt a wooden wall next to her. The wood was cold and damp. The world bounced, making her rock, causing a harsh pain in her left leg that brought her out of her grogginess. She shifted her hips but couldn't move far. Her hands wandered in the dark, finding a thick rope wrapped around her waist. *What? Why am I tied down?* She could hear voices, distant and muffled as if people were talking underwater. She was covered with something, a blanket, maybe. Her hands felt around, feeling fur, not soft like a sheep or coarse like a goat but somewhere in between. Her fingers moved through it. It was smooth and long, reminding her of one of the dogs she petted when she was younger.

Cinda tried to lift her head, but a pain in her neck made her give up and laid it back down on what felt like a fur pillow. Her hand reached up, feeling leather. The world moved again from under her as a wind blew through an opening near her feet, fluttering the material wider. She saw the leather over her. It was the hide of a large animal perched against the wood wall like a tent.

Laughter sounded from the other side of the hide flap. It was loud and deep, then more voices, but none of the words made sense. She reached up to rub her eyes, but it hurt to touch the left side of her face. She felt the swollen skin there, a numb pain as she glided her finger across her eyebrow and cheek.

What happened? Where am I? Cinda tried to remember. She tried to sit up, but her hips hardly moved. *That's right, I'm tied down.* She reached above her head to open the flap above her, but a sharp pain shot through her side. She retracted her arm back to her chest.

Thud, thud, thud. Cinda heard it from behind the hide flap. *Someone is knocking on the door.* She moved to get up, but her hips hardly moved. *Why am I tied down?* The sound of multiple people laughing deep laughs came again, with some yelling of words she didn't understand, then some more laughing. *Who's out there?*

"Hello?" Cinda tried to call out. Her voice was raspy from her throat being so dry.

She heard water, like a waterfall or rapids. "Rapids," she said to herself. She remembered going down the river, banging into rocks, clawing at anything for dear life just to breathe.

The world seemed to move again. She moved her leg to brace against it. As she did, a sharp pain went into her left thigh. "An arrow," she said out loud, remembering she was pierced through the thigh with an arrow. She began to panic as her mind became more aware of her surroundings.

More deep laughter erupted among the yelling. She realized they were speaking a different language. Her panic rose, and her breathing picked up speed. Each breath hurt her ribs, but she couldn't calm herself. She looked at the opening above her head but only saw the curved wooden wall.

Gritting her teeth through the pain, Cinda reached above her to move the flap slowly. Her first glimpse was of an arm, very large, bigger than any arm she had ever seen, covered in green skin.

Quickly, Cinda retracted her hand. Her mind flew through stories she'd been told from northerners, stories of green-skinned giants called orcs. They raided and killed people without warning, painted their skin with the blood of their victims, and ate people while they were still alive.

Her heart began to race. Her hands pulled at the ropes around her waist, but they were tight and did not budge. She shifted back and forth, trying to wiggle free, attempting to gradually pull herself out of them.

A deep voice started shouting right next to her as she felt the world move again. Cinda froze, hoping to go unnoticed, hearing only the creaking of wood and splashing of water. She reached up and lifted the flap again, seeing the arm had moved. She kept lifting it to try and see where the arm went, then suddenly, the wind caught the flap, and it slipped from her weak grasp. She froze with terror as she looked up, seeing the large orc to whom the arm belonged and him looking down at her, sitting on a bench opposite her, holding the rudder of the ship.

The orc's frame was larger than any man she had ever seen. His shoulders were as broad as a horse's, thick, bare arms as wide as her waist, and large hands that looked like they could easily wrap around her head and crush it. He wore animal furs over his shoulders with a shirt of thick leather and pants that matched but were dyed dark. His head was large like the rest of him, with a wide jaw that jutted out slightly with two large tusk-like teeth protruding from his lower lip, curled and larger than his upper one.

He had a stubby nose, bushy eyebrows, and his hair was shaved on the sides, with long hair on the top, braided and hanging to the back of his neck. His ears were rounded on the top like a human's but a little more curled along the ridge.

Cinda looked into the orc's brown eyes. They looked at each other in startled silence, not knowing what to do.

"Ahhhh!" Cinda let out a shrill.

The orc panicked, looking away from her, and yelled, "Lars!" He then looked back at Cinda, holding his hand out.

Cinda screamed again at the gesture and reached for the flap. Her hand fumbled to get to a spot to pull it back over, the adrenaline in her veins keeping the pain at bay.

"Ssss…" the orc said. Cinda looked at him in a panic. "Ssss…aaaafe," he tried hard to say in a deep voice. He looked in the other direction again. "Lars!" he yelled and then yelled some more words that Cinda could not understand.

Cinda grabbed the flap and pulled it back over her, hiding herself again. "Ssssaaafe," she heard the orc say again in his deep voice. Then she listened to the stepping of feet and the orc talking again in the strange guttural language. She curled up her arms as if to hide.

Then she heard another voice. It spoke the strange language but was not nearly as deep and sounded almost human.

"Excuse me, young lady?" a male voice said in Terrish from the other side of the large hide. The voice was kind and polite in demeanor. "Sorry if Ulrick startled you. We are still working on his language skills."

Cinda pulled the fur blanket up to her chin, wanting to hide her face, hoping they might disappear.

"Excuse me..." the voice said again. "Hello?"

"Go away," Cinda responded, trying to shout with her dry throat.

"Well, I would, but the boat is not that big, to be honest," the voice said back with a slight chuckle.

"Boat?" Cinda said out loud but mostly to herself. It all began to make sense: the sound of water, how the world was moving, and why the wood next to her felt cold and damp.

"Yep, you're on a boat,"

Cinda froze, not knowing what to do. She was afraid to even talk. She slowly closed her eyes as the pain in her head grew, making her feel nauseous. Every muscle hurt. She wanted to wake up from this bad dream.

"Young lady, are you still awake?" the kind voice asked after a long pause.

"How did I get on a boat?" Cinda asked nervously. She had never actually been on a boat. Only saw boats when she traveled with her father.

"Well, we found you on the river bank," the kind voice said. "You've been asleep for over two days."

Cinda heard the man get up and move, then felt him sit on the bench near her head. She coiled back, the rope around her waist squeezing her as she twisted around.

"Mind if I pull the fur back and check your wounds?" the man asked kindly.

"No," Cinda growled.

"Okay, we can sit and talk until you are ready,"

A long silence settled between the two of them. Cinda thought of how she could escape. Knowing her leg hurt every time she moved, making swimming a risk. Her head continued to hurt, making it difficult to think.

"My name is Lars. What's yours?" Lars asked.

"Why did you take me?" Cinda asked, ignoring the question, worry showing in her tone.

"You were badly injured, and Ulrick did not want to just leave you to die,"

"Ulrick?" Cinda asked with a raspy voice. She moved her fingers up and down the ropes around her, finally finding the loose knot.

"The orc you saw sitting near you. His name is Ulrick,"

"What are you going to do with me?" Cinda asked as she untied the ropes, loosening them from around her. The pressure in her head hurt with every heartbeat, and the pain was almost as bad as her left thigh.

"Umm… not… quite sure," Lars answered. His voice slightly trailing off.

Cinda froze in place. *Not quite sure! How can you not be sure what you will do with me? Is he going to eat me?* She hesitated to ask, but she could think of nothing else. "Is Ulrick going to eat me?" She whispered out of the flap.

Lars laughed a little after hearing the question. "No, no, no. These orcs don't eat people. The Gray Orcs of the north might. But they eat anything that has a heartbeat, really."

Cinda's mind grew more afraid, taking what Lars said as she might possibly be eaten. She looked around and noticed the large piece of hide making the tent. It could be opened from the top. *If I can get over the edge of the boat, I can maybe swim to the shore. It shouldn't be that far.* She moved her legs, testing their mobility. *Seems good enough to swim a little bit.*

"Are you okay?" Lars asked since Cinda said nothing, but he could feel her moving around through the bench.

Suddenly, the large hide flung away as Cinda emerged. She pulled herself up by the side of the boat, her good leg supporting her, ready to jump over. Her body was almost over the edge, the edge to freedom, but she stopped herself just before going over.

Cinda's heart froze, and her jaw dropped as she looked in every direction. Where she thought she would see trees or grass, all she saw was open water. Her eyes quickly looked over the horizon, seeing nothing but the blue ocean.

"If you really think you can make the swim, go that way," Lars said, relaxed on the bench and pointing south, the opposite direction the boat was heading.

"Where...where are we?" Cinda asked quietly, not truly intending for Lars to hear her.

"We are about... a day into The Crystal Ocean, but you might know it as the North Sea," Lars said as he stood up and looked over the water. "Odd how your people call it the North Sea when there are still more oceans north of us."

Cinda slowly turned her head and looked at Lars. She was surprised to see he wasn't an orc but a human. He was tall for a man, with brown hair as long as a palm on top, cut very short on the sides. His brown beard was short and full, with red hues mixed in where the sun hit it. His face was older than he sounded, with slight wrinkles of age around his eyes and some gray hairs on his temples, making him look in his mid-thirties. He wore a light brown long-sleeved shirt made of leather with dark leather pants. His outfit looked similar to Ulrick's; however, he had much more gray and white fur over his shoulders.

Cinda looked closer at Lars's face. His dark green eyes stared at her while his right eyebrow was raised much higher than his left. "You're human," she said in a surprised tone.

Lars's eyebrow dropped back to normal as he smiled. "Half-human," he said as he pointed to his ear, showing that they were pointed at the top and not rounded like human ears. "And half-elf."

Cinda felt a chill on her skin, only wearing her thin underdress as she stood on the bench. Half over the side of the boat, in position to jump. A large gust of wind came, blowing her dark copper-red hair into her face as the boat shifted to the side. Cinda felt herself start to lose her balance as the boat moved. She panicked as she began falling off the boat's edge and into the waters below.

Lars quickly lunged and wrapped his arms around Cinda's hips, grappling and pulling her off the bench. His arms hurt as they pressed against her bruises while they held her in them. He placed her down, and Cinda looked at the rest of the boat for the first time.

The longboat was around twenty paces long and about three paces wide, with both the front and back curving to a point. The large mass in the center had its green sail open and full of wind. About twenty orcs and a few humans lounged on benches that ran the boat's length while the wind pushed the boat steadily. Wooden barrels, bundles of furs, large sacks, and crates were loosely grouped on the floor. The long edges of the boat were lined with large round wooden shields and oars laying on racks.

Everyone wore something different: furs, armor, or outfits. There was no uniformity or badges or ranks. The orcs looked similar to Ulrick, taller and larger than most men, with tusk-like teeth protruding from their mouths. Even the two female orcs were large, at least they looked female, with their large breasts, gentler faces, and much smaller tusks. All of them intermingled, some with food and mugs in hand, as they stared at Cinda with confused expressions as she stood in Lars's arms.

Cinda gripped Lars's lower arm in fear as she looked back at them. Lars quickly grabbed the furry hide she had been using as a blanket and wrapped it around her. They then glanced at the bandage on her thigh.

"You need to sit back down. It's not smart to be standing on that leg," Lars said as he guided her back to the bench.

Cinda's good eye didn't leave the orcs as she moved. Her fright dulled the pain in her thigh and head. "I've never seen orcs before," she quietly said.

"They're big, aren't they?" Lars said with a grin. He took the larger furry hide that was used like a tent and placed it around her.

Cinda felt hardened leather in it and a hood. "This is a cloak?" She asked, looking at the fur as Lars tried to bundle her in it to keep her warm.

"It is," he said as he pulled the hood on her head, keeping her face visible. "It's Ulrick's cloak, so it's a bit big for you," He dragged over a barrel and sat on it across from the bench.

Cinda stared at Ulrick over Lar's shoulder. Ulrick noticed, and as he turned his head, she quickly averted her gaze, afraid to make eye contact with him.

Lars noticed her fear and softly said, "You are safe. No one here will hurt you." Cinda did not respond, holding herself tightly as she sat on the bench, the pain in her head returning along with the pain in the rest of her body. "What do you know about orcs?"

Cinda still looked down to avoid looking at Ulrick or the other orcs as she softly spoke. "I've heard that they are vile monsters, attacking and killing people at random, bathing in their blood, and taking anything of worth. Taking people as slaves, or eating people while they are still alive." She paused for a moment. "My grandfather called them marauding savages."

Lars clenched his teeth and made an awkward face while raising his shoulders. "Well…that is partially true." He then relaxed and smiled at her. "They raid, yes, but they don't slaughter people. Well, at least most don't."

"Aren't all orcs the same?" Cinda asked.

"Are all humans the same?" Lars questioned with a crooked grin.

Cinda shook her head, knowing that people were always different from the few villages she had been to.

"Orcs, humans, elves… all races have good people and bad people. It truly doesn't matter what race you are around," Lars said. "Though you do have differences in culture."

"Lars," Ulrick's deep voice resounded, interrupting their conversation. He then let out a slew of words Cinda didn't understand.

Lars turned back to Cinda. "Ulrick thinks you should eat and drink some water. You lost a bit of blood and need your strength."

Cinda nodded in agreement. She hadn't noticed how very thirsty she was. So Lars turned and grabbed a small barrel and a backpack. Reaching into the pack, he pulled out a wooden bowl, spoon, and water skin.

Cinda took the water skin and began to drink deeply, stopping suddenly when she realized it wasn't water inside. "What is that?" she asked, the sweet flavor lingering in her mouth.

"Honey mead," Lars responded as he scooped the wooden bowl into the barrel and pulled it out.

Cinda looked at the bowl. It held a light gray color

porridge with black specks. "What is that?"

"They call it "Brung" in Orcish," Lars answered. "Just a bunch of nourishment that the body needs in one simple, distasteful goop."

Cinda lifted the bowl to her nose. The smell was unpleasant, Something between a goat and sweaty feet. "What's in it?"

Lars looked at her and smiled slightly. "Honestly, it's more tolerable if you don't know. And it tastes like it smells." He then motioned to the honey mead. "You eat a bunch of it fast and then wash it down with the mead. It's how I get through eating it."

Cinda scooped some in the spoon, looking at the Brung as it dribbled back into the bowl. "I can't eat this."

"You need to. It will help you heal," Lars answered kindly. "Just imagine it as something else."

Cinda's stomach hurt, and she could not tell if it was hunger, the injuries, or the headache, causing her to feel slightly nauseous. Hesitant, she knew she should at least try. The smell of the Brung was in her nose as she drew the bowl closer. She tried to imagine anything, but nothing came to her mind. *Just get through this.* She then started scooping the Brung into her mouth. The taste of it was horrible on her tongue, but she continued to dig. *It's chicken soup. It's chicken soup.* She repeated, as her stomach turned from the taste. She stopped a moment to catch her breath. *It tastes like I am licking a goat!* Her stomach tried to heave it back, but she swallowed hard to keep it down. *Goat soup, goat soup,* She repeated in her head as she finished the bowl and quickly started drinking the mead. The sweet taste of the honey mead washed her mouth of the Brung, leaving her thankful the taste did not linger.

"So, what is your name, young lady?" Lars asked politely as he took the bowl from her. His face looked kindly at hers with a slight smile.

"Can you turn the boat around and take me back home?" Cinda asked. She was about to explain that she was a Lady and her father would pay them for the return of his only daughter. *But what if they decide to ransom me instead when they learn I'm important? But…it would still get me home.*

"I am sorry, but we can't turn around," Lars said, interrupting Cinda's thoughts. "We need to get back home before winter arrives, and there is not enough time. The wind and the tides are pushing us north." Lars moved his head lower to catch Cinda's gaze and look her straight in the eyes. "We will hopefully be able to take you home after the winter or at least get you on a boat to Miterra."

Cinda sat silent for a moment as she looked at Lars. His pleasant demeanor relaxed her slightly, and his kind eyes made her feel like he might be someone to trust. She turned and looked to the south, thinking about home and how she wanted to return, but that seemed impossible for now. She looked back at Lars and felt helpless, sighed, and said. "My name is Cinda."

CHAPTER 7

Hendric ran through the forest, dodging between trees, trying to stay out of sight. It felt like hours to him after the sun had set, only able to see the rear wagon in the moonlight and hear its wheels turning in the night air. No rear guard protected the wagon, no scouts from what he could tell. It all felt too easy for him.

The group had veered off the main road and onto an overgrown and underused path. It continued for some time until Hendric finally stopped hearing the wagon's wheels turning. *They finally stopped.* He thought to himself, knowing he should keep his distance. He heard elves could see in the dark much better than he could. So he sat and waited.

The light from a fire came through the trees in the distance, and Hendric crept closer, watching the silhouettes of the elves walking around. Pretending it was daylight in case the elves could see through the darkness. It took some time, but he managed to settle behind a few trees, a short distance away yet close enough to have a good view of the caged children. Seeing that Conner and Kervin looked uninjured with their shirts ripped, exposing their chests. Derin and Frin cried while trying to tie their shirt collars back together. Seby sat, curled up in a ball in the corner with his back to Hendric. *Why have their shirts been ripped? They were not ripped when they came out of the fort.*

Herndric's eyes shifted to the waiting elves, watching the woman in red as she walked and poured the contents of a jug into a large circle on the ground. She began pouring more within the circle, forming lines and arcs with it. When finished, she stepped out and handed the jug off to one of her guards before kneeling beside the circle.

Hendric peered through the trees, unable to determine what was drawn on the ground. He watched as she put her hand on the circle's edge above the liquid she had poured. Her eyes suddenly flared with light, painted in deep oranges and vibrant reds, like a fire roared inside her.

A burst of light and heat erupted as the circle caught fire. The flames grew, reaching up almost as tall as the woman. The surrounding elves shielded their eyes from the light and stepped away from the heat. The children backed up against the far wall of the cage. Yet the woman in red did not move. Then, as fast as it erupted, the fire died down to a small blue flame, leaving a man in the center of the circle.

He stood upright, unbothered by the blue flames at his feet. His dark, fine leather boots came halfway up his shins with his black cloth pants tucked into them. His black shirt was tucked into his pants with a leather belt fastened around his waist. The collar of his shirt was folded perfectly, with the front slit loosely tied. The shirt was sleeveless, exposing his arms but his hands resting in his pockets. His skin was a light gray, almost like marble, and reflected the light of the blue flames around him on the many curves of his lean muscles, like the scales of a snake. The dark hair on his head was slicked back and spiked on the back of his head, looking like the fur of a black dog and not like a person's hair. His face was slender, like an elf, but his ears were distinctly different. More like the ears of a bat but not as wide. His eyes were solid black, and he looked straight at Galadin as she stood up. Anger showed on his face as she took a few steps away.

"What is the reason you summoned me, Galadin?" the figure said in Elvish.

Magic. Hendric thought to himself as he watched; never had he seen magic but had only heard it described in stories. As he watched and listened, he could not understand the figure's language but knew it was Elvish. He could tell by the tone in the man's voice and the look on his face that he was angry. Hendric sat quietly and listened, unable to turn away.

"I need your assistance, Dravis," Galadin pleaded.

"Assistance?" Dravis quietly repeated as he stepped out of the circle towards Galadin.

"I need your help with these humans," Galadin said as she motioned to the children in the cage.

Dravis slowly turned his head towards the children, looking at them for only a moment, then turned back to Galadin. "You summon me like this," he said. His upper lip snarled, showing a sharp canine as his tone grew angrier. "Like some dog. Just to help you with a few human children in a cage." The hair on his head shifted to stand upright. Hendric realized it was not hair but thin black quills, much like a porcupine.

"An oracle told me the new Druid was a child and which village he lived in. These are all the children from that village," Galadin said as she looked over them.

Conner and Kervin stood before Derin, Frin, and Seby while they cowered in fear. None of them could understand Elvish, but they knew something was wrong.

Dravis slowly shook his head, his quills lowered back down to rest. "Do you plan to kill this Druid like you did the last one?" he snarled with disappointment.

"That was an accident!"

"And why can you not tell which of them is the Druid?"

"None of them bare the mark. Nor have they shown any magical abilities."

"So you need me to see which is the next Druid?"

Galadin bowed her head low to Dravis. "Please help me,"

Dravis walked past her to the wagon. The children grew more frightened as he approached. They pressed themselves against the opposite wall, the shift in weight making the wagon struts creek under them. Dravis stopped, his hands still in his pockets as he looked intently at each of them with solid black eyes. He then closed them, leaning his head back, and drew a long breath through his nose. Then he exhaled and drew another breath, then another looked at the children again.

"None of them smell of the world tree's magic," Dravis said. He then turned his head towards Galadin, his right brow raised as he looked at her. "Your Druid is not among them."

"That is impossible. All the boys of that age from the village are in that wagon," Galadin snarled. "Check again!"

Dravis looked coldly at Galadin. "The only magic I smell is yours. The smell of ash and death. Do you question my abilities…Galadin." His tone turned hostile as he spoke her name.

Galadin quickly changed her stature. "These are all the children from the village."

Dravis turned back to the caged boys. "Are there any more boys your age in your village that are not here?" He asked in perfect Terrish. His tone was entirely different, almost sickeningly sweet like he was a friend.

Conner stood out from the others like he was protecting

them. "No, it's just us," he said with slight hesitation.

Dravis smiled and spoke to Conner directly. "It is not smart to lie to me."

"We are the only ones," Conner said defiantly.

Dravis's smile sunk into a frown. He slowly nodded as he walked around the wagon, stopping at the gate to the cage. His hand left his pocket and grasped the lock to the gate. "Is there someone else?" he asked Conner. "I will give you this last chance, to be honest."

"We are the only ones," Conner said to Dravis as he moved before the other boys.

Dravis snapped the iron lock off the frame with his one hand. The gate door creaked open on its hinges. Conner raised his fists, ready to fight Dravis if he stepped into the cage. Hendric quietly pulled an arrow from his quiver and placed it in his bow as he watched.

Faster than Conner could react, Dravis reached into the cage, grabbed him by the arm, and pulled him out. Conner gasped in surprise while the other children screamed in fear. Hendric quickly pulled the arrow back to his cheek, ready to fire, as Dravis lifted Conner by the neck, blocking his shot.

Conner grasped Dravis's arm and kicked wildly, flailing desperately to escape. None of the blows even phased Dravis as he stared into Conner's eyes.

"Who is not in the wagon?" Dravis yelled so the children in the wagon could hear him. "Tell me, or I will eat this one." Dravis's lower jaw began to shake and then unhinged with a loud pop. His maw expanded, snakelike, as his teeth began to change shape, growing long and sharp. His tongue grew in length. Black veins grew from his eyes to his temples, spreading across the sides of his face while his quills stood up and shook slightly.

Conner tried to scream as he watched the transformation, but Dravis's hand was too tight around his throat to let out a sound. Hendric froze with fear, wanting to let the arrow fly but knowing he might hit Conner. The children screamed in horror as they watched Dravis' jaw separate in half along his chin to grow even wider. At the same time, Dravis' elongated tongue began to move up Conner's cheek as he lowered him closer and closer to his open mouth.

A voice suddenly pierced the screams, yelling, "Owen isn't here!"

Dravis pulled his mouth away from Conner. His quills rested again while his teeth and tongue changed back to their previous size while he growled. With a few more pops, his jaw became solid and shrank back into looking like before as he lowered Conner to the ground.

Hendric took aim at Dravis as he saw him lowering Conner, but as soon as he had a clear shot, Dravis looked straight at Hendric. Hendric's eyes opened wide at the sight of Dravis. *Is he looking straight at me?* A shiver of fear rolled down his spine. He hesitated, not knowing if he should release the arrow or not. *Why isn't he doing anything?* Dravis continued to stare at him, his black eyes not even blinking, as a thin smile crept across his face.

Conner tried to move away, but Dravis's hand around his neck held him in place.

"Who is this, Owen?" Galadin yelled at the children in Terrish. Her eyes flared with anger like a fire was about to erupt from them.

Frin crawled forward in the cage, his body trembling with fear as he closed his eyes, unable to look Galadin in the face. "Owen, son of Borin," he said softly.

"What?" Galadin yelled.

"He left the village before those elves came," Frin said, then pleaded, "Please, let us go."

Galadin shrieked in anger so loud the boys covered their ears. As she shouted, the average sized campfire behind them flared high into the air. Her teeth clenched together as she looked at the children in the cage and outstretched her left hand. "Burn in the fires of Corthus!" she yelled in Elvish as the flames of the fire twisted and bent sharply, shooting into the cage. The children's screams of fear only lasted momentarily as the intense fire burned their bodies, melting the cage's iron bars and setting the wagon on fire.

Hendric screamed in his mind as he watched the children's charred bones fall into the wagon's flames. He shifted his bow, pointing the arrow straight at Galadin, his eyes blurring and losing focus. Then he noticed Dravis still staring at him, his head slowly shaking back and forth as if telling him not to release the arrow.

"Give me that boy, Dravis!" Galadin yelled in Elvish. "His fate shall be the same as his friends!"

Dravis turned to Galadin, his eyes stern and his face straight. "No, this boy will be my snack on the long journey home I must take now," he said in Terrish.

Galadin looked at Dravis angrily. "Fine!" she snapped at him in Elvish.

Dravis then turned and looked down the overgrown road. "You should go now and find this Owen, son of Borin before someone else does," he shouted in Terrish. He then wrapped his arm around Conner's chest as two large, bat-like wings sprouted from his back. "And Galadin, the next time you summon me like this, I will not be so tolerant."

Galadin looked defiantly at Dravis, ready for a challenge, but her hands unclenched. "Will you tell Marsed about this?" she whispered in Elvish.

Dravis smiled as he looked at Galadin. "Your failure to bring the Druid Olsen to Marsed is your own doing. I will not speak of your second failure... unless he asks," Dravis replied.

Dravis slightly bent his legs and raised his wings, firming his grip around Conner. "Don't squirm. I'd rather you not be injured," he whispered into Conner's ear. Hendric watched helplessly as Conner seemed to relax. With a jump and a beating of wings, Dravis disappeared into the night sky with Conner in his arms.

Hendric slowly relaxed his bow as he sank behind some trees, entirely out of sight. *Was that monster telling me to find Owen? He had to have been, but why did he do that? Why not just kill me?* He started to slowly back up from the trees as he heard the elf woman, Galadin, begin to yell at the other Elves. Hendric wished he was dreaming but knew he was not. As he quietly snuck away, he looked at the sky. *I hope you will be ok, Conner. I'm sorry I didn't get to you in time.*

* * *

Arminiul awoke under the night sky. The stars twinkled in the heavens above. Their sight was calming as he was never one to enjoy living in one of the vast Elven cities. He preferred the deep wilderness, where he could enjoy the silence far from other elves. He listened to the wind as it whistled, passing through a crack in the wall. He missed the sound from when he was stationed there. Before he became part of the hunter units, how long ago that was.

Arminiul looked to where Sepher was supposed to be sitting and did not see him there. *I guess he actually left.* He thought, slightly happy, hoping Sepher would be okay. Knowing he would miss him in times to come. Then Arminiul realized he didn't hear anyone talking. He sat up and looked around.

The fort seemed too quiet. Even the light of the fire through an arrow slit looked to have died down. Arminiul stood up and noticed a few of his comrades lying in odd positions. He walked over to a group of them and studied their faces.

All three had their eyes open; the whites were bloodshot, and blood came from their noses. Arminiul felt for a pulse, but there was no heartbeat. *They're dead.* He began to panic as he rushed to others. Their eyes were closed, but blood came from their noses. *They are dead as well.*

Ariminiul ran past other elves, checking their faces, losing hope until he found Maltius lying on the ground. He got on his knees next to his commander's body, hoping at least Maltius was still alive, clinging to that hope until he felt for a pulse, yet felt nothing.

Arminiul's lower lip began to tremble as he wanted to mourn for his friends. He sniffed hard and shook his head to fight back the tears. *I can't do this now. Stay on task.* Then he began to inspect Maltius's body closely, checking for marks and signs of anything out of place, even opening his mouth and checking his tongue, seeing that the color had changed darker. *They have been poisoned.* He knew about the poison called Last Sleep. It took a few hours before it suddenly tricked its victims, leaving them with bloodshot eyes, bloody nose, and discolored tongue. *But how was everyone poisoned?* He looked around. Then he noticed the wine barrels. *Everyone drank the wine from Senator Galadin but me and Sepher. Why would she do this?* He then remembered what Galadin had said. *No witnesses*. The words rang out in his memory as if she were telling them to him right then.

Arminiul could not believe what he was thinking. *Why would Galadin do such a thing? Why kill so many for just a few human children?* None of this made sense. No one knew they were ordered to attack Orinton and kidnap the children except her and her Guard. They brought them to a secluded fort that the Ellious Empire abandoned. She knew everyone would drink the wine in celebration.

"Senator Galadin betrayed us," Arminiul said to Maltius's lifeless body. He looked around at the other bodies. "I'm not sure what to do," he said, expecting Maltius to direct him. He closed his eyes and let his mind think clearly for a moment, realizing he should not linger if Galadin's Guards were to come back. He quickly gathered his things and put his saddle back on his horse.

Sepher's horse slowly walked up to Arminiul. "You think we should go after Sepher?" he said to the horse as he scratched its neck. The horse nudged him with its nose. "Okay, let's go find Sepher then. It's better to take you with me anyway. If anyone counts the horses, they will notice one of us missing." He put Sepher's saddle on the horse and walked them out of the gate. He began riding north along the stream, hoping to find Sepher.

CHAPTER 8

irds chirped in the distance, welcoming the morning.
Dew weighed the blades of grass as a predawn mist
filled the air. The dark sky lightened as dawn
approached. The peaceful serenity of it all made it seem like
nothing was wrong. However, much was amiss in Sepher's
mind as he sat on his knees at the top of a hill, awaiting the
sun.

"Hyllo, Goddess of the sun and day, protector of elves.
Hear my prayer and give me your love," Sepher said in
Elvish, beginning his prayer as the first rays of the sun
peeked over the horizon. "I beg for your forgiveness, for I
have not been the man I hoped to be as of late. My actions...
I must atone for it. I need your help. I ask for your
protection, my goddess, and your protection for the boy and
young woman until I find them and can protect them
myself." He then bent down, bowing to the still-rising sun.
"I beg of you, Hyllo, hear my prayers. Be behind me as you
always have been, and I shall prove my worth once again."
He then stood up and watched the sun rise above the
horizon.

"Do you think she heard you?" Arminiul shouted as he
walked up the hill towards Sepher.

Sepher quickly turned, shocked to hear the familiar
voice. "How did you find me?"

"You cover your tracks so well I figured that would be
pointless," Arminiul said as he walked closer. "But I know
you and figured out how far you could get and knew you

would pray to Hyllo when the sun rose. This hilltop is probably the best spot in the area."

Sepher looked around, expecting more than just Arminiul. Still, all he spotted were his and Arminiul's horses tied to a tree further down the hill.

As Arminiul approached, he asked again, "So, do you think she heard you?"

"I'm not sure,"

Arminiul's expression was one of sorrow as he looked at the sun. "I hope she did," He said in a solemn voice.

"What's wrong? Are you here to take me back?" Sepher asked, seeing that Arminiul was distraught. Arminiul shook his head. "Have you decided to come with me?"

Arminiul's eyes did not look into Sepher's. "Everyone at the fort is dead," he said quietly.

"Who attacked? Are you hurt?" Sepher said in surprise as he looked Arminiul over, searching for wounds.

Arminiul shook his head again and looked off into the distance. "When I woke up... they were... They were all dead... by poison."

"How was everyone poisoned?" Sepher asked. His eyes locked on Arminiul, yet Arminiul couldn't look back.

"I wasn't sure until I found you alive, but I think it was the wine."

"But that wine was a gift from Senator Galadin."

Arminiul's eyes shifted and looked straight into Sepher's. "Exactly. Senator Galadin wanted us all dead!"

"But why?" Sepher said in a confused tone.

"When she came and gathered the children, she mentioned no witnesses. Guess that included us as well," Arminiul said as he looked off into the distance again.

"What are we going to do?"

"With any luck, they won't notice us missing. So, we will track down this boy and determine why Senator Galadin wants him. That is, if he's still alive… and then…" Arminiul paused as he turned and looked straight at Sepher, his face full of anger. "We hunt down and kill Senator Galadin."

Sepher turned and looked towards the sun. "The boy and woman are still alive. I can feel it."

"You can feel it, huh?" Arminiul said. "Are you some kind of oracle now?"

"No, just have faith that they are."

"That is too bad. I had hoped you could tell me Senator Galadin's fate," Arminiul said as he also turned and looked toward the sun.

"I don't need to see the future to tell you that," Sepher answered. "You're going to drive your arrow through her wretched heart."

"I like the sound of that," Arminiul said, wishing for it to come true.

Sepher looked down at the ground. "Everyone?" he asked quietly.

Arminiul knew what he was asking. "All of them, including Maltius."

Sepher closed his eyes as he became stricken with grief. "I can't believe it."

Arminiul grasped Sepher by the shoulder and pulled him in, hugging him tightly as Sepher began to cry into his shoulder. "Cry now for our fallen friends," Arminiul whispered. He felt horrible for Sepher and was sure it was hard enough to leave them behind, but to hear that his companions of the past few years were dead was even harder to bear.

* * *

With a loud creak, the barn doors opened, waking Owen and Tavia from their deep slumber. They lay silent with a pile of hay between them and the doorway. Tavia spotted the barn on their way to Keerike just as night fell.

"Well, hello there," a gruff voice said to the five goats Owen and Tavia had brought into the barn. "Is there anyone here?" the voice called out.

After a few moments of silence, Tavia and Owen heard the door close, and the room became silent, with only the sound of goats chewing. Tavia shifted and cringed as the hay crumpled under her. She slowly crept to the edge of the hay pile, peering around to make sure the person who had spoken had left. She sighed with relief to see no one else there.

"Are we safe?" Owen whispered as he got up from where he was.

"I think we should go before he returns," Tavia said quietly.

"I'm still here, you know," the voice said as a man stepped into Tavia's view from the opposite side of the large hay pile. He looked at Tavia, holding a short sword. "What are you two doing in here?" he asked harshly.

Tavia's heart began to race as she looked at the sharp blade. "My friend...I mean, brother...I mean..." Tavia took a quick moment to think about what to say. "My brother and I were just looking for a place to sleep," she said, her voice high in pitch, her words tripping on her tongue. She hoped the man would believe her. It was part of the story they were planning on telling people. She thought Owen and her could pass as brother and sister but had slipped up in her panic. "We were heading to Keerike when we spotted this barn."

He was cleaner than any farmer she had seen before and looked to be in his mid-twenties with a handsome demeanor. He stood slightly taller than Tavia, with short black hair and a few days of stubble on his face. His fine blue, long-sleeved tunic with yellow trim was tucked into his dark pants, held inside tall polished black boots. His posture was straight and refined like she had seen in Willhelm, the way a Lord would stand. He was only carrying an elegant leather satchel along with his short sword.

"You don't look like a farmer," Tavia said out of turn.

"And you don't look like the owner of this barn," the man retorted. He began stepping around Tavia, getting in between her and the door as Owen slowly emerged from behind the hay. "So, what are you two doing here?"

Tavia realized what they must look like. Her dress was covered in dirt with rips in many places from running through the forest. She glanced at Owen, seeing his clothes were no cleaner than hers. Their faces were covered in dirt except for the streaks that she could imagine were on her cheeks from crying herself to sleep the night before. Her once lovely, flowing blonde hair was darker and knotted everywhere. *We must look disgusting,* She thought to herself.

Tavia and Owen had rehearsed their story. Tavia knew Keerike was at peace with the Ellious Empire, and it would not be wise to say they were from Orinton or to mention what happened there. "We ran away from home," she said with conviction. "Our father is a drunk and not a good man. So we ran away for our safety." Tavia pulled part of the story from her memory of her own father and hoped some genuineness bled into her voice.

"Where are you from?" the man asked. Tavia noticed he was beginning to drop his guard.

"Green Brooke," Tavia answered. It was a village far to the south that she had visited as a little girl. It was small and not known by most, making it perfect in her mind for a place to say they were from.

"You've traveled far to escape your father," the man said. "And those goats, did you steal them or happen upon them on the way?"

"Acquired them from our father," Tavia answered. "Payment for what we had to endure while living with him," she said with spite, knowing she would have done the same to her father if given the chance. "We hoped to trade them for a place to stay."

The man looked at her curiously. "Well, I guess we can see to that. What are your names?"

"Tavia," she said, then motioned to Owen, noticing a frightened look in his eyes. "And this is my brother Owen."

"It is nice to make your acquaintance," the man said with a slight bow of his head. "My name is Vistem." He then sheathed his short sword and walked to the barn's doors. "Come, I'll take you to a place to sell the goats."

Owen looked at Tavia while Vistem walked out the doors. "Do you think we can trust him?"

"If he wanted to hurt us, he would have done it here, out of sight from everyone," Tavia said, to try and comfort Owen but also saying it for herself. "Get the goats together, and we will follow him," Tavia said as she stuffed the blankets into a sack and then flung the two burlap sacks over her shoulder that held all their supplies. Owen quickly grabbed his hatchet and slid it into his belt. He tied the goats to one cord before walking them out of the barn.

The path they walked was not well used but plain to see. Vistem walked ahead of Tavia and Owen, who kept the five goats in tow. "How is your chest?" Tavia asked quietly so that Vistem did not hear.

"It still hurts, but not as bad as yesterday," Owen whispered.

"When we get somewhere private, I will change the bandage for you. There is still half a bottle of ointment left. We will have to buy more some-" Tavia quietly mentioned. She stopped abruptly when she noticed Vistem slow his stride.

"It is not far," Vistem said as he turned and looked at Tavia. "Would you like some help with... those?" he asked cordially as he pointed to the sacks she carried.

"That would be nice," Tavia responded. The sacks were not overly heavy, but she was not about to turn down help from an attractive man.

Vistem walked to Tavia, took the larger of the two sacks, and slung it over his shoulder. They began walking the path again. "Your brother seems quite good with the goats," Vistem said, glancing back at Owen as he trailed Vistem and Tavia.

Tavia glanced back as well, seeing Owen pulling the goats with ease. "He has a way with animals," Tavia said, surprised since goats usually did not like to listen to him in Orinton. She turned to Vistem, noticing how blue his eyes were in the morning light and feeling embarrassed of how she must look to him.

As they walked around a bend, the path became cleaner and looked like it was used more often. Keerike came into view from behind some trees in the distance. The village was larger than Tavia had remembered. She counted about thirty buildings in sight, all made of wood and thatch roofing. However, there were a few different styles in which the structures were built. On one side of Keerike was a large white dome made of stone that stuck above the other buildings near it. She remembered it being the elven temple and library in the elven section of the town, a section she would like to stay away from. She could see people wandering the paths between them, going about their day. It looked like a nice place from where she was, peaceful.

"How many people live here?" Tavia asked, hoping it was enough for Owen and her to disappear and not be noticed. Because in a small village, everyone knows about anyone passing through.

"Over two thousand, I believe," Vistem answered. "But Keerike is much bigger than this, and this is just the village's market and main area. Like the barn, some scattered farms and houses are also part of Keerike."

"Why were you in the barn?" Tavia asked as she started to try and at least fix her hair. Her fingers caught in the knots on the back of her head. "You're not dressed like a farmer." She quickly lowered her hand when Vistem turned and looked at her.

"I like to go there to read. No one bothers me there, at least, not normally."

"Sounds nice to have a place to escape," Tavia said. *This man seems quite lovely and dresses nicely as well. It would be great if he would let us stay with him while Owen heals.* A slight smile grew as she looked at Vistem, thinking about the possibilities with him.

"It is," Vistem replied. He then turned his head and took

a quick look at Owen. "So, are you two just passing through, or are you thinking of staying a little while?"

Tavia smiled at Vistem. "Matters if we find something worth staying for," she said a little flirtatiously but then regretted it, thinking about what she must look like.

"I see," Vistem said as he smiled back at her. "Well, you can trade the goats, which should give you enough for maybe a month."

"Maybe we will do that then," Tavia said. She then looked back at Owen as he walked with the goats. *Maybe he will be okay with staying here for that long.* They had not really talked about what they were planning to do, nor had they really talked about any future plans. They had their sights only set on surviving the past few days.

As they approached the market area of Keerike, Tavia noticed that the people were dressed in clothes much like what she was used to, nothing like what Vistem was wearing. She then saw a few people bowing slightly to him.

Tavia stopped walking. "Who are you in this village?" she asked, thinking he was important.

Vistem paused and looked around as if thinking. "I'm just really well known."

"Hello, my lord," a man said as he walked by.

Tavia looked at Vistem with a curious expression. "My lord?"

Vistem smiled, slightly embarrassed. "It's nothing." He then started walking, but Tavia slowed her pace noticeably. "Really, it's nothing. My oldest brother is the Duke of these lands."

Tavia stopped where she was. "You mean Duke Revnar Formil is your brother?" Tavia said, slipping into a higher pitch than she intended. Vistem nodded in agreement, noticing the change in tone. Her heart began to sink. She knew Duke Revnar was one of the Dukes who refused to go to war against the Ellious Empire, claiming the peace established by the King was beneficial to all. "I think we can find our way from here," she said, slightly out of disgust. She also quickly gathered that walking with Vistem would be a quick way to be noticed.

Vistem looked sad at what he had just heard. "At least let me take you to someone who will give you a good deal for the goats."

Tavia looked at Owen, who had a look of worry on his face. Tavia knew they had to blend in, and going against the Duke's younger brother suddenly might make him doubt their story. "Okay." She said while giving a reassuring nod to Owen.

They continued walking through the village without saying a word among them. Vistem stopped to say something to Tavia, but she looked away from him each time. Still reluctantly walking the streets with him.

Owen was shocked at how different Keerike was. The plethora of smells of cooking food filled his nostrils. The sounds of boots on stone roads and merchants yelling about their wares filled his ears. The hundred or more people walking around was surprising, but he found it strange that many of them did not talk to each other, unlike their home where all the villagers were friends. Owen felt uneasy among all the people, feeling that these people were happy and had no care about the war for their freedom from the elven oppressors.

Then, the crowd seemed to part before his eyes as a male elf came into view. The elf's short brown hair made his pointed ears appear more prominent from the side. He was talking to a merchant, but that did not matter. The sight of him made Owen remember the elf that had walked by while Tavia and him were hiding between the large tree's roots. The elf looked just like the one that was hunting for them.

Owen's eyes focused on the elf. His mind was flooded with memories of the screams around him while he and Tavia held each other tight. The feeling of a bug crawling on his back as they tried to stay quiet. The crowd around them disappeared from Owen's sight as he stared at the elf while he talked. *They found us.* Owen's mind screamed as his heart rapidly beat in his chest. He let go of the ropes tied to the goats. His hand moved over the hatchet in his belt, yet the rest of him froze with fear.

"Owen," Tavia said as she grasped Owen by the shoulders, stepping in front of him. "What's wrong?"

"The elves... they found us," Owen struggled to say as he looked around Tavia at the elf who was now walking away with his hands full of rugs. "We have to stop him before he tells the others," Owen said as he began to pull his hatchet free.

Tavia quickly put her hand over Owen's to keep the hatchet in his belt. "He was not one of the elves that attacked Orinton. We are safe here," Tavia said as her right hand moved from his shoulder and rested against his cheek. "Just breathe, Owen." She said as she stared into his eyes to calm him.

"Is your brother alright?" Vistem asked as Owen began to take a few deep breaths.

"He is fine..." Tavia said as she thought about an excuse for Owen's actions. "He is just not used to so many people."

"You should gather the goats before they walk away," Vistem said.

Tavia looked at the goats behind Owen. All five of them were strangely standing still. Looking in the same direction that Owen was looking, the elf walked away and disappeared into the crowd.

"Come, Owen, we have to keep going," Tavia said as she gathered the ropes by his feet and placed them in his hand. "I told you there would be elves here." She whispered. Owen nodded his head in agreement, and they started to walk again.

It took them some time to weave through the mass of people and the center of the village to reach the small farms on the outskirts.

"This is it," Vistem said as they approached a building with a large pen and a few goats roaming inside.

"Aerlene!" Vistem shouted as they approached what looked like a counter built to the front of the building with a cloth overhang. He quickly lifted the two burlap sacks and placed them on the counter. "Aerlene, are you there?"

"Yes, yes, I'm here," an older woman said as she walked into view from inside the building. She had soft gray hair pulled back into a bun and looked in her forties, dressed in a green dress that had seen too many days since last being washed. Her kind face smiled at Vistem as she looked up at him. "What can I do for you, Lord Vistem?"

"These two are..." Vistem started to say but was interrupted by Tavia.

"We are looking to trade these goats," Tavia said assertively.

Aerlene leaned forward and looked at the goats as Owen walked them around for her to see. "They look tired," she said as she assessed them.

"They have been walking since Green Brooke," Tavia

said. "But they are in good condition."

"I mean the two of you, young lady," Aerlene said with a kind grin at Tavia.

Tavia looked at Owen, seeing his exhausted face covered in dirt. "Yes, it has been a long journey."

Aerlene then walked around the counter to closely inspect the goats. "I'll give you five silver each," she told Tavia.

Tavia looked at Owen, wondering what five silver was worth in Keerike. Orinton would trade supplies, food, and livestock. Seldom did they use a form of currency.

"Come now, Aerlene," Vistem interjected. "I brought them here because I said you were fair. These goats look like they should be worth more than just five."

"How much is a goat worth?" Tavia asked Vistem blatantly.

"Goats like the ones you have, I'd say a gold piece each," Vistem answered, though he did not have experience dealing with goats.

Aerlene sent him a glare at the price he mentioned. "Well, if most of my goats weren't taken without being paid for by some pointy-eared elves, then maybe I could afford that,"

Vistem swallowed hard as if he knew he might have crossed a line. "These times are tough, Aerlene, and they were needed," he responded.

Tavia stepped closer to Aerlene. "I'm sorry," she said in a kind tone. "My brother and I are not from around here and have never had to deal with coins for trade. I understand the elves have taken from you like they have so many other people." She took Aerlene's hand in hers. "My brother and I just need enough to get a safe place to sleep for a week or more and some good meals. If five silver each will cover that, then it is fine with us."

Aerlene looked into Tavia's eyes, pity pulled on her face. "How about I give you five silver a goat, and you two can stay with me for free."

Tavia looked at Owen. "Does that sound okay with you, Owen?" Owen nodded in agreement. "We would much appreciate that, Aerlene." She then turned to Vistem. "I thank you for your help, Vistem, in bringing us here," she said, making sure not to call him by title, feeling like his family does not deserve such things.

CHAPTER 9

The wind continued pushing the boat further from Cinda's home. She lay on the bench for hours, not moving from where she was. The pain in her side, leg, and head made her want to stay as still as possible as the boat moved under her. She sat up only from time to time and only with the help of Lars. She desperately wanted to go home but questioned what she would be going home to. The elves seemed out for blood, killing everyone for some unknown purpose. She was not sure anyone had even survived.

She began to let her guard down with Lars. His smiling, nonchalant attitude comforted her. He seemed perfectly at ease with her, unlike many in her village who always kept their distance because of her father. However, through the smiles, she still doubted her safety. He was half elf, half of those who had slaughtered her friends and grandfather. She felt trapped, unable to fight back or run if she had to.

Lars only spoke when spoken to. He never tried to pry. Cinda always spoke first, and he always obliged her, answering all her questions about orcs and reassuring her she could return home in spring when the ice melts. The conversations were short because she couldn't keep herself from nodding off while they were talking, nor did she want to talk much. It was hard for Cinda to concentrate since her headache had not wavered. Lars was kind about it, knowing her injuries were severe. He kept the conversations at her pace instead of his own, occasionally getting up from the bench to help take care of something on the boat or fetch something for Ulrick. Once in a while, he would walk to the front of the boat and speak to the two elves that seemed to be held captive.

None of the others on the boat paid Cinda any attention. It was as if they knew she was there but did not care. A feeling far from what she was accustomed to. Always being seen and bowed to, treated higher than everyone. The feeling of not being the center of attention was relaxing to her. *Always smile. You are prettier when you smile.* Cinda's father's voice said in her head. But she wasn't smiling now.

Cinda did notice Ulrick staring at her occasionally, and she would catch him in the corner of her eye. Sometimes, when she would turn and look at him, their eyes would meet for a few moments, and then he would face the front of the boat. He never spoke to her directly. Even though they did not share a language, he did not ask through Lars. However, he told Lars to do things for her to ensure she was more comfortable. It was strange to her. After all the stories she had heard about orcs yet, this one seemed different. He simply sat on the opposite bench from her, steering the boat and fiddling with small leather strips.

"It looks alright," Lars said as he finished wrapping a new bandage on Cinda's thigh. He pulled her dress over her knees and wrapped her back in the hide blanket.

Cinda, however, noticed that while Lars looked at the wound, he had a worried expression. He also spoke to Ulrick in Orcish for a while, and they both seemed to talk about her injury.

"What is wrong?" Cinda asked.

"It's nothing. We are just concerned about your leg wound," Lars answered casually as if the stiffness and sharp growing pain in her leg were normal.

"Why do you care?" Cinda asked spitefully.

Lars looked into Cinda's eyes sorrowfully. "We are worried about it being infected, is all." He then smiled. "It should be okay. We just have to keep it as clean as we can."

Cinda felt that he was lying about something with that smile. The severity of the wound or what they had planned to do with her. Ulrick interrupted her thoughts by speaking in a stern tone to Lars.

Lars looked at Cinda. "Ulrick asks how you ended up in the river." He then pulled a broken arrow shaft out from behind him. "And why did you have an elven arrow in your leg?"

Cinda took a deep breath. She knew she couldn't tell them she was the daughter of a Lord because she knew descendants of Lords were often kidnapped and held for ransom. *Why would they care if they plan to hurt me? Why would they even take care of me like this?* Cinda paused from the question. Thinking about how to answer and what Lars would do if she talked about elves attacking her home. Her eyes shifted to the two elves held prisoner. *They did not seem friends of the Ellious Empire, but could they be trusted?*

"My village was attacked by elves," Cinda finally spoke. Watching Lar's reaction to knowing that elves attacked them and hurt her, Lars only looked sympathetic. "They killed my grandpa and then started killing everyone." Lars translated for Ulrick, and they both seemed to have sorrowful faces from hearing her words. "I ran and tried to cross the river, but an elf shot me in the thigh with that arrow, making me fall into the river, passed through rapids, and then floated to where you found me." Lars continued to translate.

"What about your family? Father and mother?" Lars asked.

"My mom died a few years ago, and my dad, along with many of the other men of my village, went to fight the Ellious Empire in the south," Cinda answered. Lars translated for Ulrick again.

"I saw the rapids in the river you speak of. You're lucky you made it through alive," Lars said.

"How did you see them?" She asked, knowing she had gone a great distance floating down the river from where she was.

"Ulrick had us wait to see if someone was looking for you. I went up the river to search and saw the rapids," Lars answered. "Sadly, I didn't see anyone searching for you. But it could have been a good thing just as well since the elves did not pursue you."

Cinda was surprised to hear they had waited and searched for anyone looking for her. "Why would you do that?"

"We would have rather you go back home than come with us," Lars said and grinned. "No offense,"

Cinda looked at Lars. *That smile of his, is it genuine? Why are they being so nice to me?* "Thank you," she responded, looking into his kind, dark green eyes. They sat silently as Cinda smiled at him out of courtesy and habit. *Did they capture me... or save me?* Ulrick eventually grasped Lars by the shoulder and handed him the braided leather strips he had been working with.

"What is that?" Cinda asked.

"Let me see your right wrist," Lars said. Cinda lent him her wrist. "This is to symbolize that you are Ulrick's."

Cinda pulled her wrist back quickly before Lars could

finish his sentence. "What do you mean Ulrick's?" she said sharply. "Like his property or slave?"

Lars smiled at her as he spoke. "No, no, not quite like that. It shows that you are part of Ulrick's house...umm... his ward, you might say."

Cinda looked at the braided leather bracelet in Lars's hands. It was simple looking yet had an elegance to it. Five leather strips, three of them light brown and two black, all tightly braided together, with dark red and white beads woven into the center crossings. The braids ended in silver triangular fittings with one leather strap to tie the ends together. Then Cinda noticed Lars was wearing almost the same bracelet.

"You are Ulrick's ward as well?" Cinda asked, motioning to Lars's wrist.

"I am a member of Ulrick's house, yes,"

Cinda then presented her wrist to Lars. "Did he find you dying on a river bank also?"

Lars smiled. "No, I was a gift from Ulrick's father."

"A gift?" Cinda asked in surprise, thinking him an enslaved person.

"Yes, a gift," Lars said as he tied the straps together. "Ulrick's father, Agmit, had taken me as a slave from a temple." Lars could see the concern in Cinda's eyes as he spoke. "Don't worry. You are not being taken as a slave as I was." Lars then pointed to the two elves tied up at the front end of the boat. "They are slaves of Grumlish's." Lars had told Cinda of the orc named Grumlish earlier and warned her to stay silent around the orc, but not why.

"What will Grumlish do with them?" Cinda whispered as if not to be overheard by anyone, particularly Grumlish, who was almost ten paces away.

"Probably sell them to a fighting pit. However, a few of us have bets that the dark-haired one will make a run for it," Lars said. His casual tone shocked Cinda when talking about someone being a slave. Lars noted Cinda's face of disgust towards the subject and fell silent as he finished tying the bracelet on. "And there you go."

Cinda looked down at the bracelet with slight disgust. "So, does this mark me as a slave?"

Lars exhaled loudly and then looked at Cinda. "It's for your protection."

Cinda looked back at Lars. "So what makes you not a slave versus those elves?"

"When Agmit took me, I was a slave for a few years. It wasn't as horrible as you might think. Growing up half-elf was worse by being hated by both elves and humans. Orcs just treated me like a lower class, with a little disgust but at least no hate towards me. Then Agmit realized I had a talent for languages. I already knew Terrish, Elvish, and quickly learned Orcish." Lars then held up his wrist, showing his bracelet. "Agmit gave me a similar one when Ulrick was but a boy. It showed that I was no longer a slave but a house or family member. It allowed me to be mostly on my own but gave me the protection of his house." He then motioned to Ulrick's wrist and asked him in Orcish to show it.

Cinda looked and saw Ulrick had a metal bracelet. It was designed to look braided just like hers but had a dark silver-like metal for two strands and gold for the other three. Next to it was a leather one matching hers exactly.

"The metal bracelet was a gift from Agmit, the Earl of Tolneer, his father. It shows his allegiance and freedom to own lands and have rights. That allegiance was passed to Thrane, the new Earl of Tolneer, Ulrick's older brother when their father died." Lars then thanked Ulrick in Orcish and turned back towards Cinda. "Slaves don't wear a bracelet at all."

"So why were you gifted to Ulrick instead of going to his older brother?" Cinda asked, thinking about the traditions of her home that when a Lord dies, all their possessions go to the next in line.

"Because Thrane doesn't care to have me around him that much," Lars said with a chuckle. He then looked at Cinda seriously again. "I was a teacher to Thrane and taught him every language I know. Ulrick, his sister, and I became friends as they were growing up. And since Ulrick loved to travel, Agmit knew I would be better off with him than Thrane."

"Why don't you have a metal one if you are so close to the family?"

"Because then I would serve Earl Thrane and have to come when he calls. On the other hand, Ulrick asks me whenever we head back home if I want to stay." Lars answered. He then touched the leather bracelet. "With this, I actually have more freedom than Ulrick because I only have to answer to him, and he has no real need for me beyond friendship."

Cinda looked at Ulrick. Never really knowing an orc, it was hard for her to think how old he was. "How old are the both of you?" she quietly asked so as not to be rude.

"Well, Ulrick is twenty-five, and I'm seventy-six,"

Cinda's eyes widened from shock at Lars's age, realizing he was older than her grandfather. "But you're so young-looking."

Lars began to laugh. "Half-elf, remember."

There was a burst of laughter, and Cinda's attention

shifted to the other orcs on the boat talking loudly. "Can you teach me Orcish?"

"Of course," Lars answered with a half smile. "It is a little different from Terrish, so it could take some time, but it will probably help you since you might be with us for a few months." Lars then leaned in and whispered to Cinda. "Ulrick is not very good at learning new languages." He then smiled and laughed.

Cinda looked over the seemingly endless ocean, feeling so far from home. *They saved me.*

* * *

Arminiul and Sepher could smell the dead on the wind as they approached Orinton on their horses. Sepher felt the gods were reminding them so they never forget, searing the smell into their memories for all the days they have yet to live. Heading straight to the village center, the burned husks of the buildings came into view, and so did the dead. Lying on the ground, out in the open. Many of the bodies that had not burned had been ravaged by the scavengers of the forests. For some, only the bloody bones remained.

Arminiul stopped his horse at two bodies that were just bits of meat and bone. "We were here four days ago…" He said to get Sepher's attention. "These bodies should have more to them than this."

"Vultures, maybe?" Sepher stated as he covered his nose and mouth with a cloth, the smell becoming so strong he wanted to vomit. Arminiul continued without a cloth to his face. The stench of so much death was not new to him, so he could stomach it better.

"Maybe," Arminiul responded but doubted vultures

could have done so much.

"It's going to be dark soon," Sepher said and then gagged from breathing the smell in to talk.

Arminiul looked at the sun beginning to set behind the trees. "We should search a little while and then find a place to sleep for the night," he responded. They both dismounted and started looking for signs of anyone alive, pulling their horses with them as they walked.

The sun had just fully set when Sepher noticed something. "Arminiul!" he called out. Arminiul quickly joined Sepher as he squatted beside one of the dead bodies. "These don't look like regular animals ate them," he said while pointing at a few other bodies nearby.

"Ghouls," Arminiul said as he looked at the cleanly sliced stomach and the hollow cavity where the organs should have been. His blood turned cold at the thought of those unnatural creatures. They were once men or elves, but their dead bodies had been altered by fay magic. Making them rise again, bodies warped by the magics used to give them life and a hunger for the dead. It is one of the many cruses the fay uses on humans and elves.

"I don't know of anything else that does this," Sepher said as he stood back up. They had both fought against ghouls before. However, that was much further south than they were, almost in the middle of the Ellious Empire.

"The smell of so much death must have drawn them here." Arminiul quietly said.

"So if we did not kill everyone…" Sepher said as he looked at the defiled corpse.

One of their horses began to cry out in pain behind them. Both turned quickly as they watched a gray humanoid creature bite into Arminiul's horse. Its long, thin arms wrapped around the beast's neck while it sank the talon-like claws on its fingers into the horse's skin. The horse jumped and bucked violently, trying to shake the monster from it. Then, a second one came and jumped on its back, clawing into the horse relentlessly.

Arminiul and Sepher reacted without hesitation. Sepher pulled his bow and arrows out of their holder on his back while Arminiul pulled his sword from its sheath on his belt, spotting another ghoul coming straight at them from the opposite side.

"Take the two. I have the one coming," Arminiul said as he moved to intercept the ghoul charging at Sepher.

The horse fell to the ground from the two attacking ghouls, and Sepher let his arrow fly straight into one of the ghoul's head. The arrow went through the ghoul's skull just below its eye. It clawed at the arrow, trying to remove it, breaking the shaft. Sepher quickly grabbed a second arrow in hopes of killing the creature.

The charging ghoul shrieked at Arminiul as it approached, its fang-like teeth glinting as its long tongue swayed from its mouth. The dark black claws on its fingers were poised to cut Arminiul to shreds. Arminiul stood his ground, waiting as it grew closer in only a few moments. He gripped his sword tightly with both hands and slashed the sword wide in one solid movement. The sharp, elven steel sliced through the ghoul's bony chest, severing its heart into two pieces. The ghoul howled a death cry as it fell to the ground. Its long gray legs flailed as its bony hands clawed at its open chest while it died.

Sepher let another arrow fly as the ghoul came at him with an arrow in its face. The arrow pierced deep into the ribs, puncturing the ghoul's heart. Its body went limp and fell to the ground.

Arminiul moved around Sepher, charging at the last ghoul as it was still biting into the horse. He lept at the ghoul, thrusting his sword into the creature's chest, but the ghoul moved at the last moment. It shifted to the side and clawed at Arminiul. He quickly swung his sword up, slicing into the arm of the ghoul, severing muscle and tendons but only breaking the bone just above the right elbow.

The ghoul attacked again. Clawing at him with its left hand while its right swung limp, unaware that it was broken. Leaning its head toward Arminiul with its mouth wide. Arminiul lifted his sword, but the ghoul was too fast and gripped his shoulder, knocking him backward onto the ground. Its claws struggled to puncture his armor while its pinky and ring finger claws sunk into the flesh in the back of his shoulder.

The ghoul lunged its open mouth towards Arminiul's face as he held his sword blade up to protect him. The ghoul's teeth bit on the hard steel of the sword. Its yellow, bloodshot eyes peered into Arminiul's while it opened its mouth once more. His blade cut into the ghoul's cheeks and jaw as it neared his face. Its tongue extended, touching the side of Arminiul's nose as he tried with all of his might to keep the ghoul from biting him.

Suddenly, the ghoul jolted, and its eyes widened. Its body went limp on Arminiul as its head slid down his sword, dead.

"Are you hurt?" Sepher asked as he rolled the ghoul's corpse off of Arminiul.

"I'll live," Arminiul answered as he got up. He felt a sharp pain in his right shoulder.

Sepher grabbed his arrow that punctured the ghoul's

heart, killing it. "How many do you think there are?" He asked as he notched the bloody arrow, looking all around, waiting for another ghoul to come at them.

"I hope that was all of them," Arminiul answered moments before they began hearing guttural howling from around them, some sounding distant and some close. Both of them knew the howl well.

"That was not all of them,"

"We get on your horse and ride," Arminiul said as he started to move towards Sepher's horse.

Three ghouls came from behind some trees and charged towards Sepher's horse. The horse reared up, flailing its hooves at the attackers while Sepher shot one with his arrow, missing its chest but hitting it in the shoulder. The horse's mighty hoof struck a ghoul in the chest, sending it to the ground while the other two attacked it, clawing at the horse and biting it. The horse bucked violently to get free as it trumpeted in pain.

As Arminiul pulled out his knife and started cutting his saddle bags free of his horse's saddle, Sepher pulled his bowstring back to his cheek, aiming his arrow between the ghoul or his own horse as he watched a ghoul's claws slice deep across the shoulder of the horse. At the same time, it continued to buck around in circles until it started to run away. Sepher watched as two other ghouls came from the forest, chasing his horse as it rode away.

"My horse is gone," Sepher said as he relaxed his arms.

"We will have to run then," Arminiul said as he cut the last straps, freeing his saddlebags.

More howls began to sound deep within the forest as they both looked for a direction to head.

"There is a river to the north, through the village center,"

Arminiul said as he slung the saddlebags over his left shoulder, trying to keep the weight off his wounded one. He knew that ghouls did not like water, even fearing it from what he had seen once.

Sepher spotted two more ghouls heading their way towards them. "Wherever we go, we should start going now." He pulled back and released an arrow. It flew through the air and plunged deep into the ghoul's collarbone, missing the heart.

"Run!" Arminiul yelled after seeing Sepher had missed. They both quickly ran into the center of the village, wary of more ghouls. They could only hear them in the forest around them. As they ran between the last burned-out buildings, two ghouls stepped out from behind the ruined remains of the buildings, blocking the way. Their teeth were exposed as they snarled at the two elves.

Arminiul heard the two following ghouls running up from behind. They both turned as the creatures came at them fast. Arminiul swung with his sword, cutting deep into the ghoul's collarbone where Sepher's arrow was. His blade cut into the ribs of the creature. It shrieked as it struggled to pull the sword out. He quickly slammed his left forearm on the back of the blade, forcing it down into the ghoul's heart.

The second ghoul ran at Sepher, and he let his arrow go as the ghoul came within striking distance. The bowstring forced the arrow through the ghoul's heart while it still stayed notched in the string. Sepher grabbed the notched arrow and pulled it back while pushing the body with his bow hand. Freeing the arrow as the dead ghoul fell to the ground. He turned back towards the first ghouls that had blocked their path and had begun to charge at them.

Sepher fired his arrow at the ghoul on the right. It dug

deep into the ghoul's neck, causing it to lose balance and fall to the ground. The ghoul on the left was faster than Sepher thought, and it jumped onto Arminiul's back. Its sharp teeth tried to bite into the side of his neck as they both fell to the ground, but it bit into the thick leather of the saddlebag strap. Arminiul hit the ghoul on top of him with his left elbow in the ribs. Forcing the ghoul to the side as he and the creature rolled over the dead body of the ghoul he had just killed. The ghoul's claw scrapped into Arminiul's leather armor over his stomach as they rolled. Arminiul quickly freed his knife and slid it into the ghoul's side, driving the sharp blade into its heart. He watched as the ghoul died next to him.

The ghoul with an arrow through its neck squirmed on the ground, trying to breathe as its lungs began to fill with its thick, putrid blood. Sepher quickly grabbed Arminiul by the arm and pulled him up.

"I thought I lost you for a moment there," Sepher said between his heavy breaths.

"Just about," Arminiul said. He walked to the squirming ghoul, sticking his sword deep into its back, straight through its heart.

"We have to keep going. More are coming," Sepher said as noises in the forest seemed to be getting closer to them.

They ran faster as they heard the howls of ghouls now coming from behind them. Making their way through the forest, Arminiul spotted some sacks and crates near a stone house. He slowed down and stopped as he looked at them. "Those weren't there when we left this place."

Sepher stopped and looked at the pile on the ground. "Someone survived," he said softly. His heart felt a beat of relief that the boy and young woman might have escaped.

Then Sepher saw movement in the forest from the direction they came. "We should get going." He then started to run again, and Arminiul followed shortly behind.

CHAPTER 10

The boat had been sailing on the open ocean for three days. The sun simply rising from the water was beautiful. However, the once fantastic sight had lost its specialness to Cinda. She already longed for the smell of flowers and trees back home. Lars had kept her company, teaching her Orcish as they sat in the rear of the boat. Cinda struggled with the language even though the word order was similar to Terrish. They spent most of Cinda's waking hours learning and talking since she could not walk with her left leg. Her other injuries had been healing fine, and the swelling on the left side of her face had gone down enough that she could open her left eye. However, the dull headache was almost constant and would spike with pain, which urged her to lie down often.

Cinda continued to be surprised at how the orcs did not seem like the orcs she had imagined when hearing stories about them. She had always considered them vile beasts with greasy hair and foul smells. Yet, these orcs were none of those. The only commonality between what she had heard and what she saw before her were the large tusk-like teeth and the green skin. They were kind to one another and to her as well. Even the two elven prisoners were not mistreated. When she tried to walk the boat's length, every orc and human on the vessel was right there to catch her if she fell. However, she did not make it far with the boat rocking. Some of them even clapped and cheered as she took the two steps. Two of the orcs laughed as she fell over, however.

She watched the other people on the boat. Watched how they interacted with each other while Lars translated for her. She had spent many years observing, unable to join in games with the other kids by her father's order. Conversations between the villagers would end as she approached, making her feel as isolated as she felt now.

It was almost like watching the men in her village and how they would behave from a distance. She could spot the type of people they were: the funny ones, the quiet ones, the ones who seemed to be respected. If these orcs were not so large and did not have different shades of green skin, she would think she was with a bunch of humans.

All of them seemed like good friends. Ulrick seemed different from the rest, standing out as one respected but distant from the others. He didn't join in with the drinking and joking around. And hardly talked. He usually steered the boat and spoke or listened to Lars teach Cinda Orcish.

Cinda wondered if Ulrick was not friends with the others, with how he stood away from the rest. When she talked to Lars, he said Ulrick was not very social. Growing up as the Earl's son made him separated from other orcs his age. Learning to fight and sail from age six instead of playing childish games. He would rather sit and observe than interject, unsure of himself in conversations. Cinda felt a kinship to that same feeling.

Lars, on the other hand, was very different. He joked with the others and shared humorous stories. He was one of the funny ones in the group. However, she did not see much respect from most orcs towards him. They easily pushed him to the side when walking by him or even disregarded him while he spoke. Yet he did not seem to care. Like nothing really bothered him. She envied Lars, constantly worrying about what others thought or how she was viewed.

"Land! Land!" one of the humans yelled in Orcish from the prow. Everyone's heads turned to look, spotting tall mountains protruding from the flat blue horizon in the distance.

Cinda sat up and looked. Her heart felt relieved to finally get off the boat and onto solid land. "Soon…home?" Cinda asked Lars in Orcish.

Lars smiled back. "Very good," he said in Orcish.

Much of the crew prepared as the boat sailed closer to the mountains. Clearing the benches of crates or large blankets, they had pitched as tents. Making sure the bench areas were clear and their things secure. Ulrick began giving orders to the crew. Cinda only understood the words "oars" and "pull." Everyone moved around each other flawlessly. Two humans pulled the sails up by ropes while one of them, the smallest of the group but still bigger than Cinda, started to beat on a drum. The orcs sat on the now cleared benches and began to get the long oars into position. Each beat kept the rowers moving as one as the oars dipped and pushed the boat along. Ulrick turned the boat. The wind now came at them from the side.

As the boat traveled closer and closer to the land mass, Cinda looked at the cliffs as they rowed by. They were tall, much taller than any tree she had seen, with gray and white stones throughout. Above the cliffs were large bushes that looked the size of houses with rocks among them. The boat continued gliding across the water as Cinda kept her eyes on the coastline, seeing different birds flying in the sky with grey backs and white underbelly. Giant goat-like animals with broad shoulders and an extra set of horns from above their noses walked around the steep mountains. It was so strange to her, like seeing a different world.

She watched the coastline as the boat moved along until she noticed the shows had passed midday. Then, finally, Ulrick turned the boat into a long fjord.

The fjord was narrower than it was long. Cinda stood up as best she could and spotted buildings and columns of smoke at the far end.

"Tolneer," Ulrick said, noticing that Cinda was looking at the port.

Cinda looked in amazement as the longboat continued to get closer to Tolneer. The large, steep mountain to her left dropped to the water. She noticed a few small, flat paths because of the orcs walking them. To the right was a mountain at the mouth of the fjord, but soon leveled out to flat land and tall hills behind it. On the flatter ground were houses and small docks with much smaller boats. She saw the orcs working around their homes. She was amazed at how it looked like they were doing the same things as the people in Orinton usually did. Some tended to gardens, while others fed large pigs and chickens. Two houses were built next to the water, and the orcs were building boats like the one she was on.

"Home," Ulrick said in Terrish as he pointed to a small house near the shore.

"Home," Cinda responded in Orcish. Ulrick smiled at her kindly, then turned to the oarsmen and drummer, issuing them orders in Orcish to slow down the pace of the rowing.

The crew moved in unison with Ulrick's commands flawlessly. She remembered Lars talking about how this was the first time Ulrick sailed with half of the crew, so she was surprised at how well things were going. They had to weave between other boats in the water and maneuver to the correct dock. But Cinda was concentrating on seeing Tolneer more than anything.

The large village of Tolneer was built on a gradual slope towards the water so all the buildings could be seen as the boat approached the dock. The buildings were numerous. Most were made of wood except a few made of stone, and a wide variety of roofs looking like thatch, tile, slate, and shingle. One building stood out from the others, almost three times the size of any other structure in sight, and was nearly centered in the middle of the entire village. Cinda figured it was like the Hall of Orinton, the village's heart.

As the boat docked, a crowd began forming on the shore. It made Cinda nervous seeing the group of orcs and humans. She felt relatively safe with Lars and Ulrick on the boat, but what about with others? What if she was separated from them in the crowd or left behind, unable to walk? She covered herself more with the fur blankets, pulling part of it over her head like a hood. Her stomach began to turn, and her hands started to shake. She peeked out from under the hood, looking at the people they were heading toward. They mainly were orcs, tall and broad-shouldered, standing together; they looked like a solid wall except for the few humans among them.

Cinda shrank into herself, trying to hide as the boat bumped against the dock. The boat crew cheered as the people on the shore cheered in response. She closed her eyes and felt the longboat tip side to side while the crew disembarked and greeted those awaiting them.

"Are you okay, Cinda?" Lars asked as he squatted before her. Unsure since he could not see her face because of the hood.

"I'm...I'm scared," Cinda said quietly. "Can you take me home now?"

"Scared?"

Cinda slightly raised her head so she could see Lars's face. "I can't walk...and all the..."

Lars smiled at Cinda. "It's okay. Ulrick will carry you." He then looked at the crowd. "And don't worry, Ulrick will carry you to his house. There, you can get some real rest."

"Will you stay with me?"

"Yeah, I'll be with you the whole time," Lars said with a half smile. He stood up and grabbed some sacks and something large wrapped in a cloth. Cinda could tell he struggled with the weight but did not ask for help.

Ulrick walked up to Cinda and squatted in front of her so she could see him. "I'll carry you," he said in Orcish.

"Yes," Cinda responded in Orcish, unsure what Ulrick said but too afraid to question.

Cinda felt like an infant with how easily Ulrick lifted her in his arms. He then stepped off the boat. Each step he took, however, would cause pain in her thigh. She felt embarrassed and pathetic as she saw everyone glancing at her in Ulrick's arms. *I wonder what they are thinking?* But those thoughts faded as her headache spiked, causing her so much pain that she could not help but shut her eyes tight and clench her teeth.

It was not a strenuous walk for Ulrick, carrying Cinda to his house, but Lars needed help carrying everything from the boat, even taking a few breaks during the trek.

Ulrick's house was much simpler than Cinda had imagined since he was part of the governing family of Tolneer. It was just a plain wooden house with what looked like clay covering the outside of the walls and a thick thatch roof like all the other houses nearby. There was a nice area of flat ground in front of the house and a fenced area that looked perfect for an animal pen but was full of long logs. Lars dropped everything and opened the large door for Ulrick, who carried Cinda inside.

The interior was well-lit and radiated warmth. Furs of different animals were scattered throughout, with a small bed on one side, a table, and a few chairs on the other. In the back was a large bed with curtains to separate it from the rest of the single-room house. In the center was a fire pit that looked like it had been used in the last few days. Trinkets were scattered around the room, some hanging and some sitting on shelves. Items from distant lands that Ulrick and Lars had traveled to.

Ulrick quickly placed Cinda on the small bed and started gathering extra blankets for her. Laying on the bed felt terrific to Cinda. It was completely dry and didn't move like the boat, but it felt like it was still moving to her. The sharp pain in her head softened when she finally laid her head on the pillow and quickly fell asleep as Ulrick gently placed a fur blanket over her.

* * *

Owen stood before the large doors of the Hall of Orinton. But the doors looked different. Most of the deer antlers on the door were new. Only one or two sets had faded by the sun. A flag hung from the roof, the banner for Gustoll. The building looked different, kept up, and cleaner than he remembered. He felt a nice breeze begin to blow as he smiled. The hall was perfect. There had been no fire or bodies at his feet. It was peaceful. He slowly turned and looked upon the other buildings that made up the village center. They all still stood. One of the buildings was still being built and did not have a roof. *Strange, that building had been built before I was born.*

There was no sound except the breeze. His smile soon faded. Something felt wrong. *It's never empty here.*

"Hello?" Owen yelled as he stepped forward, standing at the top of the steps. "Is anyone there?" he yelled again. "Anyone?" he said softly, growing more worried.

Owen heard something move behind him. He quickly turned and watched both doors to the hall swing open. His eyes widened as he looked at a woman made of fire approach him from inside. With each step she took, lines of flame stretched out along the ground, moving like snakes, burning and sliding as they went, igniting anything they touched. She seemed to grin mischievously as she drew closer to him.

"There you are, Druid," the woman of fire said as she walked through the threshold of the double doors. Both of the doors ignited in flames as she passed between them.

Owen stepped back. His foot missed the first step, and he stumbled. He landed on his hip as he fell to the ground. The woman descended, step by step, toward him.

"Druid," She said wickedly as her hand reached out to him. "You're mine."

Then, suddenly, from out of somewhere, a golden eagle flew in. Its talons ripped into the firewoman's right arm and cleaved it off. Her right hand and wrist dropped to the ground, the flames extinguished, and it turned black. Shattering on the ground like a burnt log before it became entirely ash.

The woman of fire screamed and fixed her attention on

the eagle. She slung a stream of flame from her left hand, but the bird nimbly dodged and turned about in the air.

The golden eagle swooped in for another pass but veered to the side when the woman of fire sent more flames at it. As this happened, Owen turned to get onto his feet and run, but as he turned, he was startled by a face only inches away from his.

It was the face of a middle-aged man with darkness around him. As if all he had was only that face. His skin was pale, and the irises of his eyes glowed with a dark red color. Usually, Owen would be afraid of such a strange sight, but the man looked worried, almost like he was scared.

"Boy," the man's face said in a panicked tone. His fanged canines showed as he spoke. "Boy, you must find this man."

The eagle screeched, and Owen tried to turn to see it, but the pale man's cold hands emerged from the dark mass, grabbed the sides of Owen's head, and pulled his face back to look at him. "Our visions are uncontrolled. You must find this man. Go to Delmock. Search for Lord Tyris."

"Delmock," Owen whispered.

"Now, wake up. You have far to travel." the pale face said.

Owen closed his eyes tight. *Wake up! Wake up!* He yelled in his head, unsure if it would work.

"Boy, wake up and find him! Find Lord Tyris," the pale face yelled.

"Boy...Owen!" The voice began to change as it said his name. "Owen!" a female voice said.

Owen opened his eyes and saw he was standing in the middle of the goat pen. The goats gathered around him as he held their feed in his arms.

"Owen!" Tavia yelled from the other side of the pen

fence. Owen quickly turned to face her. "Are you planning on feeding the goats or just staring off into nothing for a few more minutes?" Tavia joked, but as she saw the fear in Owen's eyes, she knew something was wrong.

"Owen, what happened?" Tavia asked in concern as she walked around the fence and into the pen. Owen walked towards her with open arms, quickly hugging her for comfort.

"What's wrong, Owen?" Tavia asked as she held him.

"I had a vision." Owen whimpered into her chest.

"Was it of the white oak tree?" Tavia asked in a panic. Pulling herself from him to check if he was okay. "Did it burn you again?"

"It was not the tree." Owned said as he shook his head. "I was in Orinton, but it was strange. Kellen's blacksmithing forge was still being built, and Gustol's banner was hanging on the front of the hall."

"But they finished building the forge when I was a little girl."

Owen nodded his head. "There was no one there except a woman made of fire." Tavia looked at Owen with a worried face at the mention of the woman. "She was setting everything on fire around her, and she…" Owen paused as he recalled his vision and fear while he had it. "She called me Druid."

"Like the Seer did when you saw the tree?"

"Yes, she said she found me, but then an eagle attacked her."

"An eagle attacked the woman of fire?" Tavia asked in confusion at the thought of an eagle attacking a fire.

"I tried to run, but a man stopped me." Owen shook his head as he remembered the events of his vision. "He told me to find a Lord Tyris in Delmock."

"Did you recognize the man?"

"No..." Owen replied. "He was pale with strange red eyes... and sharp-looking teeth."

"He told you to go to Delmock?" Tavia asked, making sure she had heard Owen correctly.

"Yes. find him, Lord Tyris, in Delmock."

"But why would he want you to go to Delmock? It is ruled by the fay." Tavia responded.

"You mean like Faylend?" Owen asked. Knowing that Faylend was an island to the northeast of Effrin.

"Feylend is an island of fay. Delmock is a small kingdom ruled by fay. At least, that is what I have heard about it." Tavia said, unsure of herself.

"Is Delmock far?" Owen asked, thinking about how the man said it was a long journey.

"I think it is far. I am not sure exactly where it is."

"Should we go there?" Owen asked, worried. Not sure if he should listen to his vision or not. Hoping Tavia would have a better idea of what to do.

"Let's stay here for the winter and then see about going to Delmock," Tavia answered but had really wanted to say no since she had heard that Delmock was a nightmarish place. "Are you sure you are okay?"

Owen nodded that he was. "I am just afraid."

"I am too, Owen. You should keep feeding the animals, and we can talk about Delmock later." Tavia said as she noticed people staring at them as they walked by. Owen walked back to the feed bag he had dropped, and the goats were already getting close to eating out of it while Tavia walked back to the house.

They had been staying with Aerlene and even started to

work for her. Tavia helped with the counter, selling the livestock and eggs while helping with routine housework, while Owen was working with Aerlene's chickens, goats, and pigs.

Aerlene quickly hired Owen when she saw how good he was with animals. She needed help since her husband had left her for another woman a few months ago. She hired Tavia out of sympathy and to keep her busy. Over the next few days, however, Aerlene liked having them both around. Tavia and Owen had begun to feel slightly at ease there as well.

Tavia enjoyed it the most. She had been trying to forget the past and embrace where they were. She crammed the grief of her family and friends and the fear of what had happened to Owen deep into her mind so she did not think about them. Trying hard to make a new life for Owen and her in Keerike. She still felt stressed and on guard, particularly around the elves that resided in Keerike. Making her easily agitated.

Owen was not fond of the idea of staying. He was plagued every night grieving about his mother and the people of Orinton, or he thought about the white oak tree and the Seer's ghost. It kept him up late at night, unable to sleep. However, he found peace while working with the animals, finding himself just sitting and talking to some of the pigs as if they could understand him.

Owen finished feeding the animals and headed inside, finding Aerlene in the kitchen preparing dinner early like usual.

"Aerlene," Owen called to get her attention.

"Yes, dear?" Aerlene answered gleefully to hear Owen talk to her. The hardest part about her husband leaving her was not having someone to talk to. Her eyes never left the cutting board as she spoke while chopping carrots.

"Do you know where Delmock is?" Owen asked, never having heard of the place himself.

Aerlene paused her chopping. "Delmock," she said while thinking for a moment. "It is north of Esterra, I believe." She then turned and faced Owen. "Maybe try asking Vistem. His family travels and has many maps, and he should be able to give you better directions."

Hearing Vistem's name made Owen's skin crawl. The man had come by several times over the last few days asking for Tavia. She would hide at first sight of him. Leaving Owen to talk to him, which he didn't enjoy since the man only wanted to ask questions about Tavia. He could tell that Vistem liked Tavia, which he thought would only get in the way when Hendric finds them.

"Okay," Owen said with a fake smile and nod. He then turned around and walked back out. He sat next to the pig pen as one of Aerlene's cats approached him to be petted. His mind wandered to the eagle and the woman made of fire as he scratched behind the cat's ear. *She said she finally found me.* He thought in his head. *And she called me Druid.* Owen sat and thought about leaving, running away to keep Tavia safe. But he would need to know better directions for how to get to Delmock first, which meant talking to Vistem or hopefully finding someone else who would know.

* * *

Hendric arrived back in Orinton after a long, two-and-a-half-day walk, only stopping to rest and get some food from a kind farmer he happened upon. His walk was slow, his legs still aching from being over-exerted the last few days, but he knew he had to press on. The weather had turned and grown colder with the approach of winter. His luck held out as the darkening skies stayed distant, but a storm soon approached. Quickening his steps to avoid the impending rain, he could not help but feel tired. His mind hoped others might be as well if Owen was alive, particularly Tavia. He had longed to see her again. Though he knew the chances were slim. He clung to hope.

As he approached the outskirts of the village, he sauntered, taking the time to check everyone he saw on the ground. The days had given time for animals to scavenge. Many bodies were no longer recognizable. Hendric noted the hair, searching for Tavia by this trait alone. Her wavy blonde hair was fresh in his mind, like a memory burned deep into him. How he wished to run his fingers through her hair once more.

Then Hendric spotted a body curled up on the ground. Its gray skin made it stand out from the fallen leaves around it. He could see the bones under the creature's thin skin. Its arms and legs were longer than average. It looked unworldly. He approached quietly with his bow and arrow ready. The stench was rotten, more rotten than any of the dead bodies around him, yet the body looked fresh and untouched by anything. There weren't even flies about the creature, yet its dark blood was dry as if it had been there for a while.

Hendric kicked the creature onto its back, its open mouth revealing sharp yellow teeth and a black tongue. Across its chest was a deep wound with claw marks around the left side. *Is this a ghoul?* He thought to himself as he remembered the description Gustoll had given him one night while telling frightening stories around a fire. Telling him about how ghouls would wander battlefields at night, eating the dead. He then looked around and spotted two more ghouls lying on and near a dead horse. He walked to the closer ghoul, seeing a broken arrow below its eye and an arrow in its chest. He reached down and pulled the arrow from the dead creature at his feet. Seeing the steel arrowhead and design, he knew it was elven-made.

Hendric's heart sank as he dropped the arrow and quickly readied his bow, pulling the bowstring back to his cheek as he looked around. *Elves. But why did they come back? Could they know that Owen is still alive and got ahead of me without me knowing?* He then ran to a tree for cover, looking but not seeing anyone. Slowly, he started moving towards the village center, seeing a few more gray creatures lying dead between two burnt-out buildings. Slowly, he walked past them, taking the arrows and sliding them into his quiver, knowing he may need them. He could see footprints clearly in the ash-covered dirt. *Two elves seemed to be running.* He thought as he inspected the imprints.

Hendric followed the two sets of imprints, walking away from the village center and further into the hills. Other prints then showed up in the dirt. Barefoot with clawed toes. *The elves were being chased by ghouls… Three of them, maybe more.* Hendric followed them until he spotted a pile of sacks and small crates in front of the stone house where the Seer once lived, but the boot prints continued up the hill in the other direction. His heart quickened at the sight, knowing Tavia had slept there and she felt safe inside while no one else would want to stay there.

Hendric crept to the pile, moving slowly, keeping an eye on the forest around him as he went, afraid of the elves and the ghouls. He checked the sacks, and they were picked through. Many tracks littered the area, making it hard to tell them apart. Reaching in, he pulled out some dried meat and took a bite. The feeling of food in his mouth was gratifying since he had not eaten much that day.

His eye focused on the closed door of the stone house, wanting so badly to shout out for Tavia and Owen or anyone but knew it was wiser to stay quiet. He walked to the closed door. His heart pumping with the hope that Tavia was inside, perfectly safe. His hand reached out and pushed the door open slowly.

"Tavia? Owen?" Hendric said in a low voice. "Are you there?" The door opened with a creak as he slowly pushed it. Light filled the dark interior.

Then, faster than Hendric could even react, a clawed gray hand grasped his left arm. Its claws dug deep into his forearm as he tried to pull away, ripping through his fur jacket and into his skin. Hendric's eyes widened with horror as one of the gray creatures came into his view from inside. Its sharp fangs and lips snarled as it lunged out to bite him.

Hendric fell back as the creature leaned forward to taste his blood. The sharp claws sliced through his skin and muscles, down his arm, and through his hand. He landed on his back, freed from the grip. The creature came at him again, its hands flailing with claws out as one struck his boot. Hendric kicked as he tried to escape, but the creature's other hand soon followed, its claws digging deep into Hendric's calf. He screamed in pain and kicked the creature's hand.

The ghoul's fingers broke from his kick, making it lose its grip on Hendric's leg and began flailing again. Hendric looked up and saw the creature's eyes squeezed shut as it tried to find him by reaching out with its hands, searching just outside the threshold of the stone house. Hendric pushed himself further away from the ghoul as it let out a shriek of agitation, trying to find its prey. He then heard more howls and growls coming from inside the stone house.

Hendric rolled onto his stomach and began to crawl away, his arm and hand bleeding as he went. His leg ached with every movement. The creature retreated into the stone house and shut the door behind it. He breathed a sigh of relief. *I guess Gustoll was right about them hating sunlight.* Slowly, he made his way to the pile of supplies a short distance from the door. He rested his back against a box and moved the flaps of his sleeve, seeing the deep gashes in his skin and muscles. He looked in horror as his hand was curled and misshapen. The monster's grip was so hard that two claws went through his hand and sliced the muscle between his hand bones. He panicked, rummaged through the supplies with haste, and found some cloth small enough to be used as bandages. He quickly wrapped his arm sloppily but enough to stop the bleeding. He tried to wrap his disfigured hand as best he could. He then looked down at his right leg. His thick, high leather boot had protected him except for two slices that cut his skin right above the boot. It was not as bad as his hand, but it still needed to be bandaged quickly so he could get away before the sunset.

CHAPTER 11

Each step Ulrick took crushed the snow under his heavy boots as he walked the path along the cliff face. The snow did not bother him as he walked through it effortlessly, even with the added weight of Cinda tied to his back. Feeling like a toddler, she was embarrassed when Lars put her in the harness made of cloth and ropes for Ulrick to carry her. She knew it was necessary, as Ulrick would need his hands free for traversing the steep and rugged terrain.

As they walked the path up the cliffside, Cinda began to feel comfortable, and her mind began to drift, remembering times when she was little and would ride on her father's back as he ran around the hall, acting like a horse. She closed her eyes and rested her head against Ulrick's back, recalling when she and her father were happy, how her mom would stand and clap a beat that her dad would trot to. How full of life they all were back then, full of hope. The smile on her face from the fond memories faded as she remembered her mother. It had been so long since she thought about her, and she had trouble picturing her mother's face. She teared up as she thought of her mom and her home. The warmth of her tears on her cold face felt almost like when her mother would run her fingers over Cinda's cheeks.

"Are you ok?" Lars asked after hearing Cinda sniff hard. "Is the harness hurting you?"

Cinda shook her head. "I'm just remembering home."

"Don't worry, you'll see home again."

Lars had told Cinda multiple times they would most likely get to take her back to where they found her. But Cinda did not fully believe him, mainly because since arriving in Tolneer, she felt so far away from home.

"Where are we going?" Cinda asked, trying to get her mind to think about anything but home.

"We are going to see Ulrick's sister," Lars answered as he tried to keep pace with Ulrick's significant stride.

"Why?" Cinda asked curiously, thinking she should be in a warm bed instead of being carried in the cold. Her leg and side were still hurting with each step Ulrick took.

"We hope that she can help," Lars answered between breaths.

"Help with what?" Cinda asked.

Lars glanced at Cinda's leg and then back to the path to ensure his footing. Yet he did not answer right away as if he was thinking. "Just help us with a few questions we have," he finally responded gingerly.

Cinda turned towards the ocean to their right, peering over the seemingly endless blue horizon, wishing to be home. She sensed Lars was not being honest with her. She felt used and hopeless by her situation, not even able to run away if she wanted to, not having a choice in anything for herself. *They could just leave me to die if they wanted, and I wouldn't be able to do anything about it.*

The path began to even out as they walked around a bend. Cinda spotted a long pile of rocks with a sword sticking out of them on an outcrop of the cliff. Ulrick and Lars' paces slowed as they approached. By the size and shape of the rock pile, she could tell it was a grave, the large sword positioned like a headstone in the rocks. As they advanced closer, the sword's details came into view.

The sword was gorgeous. Its broad blade stuck up about two feet, meeting the glistening silver-colored hilt. The hilt was smooth and large, with sharp points on the ends. The handle was bigger than most swords she had seen, big enough for the two hands of a large man to hold. The handhold was black leather with gold thread spiraling throughout. On the pommel was a large red jewel set within a strip of dark silver metal. The red light shining through it made the sword look even more majestic.

The moss that had grown between and over some of the rocks made it look like the stones had been there for years, yet the sword looked freshly placed; not even the silver hilt or steel blade was tarnished by the weather.

Ulrick stopped directly before the grave for a moment and then began muttering quietly in Orcish. Cinda could not make out his words since he spoke so fast and quietly. She looked at Lars; his face looked sad as he looked calmly at the grave. Cinda took a deep breath, about to speak, but then stopped herself. She looked around, not seeing any other graves around them, just a large wooden bench on the other side of the path.

Cinda gave Ulrick a moment after he was finished with his quiet speech and then asked, "Who was he?"

"She," Lars corrected Cinda. "She was called Tallus." Ulrick's head quickly turned and faced Lars at the mention of the name.

Cinda tried to lean to her left in the harness. The pain in her thigh became sharp as she shifted, but she wanted to see Ulrick's face better. "Who... is... Tallus?" She asked Ulrick directly, taking time to say the words slowly and clearly for Ulrick to understand.

Ulrick paused, deep in thought for a moment, then

slowly said one word. "Wife."

Cinda sank back in the harness. "I'm sorry to hear your wife died," she said, unsure what to say, but the words came out of habit. Lars did not translate for Ulrick this time. They stood in silence for a few more moments. Cinda's mind was not silent as it swirled with questions about Ulrick and Tallus.

"We go," Ulrick then said in Terrish. His deep voice almost startled Cinda as she was thinking. Then he turned, and the three of them continued up the path. Cinda looked back at the large sword in the grave as they walked away.

"Excuse me, Lars?" Cinda quietly said to get his attention. Lars looked up at her. "How long ago did Tallus die?" Cinda asked, hesitant to ask about the subject.

"A little over two years ago," Lars answered. He slightly smiled at Cinda, saying it was okay to talk about.

"How did she die?" Cinda asked uneasily. Lars's face grew sad as she asked the question, and he went silent. *Did I push too far?*

"She was killed during a raid to the west," Lars said somberly.

By Lars's shift in tone and demeanor, Cinda could tell that Tallus's death was a delicate matter. She thought it best not to push. "Was she a great warrior?"

"She was… particularly with that sword. You wouldn't think that sword could be swung so fast by its size, but she was magnificent with it." A smile slightly grew on his face as he said it almost pridefully.

"How come no one has stolen the sword? It looks quite beautiful." Cinda asked, noticing Lars was okay talking about Tallus, just not her death.

Lars slightly laughed at the question. "If you steal a grave weapon, it is said the spirit of the warrior it sits for will hunt you and drive you insane." Lars looked up at Cinda. "I don't know about you, but I really don't want an angry orc ghost following me around." He then laughed.

"How come the sword looks brand new if it has been there for two years?" Cinda asked after Lars was done with his short laugh.

"Well, the sword is not normal steel. You would possibly know it as Allurian Steel. It is much harder and holds an edge better than normal steel," Lars answered. "Also, Ulrick takes care of the sword, polishing and oiling it to keep it looking new."

Cinda had heard about Allure in fairytales and legends. A magical kingdom that fell long ago. Full of great wonders, but she focused her thoughts on something else. Her mind thought about Ulrick, the savage orc. *He rescued me from the banks of that river and even sent Lars to go looking for people to help me. He could have left me there or, even worse, taken advantage of me. But he didn't. He brought me with them and helped take care of me.* The path they were walking became steep again, so steep it was almost climbing instead of walking for nearly eighty paces. The sight of it made Cinda stop thinking about Ulrick.

"Cinda, speak pain," Ulrick slowly said to Cinda in Terrish as he approached the steep path, popping his knuckles to get his hands ready to start climbing.

"Ok," Cinda responded in Orcish, impressed with how much Ulrick had spoken in Terrish since she first met them. She wrapped her arms around his neck for extra support.

Ulrick began to climb easily, even with Cinda on his back and the little snow on the rocks. Lars, however, seemed to struggle behind them, and the weight of their supplies in his backpack made climbing harder for him.

"This path was made for orcs, not humans," Lars yelled in Orcish as he struggled to lift himself up some rocks.

"Grow taller then," Ulrick yelled in Orcish as he laughed. Cinda smiled, not fully understanding what was being said, but knew it involved Lars struggling with the climb.

"You know I can't grow taller, right?" Lars yelled back at Ulrick after he climbed over a few large rocks.

Ulrick turned and looked down the slope at Lars. "Need me to carry you as well?" he laughed.

Lars looked up at Ulrick as he climbed a few more easy rocks. "If you are offering," He joked.

Ulrick slowly shook his head as he laughed. "When Cinda and I reach the top, I'll toss you a rope."

"I'm the one carrying the rope!" Lars yelled.

"Well, I guess we'll just be waiting for you then," Ulrick said while he chuckled. He then turned back and started climbing up again.

"You're an ass!" Lars yelled from below them.

Cinda wished that she understood Orcish better. She could tell they were joking, much like friends do, friends she didn't have.

Ulrick seemed to climb faster than earlier, almost mocking Lars as he fell far behind. Cinda would turn and keep an eye on him, though. It was not a dangerous climb, but it took him more effort since Ulrick's size was so much larger than his. Cinda's thigh hurt with the faster climbing, but she gritted her teeth through the pain, not wanting to spoil Ulrick's fun.

As they reached the top of the climb, the ground plateaued out to the edge of a forest. The tall evergreen trees looked magnificent with the snow on them. Ulrick turned and looked at the view from the ridge. They could see for miles through the light-falling snow. They could even make out the mouth of the fjord they entered to get to Tolneer. The town, however, was out of sight from the trees. Ulrick watched as Lars climbed, making sure he did not need help.

Cinda held out her hand, catching a few snowflakes, watching as they melted in her palm.

"Cinda…" Ulrick said as he held out his hand, letting flakes of snow land in it. "Cinda… home." He pointed at the melting snow in his hand.

Cinda did not understand what he was saying, so she pointed at the flake in Ulrick's palm. "Snow."

"Cinda, snow home?"

"Yes, Ulrick, it does snow at my home," Cinda said slowly and clearly.

Ulrick then pointed at some darker clouds on the horizon. "Big snow come." He then looked down at Lars, yelling at him in Orcish. Cinda noticed Lars started to climb faster.

Cinda wondered about Ulrick again as they stood waiting. Seeing how he watched over Lars reminded her of how they both watched over her. The memory of the grave sword popped into her head. *He polishes it.* She had not seen many grave weapons, but the ones she had seen were never cared for like that. *He must have truly loved her. He isn't a savage at all. He is kind to those around him, his family.* She looked at the leather bracelet on her wrist. *But how am I his family when he doesn't even know me? He doesn't even know who I really am.* She then spotted Lars reaching the top of the climb. He quickly turned and saw the dark clouds in the distance. His face had a look of worry.

"What's wrong, Lars?" Cinda asked.

"That storm is going to reach us before we get to where we need to be," Lars answered. He then turned to Ulrick and spoke in Orcish, "We will need to start going faster."

* * *

Tavia was cleaning the counter where customers made their purchases. It was an easy task Aerlene would have Tavia do to keep her busy. Since the counter was hardly ever actually used or got that dirty. But Tavia did it with pride and diligence, knowing she did not contribute much to Owen and her stay.

"Ex...Excuse me," a quiet voice said to Tavia as she was cleaning the shelves on the wall behind the counter.

Tavia quickly turned and saw a young man standing at the counter. She recognized him from a few days ago. He was with one of the butchers that came by. "Hello there," Tavia said with a welcoming grin as she looked over the man.

He was only eighteen or nineteen, standing a few inches short of six feet with black hair and a nervous look. As Tavia looked at him, his eyes quickly shifted away from her as his cheeks began to turn slightly red. Tavia found it cute that the young man was blushing.

"What can I get you?" Tavia asked as she stepped closer to the young man. Her grin grew wider as his eyes avoided looking at her. "Am I so hideous you can not look at me?" Tavia said in a playful tone.

"No, no," the young man said quickly. His light brown eyes then shifted to look into Tavia's. "I ummm..."

Tavia waited a few moments for the young man to speak, but nothing came out of his mouth as he stared at her. "How about we start with your name."

"My name?" The young man said nervously. "I'm Standin... I mean Stanlin," Stanlin said with a panicked correction.

"Well, Stanlin, my name is Tavia," Tavia said with a slight curtsy.

"I...I know," Stanlin said as his cheeks grew redder and his eyes looked away from her's.

"So, are you here to buy something, Stanlin?" Tavia said as she leaned over the counter slightly towards Stanlin. "Or did you just come here to say hello?" She said in her playful, flirtatious tone.

"My...my mom wanted a dozen eggs," Stanlin forced himself to say as he glanced toward Tavia's eyes and then away.

"And here I was hoping you came all this way just to talk to me," Tavia said as she turned around and got a wicker basket off the shelf with a dozen eggs inside. Stanlin put some coins on the counter for payment. She looked at him with a smile as his lips pressed together and his face flushed. "Now, why are you blushing, Stanlin?" she said as she rested her elbows on the counter, bending over enough so her cleavage would show better with her dress.

Stanlin's eyes darted between Tavia's eyes, chest, and the eggs quickly. "I umm...I should get these to my mom," he said nervously as he grabbed the basket.

"Is there anything else you want?" Tavia said in a seductive tone.

Stanlin stood for a moment, his hands shaking slightly out of nervousness while he lifted the basket. "Can I...I mean, can we..." Stanlin fumbled the words as he tried to speak.

"I would love to spend some more time with you, Stanlin," Tavia interrupted, seeing that he was having trouble getting his thoughts across.

"Ok...good," Stanlin said with a look of joy on his face. He then turned and walked away from the counter, glancing back at Tavia after a few feet, and she smiled back at him while giving a little wave of her hand.

"Telling me when would have helped, Stanlin." Tavia chuckled as she watched him walk away through a small crowd of people. She sat on the stool at the counter, thinking about Stanlin. He was handsome, but she found his innocence adorable, thinking how nice of a man he must be and how nice it was to have his attention; anything to help cure her of her boredom at Aerlene's and help her forget her old life for a little while.

"There you are!" a voice rang out.

Tavia knew the voice, and her smile faded as she became annoyed. "Hi, Vistem," Tavia mumbled as she looked over and saw him walking towards her.

"About time I catch you," Vistem said with a smirk as he stepped closer and closer, stopping on the other side of the counter from her. "Every time I come by, your brother says you are busy or gone."

"What can I get for you?"

"I just wanted to know how you are settling here with Aerlene?"

"It's fine," Tavia answered in a slightly stern tone. She then stood up from the stool. "If you will excuse me, I have some things to take care of."

"Glad to have helped such a kind woman," Vistem said sarcastically as Tavia walked back into the house.

As Tavia closed the door behind her, she saw Aerlene

sitting and weaving a basket, looking up at her with a confused look on her face. "Is there a reason you treat Lord Vistem like you do?" Aerlene asked.

The question caught Tavia off guard, but then she realized the woman probably heard every word of their conversation. "I just don't like the man," she said quietly. However, in her head, Vistem reminded her of her father. With the sheer arrogance and the way he talked to her, many others might swoon over such a man. But Tavia had her fill of witnessing such behavior.

* * *

The storm came faster than Ulrick and Lars had thought it would. The snow fell so thick it was hard to see more than five paces ahead of them. The pain in Cinda's leg had grown worse than when the arrow had hit her as she bounced around in the harness while Ulrick trudged through the snow that came up to his knees. The thick animal fur cloak covered the two of them and kept most of the frigid temperature at bay, but Cinda still felt cold. She could hardly see anything Ulrick's large hood over her head, but she did not notice since her eyes were closed tight while she gritted her teeth from the sheer pain she felt. She begged in her mind for it to stop.

"Almost there!" Lars yelled in Terrish as loud as he could so Cinda could hear him over the snowstorm's wind.

Cinda's eyes opened, and she peeked through the hood, seeing nothing but white snow and a few trees. Then, through the storm, she spotted stairs. Ulrick took them without losing stride. His body bouncing with each step made Cinda's leg throb with pain as she screamed in agony.

Then Ulrick outreached his arms and pushed open some doors.

"It's Lars and Ulrick," Lars yelled in Orcish. His voice echoed as he began to close the doors behind them. "We need some help."

Ulrick quickly took the hood off Cinda's head and removed the cloak from them as he began to shout in Orcish to Lars. Cinda was in too much pain to understand what was said, but Lars quickly ran off into the darkness of the large room.

"Free Cinda," Ulrick said as he squatted on the ground and began to untie the ropes holding Cinda to his back.

Cinda could feel the ropes around her back loosen as she looked around for something to lie down on, but nothing was nearby. The room they were in was massive and had only dim sunlight coming through the shutters on the walls high above her. As Ulrick untied the final ropes, Cinda slid slowly to the ground and lay flat on the cold marble floor, limp and tired from the pain and cold. She could feel her eyes begin to close.

"No close," Ulrick said as he touched Cinda's cheek.

"We're coming!" Lars shouted from an open door. His voice echoed throughout the room as he ran towards Ulrick and Cinda with a torch in his hand. Cinda looked over, seeing Lars and a female orc running behind him.

The orc behind Lars wore very different clothing than anyone she had seen since meeting Lars and Ulrick. A solid, white, thick robe and no shoes. The look reminded her of a few priests she had seen back home; however, they wore brown robes over white clothing.

As they got closer, Cinda touched her thigh, feeling that it was wet. She looked down and saw in the torch's light that her pant leg was soaked with blood. She screamed in a panicky shrill as she looked down at her blood-covered hand.

"It's okay. Cortay will help us," Lars said in Terrish as he got to Cinda's side, handing the torch to Ulrick to hold above them.

The female orc pulled the knife from Ulrick's belt without hesitation and started cutting Cinda's pant leg open quickly and precisely. "How long have you been bleeding?" Cortay asked in perfect Terrish as she ripped the pant leg open, exposing the blood-soaked bandages underneath.

Cinda looked at Lars in amazement and shock as she heard Cortay speak so clearly. She then looked back at Cortay, her mind unable to focus on the question she was given.

"How long have you been bleeding child?" Cortay asked again as she cut the bandages, carefully holding Cinda's leg still as the knife blade moved between her skin and the now dark red cloth wrapped around her thigh. The cold steel sliding against her skin would have sent shivers down her spine if she was not in such pain.

"I...I..." Cinda struggled to say as she looked down at her leg.

Lars took Cinda's cheeks in his hand and turned her face towards him so she could not see her leg. "When do you think you started bleeding?" Lars asked calmly, his face only a few inches away from hers.

"I'm not sure," Cinda finally said, still panicking. "It hurt the most when Ulrick started running through the storm."

"You both are idiots coming here in such a dangerous storm with her in such a condition," Cortay said. She then looked somber as she looked down at Cinda's thigh, seeing the wound's condition. "We need to get her on the table in the other room. This is much worse than you said, Lars," Cortay said in a worried tone. Lars and Ulrick both turned and looked at her. She then started to talk to both of them in Orcish. It was too fast, and Cinda was in too much pain to understand what was being said. But Cinda noticed Ulrick's expression changed. He looked frightened.

CHAPTER 12

The blood had soaked through the cloth Hendric had wrapped his arm and hand in. It slowly dripped onto the dirt road as he limped, supporting his weight on a thick stick and his left good leg. The pain of his wounds had turned to a numb feeling as he made his way down the road. His mind could not focus on anything, and the mental haze only worsened. The sun slowly set in the distance as he tried to escape from Orinton. Knowing once the sun set, nothing would keep the ghouls inside the stone house. He had been limping for some time but had no sense of how far away he was. He just hoped he was far enough. He was so tired from the lack of blood he was not even sure where he was going, just following the road south from his village. The last rays of the sun disappeared behind the dark clouds of a coming storm. *Just keep going. You have to get away.* He thought as the air around him became noticeably cold. *I hope it doesn't snow.* Hendric looked at the clouds as he walked, seeing the last light from the sun behind them start to disappear.

Suddenly, his left leg gave out from exhaustion, and his body fell to the ground. He reached out with his left hand to brace himself out of habit. The bandaged hand smashed into the ground, sending excruciating pain up his arm as the rest of his body crashed into the dirt. He screamed in agony as he grabbed the bandaged hand with his right hand. A vain effort to feel some relief. His mind slipped in and out of consciousness from the pain and exhaustion. No longer aware of how much time had passed while he lay on the dirt road, he was suddenly awoken by a shriek in the distance. Hendric's head snapped up at the sound as every ounce of breath seemed to leave his body from fear. He looked into the darkness down the road he came from as his heart strived to pump the little blood he had left.

Hendric grabbed a torch from his bag and the flint and steel in his side pouch as he did not have the energy to get up. Then, in the distance, he heard the sound of the ghouls again. This time, it was not alone as other screeches sounded as if they were telling him there were more of them, and they were getting closer. He quickly laid the torch on the ground next to him and began to fumble with the flint in his bandaged hand, but he could not grip the rod. Panic started to set in as he could not get the torch lit, knowing that without the light from the flame, he would not even see them coming.

Frustrated with his hand, Hendric stabbed the flint rod into the torch. Some of the torch's oil squeezed out of the cloth as he pushed the flint in. He then started rubbing the steel against the flint. The spark ignited the torch and the oil on the ground around it in a fireball of light. With the searing heat on his face and arm, he quickly rolled away onto his back.

Hendric took a moment to catch his breath as he looked at the night sky overhead. Then he rolled back over to grab the torch handle. He froze when he spotted a figure on the other side of the flames. Quickly, he held the torch, seeing the figure had a gray face like the monster that attacked him. Frantically, he swung the torch but noticed the figure did not move.

"Plan to kill me with that?" the figure asked sarcastically

as it moved closer to the torchlight.

The light revealed the marble skin, the sleeveless black shirt, and the eyes of nothing but darkness. Hendric knew him, the one the elves called Dravis. His expression was blank, as if Hendric's wounds caused him no pleasure or discomfort to see. Dravis simply stood with his hands in the pockets of his black pants.

A violent howl and screeches sounded from down the road, much closer this time. Hendric turned to face the noise, knowing it would only be a few minutes until those monsters were on top of him.

"They are following you, boy," Dravis said to Hendric calmly, "though it would not be hard with you leaving a nice trail of blood for them."

"Are you going to kill me?" Hendric asked in a panicked voice as he looked at Dravis, unsure of which fate would be better, to be killed by him or the monsters on their way.

Dravis's solid black eyes seemed fixed on Hendric as he lay defenseless. "If I wanted you dead, I would have killed you while talking to Galadin." Dravis then started to walk around Hendric, much like a predator observing its prey. Hendric held the torch out between them as if to try and ward Dravis away with the flame as he struggled to sit up. "Though by the looks of it, you will be unable to find the child, Owen, and take him far from here."

Several screeches sounded again, so loud and close that both Dravis and Hendric turned to face them. Hendric's arm and hand began to shake from strain and fear as it held the torch toward the darkness.

"Are they formidable?" Dravis asked in an inquisitive tone as he looked down the road.

"What?" Hendric asked, unsure how to answer the

questions or if he had even heard it correctly.

"Are the seven creatures coming to kill you, formidable opponents?" Dravis asked in an aggravated tone from having to repeat the question.

"I...I don't know. I've only heard stories about them," Hendric stated in confusion and fear. He looked up at Dravis and noticed the corner of his closed mouth slightly rise. *Is he grinning?* Hendric thought to himself with surprise.

Then, as if responding to his name being called, Dravis started to walk toward the sounds of the approaching monsters. Hendric watched as Dravis took his hands out of his pockets. His arms and hands began to change in size and shape while the quills on his head shifted to stand up. His forearms grew slightly bigger and scales like a lizard formed on his skin. While the four fingers on his hands melded into two. Claws protruding from them, and his thumbs. Looking more like the hands of a three-clawed lizard than the human hands he had before. Dravis slowly faded from the torch's light as he walked away, disappearing into the darkness.

Hendric froze in horror as the sounds of the ghouls approaching grew closer, close enough that he could tell they were within a stone's throw from him. Then, a cry of pain erupted in the darkness. Hendric's bottom lip began to tremble as he heard more sounds. Growling, shrieking, and a sudden scream, followed by a loud thud and the breaking of branches. *He's killing them.* Hendric thought to himself, and then he heard laughing. *He's enjoying this.*

The forest fell silent; no screams or screeching. Rain began to fall from overhead. The sound of the drops hitting the ground was all Hendric could hear. His mind grew blank as the adrenaline wore off, and his heart began to calm. "Hello?" he shouted into the darkness beyond his torch as the rain steamed from it.

A severed head emerged through the air from the blackness, landing and rolling on the ground. Its dark gray face, hollow yellow eyes, and wide open mouth revealed its sharp teeth. The severed head came to rest in a forming puddle only a few feet from Hendric's hand. Its neck was not cut but ripped from its body, with jagged flesh and muscles hanging from the base of its skull.

"Formidable, they are not," Dravis's cold voice said as he walked back into the torch's light. His arms returned to normal, and the quills on his head were relaxed again. He wiped the black blood from his hands and wrists with a small cloth, missing the splatter on his shoulder and neck that had begun to drip down his skin.

Hendric did not turn to face Dravis. He stared at the head of the ghoul before him, seeing the fangs that would have bitten into his flesh and ended his life. The smell and the sight turned Hendric's stomach, and he could not help but vomit in his weakened state. The strain of losing his stomach and blood loss made Hendric slowly fall back onto his side, unable to hold himself up anymore. He looked at the dirt of the road and the oil spot struggling to burn in the rain. Slowly, he closed his eyes, defeated by the sleep he had been fighting for so long.

Dravis walked and stood over Hendric's unconscious body. "Seems it is up to me to deal with Owen before Galadin finds him," he said disappointedly. Massive bat-like wings emerged from his back as he bent down and lifted Hendric's body from the ground, holding him in his arms like a small child. Hendric's eyes slowly opened, yet his body was too weak to fight. "Don't worry. I am taking

you somewhere safe to heal. You might prove useful later."
Hendric's eyes then shut, unable to stay open any longer as
Dravis bent his knees and sprung up, sending him and
Hendric into flight.

* * *

Sepher sat atop a hill, praying again to rising Hyllo.
Arminiul stood guard, feeling uncomfortable about praying
to a sun goddess he had lost faith in many years ago. The
air was full of birds chirping as if celebrating the morning.
It was a song Arminiul loved to hear, better than any bard
or troubadour. It was one of the few things that relaxed him
and made him feel genuinely at peace. He leaned his head
against a tree and closed his eyes, listing off the names of
the birds in his mind as they chirped and squawked their
lines in the chorus. A small smile grew on his face while the
melody played. Then, suddenly, the beautiful notes were
interrupted by the distant resounding screech of an animal
to the south.

Arminiul quickly opened his eyes and looked in the
direction the screech came from. He then looked up the hill
at Sepher, who had already gotten up and faced the
direction of the screech as well.

"You heard it too?" Arminiul asked as Sepher
approached.

"I did. Sounded bird-like, but bigger."

"Axebeak?"

"Louder than any axebeak I've heard,"

The screech sounded in the distance again. This time, the
two of them both were listening for it. The sound was
unfamiliar to them, but it sounded big.

"Almost reptilian, dragon maybe," Arminiul said.

"I doubt that," Sepher said, crushing Arminiul's hope since he always loved hunting dragons. "Besides, just the two of us would be foolish to go after a dragon."

"I'm sure we could take down a young one," Arminiul said gloatingly.

"It doesn't matter anyway. We need to look for the blonde boy and woman." Sepher said as he started to walk east.

"What if they did not get away from the ghouls?"

"Those crates and boxes were not there before. They must have been gathering supplies to leave."

"Or to stay," Arminiul added quickly as he walked behind Sepher.

"I am sure they are alive."

"There are so many places that they could have gone Sepher. Do you really plan to wander from village to village, in an area not fond of our kind, looking for them?"

Sepher stopped walking and turned to Arminiul. "If that is what it takes, then yes."

Arminiul could tell by the stubborn look in Sepher's eyes that this meant a lot to him, possibly even his own life. He looked at the storm soon to be overhead, knowing the rain would clear any tracks of the boy and woman if they were to go back to Orinton. "Fine," Arminiul muttered and kept walking with Sepher beside him.

The two of them walked in the rain for miles, neither speaking to each other nor hearing the screech again. The rain had finally stopped, and they spotted a small cluster of buildings in the distance, five in total, with sparse trees all around them. Sepher crouched behind a tree, getting an arrow ready, as Arminiul began to walk a wide circle around the buildings. As he walked, he did not see anyone. The only sign of life was smoke rising from a single chimney steadily.

"I don't see anyone," Arminiul told Sepher when he returned to his side. "Darker clouds are heading this way. The rain will worsen, so we should see if we can stay the night here."

"Do we just knock on the door?" Sepher asked after nodding his head in agreement.

"I guess so. Cover me from here. I'll get a closer look," Arminuil said. He then snuck to the shabby road that led to the buildings and started walking in the open, plain to see. His hand gripped the handle of his sword as the other was raised up with his palm open to show greeting. "Hello?" he shouted in Terrish. "Is there anyone there?" Sepher stayed hidden with an arrow at the ready, pointing at the door to the building with smoke.

The sound of shuffling within the building was faint since Arminiul was about five paces away. "Excuse me. I am looking for a place to wait out the storm for the night."

"Who are you?" the voice of an elderly person shouted from the other side of the door.

"My name is Arminiul," he said as he stopped, keeping some distance.

"You don't look like the normal elves that come around here," the elderly voice yelled.

Arminiul felt slightly relaxed in hearing other elves had been there before. "My friend and I are traveling through this region. Neither of us has been here before and are quite lost," Arminiul said, talking in a relaxed tone so his nervousness did not show.

"You are not with the collectors?" the elderly voice

shouted through the door.

"No, we are hunters. Trying to track down a wild beast and followed it out here," Arminiul said as he slowly lowered his hand. "We will gladly pay for our stay." He said, knowing that greed was always a good thing to count on when it came to humans.

The door began to open just enough for an old man with a bald head and long gray beard to stick his head into view. "How much will you pay?" he asked curiously.

"We do not have much, but we can give you four gold for a place to sleep and some thick cloaks to keep us warm." Arminiul knew that four gold coins were worth far more than he was asking for but knew it would be enough for the old man to agree.

The old man's eyes looked Arminiul up and down slowly as if inspecting every inch of him. He looked around, peeking his head out further from the door. "Where is your friend?"

"He will be along shortly," Arminiul answered, knowing that Sepher was in enough cover that he could not be seen.

The old man opened the door wider and took a slow step out. His back was hunched, and he shuffled with a cane. His dirty, long-sleeved shirt and pants were worn thin in spots. He squinted to see Arminul clearer. To Arminiul, he looked frail, his face wrinkled from time and his hands bony with bruising. Then, from behind him, a teenage girl came into view.

She looked completely different from the old man. Her casual light blue dress was only slightly dirty but looked new, with no faded spots. Soft brown hair was held in a silver clasp on the top of her head. She had a look of worry on her face as she stood behind the old man.

"You and your friend can stay in that barn," the old man said as he gestured to one of the buildings. "We will find something that will be suitable for cloaks."

Arminiul smiled and bowed his head slightly in thanks as he signaled with his hand behind his back for Sepher to stay where he was. "I thank you for your kindness, sir." Arminiul walked to the barn and opened one of the double doors while the old man walked behind him at a much slower pace.

"So it is just you and one other?" The old man asked curiously.

"It is. He should be here any minute," Arminiul said as he looked inside the barn, but he did not take a step inside.

The barn was nice and clean. Two pens on each side looked like they were built to hold horses. The horses had been gone for a long time, by the looks of it. The walls, roof, and door were still in good condition and would be an excellent place to stay while the storm passed.

"Is there anyone else that lives here?" Arminiul asked while looking at the three other buildings.

The old man smiled nervously. "No, it is just me and my granddaughter."

"Where has everyone else gone?" Arminiul asked, confused as to why it was just the two of them and no real sign of how they survived since there was no livestock or farmland in sight.

"They were called away some time ago. It is just me and Clair for now," the old man answered.

Arminiul was about to ask more, but tiny raindrops began to fall from the clouds above. He reached into his pouch and pulled out four gold coins. "For the barn and the thick cloaks," he said as he handed them to the old man.

"I thank you." The old man then started to head back to his house. "I will fetch what best I can for you," he said as he limped away.

Arminiul stepped into the barn and gave it a closer look, his mind already planning how they would sleep. He then stepped back out and signaled to Sepher to come join him.

Sepher quickly came out from behind the tree with his bow relaxed, walking briskly through the field toward the barn since the storm could downpour at any moment.

"You must be the other one," the old man said after opening the door and saw Sepher near the house. His weak arms held a thick blanket and a thick cloak. "These are for you and your friend," he said while struggling to hold the weight.

Sepher walked to the man and took them with one hand. As he reached, he could see the old man shaking with a worried look in his eyes. "I thank you," he responded in Elvish. The old man, not understanding a word of Elvish, forced a polite smile and closed the door as Sepher walked to the barn.

As Sepher approached the barn, Arminiul was already finishing walking around in it, seemingly to check every space the barn had. "What is it?" Sepher asked in Elvish as he approached.

"There is only one way into this barn, and the windows are too small to crawl out of," Arminiul said as he began to look at the roof.

"Is that an issue?" Sepher asked as he rested his bow against a stall door and held the cloak in one hand with the blanket in the other. "Do you not trust the human?"

Arminiul took the blanket from Sepher and shook his head slightly. "I'm not sure." The downpour of the rain began hitting the roof. "I guess it is a little late now to find somewhere else to go."

* * *

Cinda's arms and legs tingled with numbness from the herbs Cortay fed her. She would have relaxed from not feeling pain in her thigh anymore, but Cortay and an elf wearing a green robe named Sindel were inspecting her arrow wound. Both showed concerned expressions as they felt the skin and discussed things in Elvish. Lars was not even translating for her. Cinda grew worried as she heard their tones change, unsure of what was happening. Her mind thought about one of her grandfather's friends who was injured in a fight and had his leg removed to save his life from the infection. How everyone had to help him while he spent most of his time sitting in a chair from then on.

"Am I going to be ok?" Cinda asked in hesitation. The fear of them saying they would have to remove her leg was fresh in her mind.

Cortay took a deep breath, looking at Cinda with sorrowful eyes. "I'm afraid the wound is too dire, and the infection has done irreparable damage," she said in Terrish.

Cinda looked at Lars. Tears began forming in her eyes, expecting him to say anything. But Lars just sat silently, looking back at her. His eyes looked sad as he slowly grasped her hand.

"We will clean the wound to prevent further infection, but it looks like your leg will never fully heal," Cortay said, making Cinda turn and face her as she spoke.

"What do you mean? Will never fully heal?" Cinda said with worry as tears began to slide down her cheeks.

"You should be able to walk with support, but it will be difficult," Cortay said as she kindly placed her hand on Cinda's shoulder to comfort her.

"I won't be able to walk on my own?" Cinda shouted in shock. She looked down at her bare leg and saw where most of the stitches Lars had ripped. Where the arrowhead had cut through the skin seemed to hold, but where her skin was torn by the arrow shaft hitting rocks while in the river was open. Her skin around the wound was red and infected, with yellow pus forming where the skin was supposed to be healing together but wasn't.

"The arrow moving in your leg ripped up..." Cortay said until Ulrick stood up and started yelling in Orcish at her. His deep, booming voice startled Cinda. She quickly turned to face him. Cortay did not hesitate to stand up. She looked Ulrick in the eyes as she began yelling back at him. Cinda watched as both orcs argued for a moment. Cortay went silent and pointed to the door that led back into the large room. Ulrick walked out the door with Cortay, closing it behind them while they argued again.

"What just happened?" Cinda asked Lars. She could not fully understand what was being said while Ulrick and Cortay argued in Orcish. She also didn't know why Ulrick reacted the way he did.

"They argue like that quite often," Lars answered Cinda as Ulrick and Cortay could still be heard yelling at each other on the other side of the closed door.

"Ulrick won't hurt her, will he?" Cinda asked with a worried tone for Cortay since she had never seen Ulrick so angry.

Lars began to slightly laugh at the question before answering. "No, orc siblings always seem to fight the loudest."

"Siblings?"

"Cortay is Ulrick's older sister,"

"The older sister that you taught languages to?" Cinda asked, remembering the conversation they had on the boat.

"Yes, that same one,"

"Why did Ulrick get so upset?" Cinda asked in a confused tone.

Lars looked at Sindel momentarily as if waiting for her to say something, but she just looked away from Lars in disapproval. He then looked back at Cinda. "Cortay is..." He paused to give himself a few moments to think. "You've heard of magic, right?" Lars asked.

"Yes, in old stories about the Fay," Cinda answered, not understanding why Lars was asking. Her confusion showed on her face.

"Well, Cortay can use magic to heal you," Lars said.

Cinda looked at Lars with a straight face, not really believing what he was saying. "Okay," she answered, not really knowing how to respond.

"You don't believe me, do you?" Lars asked as he slightly smirked and raised his right eyebrow.

"If she can use magic to heal me, then why doesn't she just do that?" Cinda replied snidely.

"Because most do not deserve such healing," Sindel interrupted in a cold, steady tone.

Cinda turned and looked at her quickly, shocked to hear the elf speaking Terrish. "What do you mean?" she asked after a pause.

"Did I not say it correctly in Terrish?" Sindel asked Lars in Elvish.

Lars smiled and nodded, letting Sindel know that she had spoken correctly. He then turned to Cinda. "A long time ago, Cortay healed an orc warrior named Thalson. He showed up at the temple doors gravely injured in combat. Cortay healed him like she had done for many. He walked out the door the next day perfectly fine, as if the ax wound to his stomach, broken ribs, and a broken arm had not happened."

"What is so bad about that?" Cinda quickly asked when Lars paused for a moment.

"Thalson then went on to gain his title, Thalson The Butcher," Lars said. He then turned and noticed the yelling between Ulrick and Cortay had died down, then back to Cinda. "Thalson left this temple and went back to his people. He gathered many warriors and slaughtered the people who would have killed him if it weren't for Cortay's healing, the same people Thalson had blatantly attacked unprovoked the first time." Lars then sat for a moment, looking sorrowfully into Cinda's eyes.

"He killed every man, woman, and child," Sindel said in Terrish. "He then went on to do the same to two other villages. That is how he came to be known as the Butcher." Cinda looked at Sindel. The elf's face was cold as she spoke. Retelling the story caused her no grief or sorrow. "Cortay then started to learn about others she had healed from death or crippling injuries." Sindel's eyes then narrowed on Cinda's. "One human took pleasure in horrible acts with young girls. Another orc enjoyed cutting the legs off his foes and watching them crawl away from him until they bled to death." Sindel then stood up from her stool, her face angry. "And then there was Perclin, an orc slaver who killed my father and two brothers before my eyes. Then my mother was his slave until she died one night." Sindel's jaw began to shiver in rage. "He then kept me barely alive as he would…" Sindel turned and walked away in the middle of the sentence, leaving the room through a different door than the one that led into the large room where Ulrick and Cortay were.

Cinda looked at Lars sorrowfully, thinking about what had happened to Sindel. "What happened to Perclin?" she quietly asked Lars.

"Perclin brought Sindel here to get her healed," Lars answered. "Cortay killed him without hesitation after seeing what he had done to her. Guess Perclin didn't know that Cortay also spoke Elvish." Cinda's gaze went to the door that Sindel walked through. "If Cortay had not healed Perclin's broken arm and leg from a sailing accident years before, he would probably not have been able to do what he did to Sindel and her family," Lars said quietly.

* * *

Cortay closed the door behind her aggressively, her heart pounding with adrenaline. "How dare you order me to use my powers to heal her!" she yelled at Ulrick in Orcish.

"You have the gift! You should use it!" Ulrick yelled back in Orcish. "Don't make her worry about her future when you have the power to save it!"

"You don't even know this girl!"

"She is innocent and needs our help!" Ulrick's voice was so loud it echoed through the large room, louder than the wind of the violent storm outside.

"But will she be innocent when she leaves here? Will she always be so innocent?" Cortay looked straight into Ulrick's eyes. "I will not have the blood of her wrongdoings on my hands because I healed her!" His eyes shifted away from hers quickly as he clenched his jaw in anger. Cortay took a few deep breaths. "Why do you care about this young human so much?" Cortay calmly asked. "Did she save you or something?"

"No," Ulrick answered calmly in return. "We found her on the riverbank in Miterra while we were heading home." They both fell silent. Only the wind blowing outside was heard while the storm raged on. Neither of them said a word as they stood still.

Cortay slowly cupped Ulrick's cheek and chin in her hand and moved his head to face her. "You have a kind heart, Ulrick Ironhide," she said with a loving smile. "Don't think I did not notice the bracelet marking her a member of your house."

"She reminds me of…" Ulrick started, but his voice trailed off.

"Tallus?" Cortay asked, thinking that was the name Ulrick did not bring himself to say. She slowly retracted her hand from Ulrick's cheek while he looked sorrowful at the thought of his dead wife. "I noticed that about her eyes also. Those reddish-brown eyes that change color in the light, just like Tallus's eyes."

"I know she isn't Tallus, but she still needs our help,"

"Like all those hurt animals you used to bring me when we first learned about my powers," Cortay said as she looked at the closed door to the room where Cinda, Lars, and Sindel still were.

"We had hoped her wounds would have healed and that we wouldn't need to bring her here like this," Ulrick said. "But when her leg got worse, and her headaches didn't stop, Lars and I decided to bring her to you."

"Did you tell her I would heal her?" Cortay asked,

looking at Ulrick.

Ulrick shook his head. "Lars warned against it. He was not sure you would agree to heal her."

Cortay smiled. "Well, at least you have Lars to make the wise decisions. Though I have heard stories about his idiotic ideas for the sake of fun."

Ulrick began to laugh, knowing the side of Lars that Cortay was describing. "He is the best of friends I could ask for."

"That is why Father wanted him with you," Cortay said as she looked at the door sadly. "Do you ever think how life would have been if I did not have these powers?"

"I thought you loved it here," Ulrick said in concern.

"I do, but sometimes I wish I could go on adventures with you two," Cortay said in a low tone.

"You mean on the adventures with Lars," Ulrick said with a giant grin. Cortay slightly blushed at hearing Ulrick's words. "Nothing is stopping you from coming with us," he said as he placed his hand on Cortay's shoulder.

"I swore to stay and protect this temple for the next Druid," Cortay said quietly, mostly saying it to herself as a reminder of her promise.

"At the cost of your happiness?"

"At the cost of my happiness."

"Bah," Ulrick disagreed. "This temple is fine; others will stay here and watch over it." Ulrick then raised his finger in the air, having an idea. "You can come with Lars and me while we take Cinda home after the ice melts. You can see Miterra, and…" he said excitedly, but Cortay raised her hand to cut him off.

Cortay looked at Ulrick with a concerned gaze. "Things have been happening, Ulrick. The world feels off balance."

Ulrick's smile quickly faded as he looked at Cortay's fearful face. "How can I help?" He asked sternly. "Do you need me to stay here to protect you?"

An appreciative expression grew on Cortay's face as she looked at Ulrick. Her favorite part about him was how he would defend and help people without knowing what he was up against. The heart of a true hero, she would call it. "I'm sorry, Ulrick. I know you want to, but in these matters, there is nothing you can do."

"Druid problems," Ulrick muttered. It was not the first time that Cortay needed help, but he couldn't do anything. He hated the feeling of being helpless with the things Cortay faced. No matter how strong or brave he was, he was no Druid, and there was no way to become a Druid. He spent two years with Lars trying to find a way, even traveling to the dangerous land of the fay for answers, but learned that Druids were chosen by greater powers, discovering that becoming a Druid could not be attained by those who seek it.

They both stood in silence for a few moments until Cortay finally spoke. "I will heal Cinda for you. But I want to hear about your latest travels."

"Of course. I will tell you all about them. They were not so exciting this time, though," Ulrick said with a smirk, knowing that Cortay was just trying to change the conversation like she usually did when talking about Druids and the problems he was powerless to help with.

Cortay then walked Ulrick silently back into the room with Lars and Cinda. She sat on her stool next to Cinda. She looked at her kindly as she thought in her head and weighed her options, thinking if maybe Cinda's leg could heal naturally with her help but not her powers, but she did not see a way since her thigh muscles were severely damaged.

"Are you going to use your magic to heal me?" Cinda asked kindly but quickly, as her heart was pumping fast.

Cortay slowly looked up at Lars with disapproval.

"I told her," Lars said as he smiled and shrugged his shoulders like a toddler. "Sorry."

Cortay shook her head as if disappointed with the acts of a child. She looked down at Cinda, her eyes full of worry about what could happen from this act. "Yes, Cinda, I will heal you," she said quietly.

Cinda smiled as her eyes filled with excitement. She wanted to lean up and hug Cortay, but the herbs in her system rendered her arms useless. "Thank you," she said as she was about to cry with happiness.

"You three will have to stay here while we prepare the room," Cortay said as she looked at Ulrick, Lars, and Cinda. She stood and took a bottle that held a dark brown liquid from one of the shelves in the room. "Give Cinda four gulps of this." She handed Ulrick the bottle. "It's the antivenom to return feeling to her arms and legs."

"Antivenom?" Cinda asked in a confused tone.

"The herbs are poisonous, and the elixir I gave you has snake venom," Cortay answered. "With the proper amount, it will only make your arms and legs numb. Too much, and it stops your heart."

Cinda's eyes went wide again in shock at what she was hearing. *She poisoned me!* Cinda screamed in her head. *She never said anything about poison before giving it to me.*

"It's okay, Cinda," Lars quickly said, seeing Cinda's expression change. "Cortay knows what she is doing." Lars then took the bottle from Ulrick and helped Cinda drink four gulps, then gave her an extra sip to make sure while

Cortay walked out of the room.

The taste of the antivenom was bitter on her tongue, reminding her of the taste of plums that had not fully ripened. "Can I have some water?" Cinda asked as the taste lingered in her mouth. Lars quickly got her some, but while he was searching, she noticed the concern on Ulrick's face as he looked at the floor, thinking about something. "Are you okay, Ulrick?" Ulrick looked up at Cinda, confused. "Ulrick, okay?" she asked in Orcish this time.

Ulrick then forced a smile on his face and answered. "Yes." Cinda could tell Ulrick was lying but did not want to pry.

Sitting in the room, they could hear people on the other side of the door talking and Cortay yelling commands in Orcish at people. The three sat and waited as the feeling returned to Cinda's arms and legs. Unfortunately, as the feeling returned, so did the pain in her thigh. The pain was still sharp, and she began to feel other pains. Then Sindel opened the door, carrying an off-white robe in her hands.

"I will help you put this on," Sindel said as she walked to Cinda's side.

Cinda shifted herself to get up, but she did not have full use of her limbs yet and flopped back to the table.

"I said that I will help you," Sindel said coldly. She then looked at Lars and Ulrick. "You two can leave the room so she can dress."

CHAPTER 13

The rain on the shingled roof played a melody that put Sepher to sleep quickly as Arminiul stayed awake to keep guard. Wrapped in a heavy blanket, it kept him warm enough that they did not need to light a fire. He paced the barn, staying on his feet and fully alert. Each time he reached the door, he would stop and peek through momentarily. It had been a few hours since the sun had set, and he figured the old man and his granddaughter would have gone to sleep already, but he could still see shadows moving in the firelight through the house's shutters.

As Arminiul paced, his mind drifted, thinking about home and springtime, his family when he was young, and how he always loved riding his horse through the forest and meadows on his family's land. He wished for simple times like that again, to be at peace and not at war. His mind shifted to the kids he watched get put in a cage and how scared they were. It pained him to think about them and how he regretted it, wishing he had spoken up before they even raided Orinton.

As Arminiul neared the barn door again, he heard a splashing, more than a patter of the rain off the rooftop. He quickly moved to the crack in the door and looked through. The sound of another large splash reached his ears. *Someone slipped in the mud?* he thought. Then he noticed the light from a torch on the other side of the house.

Arminiul rushed to Sepher's side. "Wake up, Sepher. Something is wrong."

* * *

Clair noticed the men approaching the house, led by her little brother. They were quiet as they walked, knowing the elves were asleep in the barn on the other side of the house.

"Kaden is back with the men from the village, Grandpa," Clair said excitedly as she put a heavy cloak on, preparing to go out into the rain.

"How many are with him?" the grandfather asked as he struggled to get out of his chair.

Clair quickly went back to the window and began counting. "Looks like ten of them," she said with an arrogant smile.

"I hope that is enough."

"There are only two elves. Of course, ten is enough."

The old man looked at Clair with a severe expression. "Those elves in the barn are not like the others. They look like they haven't slept in a bed for many days, which means they have been out here for a long time." The old man stroked his beard with his free hand. "This may not be such a smart idea to try and capture them."

"There are still only two of them, and the reward will make things easier for us while father and mother are away," Clair snapped quietly at her grandpa as she walked past him to the door.

As Clair walked outside, she noticed the rain was not as bad as earlier, but it quickly soaked through her heavy cloak. The downpour of rain the last few hours had made the ground soft and soggy. Her boots would sink with each step, and she had to strain to pull her foot up. She went around the house to greet her brother Kaden and the ten men with him.

"This is all that would come," Kaden told Clair when he finally got close enough to whisper.

"This will be enough," Clair told Kaden as she touched his shoulder. She knew not many would come since Kaden was only twelve and known for making up stories. Clair looked over the men that had come, all drenched in the rain, making them look even older than they already were, but it was the best she could ask for since most of the fighting men had gone south to fight against the elves.

The ten men crowded around Clair as she spoke. "There are only two elves in the horse barn. It should not be hard to get them," she told Dewart, the group leader.

"We will take it from here, Clair," Dewart said. He then nodded at the other men. "We rush the door quietly. There are no other exits, so it should be easy to get these filthy elves." He then turned to Clair and handed her a heavy pouch of coins. "Your reward, Clair, for telling us the elves are here."

The men walked along the back of the house, Kaden following Dewart. "Can I fight too?" Kaden asked as he looked up at Dewart. Before Dewart could answer, Kaden slipped and fell in a puddle, covering himself in mud and rain.

Dewart smiled down at the young, enthusiastic boy. "How about you stay back in case the elves make it past us," he said with a smirk.

Dewart stopped the men as he approached the corner of the house. Slowly, he peeked around the corner, seeing the doors to the horse barn were about twelve paces away. He then looked back at his men. "We approach quietly and make sure to watch your footing. Don't want to slip like the heroic Kaden," he said with a glance at Kaden, who was still struggling to get up off the ground. The men took a few deep breaths as they got their weapons ready. Dewart was the only one with a sword, while the others had clubs, torches, axes, and pitchforks. He slowly took another look at the barn doors and handed his torch to Clair. "Stay back until we bring the elves out," he told her, then signaled to the others to approach the door.

Clair stayed behind them as they all moved around her to head to the barn door. Each step they took made a sound as they walked through the puddles. Clair worried that they were making too much noise. But then, about three paces from the door, they began to yell as they charged. The first two thrust the doors open as the others rushed into the small barn. Clair stepped closer in anticipation as she watched them, hoping to glimpse them fighting the elves. However, there were too many of them, and only the man in the back was holding a torch.

As the last man entered the barn, Clair watched as two slim figures dropped from the ceiling behind them. "Behind you!" Clair yelled as the two slim figures started attacking Dewart's men. The one torch they had fell to the ground, and Clair watched in horror as one of the men was thrown onto the flame, snuffing it out.

The barn's interior was pitch black as Clair froze in fear, listening to the men yell or scream in pain. "Behind us!" she heard Dewart's voice yell out in the darkness among the other shouts. Another groan of pain was followed by the sound of wood breaking and a man screaming for help. She stood and listened for what seemed like over a minute until the barn fell silent inside.

"Hello?" Clair said quietly as she took a step towards the

barn. "Dewart, are you there?" she called out. The darkness and silence inside the barn frightened her as she peered into it. She held the torch towards the barn, hoping the light might chase away the darkness. Then, suddenly, Arminiul came out of the dark, charging straight at her.

Clair turned to run away, making it a few steps until Arminiul engulfed her with his arms from behind. His right hand grabbed the torch and pulled it from her grasp as his left arm came under her shoulder, his elbow pinning her to him as his hand grasped around her throat.

Arminiul quickly pulled Clair back as she struggled to get free. "You're lucky Sepher asked me not to kill any of you," Arminiul said as he kept Clair in his grip.

"Let go of my sister!" Kaden yelled as he ran at Arminiul from around the corner of the house. Arminiul let go of Clair as Kaden slashed at his belly with his knife. The blade only scratched his leather armor. Arminiul looked down at Kaden and slammed his fist across the boy's jaw in reaction.

Clair watched as Kaden fell to the ground with a large splash. Her rage took her. She attacked Arminiul. Her nails scratched into his cheek as he grabbed her by the throat again. This time, his leg swept under her, and he pushed her to the ground, keeping his hand around her throat as she fell.

"Please, don't hurt her," the old man yelled as he limped quickly towards Arminiul and Clair. Arminiul looked up at the old man as Clair gasped for air, her hands trying to pry Arminiul's fingers from her throat. "Please, don't," the old man pleaded as he fell to his knees a few strides from them.

"We don't have to kill them," Sepher said in Elvish as he walked calmly out of the barn, blood dripping from his knuckles.

Arminiul looked at Sepher. "They were trying to kill us. It is only fair," he snarled in Elvish, feeling betrayed.

"And they failed," Sepher responded. "There is no reason to kill them."

Arminiul looked back at the old man, who was now crying and glancing back and forth between him and Sepher, his grip loosening around Clair's neck. "Why did you send these men to attack us?" he demanded in Terrish.

"There is a reward for anyone that helps capture elves," the old man answered with fear.

Arminiul glanced at Kaden and Clair, then looked at Sepher. "Are these the two we are looking for?" he asked in Elvish.

Sepher walked closer to get a better look at the young boy and girl and shook his head. "These aren't them," he responded regretfully in Elvish.

Arminiul let go of Clair's throat and stood up. She quickly rolled to her side, coughing. "Go gather our things and anything of worth from the men inside," he said to Sepher in Elvish. Arminiul then walked to the old man. "What do they do with the captured elves?" he asked angrily in Terrish.

The old man looked up at Arminiul with fear, slowly shaking his head as if he was worried about answering. "No," he quietly cried out, not wanting to respond in fear of repercussions.

"Answer me,"

"They don't survive long," the old man muttered.

Rage was beginning to fill Arminiul as he heard the words. His hand gripped tightly around the handle of his sword, pulling it from its sheath and wanting to dispatch every human around him. He stood still momentarily, taking in a few deep breaths as the rain fell around him. Slowly, he felt his rage dissipate, knowing that Sepher did not want to see more death. His mind finally pierced through the veil of anger in his heart, and he remembered why they were there in the first place.

"We are looking for a young woman and a boy, about fourteen, from a small village called Orinton," Arminiul said. "Have you heard or seen any survivors from that village?"

The old man shook his head. "No, I have not." He then bowed his head at Arminiul's feet. "Please, please, spare our lives," he cried.

Arminiul looked at Clair, who was checking on Kaden. "Have you heard of any survivors from Orinton, girl?" he shouted.

"Why? So you can hurt them too?" Clair yelled back in anger as she held her little brother.

"No," Arminiul said calmly. "So we can keep them safe." He could tell by the look on Clair's face that she would not tell him the truth even if she knew.

Sepher walked out of the barn with one of the men's heavy brown cloak and tossed it to Arminiul. "We should go before those men in the barn wake up," he said in Elvish.

Arminiul put the rain-soaked cloak on. It was long for him but fit well over the shoulders. He looked at the old man crawling up to Clair and Kaden's side. "If anyone follows us, I will take their lives," Arminiul warned. Then Arminiul and Sepher walked away into the night.

* * *

Cinda walked into the room wearing the off-white robes

Sindel helped her change into. They were plain and simple, hanging from her loosely with long sleeves and a neckline that felt almost too small. Only her feet and head showed. The clothes made her uneasy since she could feel the cold air on her bare skin.

Ulrick and Lars stood waiting near the door to help her walk. Her eyes drifted from them, gazing at the room, well-lit by braziers evenly placed throughout it. It was much larger than the Hall of Orinton, which she hadn't noticed before. The floor and walls were all made of marble. The slabs were polished and well-cleaned, showing the gray veins within them. The dark wood roof was supported by six brilliantly bright white marble columns that would take three men to reach around and stretch as tall as a tree in the air. They were positioned in two perfectly spaced rows decorated with round tables around them. Each table had an assortment of golden statues and trinkets on them. The left and right walls had five closed doors each. They were spaced wider apart as they went further away from the front entrance. Each door was painted a green color, much like the leaves of a tree in the spring. This same green color was used for all the carpets that marked the walkways of the floor, carpets going across the entrance, parallel to the side walls, and one wide carpet that stretched to the altar in the center of the room. Its marble stairs lead to an enormous altar, a large flat granite stone, with no elegant carvings or gold trim like so many things in the room. It looked out of place.

However, most of the room's details were lost on Cinda as she looked at a large white tree that took up the back half of the room. Its limbs stretched out, almost touching the sidewalls, and the top of it reached high, almost touching the supports of the second-story roof above. It looked magnificent. The branches twisted and weaved in and out of each other like an old oak tree. Its solid white color was pure, with no difference from the bottom to the tip of the branches, not a single leaf or blemish. The sheer size and serenity of the pure white tree looked otherworldy.

Others stood in the room, all wearing green robes like Sindel, except for Cortay, who was still in her bright white robes.

"The room looks different with some light, doesn't it?" Lars asked with a grin as he watched the amazement on Cinda's face.

Cinda nodded in agreement. "I had no idea," she said quietly.

"I carry," Ulrick said in Terrish as he walked to Cinda. She quickly raised her arm and let him scoop her up. She felt small in such a large room and even smaller in his arms as he carried her. She looked at Cortay, standing next to the stone altar, as Ulrick followed the carpet paths to her. As he walked the steps, Cinda could feel the pain in her thigh every time her leg bounced.

"Do I have to do anything?" Cinda asked Cortay quietly after Ulrick sat her down on the stone altar.

"Just lay down and relax, Cinda," Cortay told her.

Cinda lowered herself slowly on the hard stone, her head leaning back slowly as she looked up at the white branches overhead. The rock she was lying on was warm, the perfect temperature to keep her comfortable. It was a strange feeling to her with the cold air on her skin. Her heart began pumping harder with anticipation as Cortay stood beside her.

The pain in her leg faded as the giant stone grew warmer.

Cinda lifted her head to look at her leg, hoping to watch the wound heal. However, the robes covered her leg from sight.

"Don't be afraid," Cortay said as she watched Cinda look around anxiously. "You are safe."

Cinda lowered her head and turned it, looking behind Cortay to see Lars and Ulrick standing before the steps. Lars stood smiling while Ulrick had a pleasant expression as they looked back at her. Seeing them gave her comfort, knowing they were there with her.

"Take a breath," Cortay said to Cinda in a calming voice as she began to pull the robes up her leg. Cinda breathed steady breaths as Cortay slowly exposed the infected wound on her thigh.

Cinda lay still, concentrating on her breathing as she looked at the branches of the white tree overhead. Then she felt something, a tingling feeling moving around in her leg. Cinda quickly looked down, seeing Cortay's eyes. She was shocked to see them glowing white as if they were a bright light themselves. She then noticed Cortay's hand above the wound. The inside of her palm emanated a soft yellow glow as tiny flakes of pure light drifted in the air, reminding Cinda of snow. They continued to float around her as more came from Cortay's hand. Cinda raised her hand slowly and reached for one of the flakes. The tip of her finger lightly touched a glowing flake of light as it drifted through the air. It felt warm as the flake absorbed into Cinda's skin, causing the tip of her finger to glow and then fade.

Hundreds of different shapes and sizes of flakes surrounded Cinda as they all started swirling slowly. She looked at Cortay, who now had her eyes closed. Her lips moved slightly as if mumbling something to herself but without a sound escaping her mouth. Cinda almost asked a question about the glowing flakes but decided not to, telling herself to remain calm as she lay motionless.

The flakes drifted closer and closer to her as they swirled around like a snowstorm. She held her breath with apprehension as the flakes started to touch her. Each one made her skin glow in the spot they touched her, momentarily, as they seemed to penetrate her skin.

The sensation of the flakes on Cinda's skin was warm and comforting. As more drifted into her, she felt calm, like how it felt when she was a child being held by her mother. Her body relaxed as her eyes closed, feeling the warmth encompass her. The tingling sensation in her thigh faded as all she felt was warmth. Cinda's mind drifted. Memories of sitting with her mother came to her, of when she was young, how she smelled, the color of her bright red hair, and the sound of her voice as she hummed a lullaby. How peaceful life was then, how happy she was.

Cinda's eyes then slowly opened as if waking from a long sleep. She looked at the white branches of the tree above her. The flakes of yellow light were gone, and she felt slightly cold again, lying on the stone altar.

"How do you feel?" Cortay asked kindly as she looked down at Cinda, her hands no longer glowing by her side.

Cinda leaned up and looked at her leg. A long, jagged scar was all that remained of the injury. She gazed in excitement. The skin looked perfectly healed, as if the damage was long ago. She still paused, though, hesitant to move for fear that she would feel pain. Then she noticed the hollow ache in her head was no longer there. Her breathing no longer hurt her side. Cinda smiled gently as she lifted her left knee up. Her eyes widened, and her smile grew larger as she felt no pain in her thigh as it moved.

Cinda began to laugh happily as she moved her leg around, and it did not hurt. "It worked!" Cinda yelled. Her voice echoed throughout the large, quiet room. She quickly leaned towards Cortay, wrapping her arms around the orc's waist as she cried in happiness. "Thank you... Thank you for this," she said into Cortay's robes.

Cortay chuckled as she returned Cinda's hug, squeezing her gently as best she could for a few moments. Cinda swung her legs off the altar and stood up, looking at her legs and feet as she did. Then she stood fully upright momentarily and looked at Lars and Ulrick, who stood smiling at her.

"It doesn't hurt!" she yelled again like an excited child, raising her arms in the air in celebration. She ran down the stairs at Lars and Ulrick, her eyes full of joy as she hugged them the best she could.

* * *

The morning sun filled the large room with light through the open shutters of the windows. Cinda could not help but be in awe of its majestic appearance. The white walls and columns reflected soft light throughout the room, making the space shadowless. She walked the room, each step feeling like a blessing as she felt perfectly healthy. Hearing Cortay and the others who lived in the temple in the side rooms, preparing breakfast.

Cinda found the temple attendance to be kind. They were not worshipers of Cortay or Tresil but people who needed sanctuary. Whose lives had been destroyed and found themselves there, much like Sindel. The three humans and two elves had made lives there. Tending to the sick or injured in neighboring villages and towns or those who came to the temple. They are the ones who made sure the temple stayed clean and kept Cortay company.

Cinda did not speak to them much, but they all made it apparent that she could stay at the temple as long as she wanted. Instead, Cinda spent most of her time walking the large room, wanting to know more about what had happened, not just about the magic used to heal her but also about the tree, the temple, and how all of it was possible.

As Cinda made it around the room, she stopped at the bottom of the steps to the large stone altar. *Magic is real*, she said to herself as she touched her thigh with her fingertips, looking up at the large white tree.

"It is beautiful, isn't it?" Cortay asked Cinda as she walked into the large room from a side door.

Cinda quickly turned to Cortay and smiled as she came closer. "I have so many questions," she said, then looked back at the tree.

Cortay laughed lightly and stood by Cinda's side. "You may ask them," she said kindly.

Cinda's mind lit up with every question she had thought about since arriving at the temple. She quickly sorted through them and finally asked, "Why do you have a large tree and not an idol to a god?" She learned from Lars that all the orc gods were depicted as orcs, not trees.

"Because this is not a temple to the gods," Cortay answered. "This is a temple to Tresil."

"Tresil?" Cinda asked.

"Tresil " is the tree's name in this world's history."

"In this world?"

"Each branch of Tresil holds a different world, and through Tresil, all the worlds are connected. So, the tree has different names in each world. Names like Wovensil, which is a world full of dragons, Yggdrasil in another, or even the most basic name, The Great White Oak. There are many different names in many different worlds, all talking about the same thing: the tree that connects all of us."

Cinda looked up at the branches of the white tree, seeing so many she could not hope to count them all. "How are there worlds on the branches of that tree?"

"This tree is not even a real tree," Cortay said as she smiled and gave a short laugh. "This tree was carved from wood and painted white long ago by the elf Talizeem, who taught me about my gifts."

"Did he heal people also?" Cinda asked.

"Talizeem was not a Druid like I am but knew much about Druids and Tresil. Even trained a few other Druids before me." Cortay walked over to the steps and sat down on them.

"What's a Druid?" Cinda asked as she sat down next to Cortay. "I overheard you and Ulrick saying that word while arguing."

"Druids are those that Tresil gives its gifts to. We are the guardians or watchers of this world."

"Guardians? Guardians of what?"

Cortay looked at Cinda. "Guardians against other worlds or even threats inside of this world," she said as she lifted her hand and extended two fingers. "You see, for most branches, they have other branches coming from them." She demonstrated with her arm, hand, and two fingers. "Between the worlds with conjoining branches, it is easier to travel between them, and sometimes things come through to other worlds."

"We can travel to other worlds," Cinda said excitedly

about seeing another world. "Have you traveled to another world?" she quickly asked.

"I have not, but long ago, before I was born, a Druid from another world came here. He traveled many worlds, some like ours, some very different from ours. Some filled with majestic dragons while others with fiendish monsters." Cortay looked at Cinda with an excited face. "There is even a world of ice, as far as you can go. It is filled with giants as well. Sounds a bit cold for my liking." She remarked with a slight laugh.

"Are you the only Druid in our world?" Cinda asked quietly.

"There are never more than five Druids in our world. Each of us has control of an aspect of the world we watch over," Cortay said as she untied the collar hold of her robe. She slowly pulled the collar open and showed Cinda her chest below her collarbone. Her green skin was scared, like a brand. It resembled an oval with four lines coming from the top arch, each line evenly spaced on the outside of the oval while another line went halfway up the middle of the inside of the oval from the bottom. "It looks like a heart. The line up the middle dividing it into chambers, and the lines over the top are the arteries that bring blood throughout the body," Cortay explained as Cinda leaned in, taking a good look at the branding scar.

"How did that happen?" Cinda asked.

"When I was only a couple years older than you, Tresil came to me in a vision and branded me when I was chosen," Cortay said as she shifted her robe back in the proper place and tightened and tied the string to close it.

"How did a tree in a vision hurt you?"

"How does a tree hold the worlds together?" Cortay

asked in response. "There is much we do not know about Tresil. Talizeem says its magic is connected to all things, not just worlds. So it would not be hard to reach you in a vision when you are chosen."

"How is a Druid chosen?"

"We are not sure," Cortay replied, looking away somberly. "Some think it has to do with Fay ancestry, but I am sure I do not have any fay blood in me. Others believe the Druid who dies chooses their replacement, or Tresil decides who shall be a Druid. Then some think it is something like fate."

"Which do you believe?" Cinda asked.

"I like to think that the Druid chooses who shall be the next to take their place. It sounds nicer to think I have a choice in who will be the leader of this temple and help those I care for," Cortay answered.

Ulrick and Lars walked into the room. They wore thick winter clothing and held supplies for the return home.

"It is time we should leave before another storm comes," Lars said. "How about you get yourself dressed for the walk home Cinda." Cinda nodded in agreement as she got up and walked to the room where she could change into warmer clothes.

Cortay stood up from the step. She looked at Lars with a smile and kind eyes, and Lars returned the look before she spoke. "Lars, can you give Ulrick and me some time to talk?" She then walked out the front entrance with Ulrick as Lars stayed inside.

The thick blanket of snow from the storm the night before made the forest around the temple look surreal. The perfect, undisturbed snow crunched as Cortay and Ulrick walked on it. Ulrick followed Cortay as she distanced themselves from the temple so no one heard them.

"It was nice to see you again, Ulrick," Cortay finally said in Orcish as she stopped among some trees.

"It was nice to see you as well, Cortay," Ulrick answered in kind as he stopped by her side. "Why did you want to talk out here?" He thought it was strange that she led him so far away.

Cortay quickly hugged Ulrick around the chest, burying her face into his collar. It startled Ulrick at first, but then he wrapped his arms around her.

"Are you ok?" Ulrick asked, not expecting this kind of affection from his sister.

"I know we agreed I would never tell you about my visions of your future," Cortay said somberly, still hugging Ulrick. It was an agreement they both made since Cortay began having visions of the future when she first gained her Druid gifts. Ulrick never wanted to know them, wanting to live his life his own way, or so he thought. "I had a vision about you a little over a week ago. It was different from the others, a new one."

Ulrick stood quietly, holding Cortay in her arms. He could tell something was off with her this time since she never acts this lovingly towards him when he departs. "What did you see?" he asked reluctantly, unsure if he wanted to know his future.

"I saw a fire burning on ice and a path calling your name behind you," Cortay said quietly. She then leaned her head back, looking up into Ulrick's eyes. "I want you to follow that path, no matter where it leads you." She buried her head back into his collar, on the verge of crying. She knew she had to hold back the tears. "Promise me you will follow that path." She squeezed him tighter as she spoke, knowing, in her heart, the path for Ulrick would lead him from her, never to see her again.

"I promise," Ulrick answered as he held his sister.

CHAPTER 14

The rain had been falling for days, driving Owen stir-crazy. He was not used to dealing with two people, neither being his mother. But with Tavia and Aerlene seeming to nag him about little things like his mother did, he had grown frustrated being stuck with them for hours. It was not until a break in the storm that Owen hurried to gather the goats and take them to an excellent field he had spotted a week before. He had seen a large rock that seemed perfect to sit on and enjoy being outside, away from Tavia and Aerlene for a little bit. The goats seemed just as eager as him to be out of their pen and followed him without wandering or needing to be prodded with the wooden walking cane he carried.

Owen quickly sat on the large flat rock, banged the mud off his shoes, and placed the wooden cane beside him. He watched the goats wander about, eating the fresh grass. He closed his eyes, feeling the warm sun on his face and the light breeze wafting his blonde hair. Breathing deeply, he could smell the moist dirt and grass around him. He loved being out in the fields. It was much better than cooped up in a house.

Part of him wondered how Hendric was. After weeks of waiting for him, Owen lost hope. Thinking maybe Hendric had never checked the stone house and found the note, or even worse, the elves had found him. He missed Hendric, being able to talk to him, tell him stupid jokes, and him ruffing up his hair.

A strong breeze rustling through the trees some distance away caught Owen's ear. He looked at the tall pine trees as they swayed back and forth. They were part of the forest on the eastern side of Keerike. The sight of them reminded him of home. His stomach began to twist inside him as feelings of all he had lost came to the surface of his mind. Owen then spotted something moving in the trees. Much bigger than the wolves he had heard on numerous occasions but had not seen. He grabbed his wooden cane and watched intently. The dark mass moved back and forth but did not come out of the treeline.

Owen finally caught sight of the brown fur between a gap of trees. Its rounded ears and large head emerged into sight, followed by its thick, lumbering body. *A bear?* Owen thought to himself as he watched it pass behind another tree and out of sight. *Shouldn't it be hibernating? Hendric said that bears hibernate during the winter... unless...* Owen quickly glanced at the goats, realizing the bear could be after them *unless they were hungry.*

Owen gripped his cane tightly when he noticed the bear come back into view. Its body shifted slowly as the bear sat down. Its large brown eyes stared straight at him. *Why is it just sitting there?* He thought as he held still, poised to run if the bear moved towards him. Yet the bear did not move from its spot. Instead, it sat as if it was enjoying the sunlight and the break from the rain.

The bear began playing with a broken branch. It swung it around in its paws as it gnawed on the bark. Its enormous body fell to lie on the ground as it played with the branch. The sight of the bear playing made Owen smile. How happy the bear appeared to him.

"Owen!" Tavia angrily yelled. Owen quickly turned to

look at her as she came trudging through the muddy field towards him. She carried a thick leather backpack with a bedroll strapped to the bottom. Owen had bought it over a week ago and had hidden it in his room.

Owen glanced back at the bear, who had now dropped the branch and rolled onto its stomach. Its eyes focused on Tavia as she came closer to him.

"Why do you have this?" Tavia angrily asked. Owen stood up from the rock, and Tavia threw the backpack at him. He dropped his cane to catch the heavy load. "Why do you have a backpack full of food and traveling clothes hidden under your bed?"

"I...I..." Owen struggled to say. Not wanting Tavia to know his plans, he realized he had no choice but to be honest. "I was thinking of running away."

The words pierced Tavia and brought her anger to a boil. "You what!" She screamed at Owen.

"I can't stop thinking about the visions." Owen retorted.

"That is not a reason to run away from me!" Tavia spat. "To leave me like everyone else!" Tavia screamed with heartbreak and rage. She quickly swung her hand without thought and slapped Owen across his face. Owen's head went to the side as the sound of the slap reverberated throughout the clearing. Owen did not move, shocked by Tavia's actions. Tavia did not move either as she looked at Owen's face. Her eyes began to fill with tears. *Is this what my father felt when he slapped me?* She thought to herself in fear. "I am so sorry, Owen." She cried.

Tavia slowly reached out her hands to hug Owen, hoping to be accepted, but as she got closer, a loud roar from a large animal came from her left. Tavia and Owen turned their heads as the goats began running from the roar. Both looked in horror as the bear was on its hind legs, less than thirty paces from them. Its eyes fixed on them as it fell back to all four legs.

Tavia quickly reached for Owen's shoulder to pull him away so they could run, but as her hand gripped his arm, the bear roared again and bared its teeth as it began to walk towards them slowly. Tavia froze with fear.

Owen then noticed the bear's eyes focused on Tavia, not him. He stepped in front of Tavia as if to protect her.

"What are you doing? We should run." Tavia said in a panic as the bear glared at her. Its enormous body slowly halted its advance. "We need to run."

The bear shook its head with a loud huff, gave Tavia another glare, and turned around, returning to where it was before, among the trees.

"What was that?" Tavia asked in shock.

"That bear has been sitting and watching me," Owen answered as he turned around to face Tavia. He placed his hand on his shirt atop his right chest. "Things have been strange since…" Owen paused a moment as he looked into Tavia's eyes. "Since I got this scar on my chest. Since the vision of the white oak tree."

Tavia glanced at the bear sitting next to a thick branch and then looked at Owen. "The bear is just sitting and watching you?"

Owen looked at the bear as it sat staring at the both of them. "It was playing until you came and yelled at me."

"You think it has something to do with what's happening to you?"

"That's what I'm wondering about," Owen replied. "I don't understand what is happening, and that scares me even more." Owen stepped towards the large rock and placed the backpack on it. "The vision said to go to Delmock. Maybe this Tyris person knows what is happening and what the symbol on my chest means."

"I told you we would go in the spring when the weather improves."

"I can't wait that long." Owen blurted out. "Don't you understand? The floating orb that saved us guided us away from the elves that attacked our home. They were there for me. What if they realize they didn't find me? They will hunt for me again."

"They won't find us."

"They will! What if they come here and kill you like they killed my mom and everyone else?" Tears began to run down the sides of his cheeks.

Tavia quickly grabbed Owen and pulled him to her. Hugging him around the shoulders as he wept into her chest. "I know it is scary, Owen. I am afraid, too, but we need to be smart. Going to Delmock in the winter would be hazardous. Neither of us knows how to get there, and we can't be caught in a storm. I am sure the elves that attacked Orinton won't find us here."

"It is not just that, Tavia. I don't understand what is happening to me." Owen said as he squeezed her. "The animals around me are acting strange, and the strange visions... I can't stop thinking about them. What does it all mean? What did that white tree and the Seer do to me?"

Tavia looked at the bear as she held Owen. The bear did not pose a threat now and was just sitting, watching the two of them. "Do you mean to tell me that you think the bear was trying to defend you?"

Owen's grip on Tavia loosened as he also looked at the bear. He wiped the tears from his eyes. "She seemed upset when you slapped me."

"I'm sorry…that I hit you," Tavia said regretfully as she stepped back from Owen. "I was just so upset that you would leave. I guess I am more like my father than I thought."

Owen was trying to figure out what to say. So much was running through his head. He turned and looked at Tavia. Seeing the sorrow on her face at what she had done. "I… forgive you, Tavia." He then looked back at the bear. "The bear did seem to want to defend me."

"Does that normally happen?" Tavia asked as she looked at the bear.

"No, this is the first time I have seen her."

"How do you even know it is a female bear?"

"I am not sure… just a feeling." Owen then pointed at one of the goats. "Like, I know that goat doesn't really like the taste of seeds." He then pointed to a different goat. "Or that he has pain around his right horn, but I don't see anything wrong. It is like that with most of Aerlene's animals I spend time with."

"It could be that you have just been watching them closely and noticed."

Owen shook his head. "That is what I thought, but then I realized how well the animals behave when I'm around. I don't even need my cane to herd these goats. They all just seem to listen and follow me, something even Harrah could not do after having them for years."

"Why do you think the elves would be after you if all you know is what animals are feeling?" Tavia asked as she watched the goats around them. None of them even appeared threatened by the bear still at the tree line.

"I think the white oak tree did more to me than just give

me the ability to understand animals," Owen said as he touched the shirt over his right chest. "It feels like there is much more… much more that I can do."

* * *

The Great Hall of Tolneer was loud and full of people as Ulrick, Cinda, and Lars entered through the large doors. Everyone was celebrating Fortege, the first night after the first snowfall. It was a tradition in Tolneer, but Lars explained it as another reason to feast and drink. Orcs, some humans, and a few elves sat at the tables filling the hall's interior. All of them were eating and drinking together as though they were family. Mugs hitting each other, the occasional plate breaking, and people talking over one another made for a menagerie of noise. Yet, as Ulrick walked into the view of everyone, the room grew silent as they bowed their heads or raised a cup in his direction. Cinda found it amazing to see such respect, but then she noticed a large orc standing on the opposite side of the hall with his cup raised. The large orc, Ulrick's brother and Earl of Tolneer, Thrane The Bold, stood before his throne. However, when Thrane sat down on his large throne, everyone returned to what they were doing.

As they walked through the crowd of people, everyone would part ways for Ulrick. Cinda felt uncomfortable as many would stare at her as she walked past. She felt uneasy walking in the plain green dress Lars had found for her, believing she stuck out from the others. Her eyes looked back at Lars, making sure she did not drift far from him since many were greeting Ulrick, distracting him. The orcs gathered were much larger than she was, making her feel like a small child as they weaved through. Ulrick had led them to a spot for the three to sit together.

"Is this a spot for the family of Thrane?" Cinda asked Lars after they sat down, realizing they were close to Thrane and had no one sitting behind them, much like the spot her grandfather would sit when there were feasts in the Hall of Orinton.

"It is," Lars answered as he poured himself and Cinda a drink from a large pitcher of mead.

Cinda stared at the large, orc-sized clay mug as the amber liquid rested. She could smell the honey mead. It brought her memories back to the boat they sailed in. She looked up, seeing the orcs near them laugh, joke, and drink. The feeling of being alone set into her mind as what little Orcish she knew did not really help since the hall was so loud. It all became muffled noises in her head. Then she noticed a group of orcs across the hall staring at her.

The group dressed differently than most of the people in the room. They wore red shirts with white and gray furs on their shoulders, whereas most of the other orcs in the hall had clothes of green, and no one had furs that were so lightly colored. One of them stared at her the most, a male orc that looked younger than Ulrick by a good amount of years, yet his tusks were more prominent and his skin a darker shade of green. He wore a necklace of gold pendants, and his right arm had a gold bracer. She noticed that none of the others with him had such lavish jewelry. Cinda quickly looked away as her eyes met with his, shifting in her spot uncomfortably from still feeling the orc's stare.

"What's wrong?" Lars asked, seeing Cinda's body language change suddenly.

"That group of orcs in red," Cinda said nervously as she

looked down at the table. "They keep looking at me."

Lars casually looked over at the orcs Cinda spoke of and then back out to the crowd of the others. "I believe that is the new Earl of Glathbern, a territory to the northeast of here." He slowly took a drink as he looked out over the people. "Make sure to stay close to Ulrick and me. The orcs from Glathbern see all non-orcs as inferior and treat them as such."

"Even you?" Cinda asked in a worried tone.

"If I were in Glathbern, I would be a slave," Lars said coldly. "Ulrick's father changed the culture of orcs in Tolneer. He realized that treating other races with more dignity paid off in more trade and wealth." Lars then signaled to the group of humans that sat by themselves at a far table. They looked differently compared to all the humans Cinda had seen. These humans had prominent cheekbones, stocky builds, round faces, narrow eyes, and a darker skin tone than she was used to seeing. "They are humans from the east called Althians. Forty years ago, those humans would be seen as enemies and not welcome to wander these streets even as slaves." Lars then pulled a dagger from its sheath on his belt and showed it to Cinda. "But now we trade with the Althians, gaining the bonus of their superior steel and metal craftsmanship. These ideals have made Tolneer the largest and wealthiest city in all the Orcish lands. Thrane himself has dreams of building more trade routes with humans and elves."

"Then why do you still raid people needlessly?" Cinda asked, remembering the stories she had heard about orcs and even recalling the orcs on the boat and the elf prisoners.

"Change cannot happen overnight. Raiding and war are part of the Orcish culture, and victory in battle is how many orcs gain fame," Lars answered. "Once we become trade partners with a people, we no longer raid them. We even fight for the people if they pay enough."

"So instead of killing them, you will kill for them?" Cinda asked snidely.

Lars laughed at Cinda's question. "Yes, if they pay enough." He then looked Cinda in the eyes. "Everyone has enemies, Cinda, even in Orcish lands. They wage war against each other out of greed, for wealth, food, honor, and women."

"Women?" Cinda asked, surprised to hear that word on the list. Lars laughed again and pointed at Thrane. Cinda turned her head, noticing Thrane on his throne. To his left were two orc women and an elf woman. Each sat in a smaller chair the further it went from Thrane's. "His daughters and their handmaiden?" She asked. Having a similar seating arrangement for herself in Orinton.

"Nope," Lars said as he shook his head. "Those are Thrane's wives."

"He has three wives?" Cinda asked as she looked at the women. "Even an elf?"

"She was a gift as a slave, but eventually Thrane saw something in her, and he married her as well."

"But why does he have more than one wife?" Cinda asked, confused.

"Orcs are polyamorous with their relationships," Lars said. He could tell by the look on Cinda's face that she did not understand. "Many, the stronger and wealthier ones at least, have multiple spouses. Most marriages are for political gain or the daughter of a defeated rival. Not often are second marriages out of love, sometimes not even the first one is. Vools, Thrane's first wife, was a marriage of peace.

Vools is the daughter of another Earl who lost power soon after the wedding. Cathis is his second wife. They met while Thrane raided in the east, and she became pregnant. So Thrane married her, not so much out of love but because they had a child together."

"Why does he not have a human wife?" Cinda asked, thinking it was strange that there were more humans than elves, yet he had two orcs.

"Noble orcs cannot have human wives. It dilutes the strong, noble bloodline by having half-orc offspring,"

"But wouldn't children with an elf be the same thing?" Cinda asked as she looked at the wives. Each was dressed in an extravagant dress decorated with jewelry and furs. The amount of gold each wore seemed to diminish with their rank, as shown by the placement of chairs.

Thrane's first wife, Vools, seemed most important or influential. She sat beside Thrane with an angry scowl as she looked over the crowd in the hall. Wearing a dress that looked more like armor. Her shoulders were covered with steel shoulder plates held on with gold chains. She wore hard leather armor that had decorative gold-thorned vines swirling around. She even carried a small sword on her hip as if waiting to be called to fight at any moment. She still had a skirt on under her armor. Finely crafted from silk, the skirt was a dark green with gold trim. None of it was flattering, but she looked more like a woman prepared to go to war. Cathis wore less decorative armor and a skirt with only a golden necklace.

The elf, however, wore a different style of dress altogether. The clothes were tailored to show her feminine curves. The style made the female elf seem more delicate than the others, with extravagant feathers decorating her necklace. Her face, however, was stern and looked more like a grand queen with her head held high. The elven wife impressed Cinda. She could pass as a lady in any court she walked into.

"Elves and orcs can't produce offspring," Lars said.

Cinda quickly turned and faced him. "Why can't they?" She thought it was strange since Lars was half-elf and half-human, and she had seen a couple half-human, half-orcs.

"No one really knows, actually," Lars said. He then took a drink of mead and looked back at Cinda. "Orcs and elves can't have kids between each other, but humans can have kids with either of them." Cinda looked at Lars with a confused expression. "Talizeem had a theory about it. He thought that since humans seemed to reside in all the worlds of Tresil, they were something he called the Root Race. All other races spring from them." Lars then leaned back in his chair. "That is only his theory, though. But because of the inability to produce offspring with elves, orcs prize female elves.

"So Thane's elf wife will never have children?" Cinda asked as she looked back at the elf woman, thinking how sad it must be to never have her own children.

"If she does, they will not be Thane's, which could cause some problems," Lars said as he laughed lightly.

"So is that why Ulrick never took advantage of me, because I'm human?" Cinda said quietly so that Ulrick did not hear.

Lars began to laugh loudly. "No, Ulrick did not take advantage of you because, unlike many, he is a good person." Ulrick turned from his conversation, hearing Lars mention his name. "Orcs can still have their way with humans. Nobles can't marry them, so any offspring have no claim to titles or lands. Even Thrane has a few half-orc children, but they are bastards."

Cinda felt uneasy once again as she glanced at the orc from Glathbern. His eyes still seemed to be trained on her. Her hand moved to her wrist as she started fiddling with the bracelet, marking her as part of Ulrick's house. *They said it was for my safety, but how safe am I?* She thought as she moved the beads in her fingers.

The food began to be dispersed among the crowd, making the shouts quiet as they ate. Cinda was surprised when her large plate was placed in front of her: an entire chicken with uncut potatoes, carrots, and something that looked like thick green goop. She watched as Ulrick ripped the drumstick from the chicken with his bare hands and began eating sloppily. Scenes of barbarism were all around her. She had seen Ulrick and the others eat like this but thought that was circumstantial since they were on a boat with no table, not at a feast.

"Where are the forks and knives?" Cinda asked Lars, who had picked up an uncut carrot and took a bite. He looked at her, perplexed by the question.

"They don't use forks. You just eat with your hands," Lars said after quickly swallowing the piece of carrot in his mouth.

"Even at a feast?" Cinda asked. Lars nodded, unable to answer with the carrot in his mouth. She looked at the chicken. The smell of it filling her nose made her mouth water. She reached nervously with her hands and tore a drumstick free.

"See, it's not so bad," Lars said with a slight nudge of his elbow.

"I don't think I can eat all of this," Cinda said as she

looked at the pile of food on the large plate.

"It's okay if you don't. All the scraps get fed to the pigs or dogs or anything else really," Lars answered and then started to rip the chicken apart with his hands.

The chicken tasted amazing to Cinda as she took a bite of a drumstick. Its moist texture and seasoning made it taste like nothing she had had before. She smiled as she took another bite, closing her eyes and enjoying every moment, for this was the first thing she had eaten for over a week that she actually enjoyed.

"It's good, isn't it?" Lars said with a laugh.

Cinda smiled and nodded her head. "It really is good," she said, covering her mouth with her hand since she still was chewing on some of the chicken.

"Now, dig in with your hands," Lars said encouragingly.

Cinda reached for the chicken's body after she had finished the drumstick, sliding her thumb into the meat and pulling a section of the breast off with her fingers. She took a full bite, enjoying the flavor of the breast meat even more.

"Good bird?" Ulrick asked Cinda in Terrish with a smile as he looked at her.

Cinda smiled back. "Very good…chicken," she said clearly in Terrish for Ulrick to understand the bird's name.

As they all ate together, hands greasy from the chicken meat, Ulrick suddenly stopped, and his smile faded as the Earl from Glathbern approached him. The large orc stood across the table from Ulrick, looking at him sternly, and then started speaking in Orcish to him.

The words were different and strange sounding even for Orcish to Cinda, so she quickly turned and looked at Lars, who seemed angered by what the Earl was saying.

"What is he asking?" Cinda asked Lars quietly as Ulrick

started talking back to the Earl.

Lars's unwavering eyes did not leave the Earl as he quietly answered. "He is offering payment for you."

Cinda's heart sank, and her stomach turned as she looked back at Ulrick. As the two orcs spoke, everyone around them fell silent. Each time Ulrick answered, she felt increasingly nervous about the situation. *Are they haggling on price for me?* she thought while her mind raced to translate what little Orcish she grasped.

Ulrick looked at Cinda, and he quickly grabbed her arm. Cinda panicked, pulling away, but she could not overpower his might. He held up her arm and spoke to the Earl harshly and angrily.

"No, please, don't," Cinda cried out. She looked up, seeing the Earl's face seethe with anger as he turned around abruptly and walked away, pushing a few orcs to the side that stood in his way. Ulrick let go of Cinda's arm, his eyes not leaving the back of the Earl as he walked away.

"You're okay," Lars said frantically as he rubbed Cinda's shoulders to comfort her, but she quickly shied away from his touch. She looked at Ulrick as her wrist hurt from being yanked so hard. The chaos of the sounds of people in the room sent shivers down her spine as fear took over. She felt entirely alone. She squirmed as Ulrick looked at her, his face full of anger that she thought was directed at her.

I have to run. I have to get out of here. Cinda thought to herself as she turned and darted from her chair, away from Ulrick and Lars.

Cinda was quick to move around the large orcs. She could see the way to the hall's main doors was blocked by crowds. She quickly turned around, spotted a nearby door, and ran through it. As she cleared the door, she was stopped by a large orc looking down at her while carrying two plates of food. In a panic, Cinda ducked below his arm and passed him. She looked around, seeing she was in a kitchen full of orcs. Their green skin, large bodies, and frightening tusks made her run for another door in the room that led to a hallway. *I gotta get out of here.* Her mind screamed as she ran down the hall until she spotted an open door and ducked inside. Seeing no one in the room, she closed the door and quickly hid behind the large bed. She curled into a ball and began to cry in fear as she heard the footsteps and yells of others from the other side of the door.

Cinda was unaware of how much time had passed as she lay crying on the floor, wishing she could just open her eyes and find herself sitting in her bed. She wanted to go home so badly, to see her father and other familiar faces again, hoping most of them made it through the elven attack. She then wondered about returning to Cortay and staying with her and the others at the temple. The people there seemed friendly and accepting of humans since a few were there. Cinda wanted to be anywhere but where she was.

Then, the sound of the door opening made Cinda panic once again. She froze, holding her breath as she heard something quickly run into the room and jump on the bed. The bed creaked under the weight of it as she closed her eyes tightly, hoping to not be seen. She felt something cold touch her ear and the sound of rapid sniffing.

Cinda looked up, seeing the sizeable gray face of a wolf only inches from hers. Feeling the wolf's breath and peering into its staring eyes, Cinda sat up with a scream, pushing herself away from the wolf until her back hit the wall. She continued to scream, looking at the wolf as it lay on the bed, its gaze unwavering. Cinda spotted Thrane's elven wife in the room through the wolf's tail wagging. Behind her, in the hallway, stood Lars and Ulrick.

"Thank the gods we found you, Cinda," Lars said as he walked through the door. A look of worry was on his face.

"I don't want to be sold," Cinda cried out. The wolf moved slightly, and she quickly retracted her arms to her chest, fearing it might attack.

"Ulrick was never going to sell you," Lars said in a panic. "He was showing the Earl your bracelet. Making him see that you aren't a slave but a member of his house." Lars looked at Cinda with a sad face. "I'm sorry you thought that we would sell you like that," Cinda looked at Lars, seeing he was genuine with his words. She then looked at Ulrick, who seemed sad as he stood in the doorway.

Thane's wife began speaking in Elvish to Lars, ushering him and Ulrick out of the room and closing the door behind them.

"I'm sure that was a bit overwhelming," Thrane's wife said in Terrish when she turned around and looked at Cinda. "I do not believe we have been properly introduced," she politely said as she walked towards Cinda, holding her hand out to Cinda as she still sat on the floor. "My name is Levelith, but everyone just calls me Lev."

Cinda took Lev's hand and got to her feet. "I'm Cinda."

"Oh, I know who you are," Lev said with a smirk. "The beautiful dark red-haired human from Miterra Ulrick found on the river bank, healed by Cortay herself on the altar of Tresil. Most of Tolneer knows who you are." Lev then walked to one of the wardrobes in the room and opened it casually as if not wanting to draw attention to the fact that Cinda was crying on the floor moments ago.

Watching Lev walk through the room made Cinda

realize the space around her. She saw a vanity with a polished silver disc for a mirror, a finely crafted stool tucked under it, three wardrobes along a wall, and a large bed with a headboard decorated with feathers of different birds. The feathers fanned out in an arc along a semicircle piece of wood with birds in flight carved on it. Then there was the large wolf lying on the bed, its yellow eyes peering straight at Cinda while its tail wagged every time she moved.

"Don't be afraid of Feirdren," Lev said as she smiled at the wolf on her bed. "He seems to like you already."

Cinda looked at the giant wolf. "Feirdren," she said, seeing the dog's excitement from hearing his name. Cinda slowly reached out her hand, letting Feirdren sniff it, and as he did, he quickly licked her fingers.

"Look at that, Feirdren. He won't hurt you," Lev said while she pulled the thin silver rod from her bright blonde hair tied in a bun, letting it fall past her shoulders.

Cinda began petting Feirdren on the top of its large head, feeling the soft hair of its fur in between her fingers as she scratched. "Hi, Feirdren," she softly said to the dog as it sat and enjoyed being petted.

"You can sit and pet him," Lev said. She then removed the necklace of feathers from her neck and hung it up in one of the wardrobes.

Cinda quickly obliged and sat beside Feirdren on the bed, running her fingers along the wolf's fur. The gray coat was a little more coarse than the white fluffy fur, but it felt nothing like the dogs she had petted. They all had a slightly dirty feeling with tough hair, nothing as soft as Feirdren. She was also somewhat amazed that she was petting an actual wolf since all the wolves near Orinton were wild and something to fear. However, Feirdren seemed loving and bigger than any wolf she had seen.

Cinda turned and saw Lev standing in the room, watching her as she sat and petted Feirden. She smiled kindly at them, giving Cinda time to relax.

"Have you ever had a pet dog?" Lev asked as she walked over and sat down, also starting to pet Feirdren.

"No," Cinda answered quietly. "My father didn't want me to have a dog. Said they cause too much of a mess, but there were some in my village."

"Pets are good to have," Lev said as she stared at Feirdren lovingly. "They make the most wonderful companions and can help melt your problems away." They both sat for a moment. The only sound was Feirdren's panting and tail whacking on the bed until Lev spoke again. "I saw what happened with Beotolt." Cinda's eyes quickly looked at Lev. "The Earl of Glathbern," she said to clarify. Cinda's hand retracted from Feirdren at the mention of the subject. "I can't believe that orc really thought he could walk up and buy you," Lev said. Cinda shrank further from Lev until Lev reached out and softly placed her hand on Cinda's. "Don't be upset with Ulrick by how he acted. When he gets angry, he doesn't think well and didn't mean to hurt you when he grabbed you."

"I know," Cinda quietly said, realizing that Ulrick had been kind to her the entire time. "I shouldn't have run like that." She then looked at Lev and then quickly away. "I just get so scared here sometimes. I didn't know what to do but run."

Lev nodded her head. "I was like that too when I first was brought here." She then looked at the headboard of the bed. "You are lucky you have Ulrick. Most are not as fortunate to be found by someone so kind."

Cinda looked at Lev, seeing the sadness in her elven eyes. "But now you have Thrane," she said in a slightly happy tone.

Lev seemed to smile at the remark. "Yes, you could say that." Her eyes still looked at the headboard.

Cinda turned and looked at it as well, seeing all the feathers and carvings of birds in flight or perched on branches. "You must really like birds," she said after realizing even her necklaces were of bird feathers.

"I'm jealous of them," Lev said sorrowfully. "They can just fly away. Free at any moment to fly away." She then looked down at Feirdren and started petting him vigorously. "At least I have you, Feirdren," she said as the wolf's large body rolled onto its back, exposing its belly to be pet.

A loud knock sounded at the door. "Is the human okay?" Thrane's deep voice rang through the wooden door.

"Her name is Cinda, and yes, she is okay," Lev answered kindly.

"Good. Ulrick and Lars want to know if she is good enough to return to Ulrick's," Thrane said in Terrish.

Lev turned and looked at Cinda. "It is up to you," she said politely.

Cinda nodded her head in agreement and stood up from the bed. "Thank you," she said to Lev while she curtseyed.

Lev smiled at the motion. "I haven't seen a curtsey in years." She stood up and curtseyed as well. Lev quickly grabbed her hand as Cinda turned and started walking to the door to leave. "Remember, Ulrick will always protect you. No matter the odds."

Cinda looked into Lev's eyes as she spoke. They were sympathetic and kind, nothing like they were in the hall as she sat in her chair. They reminded her of her mother's eyes.

CHAPTER 15

Owen opened his eyes, seeing a familiar wall before him. Each board and the cabinet on the wall was home, where he was raised. He looked at the wall, seeing the small iron pot his mother used often and the paint on the cabinet. However, everything was slightly different. The pot looked new, yet he always remembered it with years of use. The paint on the cabinet had vibrant blue flowers along the bottom of the door. He always saw the flowers chipped and faded. He stepped back from the wall, expecting to hear the floorboards creak from the shift of his weight like always, yet it was silent.

A squawk behind him caught his attention. Sounding much like a crow but deeper. Owen slowly turned, and his eyes widened as most of the house's main room wasn't there. Only burnt timbers remained of the kitchen where he would eat with his mother. It was still his house, though. He knew the remnants of his home even in this state. The remains of everything he had were now nothing but ash. Where the charred wood met with the perfect wood, it was not scorched as it should be but blurred, as if looking through a stream of water that flowed and shifted continuously. Owen rubbed his fingertips against his thumb as he slowly lifted his hand to touch the oddity as it swayed back and forth along the wall.

"I don't see why you can't take me with you." a female voice said.

Owen quickly looked, his heart almost skipping a beat

as he could not believe the voice he heard, the voice of his mother.

"You know why, Cassiday," a male voice replied.

A shirtless man appeared, walking into the solid house from the burnt section. The air around him rippled as he materialized as if emerging from a water's surface. Owen took a step back from seeing him walk away from him. Not knowing who he was or recognizing his voice. The man was tall, standing around six feet, with broad shoulders and a few long scars across his back. He wore dark green pants with dark leather boots that looked worn from years of walking. Only a moment passed as he stepped away from Owen. Then, a woman entered the room from thin air, like the man did. Her arms spread wide as she hugged the man from behind, squeezing him tightly around the stomach since her head only reached the middle of his shoulder blades.

Owen recognized the woman, her short height, her brown hair curled at her shoulders, and how she moved her arms when giving a hug, hugs he once would get annoyed with but now craved.

Owen acted without thinking and rushed to his mother. "Mother!" he shouted as he took a few steps and engulfed her with his arms. As he closed his embrace, his arms went through her like she was smoke. "Mother!" Owen yelled frantically as he tried to touch her again. His hands passed through her body.

"But I love you, Olsen," Cassiday pleaded into the man's bare back as Owen took a step away, his heart crushed under the weight of being so close to his mother but unable to touch her.

Olsen slowly turned to face Cassiday, stern yet

sorrowful, as he gazed into her eyes. "I know. I love you too."

Owen watched with astonishment, seeing Olsen's light blue eyes and blonde hair, hair that was cut like his mother cut his own. He could see so much of himself in the man's face. Cassiday then shifted her head, placing her forehead on Olsen's chest. Owen's breath shortened as he saw the right side of Olsen's chest. The five triangles branded into his tan skin, the same symbol Owen had. Owen slowly took another step back. His mind could not think coherently as his hand moved up and touched the scars on his chest.

"You will be safer here with Borin," Olsen said kindly, lifting Cassiday's chin to look up at him.

"I don't love Borin like I love you," Cassiday pleaded, fighting back her tears.

"You know my duty takes me elsewhere," Olsen said.

Owen stood watching them talking and looking at each other while he stepped to the side, getting a better look at his mother's face. She looked younger, almost like she was when he was a child. Her skin was soft with no wrinkles around her brown eyes, those loving eyes. He had never seen his mother look at someone like that, the love and sorrow on her face. It made his heart ache for her. *Is this another vision... of the past?* Another squawk sounded out in the trees beyond the burnt walls, but it did not phase Owen as he looked up at the tall man. *Olsen, the name the seer said, was my father. Mother never mentioned she was in love with someone else; he has the same brand I do. Did he see the white tree also?*

"You didn't choose that life, though. Choose to have a life with me," Cassiday cried out, tears now streaking down her cheeks.

Olsen's lower lip quivered, about to start crying before he spoke. "I didn't choose, but I was chosen," he quietly said. "Chosen to wander and guard this world."

Owen's mind recognized the phrase. He had heard it for many years from his mother while she told him tales of a hero doomed to be separated from the woman he loved because there were monsters in the world. *The hero who wanders and guards the world.* Owen repeated in his mind. *It wasn't some story she heard, passed down from her parents like she said. Those were her stories. Their story.* Owen felt himself looking away, his ears and mind catching onto the yells and shouts that were going on outside the house. Yet Olsen and Cassiday did not even flinch while they held each other.

The sounds outside grew louder as a sizeable brown bear came into view from the burned section of the house. The bear reared around quickly as a giant brown lizard with dark stripes came into view. The giant lizard had four legs structured like a wolf but thicker, with three large clawed talons on each foot. Its neck stuck straight out from its shoulders, while its long, thick tail stuck out the opposite side, waving as it ran. Then Owen noticed a single red handprint on the lizard's shoulder while its large mouth opened wide, the bottom jaw separating down the middle, showing the rows of sharp teeth within.

The giant lizard lept nearly three of its body's length through the air at the bear. The bear quickly swung with its paw, digging its claws deep into the lizard's skull knocking it to the side. The bear then paused and looked in Owen's direction. As if it knew he was there but couldn't see him.

"Run, bear! They are after you!" a deep voice yelled. The yell came from a large figure, much larger than any man he had seen. Its skin was green, and it wore brown leather armor that covered its torso and most of its legs. Its hair was long on its head, forming a braided ponytail while shaved on the sides. Its bulky jaw had two large tusks protruding from its lower lip.

"An orc?" Owen said to himself out loud, never seeing one for himself but knowing the description from stories he had heard.

The orc spun around while another lizard came towards him. He raised his large, round, wooden shield as the lizard leaped. Its body hit the shield with a loud thud, but the force did not move the orc back a single step. He retaliated, swinging his large sword down and driving it through the lizard's skull.

Owen then heard something clicking behind him, like a bird. He quickly looked in the direction of the noise, just in time to see another lizard jumping through the wall of the house. Its body passed through with ease as the once solid wall turned to ripples, disappearing into the open air like a rock thrown in a river. Owen jumped back and fell through the ripple between the two visions of the house. He could feel his body falling. He shut his eyes, bracing for the impact, but felt softness.

Owen opened his right eye, fearing what he would see, but then noticed the ceiling over his head. He had woken up to the same ceiling every morning for the past few months. Owen quickly sat up and saw he was still in the room at Aerlene's house. He ran his fingers through his hair, cupping his forehead into his palm. *Another vision... but why?*

Owen's fingers reached under his shirt and touched the scar on his chest. There was no pain from the symbol anymore, but the mark still tingled occasionally for reasons he didn't know. *Olsen had the same symbol as me… my father.* He thought to himself, seeing how closely they resembled each other. *Why didn't my mother tell me Olsen was my father? And what did he mean, "chosen to wander and guard this world"?* He stood up from his bed. The dim light of the approaching dawn came through the window, bright enough for him to see without a candle. Slowly, he dressed, thinking about the stories his mom had told him when he was a kid, the strange monsters the hero would have to fight, the places he needed to travel, and the love he could not have. They seemed different now. The woman he left behind was his mother.

Owen walked out of the door to his bedroom and down the hall, wanting so badly to talk to Tavia, but as he looked into her room, she was sound asleep in her bed, legs sprawled out and half of her wavy hair tossed across her face.

"She came in late last night," Aerlene whispered to Owen from behind him. Owen was surprised to see her awake so early. He then looked back at Tavia, wondering if she knew about Olsen and his mother. *She would have been too young to remember him if he had left before I was born, but maybe she heard things.*

Owen stayed in the doorway as Aerlene walked away and into the kitchen. *Am I supposed to wander like Olsen, leaving everyone I care about behind?* The question of if he should head to Delmock had been on his mind the last few weeks. Part of him wanted to stay with Tavia, particularly after she found the backpack he had hidden. She was the last bit of home he had left, and she seemed happy in Keerike. The warning from the Seer still lingered in the back of his mind. *Death follows me, but why? Why am I the one that the elves are after? What can I do? Just bond with animals? Is it because of my father? Does the mark and the white tree pass down in my family?* He then walked into the kitchen. "When does the elven library open?" Owen asked Aerlene, knowing that the library had the most extensive collection of books than anywhere within two days travel.

It was located in the small elven district of Keerike. He knew the risk of traveling through the area. If any elves recognized him, it could bring doom for him, Tavia, or even Aerlene. But part of him needed to find out more. He needed to find out about the tree and the symbol on his chest if he stayed in Keerike and did not listen to the vision to go to Delmock. He needed to go with Tavia, not knowing, in case she would try to stop him.

"A few of them pray to Hyllo, so they should be open just after the sun rises," Aerlene answered as she started getting the baskets ready to collect chicken eggs.

"I'll be back later to help with the animals," Owen said as he turned and returned to his room, putting on a thick coat to keep warm in the frigid morning air. He paused and placed his hand over his chest. *I have to find out what you are, what I am.*

* * *

The library was part of the largest elven structures in Keerike. The center and most prominent portion of the marble building was the temple. Its large glass dome made the facility easy to see over the buildings around it that were half the height. The temple was a place of worship dedicated to the three most powerful of their gods: Hyllo, the goddess of the sun. Selentis, the god of the moon, and their mother, Astra, the goddess of the sky.

To the temple's right was the elven-run school for the children of Keerike or any adults who wished to further their education. It had multiple rooms for teaching children of different ages, with reading desks for every child. It sounded nice to Owen compared to being taught how to read and write by his mother and learning everything else by watching the other villagers he grew up around. He remembered how Aerlene would talk about the children who attended the school with some spite. Not only did the kids learn Terrish, but they were also required to learn Elvish and the elven culture, which Aerlene wasn't fond of.

To the left of the temple was the library. It was the first section built and stood alone for over a decade before the temple and school were made. The structure had three straight walls and a rounded southern wall. Most of the walls had large windows to let in light, but the south round wall only had walls up to three feet with large panes of glass up to the ceiling, allowing for the most light to read all year around. Luckily, since it was built so long before the rest, it had its own entrance and did not require walking through the temple to gain access, unlike the school.

Owen stood motionless as he looked at the buildings, noticing the temple and school were made of marble, while the stone walls of the library were only painted a similar white color. From afar, they matched, but up close, he could tell the library was built out of the stones that made up much of Keerike. As he walked up the eight steps to the double doors, the right door began to open. Owen stopped where he was halfway up the steps as a large-bellied human stepped into the open doorway.

"Well, are you coming in, lad?" the man said with a greeting smile as he looked at Owen. "It is quite cold out, and I would rather the door be closed."

Owen nodded and quickly stepped up and through the doorway. The man closed the door behind him, the cold air rushing in until the last moment.

"I do not believe you are a student of the school, are you?" the man asked as he walked past Owen.

"No, I'm just looking for some information," Owen responded as he looked around in amazement. He saw tall shelves of books before him, all filled with books and some scrolls. A single frame held more books than Owen had ever seen in one place. Far more than the collection Cinda and Lord Willhelm had. He stepped deeper into the foyer towards the shelves, unsure where he would start to look or how to start.

"First time here, I take it?" the man asked as he stood beside Owen. Owen slowly nodded as he continued to look at the immense amount of books. "I figured. Everyone seems to have that face of amazement when they first walk in." Owen turned and looked up at the man. His round face smiled down at Owen in reply. "Make sure not to touch the black pipes around the room. They are part of the heater system that keeps this place nice and warm."

Owen nodded in agreement, though he did not feel at ease as he stepped further from the door. As he walked, he saw more selves behind the ones he first looked at. Made of dark wood with decorative carvings of different kinds of flowers and leaves riddled the sides of the supports for the shelves, row after row of them. More rows of shelves than he could count at a glance. He looked around, unsure where to start, as he wandered deeper into the library, seeing ladders in some of the aisles, and then he spotted an elf male halfway down an aisle from him, putting books high on a shelf. Owen froze in fear. He had gotten used to seeing elves over the two months he had been in Keerike but always kept his distance. Never letting them get too close to him so they could see his face. He regretted not bringing his hatchet with him to defend himself if needed.

"Can I help you?" The male elf asked politely when he noticed Owen staring at him.

"No... I'm fine." Owen blurted out without thinking before stepping out of the aisleway quickly. He took a few long strides and hid behind another bookshelf. He struggled to catch his breath from the shock of being so close to an elf.

When his breath finally normalized, Owen peered around the corner and saw the elf through the bookshelves, still ascending and descending a ladder. Owen slowly moved from his spot and walked deeper into the vastness of books.

"What are you looking for?" the large-bellied man asked as he walked a few steps behind Owen.

Owen turned to see the man behind him. *How am I to find what I am looking for? I don't even know how to describe it.* "I'm looking for stories about a white tree,"

"Like a birch tree?" Asked the man.

Owen shook his head. "A magical, white tree."

"Ah," the man said in realization. "I would have to get Vallous, the head librarian, to find such a request." The man then ushered Owen to a table with four chairs around it, located at the end of some shelves near the window. "Have a seat, and I shall fetch her for you." The man walked away.

Owen walked to the table and sat down with his back to the window, making sure if anyone were to spot him, he would see them as well. As he sat, he could feel the heat from the black pipe that ran along the corner of the floor and wall. The heat from it and his thick winter coat made him grow uncomfortable. He looked at the pipe and saw that it led to a large black cylinder with a swinging grate on the front with the glow of orange embers coming from within. Owen waited a few minutes until he no longer felt comfortable due to the heat. He removed his coat and undid the string around the slit collar of his tunic. He let out a long breath, flapping the fabric to feel cooler air on his sweating chest as he leaned back in his chair.

"Sorry about the heat. I have lived here for almost fifteen winters and still can't get used to the cold," Vallous said as she walked up to Owen from the side. Owen quickly sat up and looked at the elven woman as she approached. "Fredrick said you are looking for stories involving white trees?"

Owen looked at Vallous with unease. She was kind-looking with white shoulder-length hair, light green eyes, and a welcoming grin. The elf looked to be in her thirties if she was human, but he had no idea how old she was being an elf. "Yes," Owen said cautiously. He was nervous about being so close to an elf, let alone talking to one, but he didn't see another option, with the only library in Keerike being elven-run.

"Well, do you have anything more specific besides being a magical white tree?" Vallous asked.

Owen had worked on these questions when walking to the library, figuring they would ask. Most of them escaped his mind as he became more frightened with each step the elf took toward him. *Relax. If she sees you nervous, then it will draw more attention.* Owen thought before speaking, "My mother used to tell me and my sister a story about a giant white tree, and I was hoping to read it again."

"Was there anything special about the white tree?" Vallous asked kindly. "I read to the children in the neighborhood often and know all the children's stories we have here."

Owen looked around nervously at the question. He had wanted to be as vague as possible and try to find the books himself, but with the size of this library, it might take him weeks just to search all the titles. He looked up at Vallous. Her kind face relaxed his concerns about her being an elf. "A huge, magical white tree," he said, slightly wishing he had whispered the statement to keep it between them.

"Do you remember the name of the white tree?"

Owen shook his head. "I…" His mind thought nervously about the symbol that formed on the tree but decided not to add that detail. "I don't know the name of it."

Vallous lifted her hand to her pointed chin and slid her finger along her jaw as she thought. "There are a few fay legends that involve a magical white tree. Could it be one of those?"

Owen quickly nodded his head. "Yes, if I could see those," he said excitedly, hopeful they could illuminate his many questions.

"I will be right back," Vallous said, and she walked away with purpose, deeper into the shelves and out of sight.

Owen sat back in the chair, watching Fredrick, the man who let him into the library, scoop what looked like black rocks into the black cylinder. The man strived to breathe as he shoveled. Each scoop was going slower than the last. Owen then heard the elf in the aisles sliding his ladder along the floor. Owen waited to see if the elf was watching him but did not see him through the shelves. Owen began to get nervous as he waited. His thumb rubbed against his finger, wondering what Vallous was doing.

Vallous finally walked back into view, holding five books in her hands. "These all have stories about a white tree with magical properties," She stated as she put the books on the table. Slowly, she shifted the books off each other and opened them. "These are compendiums of stories. Four of the books are fay legends while this one..." Vallous then walked around to the same side of the table as Owen and opened one of the books, "This one has stories about a human who wandered Effrin and wrote down the wonders he saw."

Owen leaned forward quickly as he heard the word "wandered" and thought of Olsen. His eyes focused on the pages as Vallous flipped through them and stopped at one with a printed painting of a large tree. He shifted in his chair, anticipating what story would be held within.

"Do you think this is the story you are looking for?" Vallous asked.

"It might be," Owen answered. "Could I also read the other books?" he asked as he leaned back in the chair, looking at the other books.

"Of course, take your..." Vallous began to say but then paused mid-sentence.

Owen slowly turned and looked at Vallous after a few moments of her silence. He saw her eyes focused on his chest. Owen quickly pulled the collar of his tunic closed and looked away from her. "It was an accident with a cattle brander," he said. It was the same lie he and Tavia had told Aerlene when she spotted a bit of the symbol on his chest.

Vallous quickly snapped out of her gaze when Owen covered himself. "You can take as long as you like," she promptly said and stepped back from Owen. "Is there anything else I can help you with?"

"No, thank you," Owen responded, covering his chest with his shirt. Vallous gave him a nod and walked away. Owen watched her every step until she was out of sight. He sat for a moment, waiting to see if she returned. Eventually, he calmed himself and started flipping through the pages of the books.

* * *

Owen had been left alone for all morning. He sat and read through the stories, only distracted by Fredrick, who walked by and commented about him reading so many stories about fay. Owen only looked at him, grinned in response, and then returned to reading.

The stories were captivating, but none described a white tree as large as the one in Owen's vision. The one about the human wanderer, Bethill Snash, talked about a white tree with leaves that stayed green year around, though by the description, it was small compared to the tree he was looking for. The other fay stories seemed strange. One talked about a tree long ago that the local fay worshiped but was chopped down by the king of Terrasin, the kingdom that was Kelterra, Miterra, and Esterra before it split apart over two hundred years ago. The other story talked about a white tree that fairies were born out of; however, it described the tree similarly to how a birch tree looks.

There was only one story so far that came close. The tree fit the description but was not as large as the one in Owen's vision. This tree was in Faylend, and the keeper, or protector, of the tree, would kill people who came too close. Hanging the bodies by their ankles from the thick branches so the blood would nourish the tree's roots. It was a grim, cautionary tale, but it was the closest tree Owen could find. However, it gave no reference to any symbols or Druids.

As Owen opened the last book, he realized something had changed. There was no longer the sound of books shuffling that he had grown used to. Fredrick's heavy breathing seemed to not be within earshot. The large room had become silent. The sudden sound of a metal latch locking into place startled Owen as he sat in the chair. *Did they forget I am here?* He could hear the sound of light footsteps coming down the aisle towards him. Owen quickly got up from the chair and moved behind one of the endcaps of the shelves. *They found me!* Owen held his breath as his heart and mind began to race.

The footsteps around the corner had stopped. Owen looked out the window. *If I jump through the glass, maybe I can get away.*

"Druid?" Vallous whispered.

Owen's eyes opened wide as he heard Vallous say the word. *They did find me. They know what I am.* Owen then took a stance to run through the large window only a few paces away from him. *Tavia...* He realized. *If I run, then they will just hurt Tavia and Aerlene.*

"Druid, are you there?"

Owen took a deep breath as he stood straight and stepped out from behind the shelf. "I surrender." He sorrowfully said and looked at Vallous. "Just please, don't hurt Tavia and Aerlene."

Vallous stood before Owen, looking at him with a face of shock and fear as if she had seen a ghost standing in Owen's place. Owen did not know what to do since she looked more frightened than he felt.

"Are you…" Vallous asked. "Are you a Druid?"

"Yes…I think so." Owen said, not knowing what to do next, but he found it odd that Vallous was not carrying a weapon, just something wrapped in rigid leather in her arms. "I will go with you. As long as you don't hurt Tavia and Aerlene."

"Why would I hurt Aerlene?"

"Because you have already killed everyone else I care about."

Vallous stood, looking at Owen inquisitively for a moment before speaking. "Who killed everyone you care about?"

"Elves," Owen said spitefully. Vallous looked at the ground before Owen sorrowfully. "Elves came and killed everyone in my village."

"Because of the war between Duke Chalin and the Ellious Empire?"

"I am from Orinton, far from the fighting. They came for me and slaughtered everyone else."

Vallous looked down at what she was carrying and then back to Owen. "Did your village know you are a Druid?"

Owen pulled his collar to show the brand on his chest. "I did not get this until after the elves attacked."

Vallous took a step towards Owen. Her hand reached out to touch the brand on his chest, but Owen quickly covered it with his arm and hand. Vallous's eyes looked into Owen's as she retracted her hand. "You became a Druid… after they attacked?"

"Yes,"

"I'm sorry about your village," Vallous said. "Why did you come here, to Keerike?"

"Why does that matter? If you are here to take or kill me,

just do it and leave Tavia alone."

"I am not here to hurt you," Vallous reassured. "I am interested in you, your abilities, and the magic of the Druids."

"I don't even know what magic I have."

Vallous stroked her chin with her fingers as she was deep in thought. "What do you know about how the elves came to this world?" she asked cautiously, hesitant to say the words as if asking the question were wrong.

Owen looked at Vallous with a confused expression. "A few hundred years ago, your gods sent you down from the sky on a falling star," Owen replied, almost tempted to add what Gustoll told him about the elves being banished by their gods for being such cruel people, though he used harsher words.

"Is that the only story you know of?" Vallous asked as she took another step forward, almost close enough to reach out and touch Owen. Her arms were still clenched around what she held, like a mother holding a baby for protection.

"Yes...why?" Owen asked, confused about what was happening but no longer feeling threatened by Vallous.

"Why are you looking for a white tree?" Vallous asked as she squeezed the thing in her arms a little tighter. Her face no longer looked frightened but more inquisitive.

Owen paused for a moment as he looked at Vallous. *Do I just tell her the truth, tell her everything?* Owen looked down at the table as he thought about his options and repercussions until he answered. "I keep having dreams about it," he said, wanting to tell the truth but holding back the complete truth.

Vallous lessened her grip on the object she carried and looked down at it. She lifted a leather flap and revealed a large, thick book. Owen stared, seeing that it was old, so old the pages inside the broken binding were much thicker than any book he had seen. She walked to the table and placed the book down, slowly unwrapping it from the rigid leather that protected it.

The book looked hundreds of years old, its spine only held together by a few leather sections still intact. The rugged leather cover was blank, with the edges worn away around the corners and some damage at the bottom from being smashed.

Vallous looked at Owen with her lips pressed firmly together and her brow scrunched. "So you don't know the truth of how or why the elves came here?"

Owen's eyes left the book and met with Vallous's. "There is another story?"

Vallous looked back down at the book and slowly opened it. The hard binding creaked under stress. Owen looked down as Vallous reached to turn the first page carefully. The pages within were not like the paper pages Owen had seen his whole life but were much thicker, almost looking like the thin skin of an animal. As Vallous lifted the page delicately, Owen's eyes widened in shock as the next page was a painting of a tree, almost the same tree he saw in his vision. He could tell, even with the faded paint, the tree was painted white, its branches gnarled in different directions, and the leaves still held a shade of green color within them.

"It was a little over five hundred years ago. The elves did not come from the stars," Vallous said quietly as she looked at Owen.

"Then where did they come from?" Owen asked in confusion while his mind and heart raced about seeing the white oak tree in a book so old.

Vallous then turned the page delicately. On the next page, it had the tree, but near the tree's base and halfway up the trunk, the tree bulged out, showing a faded red color as if it was inside the tree. Around the tree was writing. The writing was different, not inked by a printing press like most books Owen had read. This writing was painted by hand and in Elvish but had more harsh angles than the flowing lines he had seen in a few books he just looked through.

"The elves came here through a gateway inside an ancient white tree," she whispered as if to keep the information a secret. "There was no falling star or gods involved. My ancestors that came through the gateway were running away from their world to this one." Her tone changed as she spoke the words sorrowfully.

"Why are you telling me this?" Owen asked as his eyes shifted towards Vallous.

"They called her a Druid," Vallous said as she turned to the next page.

Druid, the name the Seer said in my vision. Owen thought as he stood straight from amazement, excited to see a painting of the tree and hear the word Druid spoken.

On the next page, half was more of the painted writing, and the other half was the painting of an elven woman, her hand raised in the air and a white staff with a blue jewel on the top in the other hand. She wore flowing red robes over her left shoulder to her feet. Vallous moved her hand over the page and pointed to her right chest. Owen looked closer. His breath left his lungs as he saw a symbol painted on her bare skin. A symbol that looked similar to his. A trapezoid with four smaller triangles above it in almost a row.

"She has the same looking mark on her chest you have,"

Vallous said with concern.

"Does it talk about her?" Owen asked as he looked over the page, hoping he might recognize some words in the text.

"It just calls her a Druid, and she opened the gate for people to escape through," Vallous answered, seemingly confused. "Do you not know about this?"

Owen looked up at her. "I don't know anything about this. I didn't even know if the white oak tree was real," he answered frantically. "Does the book say anything else?"

Vallous shook her head. "I'm afraid not. Just the story about why they were running away." Vallous shook her head again and muttered almost to herself, but Owen could hear her. "I was hoping you could have told me more about the magic."

She turned to the next page, showing it full of more Elvish text.

"Why were they running?" Owen asked in confusion, wondering what could drive someone from their home so far that they needed to go to a different world. Then he realized. *People came and killed their people... just like me.*

"Religion. The book says they ran from the Flame Bearers of Corthus," Vallous said sadly as if mentioning it tore into her heart.

"That isn't a reason to hurt people, though, is it?" Owen asked.

Vallous eyes were sad as she spoke. "You are young and not tarnished by the years of your life to come. Wars and the slaughter of innocence have been done for far less than just religion, even in your human histories."

Owen looked down at the book, his mind processing what Vallous told him for a moment. "Is there anything else talked about in the book?" Owen asked, realizing it still had many pages left to turn, and hoped there was more information.

"That is all the information given," Vallous said as she turned the page, showing it was no longer the Elven text but elven signatures of names, two columns from top to bottom. Vallous then started turning more pages, showing the signatures on each one. "The rest of the book is just the names of the people who traveled through the gateway." Owen watched as she continued to turn page after page until she reached the end of the signatures and pointed to the final two. "My great Grandfather and Grandmother. The last to sign the book."

"How many names are there?" Owen asked after Vallous turned a little over twenty pages and then stopped.

"There are twelve thousand, nine hundred, eighty-three names written in this book," Vallous answered.

Owen's eyes widened as he looked at Vallous. His mind tried to picture that many people all at once. Even Keerike had a population of around two thousand, but having over twelve thousand people seemed overwhelming. "Where is the tree?" he asked.

"The tree was in Helflin, an island south of Effrin," Vallous said as she slowly shook her head.

"What do you mean, was?" Owen asked.

"After the elves came through the gateway, they burned the tree to the ground, afraid the Flame Bearers might follow them," Vallous said quietly.

"Why would the Druid let them burn the tree down?" The news felt like a blow to Owen's heart.

"The Druid stayed in the other world and did not come with them," Vallous said.

Owen stepped back after hearing what she said and sat

in a chair. "So the white oak tree is gone?" he whispered.

"No," Vallous said reassuringly as Owen looked up at her. "I believe there are others. Not only the tree mentioned in Faylend," she said as she pointed to the book with the fay legends. "But also there are reports of carvings of white trees like these being found at some dig sites of Allurian ruins."

Owen looked up at Vallous, a smile growing on his face, knowing now the white oak tree was real and there might be more of them. He looked down at the old book as Vallous closed it and wrapped it in the leather.

"Don't mention this book, or any of this, to anyone," Vallous said sternly.

"Why?" Owen asked, not understanding if the book had the answers to why the elves came to this world.

"My great grandfather was the one that wrote this book, and five others like it. He passed this one, the original, down through the family for safekeeping, hoping someday my people would want to know the truth of how we came here and why,"

"What is wrong with people knowing the truth?"

"Propaganda," Vallous said as she shook her head with discontent. "Some elves still believe they are higher beings, sent by the gods themselves, making their actions of how they treat others excusable since they feel they are divine. Luckily, things are changing within the Empire. Elves are changing their ways, but not enough for the truth to come out and not be challenged."

"So what would happen if the truth came out now?"

"My father tried to tell the truth of our origin," Vallous said as her gaze shifted to the floor and her eyes focused on nothing. "They crucified him for being a heretic and traitor to the Ellious Empire and the elven people."

"Do you think that is why elves came and killed my people? Because I am a Druid, and that could help prove where your kind came from?"

"How would they have known if you did not even know until after they attacked?"

"Then why did they kill everyone!" Owen shouted.

Vallous took a step back from Owen in fear. "I don't know why your village was attacked, but I.."

The door to the library began to shake, interrupting Vallous in mid-sentence and made Owen jump with fear. She and Owen fell silent as they heard a loud knocking at the door soon after. "Vallous, let me in! I don't have my key to unlock the door!" A muffled male voice shouted from outside the door.

"That is Fredrick." Vallous rushed to say. "I sent him away for lunch so we could talk privately. You should go." Vallous said as she wrapped the old book in its leather cover. "Come back in four days. We can talk more about the white oak tree then. Just make sure not to mention the book to anyone."

Owen looked at Vallous with sympathy. "I won't tell anyone about the book or what is in it," he said with kindness and worry for Vallous's safety, the first time he ever felt concern for an elf. Owen gathered his jacket to leave while Vallous walked away to hide the book and then opened the door for Fredrick.

CHAPTER 16

A cold front had descended on Tolneer the day after the festival. It was so cold that those in the city with livestock brought them into their homes. Ulrick had been chopping wood all day, preparing it for families needing to be well-stocked for their fires. Lars helped with delivering the wood since the temperature was already dropping steadily. Cinda helped when she could, picking up wood scraps for kindling while Ulrick moved logs to be cut. The work was tiring and far from what Cinda was used to, but she had to keep up, trying hard not to show what kind of life she came from. However, part of her began to think Ulrick and Lars would not care if she was a lady of noble birth.

The three of them moved inside as the temperature dropped. Cinda quickly got into her makeshift bed, a pile of furs. It was not as comfortable as her bed in Orinton, but she was happy to have something. She reminisced about her bed, wishing she could return to it, but she knew she would find herself there eventually. Hoping many of her people had survived the attack. She was comfortable enough for now, surrounded by the furs of bears, wolves, and deer. Ulrick and Lars quickly built a fire and tried to keep the inside of the house warm. Cinda sat silently as they spoke in Orcish, trying to follow along with the conversation. She understood Lars would leave at first light, but for what, she did not understand. Ulrick then started talking about going somewhere, but she could not understand where.

"Are you making plans on taking me home?" Cinda asked, hoping that was where he was talking about sailing.

Lars looked over at Cinda. Seeing her lying in the furs with only half her face showing made him grin, finding her adorable looking under the thick hides. "Sadly, no," he responded. "I heard the raids after winter are being discussed…"

"Will you still be able to take me home?" Cinda interrupted.

"I'm sure we can make a stop in Miterra on the way," Lars said.

"Where will you two be going?" Cinda asked. The idea of them dropping her off in Miterra worried her since she would have to return home without them.

"Thrane wants to raid to the east, but Beotolt wants to raid Kelterra in accordance with their new alliance," Lars answered. "So, for now, we don't really know."

"What is the difference?" Cinda asked, confused, thinking both options sounded dangerous.

"Territories to the east normally pay us to leave, making it less risky. However, the reward is not as great. Kelterra, on the other hand, we have not raided in many years. They would put up more of a fight, so there is more wealth and fame to be had." Lars looked down at the fire as it crackled. "Beotolt is looking for fame over anything. He wants to solidify his right to be Earl even if it costs him the lives of his people. I even heard he wants to raid Delmock."

"Beotolt, young fool." Ulrick said in Terrish as he looked at Lars. "Like Trent."

Lars nodded in agreement while Cinda recognized the name Trent. It was Thrane's oldest son. She had not seen much of him except at the feast. He was not at the family table and seemed to mingle with other groups in the hall.

"Does Trent have a say in the raids?" Cinda asked.

"Trent agrees with Beotolt, wanting to raid Kelterra. He has always wanted to prove himself in battle but has yet to get the chance," Lars answered. "Luckily, Thrane is smarter than both of them and sees it as a bad idea to commit to such action."

Cinda lay flat on her bed, looking up at the ceiling as she imagined how far of a distance it was to get home from Kelterra if they were sent there. Then Ulrick and Lars started talking in Orcish again, and their voices lulled Cinda to sleep.

* * *

Cinda's eyes opened slowly. She looked around and saw no one in the house with her. The overcast light of the sun coming through the open shutters of the two windows let her know it was morning. She got up from the bed. Her hands and arms hurt from being scratched and sore from the work the day before. She could hear the wood being sawed by Ulrick outside as she got some dried pork and a handful of berries to eat. She was tired and did not want to join Ulrick outside for another day, making logs for fires.

The brisk air refreshed Ulrick as he finished sawing some logs to split them with his ax. He looked out. The fjord's waters had frozen over from the cold during the night. It was no surprise to him that it happened, but it was earlier in winter than he was used to. He watched as some orcs began testing how thick the ice was on the other side of the bank.

"Ulrick!" a deep voice yelled.

Ulrick knew the voice well and kept his eyes on the iced-over water. Not wanting to face the orc that was calling his name. It was not a voice he wanted to be hearing again. *Beotolt.*

"You insulted me at the feast," Beotolt shouted in Orcish as he walked to Ulrick. Ulrick slowly turned and faced him, seeing four other orcs from Glathburn behind him.

"I didn't mean to insult Earl Beotolt," Ulrick said in Orcish, looking at the orcs following Beotolt. They seemed dressed for a fight, wearing their hide armor and carrying shields. Ulrick even spotted two of them with their hands on clubs strapped to their belts. Ulrick glanced around, looking for a weapon, but all he could see was his wood-cutting axe a few strides away and thick branches by the house. *If I grab the axe, they will use real weapons, not the clubs.* He thought to himself.

Beotolt neared Ulrick. His face was angry and arrogant. "I would have made you rich for such a woman," He then turned his head so the other orcs with him could hear him speak. "But for insulting me like you did, I will take the human and leave you with nothing." The other orcs grunted in agreement as if to intimidate Ulrick.

Ulrick took a steady breath. "I cannot let you take her," he said calmly.

Beotolt stood, slightly surprised by Ulrick's defiance. "You are outnumbered and unarmed," he said. "Only a fool would fight, so just give me the human."

Ulrick looked into Beotolt's eyes, his face and voice calm as he spoke the single word. "No."

The arrogance left Beotolt's face as he looked at Ulrick. The sheer size of Ulrick was larger than Beotolt, and his face showed no fear of the situation. Beotolt took a step back from Ulrick as he gained composure. "Get him!"

The four other orcs from Glathbern charged around Beotolt like a wave of water around a rock, their clubs, and shields at the ready. The first orc swung his club. Ulrick dodged the swing and drove his right fist straight into the orc's face before he could recover from the swing. The blow knocked the orc's head back, and he stumbled to the side. Another orc bashed into Ulrick with his shield. The impact hit him in his arm and ribs, pushing him back but not knocking him down. Ulrick grabbed the rim of the shield and spun it. Taking the orc's arm with it, making his whole body twist and fall to the ground. The third orc swung his club at Ulrick's head. Ulrick quickly blocked with his left arm as if he had a shield. The pain was severe like it had broken the bone. Ulrick yelled in pain as he jumped at the third orc, driving his shoulder into the orc's shield with such force that it knocked the orc onto his back. Beotolt quickly took advantage and swung his club, hitting Ulrick along his back, just below his neck. The pain of the strike caused Ulrick to fall to his hands and knees, feeling the shock to his nerves throughout his body.

Beotolt kicked Ulrick in the side, making him roll onto his back. He waved his men back as Ulrick struggled to breathe. "This was your choice, Ulrick," he snarled as Ulrick tried to roll back over to get up. "You're beaten," he yelled, kicking Ulrick in the side again to keep him on his back. Beotolt threw his shield and club to the ground and knelt over Ulrick. Lifting him by the collar of his shirt, he punched Ulrick in the side of the mouth. Blood shot out from his lips, the red clearly seen in the white snow. "So Ulrick Ironhide does bleed," Beotolt said in a snide remark.

Ulrick began to laugh. "It took five of you to make me

bleed," he said, reminding Beotolt it was not just him he was fighting.

Beotolt leaned closer to Ulrick in anger, his face almost touching Ulrick's as he roared as loud as he could, a demonstration of dominance, much like large cats. Ulrick still had fight left in him and roared back. He could feel the pain in his ribs while he roared.

Both looked at each other with relentless anger. Then suddenly, a thick branch swung in and cracked on the side of Beotolt's face. The impact split the skin of his eyebrow. His head snapped to the side. He looked up and saw Cinda standing over them, holding the broken end of a branch, her face stricken with fear as she saw Beotolt was not severely hurt. Beotolt quickly sprang from Ulrick and headed straight at Cinda, grabbing her by the arm and pulling her towards him.

Ulrick moved to get up and help Cinda, but two of Beotolt's men grabbed him by the arms and held him back. He struggled in their grasp as he watched Beotolt grab the side of Cinda's head by the hair.

"Fight!" Ulrick yelled in Terrish to Cinda as he looked at her.

"She is feisty!" Beotolt yelled in Orcish as she struggled to get free. He then held her still and looked down at her. The blood from his eyebrow ran down the right side of his face. "I will take pleasure in breaking you of that spirit," he said in Orcish.

Cinda looked up at Beotolt as he spoke. She did not understand what he said but knew by his tone that it was not good. She noticed his tusk-like teeth sticking up from his lips as he spoke. Before she could second guess herself, she reached with both hands. The change in direction made her arm slip from his grasp. Her fingers wrapped around the sizeable protruding tooth. Her fingers were so thin they avoided his upper teeth. She pulled with her entire body, falling backward. The weight on Beotolt's jaw made his head follow, causing him to lose balance and be pulled by Cinda to the ground.

Cinda hit the wet snow and dirt hard, but not as hard as Beotolt. His hand came from her hair, pulling a chunk from the side of her head as he tried to brace himself but did not make it as his face met the ground. She struggled to get out from under his arm. Clawing at the dirt, she felt his large hand grab her by the hip. She looked up for help from Ulrick but saw Feirdren standing before her. The giant wolf's eyes looked past her at Beotolt. His sharp teeth were bare while he growled aggressively, poised to attack.

"I would not hurt the girl," Thrane yelled in Orcish from behind Feirdren. "My wife says the wolf has taken a fancy to her."

Feirdren's front paw took a step closer to Cinda. As the large wolf moved, she felt Beotolt's grip on her hip disappear. The wolf continued to growl as Cinda crawled through the wet sludge of snow and dirt, moving past Feirdren before she looked behind her.

"What are you doing here, Beotolt?" Thrane asked sternly as eight of his orc guards began moving towards the Glathbern orcs, each with a spear and shield in their hands while Lev and Trent stood behind him.

Beotolt looked at his men as he got up from the ground, waving them away from Ulrick. "It was just a simple disagreement," Beotolt growled as he whipped the blood from his face.

Thrane looked at Beotolt doubtfully. From what he could

see, it was not a simple disagreement. He, however, did not want to accuse the Earl of Glathbern of lying. "Is that all it was, Ulrick?" Thrane asked as he looked at his brother.

Ulrick looked at Thrane and then back at Beotolt while he gripped his forearm. He knew that the peace between the two territories was an uneasy balance. If he were to demand justice for the attack, Thrane would have no option but to let him and Beotolt fight. That action could cause a significant rift between the two Earldoms. "It was a disagreement of culture," Ulrick said coldly. "Earl Beotolt and I are finished with the subject."

Beotolt's face skewed with anger as he spat at Ulrick's feet and started to walk away from Ulrick, passing through Thrane and his men.

"Is this disagreement over with?" Thrane asked Beotolt as he walked by.

"It is," Beotolt answered.

Cinda watched Beotolt and his men walk away. Beotolt's eyes did not look at Thrane as he walked by. But he did look up at Trent, who gave a slight nod as he passed. She noted there may be more between them than she had been told. The thought went out of Cinda's mind as she noticed Lev standing behind everyone in a thick, light blue dress, holding the leash of a young wolf in her hand.

After Beotolt and his men were far away, Thrane looked to his guards. "Keep an eye on them," he ordered. "Something tells me they will continue to cause problems." Six guards nodded and walked away, following their orders without hesitation.

"You could send them away," Ulrick said with a wince as he tried to smile.

"We need to keep them here until the raids are decided,"

Trent answered before Thrane could speak.

Trent was a young adult by orc standards and dressed like an orc ready for war. However, Trent did not have the warrior demeanor that Thrane and Ulrick had, making him almost seem like a child wearing his father's armor. Trent was well kept, his short hair always clean and combed without a single scar on his skin. Seeing him reminded Cinda of herself, a figurehead who does not actually do anything but look good.

"Tolneer needs this alliance, Ulrick," Thrane said with regret. "We cannot fight against all the orc territories if they decide to raid us next."

"You could have picked a better ally then," Ulrick said with a labored laugh.

"They have the soldiers, and with their backing, none of the other Earls would dare attack us." Thrane smiled and patted Ulrick on the shoulder. "You stick with your childish adventures, and I'll stick with being the responsible one."

"You could always come on my childish adventures," Ulrick replied.

"Tolneer is too important for me to leave," Thrane said. He then turned to Trent. "And eventually, when Trent is ready, he will lead."

"I can lead now, Father, while you go with Uncle Ulrick," Trent said with revealing eagerness.

Thrane began to laugh loudly as he shook his head. "In time, Trent. You are not ready yet."

Thrane, Ulrick, and Trent continued talking as Lev walked to Cinda while she wiped the mud from her now-soaked dress.

"Are you alright?" Lev asked in Terrish.

Cinda looked up at Lev with a smile. "I'm so happy you

all came when you did."

"Earl Beotolt came to try and take you?" Lev asked as the wolf on the leash began to squirm. She gave it more slack as it quickly tried to play with Feirdren.

"I think so," Cinda said sorrowfully, still feeling the pain of the fall on her back. She was surprised to see how calm Lev was about what had just happened but then remembered she was once a slave and probably treated worse in similar situations.

"He won't cause you any more problems," Lev said. She then smiled kindly. "We were already on our way here when we heard Beotolt was heading this way."

"Are you sure Beotolt won't try again?"

Lev looked at Thrane for a few moments and then back at Cinda. "I am sure. Thrane was talking about it while we rushed here."

Cinda was interrupted from asking another question as the young wolf jumped up her leg to get attention. "You have more than one wolf?" she asked as she looked at the wolf that stood at her feet, shocked to see that it was not an ordinary dog but a wolf puppy.

Lev reached out, took Cinda's hand, and placed the leash in it. "This one's for you," she said gleefully. "It is one of Feirdren's daughters." Lev smiled at Cinda. "The runt of the litter. I figured she would be a perfect size for you."

Cinda looked down at the puppy. The pain she was feeling disappeared as she smiled. "Really? I can have her?" She knelt down and started to pet the wolf while it tried to lick her face. Its fur was soft like Feirdren's, but it was a darker gray with sporadic black hairs along the ridge of its back and tail. The white underbelly was more defined from the dark gray and wrapped around all four legs. Its blue eyes were kind and excited, like all puppies when meeting new people.

"I will talk to Ulrick and make sure you can keep her if he says no," Lev said as she watched Cinda and the young wolf introduce themselves. "For now, let's get you inside and into some dry clothes."

Cinda quickly agreed, feeling the cold piercing into her skin through the wet dress and a stinging on the side of her scalp where the hair was ripped out. As Cinda, the puppy, Lev, and Feirdren walked toward the house door, she looked back at Ulrick. Sitting on a log beside Thrane, he talked and smiled like brothers do. She smiled, seeing him like that, seeing him happy. His soft eyes looked up at her, meeting her gaze. She smiled widely and pointed to the puppy and then to herself, hoping Ulrick would understand the signal that the puppy was hers. Ulrick kindly smiled and nodded. Cinda was about to jump for joy at the prospect of owning a wolf as they walked through the door.

"So, what is her name?" Cinda quickly asked Lev as they entered the house and closed the door. Feirdren promptly walked across the large room and jumped into Ulrick's bed to lie down while the puppy sniffed everything in sight.

"You can name her whatever you like," Lev answered as she looked around for Cinda's clothes. She had been in Ulrick's house many times and would even stay there while he was away, so she already knew where everything was. It was a peaceful place for her and Feirdren. The giant wolf was always fond of Ulrick's bed.

"How old is she?" Cinda asked as she grabbed a shirt and pants from her pile of clothes near her bed.

"Six months, I believe," Lev said as she sat on one of Lars's stools. The puppy quickly came to her side for attention.

Cinda was shocked to hear the wolf was so young. Its shoulders had already reached her knee. "How much bigger will she get?" Cinda asked, thinking that Feirdren's shoulder almost came to her chest and she could not control an animal so big.

"She should not get as large as Feirdren, a few inches shorter or more," Lev answered as she smiled and petted behind the puppy's ear. "She is a trained hunter," she said as Cinda undressed. "You let her go in the forest; she will hunt rabbits and rats and bring them back to you." Lev then pulled out a small wooden cylinder with a thin leather strap attached. "She is also trained to return when you sound this whistle." The puppy excitedly sat at Lev's feet as it saw the whistle in her hand. "That is until you teach her a name. Then she will respond to both with practice."

"So the dog is trained to hunt for me?" Cinda asked as she continued to change behind a hanging blanket.

"She can and does it quite well, actually," Lev answered. "Probably better than Lars and Ulrick ever could," she laughed.

Cinda stepped out from behind the hanging blanket, wearing leather pants and a green long-sleeved shirt. She looked at Lev with curiosity. "Why are you giving her to me?" she asked quietly.

Lev turned and looked at Feirdren, her face growing sad. "Tolneer is still mostly orc culture," she said quietly. "Even after being here for as long as I have, I still don't understand some things." She then looked down at the ground. "The first few years here were hard, very hard. Then Thrane gave me Feirdren a few years ago." She looked back at Feirdren with affection. "You could say that Feirdren saved my life. Things don't feel as bad or scary with him, and he truly belongs to me." Lev looked at Cinda with kind eyes. "I hope this puppy will help you feel safe and comfort you."

Cinda knelt down and clapped to get the puppy's attention. It quickly ran to her with its tail wagging in the air. She began petting her with both hands around the head and neck. "You said she is trained to hunt, and I need to pick a name?" Cinda asked.

"That is right. The trainers say that giving her a name helps her know she is yours and you are hers."

Cinda peered into the sky-blue eyes of the puppy as she smiled. "Then I will call you Huntress." She looked at Lev for approval.

"Huntress is a fitting name," Lev said kindly with a smile.

"My little Huntress," Cinda said quietly as she vigorously petted the sides of the wolf's face while its tail wagged.

Thrane then opened the door and stepped into the house. "We should leave, Lev. I have to ensure all the boats are secured," he said in Orcish.

Lev nodded in agreement and stood up. "I will see you and Huntress later, I hope," she said in Terrish to Cinda.

"Huntress, is that the name she decided on?" Thrane asked in Orcish.

"It is," Lev answered as she snapped her fingers, and Feirdren quickly joined her while Thrane and her left. Cinda could hear them saying their goodbyes to Ulrick before he came into the house.

"Are you okay?" Cinda asked Ulrick with concern. His lip and jaw were already swelling from the altercation.

"I okay," Ulrick answered as he slowly sat on the floor near Cinda and Huntress, lowering himself gingerly to guard his ribs. "You hurt?" he slowly said in Terrish as he labored to breathe. He pointed to the side of Cinda's head, where the bald spot was slightly bleeding and red.

"I've had worse," Cinda said. She then realized Ulrick had a slightly confused look from hearing the expression. Cinda smiled politely. "I'm okay, Ulrick."

Huntress then went to Ulrick and began smelling his hand. Cinda was amazed at how small the wolf pup looked next to Ulrick as he began to pet her slowly.

"What name?" Ulrick asked as the wolf sniffed his legs.

"Huntress," Cinda said with pride. Ulrick repeated the name as he watched the puppy walk around. "Is it okay if I keep her?" Cinda asked hesitantly, worried Ulrick might say no. Ulrick nodded. Cinda felt excited and quickly crawled to Ulrick and hugged him around the neck. "Thank you," she softly said to him as she squeezed. Cinda held on to Ulrick briefly as his large hand lightly patted her back.

"No pee," Ulrick said as his hand went from her back and pointed at his bed. Cinda retracted herself from him to look where he was pointing.

"Bed. That is called a bed," Cinda said, so Ulrick knew the word.

"No pee bed,"

Cinda nodded and laughed. "I won't let Huntress pee on your bed."

"Good. Huntress stay. Pee Lars bed," Ulrick said as he looked at the puppy with a wide smile.

Ulrick then started petting and playing with Huntress, letting the wolf puppy nip his fingers and hands. Her jaw was not yet big enough to get ahold of his forearms, but she still tried. Cinda watched, seeing Ulrick still not fully move like he usually did.

"Where learn..." Ulrick paused momentarily, gently took Cinda's hand, and put it on one of his large protruding teeth. He then motioned that she was pulling him.

Cinda smiled at the gesture. "Where did I learn to pull an orc by the tooth?"

Ulrick nodded with a grin.

Cinda looked down at her hands. "My grandfather told me once that if a goat is causing you problems, you can grab it by the horns and force its head into the ground. Beotolt's tooth reminded me of a goat's horn," Cinda said somberly as she began to remember other things her grandfather taught her and the last thing he taught her. *If you have to run, make sure most of you run in the same direction.* Gustoll's voice lingered in her head. "If only I knew how to fight," Cinda quietly said to herself.

"What?" Ulrick asked, hearing Cinda mumble.

Cinda looked up at Ulrick with a sad expression. "When the elves attacked my home." She looked away quickly. "If I could fight like you, maybe I could have saved some people instead of just running away," she said as she started to tear up. Part of her always wished she was stronger like Tavia or some of the other girls in Orinton. She looked at the ground, thinking about how Tavia would have stood up to the elves. Even though she might not know how to fight, she would have still tried. Huntress quickly trotted over to her and attempted to snuggle and play, seeing her distraught.

Ulrick slowly put his hand on her shoulder and back. "I teach you fight," he said in a kind tone.

Cinda turned her head towards Ulrick, surprised by what he said. "You will teach me how to fight?" she said as she wiped away some tears.

Ulrick nodded with a smile. "You teach Huntress. I teach you."

Cinda looked down at her hands. Hands that were once manicured and pampered now had dirt under the nails, scrapes, and were sore from being used. These weren't the hands of a lady anymore. That life seemed so far from her, a memory that felt like years ago. How much had changed for her since that day, and how much more would there be. She turned towards Ulrick. "I could go in that direction."

CHAPTER 17

The cold air made the light snowfall at night stick to the ground in patches. By the dark clouds on the horizon, everyone knew more would be coming. The goats did not seem to mind the small amount of snow as they found their way around it, eating what little grass was left in the small field. Owen knew that soon, he would have to move on to another place for the goats to eat. He looked at the nearby treeline for the bear, but it was not there. *Maybe she is hibernating for the winter.* He thought, feeling slightly sad about her absence, like someone else had left him.

"How long until you leave me?" Owen asked a goat that looked up at him with a blank stare from its rectangular-like pupils. "My mom is dead. Hendric is probably dead as well. It seems like what the Seer said is true. Death does follow me." He looked at the dark clouds coming in. "Maybe I should go before anyone else dies." He then looked at the goat as it still stood staring at him. Its jaw moved from side to side as it chewed the grass in its mouth.

"And now I'm talking to a goat," Owen said as he shook his head. He looked out over Keerike and at the domed roof of the elven temple. It had been two days since Vallous talked to him in the library, two long days. He was eager to return to the library the next day but understood the dangers. The fear in Vallous's eyes stuck with him. So much so that he never mentioned the library to Tavia.

The goat's ears quickly shifted, and its head turned, looking over a slight rise. Owen also turned, sensing that something was going on from the goat's movements. He listened as the wind carried a distant sound, the sound of a scream.

Owen quickly ran to the top of the rise to look at what was happening, still carrying the cane he used to direct the goats. As he reached the ridge, he heard more screams, sounding like children. Owen looked about and saw a dozen kids running from some trees towards a cluster of large boulders in a rocky grass field. Owen did not stop to think. His legs swiftly carried him toward the kids.

As he approached, he noticed five wolves emerging from the trees in a coordinated attack. The first few kids reached the rocks, and the wolves gained on the one trailing behind. Her legs moved fast, but it was not fast enough. Owen feared not making it in time to save the girl while he ran with all his might.

The kids who had already climbed the rocks yelled as the wolves closed on their friend. "Come on!" and "Run faster!"

The lead wolf opened its jaws as it neared the girl's heels. Owen threw his cane in a large arc. It spun in the air and hit the back hip of the wolf. The wolf yelped. Its stride dramatically decreased while it tried to steady itself after the blow. The girl gained some distance, and her hand reached out for her friends. Then, suddenly, another wolf caught up. Its jaw wrapped around the girl's leg. Its teeth sunk deep as blood came from the wound instantly. The sudden jerk of her leg made her fall to the ground and slide on the wet grass, only a leap from the safety of the rocks. The wolf quickly turned, its teeth showing while it moved in to finish its prey.

The sound of Owen's feet startled the wolf from ending the girl's life. Its head turned just in time to see Owen driving his foot into its side. The wolf jumped back, avoiding the kick, while Owen slipped on the grass and fell to his knee.

"Stay back!" Owen yelled frantically at the wolves, waving his arms as if to appear bigger than he was while scooting closer to the girl. The five wolves seemed unafraid of Owen's gestures. They circled the girl and him, their heads dipping low, looking straight at Owen and the girl.

The girl screamed in pain and fear as she tried to get away, kicking herself closer to Owen while he opened his arms and pulled her to him. She buried her head into his chest as she awaited the wolves to pounce on them, knowing the end was near.

The lead wolf slowly moved forward from the others. Its jowls flared as it growled and bore its sharp teeth. With each step closer, Owen felt his death approaching.

"Go away!" Owen yelled at the wolf while he squeezed the little girl. He covered her as best he could with his arms, shoulders, and head, hoping the wolves would take him and leave her as his eyes closed. He heard the wolf's breath as its open mouth came closer. "Just go away and leave us alone," he quietly said through gritted teeth.

Then, the growling stopped. All Owen could hear was the crying of the little girl. He slowly opened his eyes, hesitant to let go of the girl in his arms. He turned his head and saw the wolves start to walk away. *Why didn't they eat us?* He looked around, thinking someone had come and scared them off, but he did not see anyone but the other kids looking at him with amazed eyes from on top of the boulder.

"Are they going away?" the little girl in his arms quietly asked.

Owen nodded his head. "They are." His grip around the

girl relaxed. *But why?*

The little girl grunted in pain as she tried to lift her leg. The blood from the large bite soaked through her ripped pant leg and dripped on the grass.

"We need to get you to a healer," Owen said as he knelt before her. She circled her arms around his neck. He picked her up on his back while other kids ran to get help.

Owen walked with the girl on his back until a few adults ran to his aid, lifting her off him and carrying her the rest of the way.

"It was like the wolves listened to him. Like they were his pet dogs or something," one of the children said quietly, but Owen could only slightly hear the distant conversation.

The wolves listened to me? Owen thought in his head as his hand reached up and touched the brand under his thick clothing. *Is that even possible?* His mind began thinking about the bear and how it seemed to defend him against Tavia, and then the goats, how they have been cooperating with him since they left Orinton, now the wolves, and how they left him alone when they could have should have attacked him and the little girl. *Do I have control over animals?*

Owen turned and saw the crowd that was beginning to gather while the kids kept telling the story. Some of the adults had a look of amazement or disbelief, thinking the kids were just telling the story wrong. Then he noticed the faces of a few of them looking almost afraid.

Owen began to feel alarmed. He watched one of the men pull out a dagger, looking straight at Owen. He quickly turned and walked away hastily towards the field where he left his goats. As he walked, he glanced over his shoulder and saw two men had separated from the rest. They sauntered after him, their gaze never leaving Owen's back.

He got to the goats and was surprised that many had stayed in the area while a few had drifted off but not too far.

"Come, come," Owen shouted to the goats. It was his typical call to get their attention, and they all turned to look at him, even the few that had wandered further away. *They do listen to me.* As the goats began walking towards him, he patted his leg, repeating the phrase, "Come, come," getting the goats to follow him as he began to return to Aerlene's.

The two men continued to follow some distance behind him. They walked with purpose but kept away, seemingly not caring that Owen had spotted them. As he walked closer and closer to Aerlene's, he felt uneasy, not knowing what to do or why the men followed him. Owen began to run, fear gripping him as he left the goats behind and headed straight to Aerlene's house.

* * *

"Tavia!" Owen shouted in a panic as he entered Aerlene's house, hoping she was there. He glanced behind him through the door as he shut it, seeing the same two men standing near another house on the other side of a field. His heart raced, and his breath was heavy as he locked the door.

"What is it?" Tavia said as she quickly ran into the kitchen from the other room. Hearing how distraught Owen was.

Owen looked at Tavia with a frightened face. "They found me," he said as he tried to catch his breath. His lower lip shivered as he looked wildly around the room.

"Calm down and breathe, Owen," Tavia said as she put her hand on his shoulder to calm him, but she also began to panic, thinking the elves that attacked Orinton had found them.

Owen dashed away from Tavia to the window, peeking out and seeing the two men still watching the house. "They are going to kill us," Owen said in a panic.

"Who's going to kill us?" Tavia asked as she, too, peeked out the window.

"Those two men out there," Owen said as he ran from the window and grabbed one of Aerlene's cutting knives.

Tavia stood at the window and looked at the two men. "Owen, I don't think they are with the elves that attacked Orinton," She said, recognizing them both as customers she had served. "They are both human and have seen us before."

"They drew their knives and started following me," Owen said as his hand shook, holding the knife.

"Owen, what happened?"

Owen looked at Tavia, his eyes showing how frightened he was. "I think the tree did something, something that involves gateways and... and..." He paused, almost unsure what he was about to say was real or his imagination. "I think I can command animals."

Tavia looked at him doubtfully and confused by his mentioning of gateways. "Is this because of the weird bear?" she asked.

Owen shook his head rapidly. "Some kids were being attacked by wolves, and I ran to help," He explained. "One girl got bit, and I was shielding her to protect her. The wolves surrounded me and were about to attack." Owen's face went blank as he stared into nothing. "I told them to go away, and they did," He said in disbelief.

Tavia sat back a few moments, confused about what she was hearing. "Are you sure the wolves just weren't hungry?"

"Tavia," Owen said as he looked at her concernedly. "The goats have been working with me. The same with all the other animals here. Even that bear was protecting me from you, and now a pack of wolves just…walked away from me."

"But we know you seem to have some connection with animals," Tavia said, trying to bring some sensibility to the conversation.

"Not like this, though," Owen said with concern.

"Are you fay?" Aerlene asked as she entered the kitchen, her voice startling Tavia and Owen so much they both jumped.

"How long have you been there?" Tavia asked harshly.

Aerlene looked at Tavia with a kind expression. "Soon after, Owen shouted your name. I thought he was hurt."

"And you didn't feel like telling us you were eavesdropping?" Tavia barked.

Aerlene looked at Owen. "I won't hurt you, even if you are fay."

"He isn't fay," Tavia fiercely said as she stepped between Aerlene and Owen, knowing that if the people thought he was a fay just because he could talk with animals, they would burn him alive or try and kill him on sight.

Aerlene looked at Tavia admirably at how defensive she was of Owen. "News about Owen being a fay will travel fast, and others will come here for him," Aerlene said as she walked around the room, looking through the windows. She spotted some more people watching the front of the house. "You need to go, Owen," she said dreadfully.

"What do you mean he needs to go?" Tavia protested.

Aerlene looked at Tavia and then Owen. "Climb out the back window and crawl through the pig pen. From there, the grass should be tall enough for you to crawl away without being seen."

"But he isn't fay," Tavia said sternly as Aerlene began throwing food into the burlap sack Tavia and Owen brought when they arrived.

"It doesn't matter, Tavia," Aerlene said. "If they remotely think he is fay, then they will come for him." She looked at Owen, her face showing the worry she felt. "Owen, you need to go." Owen nodded. Aerlene handed him the sack and looked caringly into his eyes. "This should be enough for you to buy passage away from here and then some," Aerlene said as she pulled a small pouch from a drawer and handed it to Owen. Tavia and Owen already knew it was money Aerlene had set aside for when she grew too old to manage the animals. "I will try and distract them the best I can." She touched Owen's cheek as he shook his head, not wanting to take the money. "Now go."

The sound of shouting from outside the front of the house made Tavia panic. She grabbed Owen by the arm and started pulling him, leading down the hall, away from the front door. Tavia quickly entered Owen's room and grabbed the backpack and hatchet from under his bed. She handed them to him even while her hand trembled from fear. Together, they entered the room at the back of the house. Tavia opened the small window and looked out. A shed blocked one side, and she could see no one on the other side.

"You have to go, Owen," Tavia commanded.

"What about you?" Owen asked confusedly. Realizing the window was so small it would be hard for him to crawl through alone and impossible for Tavia to make it through.

"I'll be okay," Tavia replied, looking out the window again, forcing the backpack and the burlap sack out of it.

"They are after you, not me."

"But I'm not fay!" Owen cried out.

"We don't know what you are, Owen," Tavia said as she handed him the hatchet and jerked him to the window. Owen quickly wrapped his arms around Tavia, burying his head into her chest as he began to cry. Tavia pulled him away so she could look him in the face. Her face was not only stricken with concern for him but also love. The look reminded Owen of the look Olsen gave his mother in his vision.

"You need to run, Owen, far from here and as fast as you can," Tavia said as tears glided down her cheeks.

Owen turned around to the open window. He tossed the hatchet and his heavy coat through it. He then climbed out the window with Tavia's help. As he stood up, he looked at Tavia.

"I'm going to Delmock, but I promise I'll come back," Owen said as the tears streamed down his face.

Tavia nodded, unable to say the words to describe how she felt, but she hoped Owen knew how much he mattered to her. She then closed the window as Owen crawled through the pig pen.

"Open this door. We know the boy is in there!" a loud voice commanded from the front of the house.

Tavia quickly ran back down the short hallway, signaling to Aerlene that Owen had left.

Aerlene opened the door. The man on the other side was one of the town guards, dressed in his uniform with a silver breastplate and chainmail sleeves. The man was in his mid-thirties and well-built with a scar on his face, running from his eyebrow to his jaw.

"Where is the fay boy?" The town guardsman asked as

he pushed his way through the front door, looking around with his sword drawn as two others walked in behind him, pushing Aerlene to the side.

"He isn't fay," Tavia yelled."And he isn't here anyways."

The guardsman looked at her with distaste. "Haul them outside," the guardsmen ordered the men. "Chain this one," he said, pointing at Tavia. "She may be fay as well."

One of the two guards walked to Tavia and grabbed her by the arm, pulling her with force as Tavia struggled against his grip.

"Don't fight them, Tavia," Aerlene shouted as she watched the guard taking Tavia, growing angrier as he pulled her outside.

Outside, she saw many townspeople had gathered to see what was happening. More guards entered the house after Tavia and Aerlene were in the street.

"Search the house. Those men said they saw the fay boy enter, but he didn't leave," the commander of the guards yelled from inside the home. The sound of furniture and wood breaking made Aerlene cringe as they destroyed her home.

No one saw Owen climb out the back window. Tavia thought to herself as she breathed a sigh of relief. The guard beside her forced her to her knees and placed her wrists in chains, keeping her hands behind her back as she heard the click of the iron lock.

"Where is the fay boy, Aerlene?" the commander yelled angrily as he walked back out the front door. He glared as he approached her with a heavy stride.

"Owen isn't fay," Aerlene protested loudly as she stood tall, not flinching as the heavily armored man approached her with angry eyes. "And even if he was fay, he means no harm."

"The boy can speak to animals! We have multiple witnesses of him having control over a pack of wolves!" the commander yelled.

"He saved a girl," Aerlene snapped back.

"He probably ordered the wolves to attack the kids in the first place!" the commander shouted, gesturing with his hands as if to emphasize his point. "We cannot have another fay controlling people to commit murders here!"

Tavia just sat on her knees, looking through the crowd at the open fields behind Aerlene's house. *I hope you are safe, Owen.*

* * *

When Owen cleared the field and found himself atop a ridge overlooking Keerike. He stopped, low in the grass, to not be seen. He could see the tiny house that belonged to Aerlene and that the crowd gathered in front of it had already dispersed. "I hope you are safe, Tavia," he quietly said. Then, he turned around and started heading north to Delmock, feeling truly alone.

* * *

The forest was silent. The blanket of snow gave it a sense of peacefulness as a rabbit rose from his burrow. It sniffed the air; the sweet cold filled its nostrils, but no alarming scents were in the air. It hopped, clearing the wall of snow and landing on the soft surface. Its long ears quickly twitched around, listening for the slightest of noises. Hearing only the rustling of trees and feeling the breeze, it crept forward. Its tiny paws settled lightly in the snow as it went.

The sound of snow being crushed cut through the silence. The rabbit's ears twisted in the direction before it turned its head to look. Still, with every muscle tensed, It readied itself to spring back to its burrow. But no other sounds came. The rabbit hopped over the snow, spotting an area under a thick tree where the grass was visible a distance away.

The rabbit froze again, listened, and looked at its surroundings, assessing if any threats lingered nearby. The rabbit leaned down, its sharp front teeth nibbled the green grass. It swallowed and took another hearty mouthful, then another. The taste of the grass was so satisfying the rabbit could not resist eating its fill.

A loud thud and the feeling of something touching its fur made the rabbit jump. Its eyes focused on the arrow in the ground that barely missed the rabbit's body. It bolted back towards its burrow. Unaware of where the threat came from, it jumped from cover to cover as it panicked.

Its burrow finally came into view, and the rabbit darted. Its hind legs were pumping fast, but the snow slowed it down. Then, from the left, the rabbit spotted something springing through some bushes. The giant beast came faster than it could react, its sharp teeth being the rabbit's last sight.

"Damn it, Huntress, that was mine," Lars yelled, relaxing his taut bow.

Huntress looked up at Lars, responding to her name being called with the head of the rabbit crushed in her teeth.

"Guess you win that one, Huntress," Lars said reluctantly. He looked up at the sky, seeing the sun through the canopy of pine branches. "Well, looks like it's time to head home," Lars told the wolf. However, Huntress had already started heading that way before he finished the sentence. "Don't bother waiting for me then," Lars said as she disappeared around a tree. He shook his head a few times as he went to collect the arrow from the patch of grass, then turned to head home.

The sound of a wooden shield being hit by metal echoed through the trees as Lars returned to the house. Cinda was waving an Orcish training sword, and Ulrick deflected every sloppy blow aimed at him with his shield.

"Breath, Cinda," Ulrick said in Terrish. Cinda's tired swing of her sword only lightly hit his shield.

It had been almost two weeks into Cinda's training. They trained three times a day for over an hour each time. Ulrick had a difficult time since Cinda was far from having an orc's strength and stamina that he was used to, but she was improving. She enjoyed the training, however. Since she had started, she felt closer to Ulrick. His teaching her opened the door to more conversations and grew their commonality. Even mimicking his hairstyle slightly since Beotolt ripped out the hair on the side of her head. Her hair was cut short on the sides while leaving the top long. However, she did not braid the hair like he did. Instead, Cinda let her long copper-colored hair down or put it in a single ponytail on the back of her head.

Lars also had become more of a friend during these weeks, joking with her more often and including her in pranks he would pull on Ulrick or others in the village, always laughing together when they saw the person's face. It felt refreshing to Cinda; she even began to feel like they were all true friends, unlike those in Orinton, who mostly placated her because of her status. Things felt easy with the two of them, making her worry even more about telling them the truth of her noble lineage, thinking they might treat her differently if they knew.

"Hold on," Cinda said to Ulrick as she put the tip of the heavy sword in the ground and used it as a crutch, shifting her weight. "I need a break," she said in between her deep breaths.

"Do you think maybe that sword is a little too heavy?" Lars yelled as he walked towards them.

Cinda's head turned quickly from hearing his voice. "I want to be as good as Ulrick," she said with an exhausted smile.

"Sure, but Ulrick is four times your size. Maybe a lighter sword would be smarter," Lars said as he approached the front of the house.

"One rabbit?" Ulrick interrupted, seeing Lars carrying the single rabbit he managed to kill while hunting.

Lars looked down at the rabbit. "Well, I would have had two, but Huntress got in the way." He then turned his head and spotted Huntress on a bench. Her legs sprawled out, the side of her head rested on the wood, with her tongue hanging out the side of her mouth while she panted.

"Huntress got four rabbits," Cinda said as she pointed at a pile of rabbits not far from the bench Huntress was on.

Lars looked at the rabbits, knowing the wolf was for sure the better hunter out of the two of them. "Well, one of those rabbits was a team effort," Lars said with a smile.

"I think Huntress still wins the competition," Cinda said as she walked over and sat beside Huntress. "Good girl, Huntress," she gingerly said as she scratched the neck of the wolf, knowing that was her favorite place to be scratched.

Lev was right about the wolf helping Cinda cope with her situation. Having Huntress around made her feel safe and happier. She still stuck to Ulrick and Lars whenever going anywhere other orcs would be, even though some orcs were kind to her since word spread about Cinda pulling Earl Beotolt to the ground by his tooth. Though the story had won her some respect, it made her more afraid of retaliation from Beotolt. She even sat up at night, worried Beotolt might return and try to retake her. She had seen him twice since the fight, and both times, she grew so afraid she would run back to Ulrick's house without stopping.

The most significant test would be that evening when the orcs would celebrate what they called Dortis Brawn, the celebration of Tolneer becoming an independent earldom and plans for the coming year. It was a large feast in the hall, with many orcs coming to pay respect and hear Thrane's final decision on where they would raid in the spring. Lars and Ulrick had warned her that there would be orcs she did not recognize, thinking it would help. However, it only made her more worried.

* * *

The snowfall was thick with hardly any wind, collecting on the limbs of trees until the branches could no longer hold it. The sound of the snow crashing into the ground would echo in the darkness of the night. Arminiul did not mind the lack of wind as he stood in the mouth of a shallow cave where he and Sepher took refuge until the storm passed. A wind in the wrong direction could make for a frigid night.

"Do you see anything?" Sepher asked from his comfortable spot, sitting close to the small fire he built.

"I don't see anything," Arminiul said as he looked out at the white landscape, riddled with a sparse amount of large trees.

"Then come and get warm. We haven't seen signs of anyone for some distance," Sepher said as he readied a rabbit and a snake for cooking over the fire.

Arminiul looked at the ground with a face that looked as if he was deep in thought. *Nothing. We haven't seen or heard anything. Even the people we have asked did not know where Orinton was or had heard of it.* He thought in his head. "That is what I am worried about," he said quietly.

"Why would that worry you?" Sepher asked, barely hearing what Arminiul said.

Arminiul walked into the cave, sitting on a large rock. He looked at Sepher with a serious face. "I am worried we will not find these human kids we are looking for," he said sternly.

The tone of Arminiul's words made Sepher want to avoid eye contact with him. He knew Arminiul thought searching for the humans was a hopeless endeavor, doubting it more frequently in passing, almost like a joke. This time, however, Arminiul did not sound like he was joking.

"We have scouted out five villages and walked through two elf-friendly villages. I did not even count all the small settlements we have been to," Arminiul recounted as he watched Sepher not say a word in response. "People don't know about Orinton being attacked or that the village even exists, and no one has seen anyone fitting the descriptions of them."

"What are you getting at Arminiul?" Sepher asked.

Arminiul turned his head and looked out the mouth of the cave. "If a worse storm than this comes and we don't have shelter, we won't make it through," he said, returning to Sepher.

"You don't have to come. You can go back home if you

want," Sepher responded sorrowfully. He then looked up at Arminiul. "Find Senator Galadin. Get your revenge. I will keep looking for the kids."

"Bha," Arminiul said in frustration as he got up from the rock and walked back to the mouth of the cave, looking out into the nothingness.

The fire crackled, and a few sparks flew from the popping wood. Sepher sat in silence, looking at the flame as it danced. "I have to try and find them,"

"You could die trying to find them," Arminiul stated, not even turning to face Sepher.

"If that is Hyllo's wish for me, then so be it," Sepher said coldly. Arminiul did not respond, only shook his head slowly a few times while still looking away from him. "You should go. I'll be fine." Sepher then laid the snake down on a cloth and started to cook the skinned rabbit.

"You really think those two humans are still alive?" Arminiul asked as he turned around and faced Sepher.

Sepher looked up at Arminiul, sincerity in his eyes as he spoke. "I do." He then looked away, back at the fire. "Besides, I have nowhere else to go," he said quietly.

"We can at least go somewhere warmer," Arminiul said, making a small joke though he knew what Sepher was implying. He was sure the missing hunters had been noticed by now, so options for them were few. If they were declared dead like the rest of their comrades, then people would see them returning home, and Senator Galadin would surely get word. If someone noticed they were missing, people might hold them responsible for their deaths, making them fugitives or deserters since they did not return. Their only option was to find somewhere else to live, somewhere no one would think to look.

"I have heard summers in Miterra are not that bad," Sepher said with a smile.

"You plan to keep looking for that long?" Arminiul asked as he walked back to the rock and sat down. The smell of the cooking rabbit made him grow hungry.

"I'm sure we will find them before that," Sepher said as Arminiul leaned over and grabbed the snake, pulling half its body off the stick and cutting it off for him to eat.

"Your Goddess tell you that?" Arminiul said right before taking a nibble of the snake.

"My gut tells me that,"

"Well, I hope your gut is right about them heading east. If they went any other way, we will never find them," Arminiul said as he ate.

"Oh, my gut didn't tell me they headed east," Sepher said calmly. Arminiul looked at him with an eyebrow raised. "That was Hyllo, the beautiful Goddess of the Sun, who told me that. My gut just tells me they are still alive," he said with a wink.

"Well, next time you two have a conversation, could you get better directions?" Arminiul said jokingly.

"Sure, I'll ask her tomorrow when she rises," Sepher joked back, smiling as he finished cooking the rabbit.

CHAPTER 18

The stone dungeon was silent except for the mice that scurried around in the dark corners. The guard didn't say a word as he sat in his chair, watching Tavia from a distance. She had tried to gain his sympathy, pleading with him that she was not fay, but the guard only grew agitated the more she spoke to him. She finally stopped trying and lay on the flat, uncomfortable mattress with her wrists bound by heavy iron chains over her stomach. Her captors thought the pure iron would prevent her from using magic, but they were just cumbersome. Time in the dungeon became a blur. She was unsure how much time had passed, but it did not matter. All she could think about was if Owen was safe.

A loud groan from the hinges of the dungeon door opening sounded, almost deafening in the utter silence. Tavia heard fast-moving footsteps as someone walked into the room, hidden from her view. She looked at the wall made up of iron bars and a gate.

"I have been requested to talk to the prisoner," a familiar voice said. Tavia's heart began to race as she sat up, recognizing the voice.

The guard quickly stood up and bowed. "Of course, Lord Vistem."

Tavia watched as Vistem walked to her cell, his face stern and unwavering as he passed the guard. When he finally stood just a few feet from the bars, he gave Tavia a quick wink, then slightly turned his head towards the guard. "I shall speak to the prisoner alone," he said strictly.

"But my lord, I have orders to keep a constant eye on her," the guard protested.

Vistem turned to face the guard. "So you have been here this whole time?"

"Yes, Lord Vistem. I have not taken my eyes off her."

"You know who I am, don't you?" Vistem said snidely.

"Yes, Lord Vistem," the guard replied with a bow of respect.

"Then leave me with the prisoner until I have concluded my questioning," Vistem said with a serious look that faded to a smile. "Besides, you look like you could use a quick break. Get something to drink. I will be fine. She is bound by pure iron."

"I am sorry, Lord Vistem, but until my commander comes to relieve me, I can not go," the guard said as he stood still, looking Vistem in the eyes.

Vistem walked to the guard, getting close enough for him to hear him whisper. "I am friends with this woman," he whispered softly. "They chose me to talk to her, thinking our relationship could help, but she is shy and will not be as forthcoming if you are in the room."

The guard looked at Vistem and then at Tavia. "Do you think she is fay?" he whispered back.

Vistem slowly shook his head. "I doubt it. Perhaps her brother was replaced by one. Who knows what fay can do with their evil magic," he whispered and slowly turned to look at Tavia. "That is why they sent me to question her, but I need her to be as honest, and the best way for that is if we are alone." He looked the guard in the eyes. "Do you understand why it is important you wait outside?"

The guard looked at Vistem momentarily while thinking

about what the Lord was saying. He then nodded reluctantly. "I will be outside if you need me."

Vistem returned to Tavia's cell as the guard walked out the door. The groan of the hinges and the echoing thud of the heavy wooden door reverberated throughout the room. It was the signal that they were alone.

"Tavia," Vistem said with a smile as he got up to the bars of the cell.

"Vistem." She slowly got up from the bed and asked, "Why are you here?"

"I came here to talk to you," Vistem answered as he watched Tavia struggle to stand up and walk closer to him.

"Did they find Owen?" Tavia asked in a panic, thinking that would be the logical reason he had come down to talk to her.

"No, they have not found your brother," Vistem answered.

Tavia's heart began to calm and fill with hope, hearing Owen had not been found. "Then what is it?" Tavia asked.

"Tomorrow, there will be a trial for you and your brother," Vistem whispered as he stepped closer to the bars, hoping anyone eavesdropping wouldn't hear him. "There are multiple witnesses who say they saw your brother commanding the wolves. There is also another witness about a different incident I am unaware of."

"But I have not done anything that could make me be seen as fay," Tavia said quietly as she stepped closer to the bars, only a few feet from Vistem.

"You are his sister, and so the Lord of Keerike, Lord Mave, is investigating you as well," Vistem whispered.

"What should I do then?" Tavia asked in confusion, thinking they would not find her guilty since she had done nothing wrong.

Vistem smiled at Tavia. "I could try and convince Lord Mave you were tricked by Owen into believing he was your brother. Then they should go easier, but you would need to be watched closely for a time."

"How would I be watched closely?" Tavia asked.

"You would come to live with me. I'll watch over you." Vistem stated as his grin grew insidiously. "Maybe we will watch each other in my chambers."

"I will never love you, Vistem," Tavia said automatically before she thought of the consequences of uttering those words.

Vistem leaned forward, only a few inches from the bars, as he glared at Tavia. "You will learn to love me," he stated as if it were fact.

The sheer arrogance on his face and tone made Tavia seethe with rage. *Learn to love you.* She was disgusted. The phrase reminded her of her father and filled her heart with hate.

Tavia reached through the bars, snatched Vistem's green tunic, and yanked him towards her with all her might. His face slammed into the iron bars, the sound reverberating through the air.

"You bitch!" Vistem yelled as he cupped his hand on his injured face. Stumbling back from the cell bars.

Tavia held no regret. "I would rather rot in this cell than lose my soul rotting in your arms," she spat. "No one can love such a pathetic man like you."

Vistem stared at Tavia, blood running down his face from his split forehead. The anger on his face began to soften, deepening into a grin stretching from ear to ear, a plot sparking in his eyes. "You will burn for this, you bitch," Vistem whispered. He wiped the blood from his face, smearing it across his temple as he tried to compose himself, and walked out of the dungeon.

Tavia sank to the floor, knowing that taking Vistem's offer would have kept her safe, in a sense, but she could not accept such an offer, a similar offer that had been extended to her mother. An offer that would make her detest herself. Instead, she had sealed her fate.

* * *

All of Tolneer was in celebration of Dortis Brawn. Many priests and priestesses walked the streets, blessing people for the coming year. Orcs danced around large fires. The smell of ale and cooked meat filled the streets as everyone was friendly with each other, with a few groups being more than friendly in public.

"Do they just do that wherever they please?" Cinda asked Lars as they walked by a table with a female orc and a male orc having their way with each other.

"Yep, tonight is a night of pure celebration," Lars said sorrowfully.

Cinda looked at Lars as she picked up on the inflection in his voice. "Do you celebrate in such a way?" she asked gingerly.

"I have from time to time," Lars said as he smiled and shrugged his shoulders. "But not tonight. Gotta keep my eye on you."

Cinda looked at the two orcs, her eyes unable to look away as she watched the female orc enjoying each moment. Cinda felt sad about herself, having never been touched by a man in such a way, even afraid of such intimacy. Yet this was happening in public, and no one seemed to watch or care. Everyone walked by as if the orcs were just having a normal conversation and not doing what they were doing.

"If you stare too much, the guy might think you want to go next," Lars said to Cinda, leaning close to her ear as she stood like a statue, watching.

"No, no," Cinda said quickly as she turned her head and started walking faster to catch up to Ulrick. She quietly asked Lars when he got next to her again. "Does Ulrick celebrate in such a way?"

"Nah," Lars responded. "Ulrick is not your normal orc when it comes to things like that."

"Why not?" Cinda asked, interested in what made Ulrick so different.

"Not many orcs have fallen truly in love like Ulrick has," Lars answered.

"Have you been in love?" Cinda asked Lars as she nudged him with her shoulder.

Lars smiled at Cinda. "It may shock you, but I have," he said pridefully.

"Well, where is she?" Cinda asked as they both turned around a corner, catching up to Ulrick.

Lars shook his head slightly. "Obviously, they are not here," he said as he laughed, trying to joke the conversation away.

"Seriously, tell me about them," Cinda protested, wanting to know.

"Her name was Tina, a human whom I met as a slave. She was always looking at the positive side of situations." Lars then looked down at Cinda. "And her laugh, oof. She had a laugh that made you want to laugh even when you didn't know the joke." Lars looked away as he smiled, remembering Tina and his time with her. "We had years of laughing together. She even smiled at me as she met the end."

"Did she die in battle like Ulrick's wife did?" Cinda asked.

"No, no, she was not a warrior."

"Then how did she die, if you don't mind me asking?" Cinda asked, worried it might be a touchy subject.

"She had gotten very sick, and that took her from me," Lars said somberly.

"I'm sorry," Cinda responded, not expecting that as an answer.

"It's okay."

They continued to walk behind Ulrick, who was busy greeting others as he walked the streets toward the hall. Cinda looked up at Lars a few times and waited for him to say more, but he was quiet.

"And the other one?" Cinda asked politely. Lars quickly looked at her with a questioning look on his face. "You said they are not here," she said, emphasizing the word, they.

Lars smiled as he looked down at the ground. "I did, didn't I?" He said regretfully.

"If you don't want to talk about her, you don't have to," Cinda said, not meaning to pry, but she was very curious.

"There isn't much to say," Lars responded. "She grew up with me around, and when she became an adult..." Lars paused, shaking his head and shrugging his shoulders. "Something just clicked, and I fell in love with her."

"Did she fall in love with you?" Cinda asked.

"It doesn't matter if she did," Lars said sadly. "Our fates are on different paths, she said."

"Well, that isn't a good excuse," Cinda thundered. "If you love her, then you should fight for her."

Lars laughed, seeing Cinda holding her clenched fist slightly in the air like a champion. "Oh, to be sixteen again and see the world so simply," he said, shaking his head and smiling. "She has a very important job, and I would only complicate things if I stuck around." He said in a somber tone. They walked in silence. Cinda did not want to pry any deeper now.

"So what about you, Cinda?" Lars asked as the hall came into view. "A beautiful girl like you. I am sure men were lined up for a chance with you."

Cinda pressed her lips together as she shook her head slowly. "No. Boys my age were not allowed to talk to me."

"Strict father?" Lars asked.

"Yes, very strict," Cinda said as she watched the doors to the hall open for the three of them to enter.

* * *

The celebration inside the hall was tame compared to the streets of Tolneer. There was laughter as new people entered the hall. Cinda felt relieved when one group came in. Representatives of a small community that was made up of almost a third of humans. She found them comforting because they also spoke Terrish. Some even spoke a hybrid of Terrish and Orcish.

Cinda felt at ease as she sat at their regular table, watching everyone from a distance while Lars translated their conversations for her. Lars even translated the conversations Ulrick was having with other orcs. She felt more comfortable knowing what was being said around her.

The dynamics of the hall were strange to her. Thrane, his three wives, and four of his five children sat at their tables.

They only greeted those who approached the table to talk to them, unlike before when Thrane would greet certain people as they entered, and the children were free to meander the hall. Trent wandered through the groups, talking to them individually, seeming to talk into their leaders' ears while others around them were shouting and laughing.

Then Beotolt and the other Glathbern orcs entered the hall. The laughter and loud voices seemed to die down as they joined the menagerie of the others. Many occupants looked at Beotolt and then at Cinda while talking. Their shifting glances back and forth made her feel uncomfortable. The memory of him pulling her hair and hurting her became fresh in her mind, and the onlookers were not helping.

Cinda's eyes could not help but keep wandering back to Beotolt in the crowd as he smiled and joked with others around him. She hated seeing him, his smile, his arrogance. The only positive was the gash in his right eyebrow that was not healing well and looked like it would leave a hideous scar.

Luckily, Beotolt seemed to stick near the back of the hall, far away from her. He didn't even look at her, as if what had happened did not even matter, but it mattered to her. She looked at Ulrick, who seemed just as upset as she was.

Everyone in the crowd began to turn their heads as Thrane stood up from his throne and took a few steps towards everyone, still standing on the raised platform so that all could see him. Slowly, he raised his hand, hushing the loud ramble of people in a few seconds as they all sat down.

"I believe you are all here finally," Thrane said in Orcish with a deep, loud, commanding voice that could be heard around the large hall. Lars quietly translated every word for Cinda. "I am happy to see my friends gathered here on this Dortis Brawn. Welcome!" he shouted with his mug held high in the air. Everyone lifted their drinks and shouted in reply, then drank in salute. "I know you do not just come here for my company, or I would see many of you more often," Thrane said with a billowing laugh.

"Who cares about you, Thrane. I came to meet your newest human warrior," an orc yelled in Orcish with a loud laugh as he stood up and pointed at Cinda. The orc looked older than most in the crowd, with his long gray braided beard, wrinkled face, and bald head. Yet the orc stood proud and strong, reminding Cinda of her grandfather Gustoll. "I heard a tale of how she brought down a great orc with just her little bare hands," he said as he looked around at the others, holding his open hands out. Some in the group cheered and laughed along with the old orc.

Cinda blushed uncomfortably as the entire hall looked at her, some with admiration and laughter, others with anger and disdain, particularly Beotolt and those with him.

"Yes, a great warrior indeed, Palton," Thrane said as he admired Cinda while more of the orcs cheered.

"Give her a name," one of the orcs among the crowd shouted, and a few others cheered at the idea.

Cinda looked at Lars after he translated what the orc had said. "What does he mean, give me a name?" she asked quickly.

Lars smiled. "Famous orcs get names. Like Ulrick Ironhide or Thrane The Bold."

"Do you have a name?" Cinda asked Lars as other orcs began shouting.

"I am not famous like you are," Lars said, his smile

broadening. He turned to look at Thrane, who was watching both of them talking.

"So, many of you have heard the story of Cinda?" Thrane asked. Many of the orcs cheered and nodded in acknowledgment. Thrane waved at Cinda to stand next to him. Lars nudged her enthusiastically.

As Cinda slowly walked from her chair to Thrane's side while many cheered and shouted, she felt smaller with each step as she approached Thrane. She could feel herself sweating and her hands shaking as all eyes were on her. She looked at the ground as Thrane's large hand rested on her shoulder. His hand was almost as broad as her shoulders. Slowly, she tugged at the threads of her green dress, feeling entirely out of place. Part of her wanted to run away into Lev's room again like before.

"So what shall we name Cinda?" Thrane asked in a loud voice. The room erupted with the shouts of orcs and humans. Some shouted names in Orcish, hoping for the honor of their name being chosen. Cinda shrank under the cacophony, but she felt reassured by Thrane.

Thrane then halted the noise with a raise of his other hand. He looked at the old orc. "What name would you choose, Palton? Since you are the one who traveled all this way to meet her and not me,"

Palton stood proudly from his bench. "Cinda Tand Rycker,"

A roar of laughter followed. Cinda panicked, looking at Lars and Ulrick and then at Thrane, not knowing what the words meant. Thrane looked down at Cinda kindly.

"Tand Rycker. It means tooth yanker," Thrane said in Terrish as the room fell silent again with anticipation. "Do you accept this name?"

"Tooth yanker?" Cinda asked in confusion.

Thrane laughed as he quietly spoke to her in Terrish again. "For bringing down Beotolt...by the tooth," he laughed again.

Cinda looked at all the orcs who were looking straight at her, many of them in anticipation of if she would agree to the name. "Is that why I am famous?" she quietly asked, looking over the crowd.

"The story of the small human girl who stood with defiant pride against the great Earl Beotolt, pulling him by the tooth to the ground, standing over his body in victory. The tale has spread rather quickly," Thrane explained in Terrish.

"But that is not how it happened," Cinda whispered as she remembered the terror she felt, how hopeless she was, and how things would have been much different if Thrane and Lev had not arrived when they did.

"But that is how it will be remembered," Thrane said. "Besides, that is pretty close to what happened from what I saw."

Cinda looked at the ground, thinking about the name and how different her life was becoming. Only a few months ago, the most nerve-racking thing she did was talk to Hendric because she had a crush on him. How long ago those problems felt. Now, she was famous for fighting an orc Earl. "Cinda Tand Rycker," she said to herself, hearing how it sounded from her own voice. "Tooth yanker," she said as she turned to look at Palton. His kind eyes and smile reminded her even more of her grandfather. She smiled and curtseyed to the old orc, saying in Orcish with a loud voice. "Yes."

The hall erupted in cheering and clapping. Cinda

laughed to herself as many around Palton patted him on the back in celebration. She slowly turned to return to her chair. She froze in mid-step at the sight of Beotolt seething with anger. His hand flexed and broke the cup he held. His eyes never flinched from her as ale spilled over his arm and table. A shiver ran up Cinda's spine. She held her breath, watching the massive orc's lip curl into a snarl.

"You can sit back down, Cinda Tand Rycker," Thrane said, lightly pushing her, snapping her out of her frozen state.

As Cinda seated herself, Thrane continued talking in Orcish. She tried not to look at Beotolt, keeping her eyes on the ground to avoid his angry gaze.

"Cinda, okay?" Ulrick asked in concern. Cinda slightly shook her head

"What is wrong?" Lars asked as he looked at Cinda's face.

"Beotolt…he's angry," Cinda softly said, as if afraid Beotolt could hear her from across the room.

"Maybe he should not have challenged Cinda Tand Rycker then," Lars said jokingly as he nudged her elbow with his, a hollow attempt to make her smile.

Cinda looked up at Thrane as he continued to talk. "What is he saying?" she asked Lars, trying to talk about anything else and pushing the thoughts of Beotolt into the back of her mind.

"He is talking about what is prepared for the spring and summer raids," Lars answered.

As Thrane finished the number of boats everyone provided, he paused thoughtfully. "After this winter, I have decided that we shall head east and raid the shores of Rustall."

Some groups in the hall cheered at the news while others clapped. A few, however, did not make a sound at all. They had a look of disapproval on their faces when they looked at Thrane.

"Are they not happy?" Cinda asked Lars, not understanding why.

"No, they are not happy," Lars answered with concern. "We knew some would be disappointed by the choice, but not this many," he said as he reached over and tapped Ulrick on the arm, looking at him with concern. Ulrick looked back at Lars, shaking his head slowly, unsure what to do either.

An orc stood up from among the crowd and questioned Thrane. "Why are we raiding Rustall again? Those people have little wealth and few warriors. There is no honor in attacking them," the orc protested. He then looked over at everyone around him. "We want riches. We want fame!" he yelled, rallying many behind him with their shouts of agreement.

Cinda leaned forward in her spot, and she recognized the orc that was talking. "That is one of the orcs Trent was talking to," she said to no one in particular.

"What do you mean?" Lars asked quickly.

"Trent was talking to that orc a while earlier,"

"Well, where would you like to go, Kalrin?" Thrane asked the orc that was speaking.

Kalrin looked at Thrane with a stern face. "We should raid Delmock."

Many orcs agreed with this idea with cheers and pounding on their tables with their fists. Thrane, however, took a step back from the shock of hearing such an idea. Many had said to raid Delmock over the years, but this was the first time it had been said publicly in front of so many people.

"You know why we should not," Thrane responded as he looked at Kalrin.

"Because your father was defeated there by the fabled Warrior of Delmock?" Kalrin said with not a little accusation. "That was more years ago than many can remember. That warrior is long dead or too old to even lift a sword." Karlin then paused for a moment. "Unless you are afraid of an old human?" he snidely said.

Thrane looked at the faces of everyone around him. Many seemed to agree with Karlin. Taking a deep breath, his eyes settled on Ulrick, who slowly shook his head. Thrane then looked back at Kalrin. "We do not know what we would face if we raid Delmock. It is too risky. We shall plan for it next year."

Cinda looked at Ulrick's face, seeing the stern look in his eyes as Delmock was mentioned. She then turned to Lars and was surprised. Unlike Ulrick or Thrane or many other orcs in the hall who had a look of concern, Lars looked scared. A look Cinda could not remember seeing on the half-elf's face before.

"What is it?" Cinda asked, growing concerned since he had stopped translating for her after the name Delmock was said. She touched Lars's shoulder as Thrane and the other orcs began to argue.

Lars shook his head. His breathing was unstable, and his eyes were wide as he turned and looked at her.

"What is so frightening about that Delmock place?" Cinda asked.

Lars looked down at the table as if trying to avoid Cinda's eyes. "Delmock is a peninsula to the south of here, populated by humans and fay. It is where Ulrick and Thrane's father wanted to establish a colony because the soil there was so rich," Lars explained, his face still showing the fear within him. "It is there that Ulrick's father faced the only defeat he had suffered while he was Earl of Tolneer."

"What happened?" Cinda asked, no longer caring about the arguing in the hall between the leaders of the orc groups.

"The first two days and nights, everything went as expected," Lars said as he turned towards Cinda so she could hear him better. "We knew monsters and fay lived there, but Delmock had no army. It seemed we would be able to hold it since the few beasts there were easily handled." Lars's eyes then went cold as he stared at nothing on the floor. "The third night, however, everything changed. We had been holding against a pack of wolf-like monsters, but then a man came. He was human and wore a black suit of armor with red trim. It was unlike anything we had seen before. He did not even have a weapon as he approached our shield wall, so we thought he may be an emissary to discuss terms of surrender." Lars then fell silent as his lips pressed together.

Cinda reached out her hand and took Lars'. His eyes quickly looked into hers. "What happened with the emissary?" she asked.

Lars slightly shook his head and then started talking again. "He was no emissary. I watched as he attacked the shield wall," Lars said as his expression turned to sadness. "He alone pushed through the shield wall of twenty orcs like they were children, killing them with ease, even the ones that tried to retreat after he had already taken down half of them. Earl Agmit, Ulrick's father, called for reinforcements as the man walked through the first line of defense like it was nothing." Lars then looked into Cinda's eyes. "By the night's end, that one human killed over a hundred orcs by himself. Then, before the sun rose, he challenged Earl Agmit. The Earl accepted, and after only a few swings, he knocked Agmit onto his back and held the Earl's sword against his throat. Then, as if perfectly calm, the warrior told Agmit he was to leave Delmock that day and never returned." Lars's voice rested for a moment as he clenched his jaw. "Agmit ordered his orcs to flee, but the other Earls that decided to stay were never heard from again."

"So, just one man stopped the orcs?"

"We arrived with almost a thousand. Only a few hundred left the shores of Delmock because of that one man, the Warrior of Delmock,"

Cinda and Lars then turned and looked at Thrane, who had been arguing against raiding Delmock, knowing from his father, Earl Agmit, what could happen if they raided those shores again.

Karlin did not flinch from Thrane's gaze. "What does it matter what we face? We are orc and shall face whatever Delmock sends against us."

"I am the Earl of Tolneer, and I say we will not raid Delmock," Thrane spat, stomping his foot as he stepped closer to Kalrin, the sides of his lips raised as if about to start yelling out of anger at the orc's insolence.

"Then we will not raid with you, Earl of Tolneer," Beotolt yelled above the crowd as he stood up from his chair. His face contorted with anger as he looked at Thrane.

"Neither will we," Karlin yelled. He then turned around and began to walk out of the hall, his men following quickly behind him. Beotolt also walked from his table towards the exit with his men. Then, a few other smaller groups stood up and walked out. The hall fell so quiet the only sound was of boots hitting the wooden floor.

"Can they do that?" Cinda asked Lars as no one stopped the groups from walking out. "Just leave like that?"

"They can. It doesn't happen, though," Lars answered as he looked at Thrane with concern.

When the defiant orcs had left, Thrane looked at everyone else in the hall who had stayed. His mind faltered, trying to figure out what was left of boats and men since a third of the people in the hall had walked out. "We shall raid Rustall," he said without cheer or applause in response, a slight tinge of sorrow in his tone as his shoulders slumped down. He slowly walked back to his throne and sat down. His eyes looked at the ground.

The noise in the hall did not return to what it was before. There was still some laughing and joking after a time, but most of it was murmured conversation as they talked. Thrane sat, not talking to anyone, and simply waved people away when they approached.

"Will Thrane be alright?" Cinda asked as she looked at the once proud orc who sat dejected and alone on his large throne.

"Thrane is strong and a good leader. I am sure he will figure this out soon," Lars answered.

CHAPTER 19

The morning light crept over the rolling hills. The sky slowly turned blue on the horizon, but none of the sparse trees had cast a shadow. The air was still and silent as if life awaited the sun patiently. Only a few clouds drifted through the sky, clearing out over the last few days after the snowstorm drove Sepher and Arminiul into a shallow cave.

"Come and pray with me?" Sepher asked Arminiul as they reached the top of a hill.

"Someone has to keep guard," Arminul replied as Sepher knelt on his knees, placing his bow on the ground by his side.

"Oh yes, wouldn't want the birds to get the jump on us,"

"I'd still rather not,"

"One day, Arminiul, you'll pray to Hyllo," Sepher said as he faced the coming sun, waiting for the first rays of light to come into view.

"I highly doubt that,"

They sat silently before the sun peeked out from behind some hills. Then, Sepher started his prayer.

"Hyllo, my Goddess, I seek your aid," Sepher spoke out loud. "We have traveled far to find the two humans from Orinton. Yet now we find ourselves lost, and hope is fleeting." Sepher bowed his head towards the rising sun. "I beg of you, give us a sign or anything to help us find those that need our help. Please, Hyllo, do this for us. Guide me to be better and deserving of your light," Sepher pleaded in a low voice. He then sat back up, the sun shining on his face. "Thank you for your blessing to see you rise again."

Sepher rose to his feet as the sun came entirely into view. The sound of a screeching roar sounded in the distance. It pierced the silence around Arminiul and Sepher, and they quickly turned to listen.

"Did you hear that?" Arminiul asked quietly, waiting to hear the strange creature once again.

"It's the same roar we heard weeks ago," Sepher said.

"But we have gone a great distance from there."

"It's a sign from Hyllo," Sepher said with hope.

"Your goddess roars like that?" Arminiul asked jokingly.

The roar sounded in the distance again, followed by a few more short howls.

"We should find it," Sepher said as he grabbed his bow and jogged down the hill.

"Hey, wait!" Arminiul yelled. Sepher quickly stopped and turned around to face him. "You want to go running after whatever that thing is just because it roared when the sun came up?" he said as he walked closer to Sepher. "How do you know this is a sign from Hyllo?"

"What else could it be? We ignored the strange roar the last time we heard it. This time, we should follow it," Sepher pleaded. Arminiul stared at him with a blank face. "Have faith Arminiul. I know you do not care for Hyllo. The things you have seen have made you turn your back on her light. She still has not turned her light away from you, my friend." Sepher then took a deep breath and calmed himself. "Besides, you wanted a direction." He then pointed in the direction the roars came from. "Do you have a better idea of where to head?"

Arminiul could tell by the look on Sepher's face and his

tone that he would not budge easily about this. He took a breath, looked around, and saw no sign of civilization or clue where to go. "Well…" he began to say, slightly annoyed, not wanting to admit to Sepher that possibly Hyllo did send them a sign. "Do you think her light could send us some horses?" he said as he followed Sepher. "Or some new boots? Mine are getting a little worn from walking for months,"

They both started to jog down the hill, keeping pace with one another as they went, moving swiftly but conserving energy as they could.

It was almost midday when they began cresting a hill they both hoped was the last. A small valley appeared. A large pond with several trees around it sat near the valley's northern end with a road traveling north to south. In the middle of the valley sat eight structures with large pens populated by numerous cattle. Arminiul quickly stopped Sepher with his hand before they came into view from anyone from the valley below. They both stood, catching their breath and observing. They sensed something was wrong as one building had half its walls knocked down and the roof slightly caved in. Debris was scattered about the house. Another building had a large hole where once a door stood. They saw a couple of bodies lying motionless on the ground in the grass. Suddenly, they heard the cries of a woman coming from another house.

"We should go help them," Sepher said, running at full speed towards the settlement.

"Damn it, Sepher," Arminiul loudly whispered. He then began to run down the hill. *He is going to be the death of me.* He thought as he remembered the humans who betrayed them and worried these people might do the same.

As the two elves made it deeper into the valley, Arminiul slowed by the cattle enclosures, noticing none of the fencing was damaged nor a single cow injured. He then saw a body lying on the ground. The man looked partially eaten, half his chest and arm gone, with his bloody flesh and muscles torn out of place around the large wound. Arminiul continued to follow Sepher, finding him standing in front of what looked like a house, except the front wall had been smashed, and there was the sound of a woman crying within.

Sepher slowly turned and looked at Arminiul. His face was stricken with misery as he stood still. The same face Amriniul saw when he found him sitting on the wall in the Fortress of Theris.

"Can I help you?" a young man said in Terrish angrily as he stepped out through the large hole and onto the porch.

"He doesn't speak Terrish," Arminiul answered as he walked to stand next to Sepher. He spotted a woman inside the house, kneeling over a blood-soaked white sheet. Arminiul felt the air leave his lungs as he spotted two small feet sticking out of one side, the feet of a child. "What happened here?" he quietly asked, not to disturb the woman.

The young man looked down at Arminiul and Sepher from the raised porch. His dark brown eyes were sorrowful, yet his voice was angry. "It was a monster," he said, then looked back at the woman crying. "A hellish monster like nothing I've ever heard of."

Sepher slowly looked all around and then spoke to Arminul in Elvish.

"Did anyone else survive?" Arminiul asked.

The young man shook his head. "No, just me and Jez.

Everyone else is dead. I just started working here as a ranch hand a month ago, and now this." His anger diminished and became mournful as he spoke.

"Can you describe the monster?" Arminiul asked as he looked at the ground, seeing the large footprints. They differed from anything he had seen, one large pad with three clawed toes. By the impression of the hard dirt, it was running and very heavy.

"Like... like..." the young man paused as he thought about the monster. "Like a giant lizard but a shell on the top of its head. It was huge, larger than a horse." Arminiul looked down at the tracks. "It had four thick legs and two arms with long scythe-like talons on the ends."

Arminiul glanced at Sepher with a questioning expression. Maybe the young man had hit his head or not gotten a good look. "Were any of the livestock attacked?"

The young man shook his head. "No, it..." He turned and looked at Jez, his face growing sad. "It came after the kids," he said somberly. "Anyone who got in the way, it went through, even the walls of the houses they were hiding in," he said quietly as he looked at the destruction around him. Arminiul's face went from questioning to blank as he heard the man say the monster came for the kids.

"What is it?" Sepher asked in Elvish after noticing Arminiul's expression change.

He turned and looked at Sepher. "The man is describing...I'm not even sure, some kind of giant lizard," he said in Elvish and paused. "He also said it was just after the children."

"Ask if the boy and girl were here," Sepher quickly said. There was such panic in his voice even the young man could sense the urgency in the foreign Elvish he spoke.

"What is it?" the young man asked.

"We are looking for two humans. A blonde girl who is a young adult and a young boy, about fourteen, with blonde hair," Arminiul answered.

"Did he bring that monster here?" the young man asked, his voice ripe with concern.

Arminiul noticed the strange statement. "Were they here?" he asked quickly, excitedly stepping towards the young man.

"I don't know about the girl, but a boy named Owen came through and left yesterday morning. Said he was going to Delmock," the man answered.

"Blonde, medium-length hair, from Orinton?" Arminiul asked quickly, trying to make sure.

"Yeah, that sounds like him. Didn't say where he was from, but when we asked, he looked sad," the young man answered.

Arminiul looked at Sepher with an expression of hope. "The boy. His name is Owen, and he was here yesterday morning. Said he is heading to Delmock," he said in Elvish.

"Did he bring that monster here?" the young man asked harshly, aggravated that his question was not being answered.

"The boy doesn't even know the monster is after him," Arminiul said sternly.

"If it finds him, he won't survive long," the young man said.

Arminiul looked around, hearing the sound of horses coming from a barn. "Can we buy some horses?" he said after turning back towards the young man.

The young man looked at Jez as she mourned over her dead son. He then turned back towards Arminiul. "Do you plan to kill that thing?"

Arminiul looked at Sepher and then back to the young man. "We do," he said calmly.

The young man nodded. "You can take the two horses. Just make sure to kill that thing."

* * *

Lars and Ulrick demonstrated how to use a spear and shield against someone with a sword while Cinda sat with Huntress and watched. Lars showed how to use the shield defensively and hold the spear, keeping Ulrick at a distance.

"If you keep the point facing your opponent, they can't just walk up to you," Lars explained as he walked a semi-circle around Ulrick. "Keep the spear out only a little in case they swing to hit it away. That way, you can pull it back." Ulrick swung his sword at the spear as Lars pulled it back, its edge resting on the shield. Ulrick then held still after the missed swing. Lars thrust the spear, almost touching Ulrick in the ribs. "So when they swing and miss, you poke." Cinda nodded in acknowledgment. "Make sure to try and pull the spear back after each poke. Spears tend to get stuck in people easily."

Cinda spotted Thrane's son, Thetin, running towards the house. He shouted to Ulrick and Lars. They turned and saw the young orc running towards them. "Uncle Ulrick!" Thetin yelled in Orcish. "Uncle Ulrick!"

Ulrick slowly walked to Thetin. "What is it?" he asked in Orcish.

"It's Father," Thetin said in between panting breaths. "It's an emergency," he gasped.

Ulrick turned to Lars. "You two stay here," Then, before

Lars could even answer, Ulrick ran towards the hall.

"What happened?" Cinda asked in Terrish, watching Ulrick and Thetin run away.

"I don't know, some emergency," Lars responded, deep in thought.

"What should we do?" Cinda asked, growing worried.

"First thing… find you a weapon with a sharp edge,"

Cinda was shocked by what he said. "Are we going to be fighting?" she asked quietly, knowing she was not very good at fighting and would likely be useless.

"With what happened last night at the feast and so many groups leaving, it would not surprise me," Lars answered somberly, a tone Cinda hadn't heard him use before.

* * *

Ulrick ran as fast as he could through the streets of Tolneer. Many of the townspeople still asleep or tiredly continued the night's celebrations. His long stride pushed him forward, leaving young Thetin far behind. Nothing was on his mind but to get to his brother, knowing something was very wrong.

The hall doors were wide open, and he ran into the main room expecting to see Thrane. Quickly, he looked around and saw the sad faces of orcs and humans around the vast space, but not Thrane's.

"Where is Thrane?" Ulrick bellowed in Orcish. Lev stood on the platform next to the throne and pointed toward the doorway to the private chambers. "Is he in his room?" Ulrick asked as he made his way toward Lev.

"Ulrick, Thrane is…" Lev said quietly as Ulrick neared her. She looked up at him, her eyes red and tearful as her lower lip began to tremble.

Ulrick felt his heart drop. "Where is my brother?" he asked harshly.

"In his room," Lev answered quietly as she shrank away from Ulrick, tears streaming down her face.

Ulrick quickly moved towards Thrane's room. His heart began to ache, and his stomach turned as he walked. Each step brought him closer to the answer to a question he did not want to ask. He threw open the door, almost breaking it off its hinges. Everyone in the room quickly turned and faced him with surprise. Everyone except Thrane, whose lifeless body remained motionless with eyes closed. Ulrick closed the distance between them as he looked down in horror, seeing his brother.

"Thrane," Ulrick whispered as he fell to his knees next to him. "How?" he asked aloud to anyone in the room as he took his brother's cold hand into his and gripped it tight.

"He died in the night," whispered Vools, Thrane's first wife, who stood a few feet from the bed.

"How could he have just died in the night? Thrane was fine last night," Ulrick said, his sorrowful tone growing angry from frustration with the onslaught of emotions he was feeling.

"He had been complaining of breathing issues and chest pain of late," replied Eldron, the high priest of Tolneer and Thrane's healer.

Ulrick looked at Thrane, his face at peace as it rested on the pillow. "Why didn't you tell me, brother?" he whispered and then looked at everyone in the room. "I need a moment alone with him," he calmly said, his eyes not turning away from Thrane as he spoke.

"Of course, you can have a moment. Eldron will need to

perform the rituals soon, however," Vools responded with a bow and motioned to the others to leave the room. As they walked out, Ulrick sat on the bed next to Thrane's body.

"I suppose you are with our father in The Hall of Halls, drinking and telling stories of your life since he departed from us," Ulrick said sorrowfully. He looked at the ground, not sure what to say. "I don't know what to do, Thrane. There is so much left to do, so many more places for me to tell you about. You won't even see Trent grow into a great warrior." Ulrick wiped a tear from his eye. "Why didn't you say anything about your heart? We could have gone to see Cortay and see if she could have helped." Ulrick paused for a moment, thinking of their sister. "Cortay is going to be devastated to hear you have died. Everyone will be devastated." He then wiped more tears from his eyes as they rolled down his cheeks. "You left at a horrible time, you know," he quietly said as his eyes shifted to the side, seeing Thrane in the corner of his vision, looking at him as if expecting him to say something.

"Excuse me, Ulrick," Eldron said as he opened the door slightly. "I must begin the rituals."

Ulrick looked at the high priest with slight disgust but knew that since Thrane did not die in battle, more was needed to see him off into the next life. He then turned to Thrane and grasped his hand again. "I will see you in The Hall of Halls someday, brother," he said quietly. Ulrick rose to his feet and walked past Eldron into the hallway. Standing and taking a deep breath, he noticed Lev looking at him down the hall. Slowly, she moved her head towards the door to her room, signaling for him to come in. Ulrick walked into Lev's room, and she quickly closed the door behind him.

"I think Thrane was poisoned," she whispered so as not to be heard by anyone but Ulrick.

Ulrick was shocked to hear Lev say those words and quickly looked at her with disbelief. "Why would you say such a thing?".

"Thrane has been fine. Not once did he mention to me about his heart or breathing, and I think I would notice if he was having problems," Lev quietly said as she looked at Ulrick, her eyes unwavering.

"What you are implying is…" Ulrick began to say, but Lev interrupted him, placing her finger over his mouth to quiet him as the floorboards creaked in the hall on the other side of her door. Feirdren's ears perked up, and he also looked at the door.

Lev started walking to the door quietly, but then Feirdren jumped off the bed and walked to the door loudly. His large feet and nails sounded with every step as he lumbered to the door. Lev and Ulrick heard someone dash away up the hall. She quickly opened the door and looked out, seeing a few other priests in the hallway, beginning to do the ritual.

After she closed the door, Lev repeated quietly, "I really think Thrane was poisoned," She walked across the room to start collecting her things.

"What are you doing?" Ulrick asked with a confused tone.

"With Thrane dead, I am sure Vools will act against me," Lev said quietly as she gathered her jewelry into a backpack.

The bellowing sound of Eldron's voice could be heard through the wooden walls, reverberating into Lev's room as he began the ritual, praying to the gods to give Thrane acceptance into The Hall of Halls, where all dead warriors gather in celebration.

"Who do you think would poison Thrane?"

Lev paused and looked at the wall before her. Slowly, she took a long breath before answering. "Beotolt."

"Beotolt?" Ulrick asked in disbelief. "The Earl might be rough and horrible, but he believes in the orc ways. He would have challenged Thrane. No way would he have stooped so low as to poison someone."

Lev turned and faced Ulrick, her face stern and eyes focused on his. "After last night, when so many others left, Thrane knew there could be a power shift. He even told me if anything were to happen, I am to leave for Horn Mountain." She paused momentarily, seeing Ulrick thinking about what she had said. "Why would he say that if he was not concerned?"

"But Trent will protect you," Ulrick said.

Lev scoffed at the statement. "Trent?" she said. "It is his mother I am afraid of. Vools has always resented me. This will be her chance to sell me off to the highest bidder. Might even sell me to Beotolt." Lev lowered her gaze from Ulrick, sadness overcoming her face. "Thrane stood up to Vools. Trent, on the other hand, will agree with his mother and sell me off."

"You aren't a slave, Lev,"

"I am an elf woman," Lev said, slightly shaking her head. She then looked at Ulrick, her face almost spiteful as she spoke. "We are all slaves here, no matter how much jewelry we wear."

Ulrick looked at Lev sympathetically. He knew why orc nobles had female elves as wives and how they usually were treated. Thrane was among the few good ones that gave her many freedoms even though it was not expected of him.

"Will you stay for Thrane's voyage to the Hall of Halls?" he asked somberly.

"I am leaving once they take Thrane out to the main hall when no one is back here," Lev answered. She slowly approached Ulrick and reached up, placing her left hand on his cheek. "I wish you were next in line to be Earl," she quietly said. "I would stay for you."

"Trent is next in line, not me," Ulrick said, knowing the Earldom goes to the eldest son.

"I know, but if you do become Earl, send word, and I will come back,"

Ulrick smiled at her kindly and placed his hand on hers. "What route will you be taking? The bay is still iced over, and no ships are leaving Tolneer."

Lev retracted her hand, her face going blank momentarily as she looked away, not wanting to look into Ulrick's eyes. Hoping something else was said by Ulrick. "We are heading over the eastern mountain to Doordom. From there, we will take a boat to Horn Mountain. I will probably stop and see Cortay, tell her the news of Thrane... and say goodbye."

Lev quickly returned to packing her things silently as Ulrick stood and watched. The sounds of the ritual had stopped, and it sounded like the procession was beginning to leave Thrane's chamber. Lev put her arms down at her side and looked at the door as the noise came through.

"You should go and help with Thrane. Be with him now and say your goodbyes," Lev said quietly and sorrowfully. Her lips formed a frown as tears began to drip from her jaw.

"Will you be here when I return?" Ulrick asked, hoping Lev would say yes.

"I need to hurry. Dernum and his group of Althians are

waiting for me already," Lev said, still not turning to face him, knowing that saying goodbye to Ulrick was hard enough.

Ulrick stood behind her, looking at her, sad at the idea of her leaving. He slowly walked past her to the door and opened it. The procession of priests was already gone from the hallway. He turned and looked at Lev. "Goodbye, Levelith," he whispered.

Lev's eyes shifted towards Ulrick. "Goodbye, Ulrick Ironhide."

Ulrick stepped out the door and slowly closed it. He looked down at his hand as it gripped the door handle, standing motionless momentarily as he heard Lev start to cry within. "Maybe someday I will see you again," he quietly whispered.

"Ulrick, you are needed," a priest said as he walked into the hallway, searching for him. The words made Ulrick realize where he was as his mind drifted about what might have been between Lev and him.

Ulrick looked at the priest and followed him into the hall's main room. His breath escaped as he looked at Thrane lying on a large table, dressed in dark green robes trimmed in gold with braided designs. In his lifeless hands, Thrane gripped his sword on his chest. Ulrick walked to Thrane's side, his eyes fixed on the sword his father had given Thrane all those years ago when he had gone on his first raid. From then on, it had been by his side, always sharp and well cared for; the simple hilt was polished, and the blade reflected the sun coming through the large open doors of the hall. He looked at Thrane's family. They all looked as if they had been crying for some time, mourning their fallen father and husband. One, however, stood with pride. Vools showed her strength in such a time. While Trent looked at Ulrick with a ponderous expression. Ulrick looked around the room. Many others gathered already to say goodbye to Thrane and show respect while more rituals were being prepared.

"Goodbye, brother. Until we meet again in The Hall of Halls," Ulrick said softly as he stood beside Thrane's body. He then turned and started to walk out the main doors.

"Ulrick," Vools summoned. Ulrick turned and looked at Vools questioningly as she held her chin up, staring at him. "You forget to swear fealty to the new Earl."

Ulrick looked at Trent, who stood beside her, his eyes looking sympathetic towards him. "It is alright, Uncle. We both lost today. Mourn my father and remember him," Trent said with a slight bow. Vools quickly turned and faced Trent with a look of disappointment.

"Thank you, Earl Trent," Ulrick responded and continued walking out of the hall, seeing the line of people forming to say goodbye to Thrane. As he walked home, many would stop to pay respects to him for his loss, but all Ulrick could think about was what Lev said. *I think Thrane was poisoned.* Her voice repeated in his head. *But why would someone poison Thrane? Why would someone disgrace their honor by using poison? Beotolt was angry, like Kalrin, but both would not stoop to poison. Trent would gain from Thrane's death but wouldn't take his father's life. Vools could have convinced Trent. I have no proof, however.* Walking by the shoreline, he spotted Thrane's personal guard and a few priests preparing a boat while it stood in its stand.

The boat was small, only fitting a handful of orcs. Ulrick thought it strange as he walked towards them. "What are you doing?" Ulrick asked everyone around and in the small boat.

The priest looked at Ulrick. "Eldron said to prepare a boat for Thrane's body to join his spirit in the afterlife this evening."

The statement shocked Ulrick. The tradition was to wait a few days before burning an Earl's body. This gave boat builders time to craft him a funeral boat and for the word to spread so people from all over the Earldom could come and pay respects. Never had he heard of this tradition being rushed, let alone happen on the same day. The boat they prepared was not worthy of Thrane to move on to the next life. Ulrick, however, did not protest. He looked past the other orcs as they prepared the boat, walking straight to his home.

Lars caught sight of Ulrick as he approached, the large orc's face stricken with anger as he clenched his fists. "We heard what happened," Lars said. "I am very sorry, Ulrick," The words fell on deaf ears as Ulrick walked past Lars and Cinda, making his way to the house and inside.

Once they were all inside, Ulrick turned to Lars. "Shut the door," he said brusquely in Orcish.

"I did not know Thrane was ill," Lars said as he closed the door to the house.

"Lev believes Thrane was poisoned," Ulrick said.

Lars's face turned to shock as he heard the words. "By who?"

"I'm not sure. She thinks Beotolt, but he would never use poison," Ulrick said and then looked at Lars. "I think it might have been Vools or maybe Trent."

"It could have been both of them," Lars said as he shrugged. "Some poisons show evidence they were used. We can check Thrane's body when we have a chance."

Ulrick slowly shook his head. "They are burning the

body tonight. Eldron ordered it."

Lars's eyes grew wide. "That's not keeping with tradition. What if this is a cover-up? Ulrick, if your brother was murdered by Trent and Vools, you should contest the Earlship."

"Do you think that would be smart without proof?" Ulrick asked.

"There isn't proof that it did not happen. Besides, many in Tolneer would follow you before Trent. He is still young and unproven,"

"But Trent is the rightful heir," Ulrick reminded Lars.

"Not if he killed Thrane to get the throne," Lars said, knowing the simple rule among noble orc families is that if a son kills a father outside of a challenge, their title was not passed down to them. "Maybe Lev will know more."

Ulrick looked at Cinda and then back to Lars. "Lev left with Feirdren and is heading to Horn Mountain before anyone notices she is gone." He felt terrible for Cinda. Lev was the only friend she had outside of Lars and him. Having her depart so quickly without saying goodbyes might crush her spirit.

Lars' eyes opened wide as he listened. "Are you sure *she* didn't poison Thrane?"

"Lev would not do such a thing. She is leaving because she is frightened for her life, " Ulrick answered confidently, knowing Lev was genuine in their conversation.

"Well, if she slips away without anyone knowing, then most will figure she is the one that poisoned Thrane," Lars pointed out to Ulrick. Ulrick turned towards a window and looked at the shore of Tolneer, his mind racing with thoughts on what to do next.

"You can always challenge Trent for the throne," Lars

said quietly. Ulrick quickly turned towards him. "Trent has not solidified his Earlship, and many would follow you instead of him. You could rally those who would back you and take the throne from Trent."

"And what? Wage war through the streets of Tolneer?"

"If Trent does not accept the challenge, then yes," Lars said. Ulrick gave him a grim look. "You and I both know your father's dream for Tolneer has a better chance with you as Earl and not Trent."

Ulrick's fingers began to ball into fists. "Yes. I know."

CHAPTER 20

The noise of the increasing crowd filled the streets as many approached the town center. The sounds were muffled through the ceiling of Tavia's cell. She sat up in her bed, hearing the people cheering outside. Then she listened to the door to the dungeon open.

"Lord Mave," the guard said with a bow.

Mave walked past the guard without reply and went to stand in front of Tavia's cell. Tavia looked at the Lord of Keerike, confused in her exhausted state, wondering why he was dressed so eloquently for a dungeon visit. His dark purple coat with yellow piping was finely pressed, his black boots polished to perfection, and his black pants seemed made of the finest fabric Keerike could provide. She thought it was a strange outfit for a trial.

Mave stood before the cell and pulled a handkerchief from his pocket as he looked at Tavia. He covered his nose and mouth to deter the smell of her and her surroundings. "Has she said anything?" Mave asked the guard.

"No, my Lord, hadn't spoken since last night when she begged for water. Long after Vistem had left," the guard responded.

Mave nodded slightly in response to the guard's answer and then turned his attention to Tavia. "Your trial awaits," he announced as he waved his hand toward Tavia. Two prominent men then came into Tavia's view. They unlocked the gate and made their way toward her. She raised her hands in protest, but the lack of food and water for the last two days rendered her weak, so weak she didn't have the strength to fight back. One of the men grabbed her by the arm while another placed a black cloth bag over her head.

Tavia flailed her arms against the men but was quickly subdued as they grabbed her by the arms and lifted her from the bed. Her heart raced as she could no longer see. Then the men pulled her through the cell doorway, and her leg smashed into an iron bar as she blindly kicked at the men. She clenched her teeth in pain as she tried to stand, but as she did, the men jerked her along, dragging her up a set of stone steps. Outside, the sun only showed dimly through the black bag over her head. She heard the yells, curses, and cheers of the people growing as the men pulled her through the crowd.

"Ow!" Tavia yelled as something hard suddenly hit her in the head, followed by something hitting her on the back. *They are even throwing things at me.* Tavia thought in her mind as something else hit her in the stomach.

"Fay bitch!" a man's voice yelled moments before she felt someone punch her in the face. The surprise of the blow made it hurt even more as Tavia began to taste blood in her mouth. The crowd roared with cheer.

Tavia's entire body went limp as she could feel herself slipping in and out of consciousness. The guards jerked her body around more as she heard them yelling at the people to get back. They carried her faster and then stopped abruptly. Tavia slowly reached to take the bag off her head, but as she did, a hand grabbed her wrist, and another grabbed her other arm. Hands came from what felt like everywhere, lifting her into the air, and then, as she felt her feet under her, they slammed her back against something hard. Her head bounced off the object with such force that even her eyes hurt. She felt heavy ropes tied around her body, from her slacked wrists to her shoulders.

The cloth bag over her head was removed, and the bright sunlight blinded her for a few moments as the crowd hushed at the sight of her face. Her eyes slowly gained focus, and she saw the great mass of people gathered before her. Many of them glared at her as if she had offended them personally. Slowly, she turned her head to the right and saw Lord Mave and Lord Vistem. Vistem, with his eyebrow swollen and bandaged, standing on a raised platform with another heavy-set man she did not recognize. She then noticed in her dazed state that she was tied to a thick wooden pole. Looking down, she saw she was on a raised platform with large bundles of dry sticks placed around it and underneath.

Tavia began to panic when she realized what Vistem had promised was coming true. *This isn't just a trial. This is an execution.* Tavia screamed in her mind as she started to fight against the ropes that bound her, struggling with what little strength she had left. Her only thought was of getting free, her animalistic instinct kicking in to save herself. Her wrists ran bloody as she yanked against the iron chains, reaching for the ropes.

"See how the fay struggles to cast her magic!" Mave yelled to the crowd and then began to laugh. "You will not be getting out of this that easily."

"Let me go!" Tavia tried to yell, but her dried throat burned.

The crowd cheered at the sight of Tavia's powerlessness until Mave began to quiet them down by raising his hands. "This is the trial of those known to us by the names of Tavia and Owen from Green Brooke." The crowd began to applaud at the words.

Hearing Owen's name, Tavia quickly began to look around, hoping they had not found him. Turning to the left, she noticed another long stake with branches around the base and a platform much like hers, except no one was on it. She looked around the crowd to see if Owen was anywhere. *They haven't found him.* She thought as she gave a sigh of relief.

"Owen of Green Brooke is on trial for accusations of being fay. We have multiple witness accounts of him having the magical ability to command wolves," Mave said as he stood before the crowd. "We also have an eyewitness account from Fredrick Galthorn of Owen reading a multitude of fay legends as if trying to gleam more magic." Mave then motioned to Fredrick, who was also standing on the platform with him, and Vistem with a quick wave of his hand. "With such compelling evidence, by order of me, Lord Mave of Keerike, the fay known as Owen shall be hunted down and his head returned as evidence of his death." The crowd cheered as quickly as Tavia's heart sank as they heard the words.

Mave then raised his hand to shush the crowd once more. "Now to the trial of Tavia of Green Brooke," he yelled as the crowd shouted curses and angry remarks at Tavia. A fist-sized rock emerged from the crowd, striking Travia in the lower ribs. The blow knocked the wind out of her chest. The crowd cheered and laughed as she hunched over in her bindings, struggling to breathe.

"Being the sister of Owen made it questionable if she was fay or not since he may have tricked her as well," Mave said to the crowd. Some of the people looked confused by his words. Mave then nodded his head and spoke again, even louder than before. "However, just yesterday, while in her cell, we have a witness to her attempting to use her magic on Lord Vistem."

Tavia's eyes widened in shock as she turned towards Mave and Vistem after hearing the allegation. "I did not..." Tavia tried to yell, but the pain in her ribs made her begin to cough instead of finishing the sentence.

Vistem stepped forward on the platform to address the crowd. "It is true!" he shouted. "In an effort to see if Tavia was or was not fay, she tried to use her magic against me. Luckily, the iron shackles on her wrists prevented her from taking control of me." The crowd began shouting at Tavia again. She clenched her teeth and what muscles she could, expecting something else to be thrown at her.

Vistem took a step back as Mave stood to address the crowd. "With such compelling evidence, I have no choice but to find Tavia of Green Brooke guilty of being fay. I hereby sentence her to death by fire." He waved to Vistem as one of Mave's men handed him a torch.

Vistem took the torch from the man and walked across the platform towards Tavia. "You should have agreed to my terms," Vistem quietly said as he stood only a few feet from Tavia.

Tavia looked at Vistem, defiant strength growing within her. "I hope you die never knowing what it is like to be loved, Vistem, Lord of Lies," she said spitefully and then spit at him with the blood of her now swelling cheek.

Vistem's lips grew stark as he looked at Tavia, his grip on the torch shaking. He tossed the torch into the dry branches below Tavia's feet. Tavia gritted her teeth, stood as straight as she could, and looked out over the crowd as she heard the fires begin to spread below her. She refused to give them the satisfaction of looking afraid as she felt the air around her growing hotter and hotter. Her mind thought only of Owen, of home, of days she spent running among the wildflowers, of peaceful times and not where she was now.

* * *

Tavia's screams of agony echoed through the streets and were heard faintly by Aerlene, who sat crying in a room in a nearby building, under guard so she did not interfere with the proceedings. She looked up at the young guard through tearful eyes.

"They are burning an innocent woman out there," Aerlene whimpered. "Does that mean nothing to you?" The guard stood by the door, avoiding Aerlene's eyes as she spoke. "Even if Owen is fay or part fay, he saved that girl from the wolves." Aerlene then stood up from the chair she was sitting in. "Do you even hear me?" she yelled at the guard. "Those screams… those are the screams of a woman being murdered because her brother saved someone's life."

Tavia's screams fell silent, as did the crowd in the distance. Aerlene fell to the ground, her heart breaking from the silence. "This is what happens when fear and hate are stronger than sensibility and compassion," she said quietly.

* * *

Many in Tolneer came to the shore where the boats were in stands so they would not be damaged by the freezing of the water. The mass of people was blanketing the ground and even in between the nearby buildings to watch. A few stood in the frigid water as the tide came in but could not move as everyone was packed near the shore. Even the groups that had walked out of the hall the night before in protest of Thrane's decision were in attendance out of respect for their Earl. Together, over a thousand people stood watching the light of day fade. The sun seemed to set faster than it usually did over the mountains as the people waited for the evening star to appear, the fabled place where The Hall of Halls resided. No one was cheering or celebrating this evening like so many others. The quiet hush of the wind coming through Tolneer was all that was heard as many stood motionless.

Drums sounded from the hall, and each beat told the people of their approach, the approach of the funeral procession. People parted as the drummers came through. Each beat kept them in perfect step, much like the drum on the longboats for the oarsmen. Behind them came four priests, flinging blood from bowls with long blades of grass at the people on either side, a blessing from the gods. Then came two of Thrane's personal guards, walking in formation with clean, polished metal armor. Behind them was the wooden table Thrane himself laid upon, carried by four of his personal guards. They held the table high so all could see their beloved Earl one last time. Eldron brought up the end of the procession. His long green ceremonial robes flowed around him with each step. He sang songs of prayer, blessing, and asking for Thrane's acceptance into The Hall of Halls, singing stories of his great deeds and how grand of a warrior he was.

Cinda, Lars, and Ulrick watched the funeral procession as it made its way between the last of the buildings and onto the beach. The three of them were standing on a dock a distance away from the funeral boat so no one could be in their sight. Thrane's two wives and children stood on a raised wooden platform closer to the boat Thrane was to be loaded in, giving them the best view.

None of this is what Thrane wanted, nor was it normal. Ulrick's father had many games and tournaments held in the days leading to his final journey to the Hall of Halls. Thrane wanted spectacle, games to be played, tournaments to see who would be honored to carry him, and poets to tell of his victories and defeats. For those defeats are what truly tested him as an Earl. He wanted his people to walk with him from his hall to the boat. Not stand on a beach and wait for him to come.

"Why is Ulrick not with the rest of Thrane's family?" Cinda quietly asked Lars.

Lars leaned in close to Cinda so no one could hear him. "It was asked of him, but he refused."

Cinda fell silent, looking around and noticing that no one around them was crying. All had stern looks on their faces, particularly Ulrick. Cinda thought about what Lars told her, that crying during a funeral is something orcs do not do. They need to be strong so the departed know they will be fine when they leave them behind. She wanted to cry, however, not just for Thrane but for Lev, knowing that she would never see either of them again when they had just started to make Tolneer feel welcome to her. Lars and Ulrick had spent most of the day talking in Orcish, meeting with others who came by the house, making less time for her in the confusion. She could tell they were preparing for a fight since she had watched her father do similar things before he left to fight the Ellious Empire.

Ulrick was not confused or holding back sadness. The

only emotion he held back was anger as he stood and watched Trent and Vools from a distance. The thought of them poisoning Thrane stuck in his mind. He was almost willing to wade through the crowd and challenge Trent to the death on the platform he now stood on. But he knew he must not, a part of him thinking Thrane would not want Ulrick to kill his son.

"Ulrick," a voice whispered behind him as an orc hand grasped his shoulder. Ulrick turned to see Warrel, one of the orcs he had talked to earlier about challenging Trent for Earlship. "I have talked to my house about your plan," he whispered in Orcish. "We will stand behind you when you ask that of us. The same for the Gromneer and the Veraslen houses."

Ulrick stood, facing Trent. "I thank you, Warrel. Hopefully, the only axe to be raised is mine and Trent's."

Warrel nodded in agreement and shrank away into the crowd of orcs as Ulrick's eyes drifted to Thrane's personal guard. They had carried Thrane and the table to the small boat while priests climbed in and hoisted the heavy wooden table into its resting place. The wood frame holding the boat a few feet from the ground creaked and shifted under the additional weight.

Eldron stood before the boat. Giving one last blessing to Thrane, his voice reaching out over the silent crowd like thunder. He looked down at the lifeless body, quietly saying his own goodbye. "I will miss you, Earl Thrane, the Bold. May the gods greet you with open arms and goblets full of ale."

Trent then walked from the platform to the small boat. Carrying a torch, he looked down at Thrane, seeing his father lying on the table. He did not say a word but began to light the dry reeds laid out inside the boat.

The crowd watched quietly as the flame spread within the boat's hull, the wood cracking from the heat, sending flakes of burning ash high into the air among the stars. Then suddenly, the boat moved as the tide reached the front supports, the water sucking the sand away from their foundations, causing the boat to tilt from the additional weight. The crowd pushed forward in shock to watch as the small boat jostled and slid down the fallen support logs and into the water.

Cinda panicked as the orcs moved forward against her, almost knocking her off the dock. She quickly squeezed herself into the crowd, finding her way without being able to see much as she only saw the large orc's backs and stomachs, some not even noticing she was there.

"Even the Gods are impatient to have Thrane join them!" Eldron yelled as the boat drifted slowly from shore, trying to make it seem like divine intervention and not poor planning to have the boat on the wooden rack. Everyone watched without a murmur as the small burning boat entered the water. Its flames grew higher as the ice in the fiord floated around it as if parting for Thrane himself.

Ulrick watched in amazement, remembering the last few things Cortay had said. *I saw fire on ice.* He watched the reflection of the fire on the floating ice. He felt a shiver, realizing her prophecy was coming true.

"Ulrick," a muffled voice called his name from behind him. His eyes opened wide. *A path calling your name behind you.* Cortay's voice rang in his head. Ulrick stood where he was, afraid to turn around. "Ulr..." the panicked, muffled voice spoke again, trying to complete his name. Ulrick finally turned around, seeing Warrel standing behind him, watching Thane's boat burn. Ulrick froze as he looked at the orc. *Am I to fight? Is my path to lead Warrel and the other families against Trent and avenge Thrane? If this is the path Cortay tells me to take, then I will. I will challenge Trent and become Earl of Tolneer.*

"Ulrick," the voice yelled clearer as Cinda's arm stuck out from behind Wassel. "Help me, Ulrick," Cinda shouted as she reached for him.

Ulrick quickly moved Warrel to the side and grabbed Cinda's hand, pulling her out of the wall of orcs around them. He looked down at her panicked face as she looked up at him. *I want you to follow that path, no matter where it leads you.* Cortay's voice said again in his head.

"Thank you, Ulrick," Cinda said with a smile as she strived to catch her breath from being crushed among the orcs.

Ulrick turned back and faced the burning boat as he kept his arm around Cinda to protect her from being swallowed up by the horde around them. He watched as the flames nestled themselves among the ice. *Is this really the path I am to take? To turn my back against Thrane's honor?* He looked down at Cinda. *Is Cinda the path?*

* * *

The wagon creaked and shook as the wooden wheels rolled over the dirt road. The two horses sauntered down the road they had been on hundreds of times before, knowing each pump and rut in the road better than the man who steered them. The man, in his thirties, drove the wagon between small villages, transporting people from place to place. It was an easy job since he was a farmer until the soil had gone foul in his fields, something he blamed on fay. Now, he carried people instead of produce in his covered wagon. It was more profitable since he was the only wagon transporting people between the five villages.

The wagon had been changed to hold people. Makeshift benches were installed inside, but the wagon had rigid axles, making it a bumpy ride. However, the thick canvas arched over where people sat, giving the patrons some reprieve from the sun.

Whereas the two teenage girls and their mother found the ride to be bothersome from the jostling, Owen found it quite relaxing, giving his feet a break from all the walking he had been doing since leaving Keerike almost a week ago, counting himself lucky the wagon had been passing by while he was eating his dried meats and an apple for lunch. The ride was not too expensive for him compared to all the money Aerlene had given him, only five silver coins to take him to the furthest village north, a price a tenth of the goats he sold to her.

The worst part about riding in the wagon was it gave Owen time to think, something he had not done much of the past few days while he walked. His eyes looked out over the road behind them, looking at nothing in particular while his mind wandered back to Tavia and Aerlene, hoping they were okay. He also wondered how all her animals had been doing since he left.

"Excuse me," the mother of the two girls asked, the first time anyone in the wagon had talked in almost an hour. Owen looked at the mother, seeing her sitting and smiling at the back of the wagon across from him. "Are you alright?" she asked kindly, seeing Owen look sad as he thought about what he had left behind... again.

"I'm okay," Owen responded with a single nod.

"My name is Sasha, and this is Cathay and Pennelope," she kindly said as she pointed at the two daughters; Pennelope was the youngest and sat right next to her mother.

"My name is Ow…" Owen stopped in the middle of his name. He knew he shouldn't use his real name since people could be after him, which he did use by accident at a ranch he had stayed overnight in. His mind quickly searched for a name that started with "Ow" until he blurted out, "Olsen, my name is Olsen," Owen said, regretting it immediately since the name was so close to his own.

"Well, it is nice to meet you, Olsen," Sasha responded.

Owen looked up at the mother and two daughters. They all had the same dark complexion and black hair that hung down to their shoulders. The older of the two daughters, Cathay, wore hers up in a ponytail, unlike her mother and sister. Their outfits were also different, lighter cloth but layered instead of one thick fabric like Owen's. He had seen people dressed like them in Keerike. It was Esterrin's style, he had been told. "It is nice to meet you as well," Owen responded with a fake smile. He then turned and looked back at the road, not wanting to talk to them. He felt there was little point, thinking the fewer people he let into his life, the less pain he would feel when they left or he left them.

"You seem a little young to be traveling on the road by yourself," Sasha stated as she looked at Owen, her eyes sympathetic, but her voice had a questioning tone.

Owen slowly turned towards Sasha. "I have no one to travel with," he answered, looking at the road.

"How old are you?" Pennelope asked with urgency as if she had been thinking about the question for a long time.

"I think I might be fifteen now," Owen answered. His eyes did not even shift from the road.

"Might be fifteen?" Cathay asked inquisitively.

"My mother was the one who told me the exact day of my birthday. It is sometime this week or last week," Owen answered, unsure of the date.

"Well, why didn't your mother tell you if it was last week?" Pennelope asked without tact. Sasha quickly nudged her.

Owen turned and looked at Pennelope, his eyes looking mournful. "She died a few months ago." His eyes then shifted toward the floor of the wagon.

"Are you on your way to see family or someone who will care for you?" Sasha asked, concerned.

Owen's eyes quickly shifted to Sasha's, and his mournful expression faded into a stern look. "My entire family is dead. Everyone I know is dead. Everyone except my friend who wanted me to leave," He said coldly. As Sasha sat back from the surprise of such a statement, Owen turned his head and looked back at the road.

The wagon fell silent for a few minutes until Sasha spoke again. "Where are you hoping to go then?"

Owen turned to answer but was distracted by the horses at the front of the wagon beginning to squeal. The wagon stopped and began to shake as the horses writhed in the tracks that held them to the wagon. Owen looked past the wagon driver and saw both horses rearing their heads. He could feel the fear of both horses, knowing they were afraid of something and wanting to bolt.

Suddenly, the wagon shifted to the side. The sound of the front wooden wheel snapping startled Sasha and her daughters. The wagon tilted downwards, causing the screaming family to tumble to the lower front corner as

Owen gripped the bench to stop himself from falling on them. The horses continued to pull the broken wagon, trying to escape.

"What's happening?" Pennelope screamed as she struggled to get off of her mother and sister.

"The horses are scared," Owen answered right before the wagon shifted suddenly from the horses, giving it another good pull. The second front wheel broke under stress and sent the entire front of the wagon into the ground. He heard the wagon driver scream as the harsh impact jostled Owen so much that he lost his grip and fell into the front of the wagon. Looking out of the wagon cover, he watched the horses strive to run, still attached to the wagon by their tracks. He then looked down, seeing the wagon driver's broken body pinned under the wagon. The driver's eyes were wide open, and his face was stricken with the fear of being crushed to death.

A screeching roar was heard above the horse's squealing and Pennelope's cries. Owen panicked, looking around as best he could, but did not see where the strange roar came from. The roar came closer, so loud it almost made Owen cover his ears. Sasha and the girls froze.

The horses pulled the wagon again, crushing the front of the wagon into the ground as it slid through the dirt. Then, with a loud snap, the wooden track that secured the horses broke. The horses came loose from the wagon and ran away with half of the thick wooden track still attached. The sound of the roar came again, followed by a low growl. Owen froze as he heard heavy footsteps behind the wagon canvas a short distance away.

"What is that?" Sasha whispered as she shifted to get off of Cathay.

"I don't know," Owen whispered, knowing the roar was not from a bear. It sounded much larger.

The rapid sound of heavy feet hitting the ground came closer to the wagon, sounding like a few horses running toward them. Owen held on to anything around him as something suddenly bashed into the wagon's side. The impact cracked the side planks almost in two. The massive force lifted the side of the wagon, its weight splintering the back right wheel as the wagon fell to the ground. Cathay and Pennelope screamed in terror as Owen slid onto Cathay.

"Run, girls!" Sasha screamed as she tried to help Pennelope to her feet. Her leg was stuck between the canvas and the wooden side of the wagon. Pennelope's foot stepped onto Owen's chest as she ran over him to get out of the front of the covered wagon. Owen tried to go after her as a large black talon pierced the canvas from above, coming to a stop only a little bit from Sasha's shoulder, and then ripped a large hole in the cover. Sasha fell to the ground, screaming as another black talon broke through the wagon's wooden side, tearing the planks away.

"Save my daughters!" Sasha yelled at Owen as a large lizard-like face looked through the hole in the canvas roof while it rocked the wagon.

Owen looked for his hatchet among the mess of items that had been spilled inside the wagon. Not seeing it right away, he begrudgingly lept out of the front of the wagon, seeing Penelope pull Cathay by the arm as she limped, trying to escape. He started to run to them as he heard more wood breaking and the monster's horrid roar coming from behind him.

"Run!" Owen yelled as he got close to the daughters, wishing he was strong enough to lift Cathay. When he caught up to them, he turned to see the monster that was attacking the wagon.

The beast was something from a nightmare. Its large lizard-like body had four legs, much like the legs of a dog or a horse, yet had three-toed feet with claws on the ends. Its sleek, bending body then had two arms, much smaller than the legs, but still looked strong and had the structure of human arms. Where the hands would be was a single large talon, curved like a bird and about the length of his arm. Its long, thick tail swung back and forth as its head was inside the large hole in the canvas roof of the wagon.

Owen froze, recognizing the giant lizard. It was similar to the wolf-sized ones in his vision. However, this one was much larger and had arms and four legs. He watched as Sasha tried to shrink into the ground, making herself as small as she could to escape the monster's open mouth, but it halted. Slowly, the head of the beast lifted from the hole. Its head was broad like a lizard and had a large frill in an arc covering the top of its head and neck. Its dark yellow eyes narrowed on Owen. The monster's jaws opened, revealing its numerous sharp teeth. Then, the bottom jaw separated down its chin, making its mouth even more extensive. A hellish roar sounded from deep within the monster's throat.

Fear ran through Owen as he stared into the beast's eyes. Yet he also felt something else: something was wrong with the monster. Like the knowledge within someone that when something smells rotten, you know not to eat it. He had never felt that way when seeing other animals he had seen after becoming a Druid. Not even the wolves gave him this sense of being out of place.

The monster moved off the wagon and headed toward

them. Owen turned and ran. Seeing the daughters heading to a group of trees for cover, he followed, hoping for safety or anything to save him. He looked for the bear that had watched over him in Keerike, part of him hoping it would come and rescue him.

Then Cathay tripped and fell to the ground a few feet from the trees. She yelled at Pennelope to keep running, but the little sister would not let go of her hand. Owen turned as he caught up to them and saw the monster gain quickly, its upper body high in the air as it prepared to come down on Owen and Cathay, its mouth open and talons poised to end them.

Suddenly, an arrow cut through the air, its sharp arrowhead punctured into the side of the monster's neck below the frill. It reared in pain as it tried to knock the arrow free with its talon. Owen turned and saw two elves riding horses at full speed towards him. One had a bow and was already notching another arrow while the other pulled out his curved elven sword.

The monster turned towards the elves. Its jaws opened wide towards the threat. A second arrow flew but bounced off the monster's hard frill.

"Get the kids!" Arminiul yelled as he urged his horse toward the beast. It roared, and the horse began to fight against Arminiul. He knew he did not have time to deal with the horse and quickly dismounted from it, not losing any speed as his feet hit the ground and went straight into a run.

The giant monster charged at Arminiul as he ran at it, sword in his right hand, and he pulled his dagger out with his left from his belt. The legs of the monster carried it quickly as it lifted one of its arms to strike. As the talon came down, Arminiul dodged to the right. Barely avoiding the blow, he quickly slashed at the monster's legs with his sword. The blade sliced deep into the front leg but only cut lightly into the back leg. The wounds did not bother the monster as it turned around and slashed at Arminiul again. With his dagger blade against his forearm, he blocked the talon, forcing it to the side as it went deep into the dirt.

"Owen!" Sepher yelled as he spotted the boy he had been searching for for many weeks. He quickly dismounted from the horse as it fought against him, trying to run away from the monster.

Owen looked at the elf that called his name. His eyes widened with surprise as he recognized the elf that had saved Tavia and him. "It's you," he said out of shock as Sepher ran to his side.

Sepher looked down at the girls and did not recognize them, but his heart filled with hope seeing Owen at least. "Run and hide," Sepher yelled at them in Elvish, not realizing they would not understand him. He then turned towards the monster and fired another arrow as it attacked Arminiul.

The arrow flew through the air and hit the monster in the side of the skull. The beast growled in pain and turned away from Arminiul. Quickly, Arminiul saw his chance and charged at the monster. He raised his sword in the air to swing down into the beast, but just as its enormous body turned, its tail followed like a whip. Smashing into Arminiul's legs and hip, tossing him into the air

Owen tried to pull Cathay more into the trees as the monster spun around and faced him. *If only I was strong like the bear.* Owen thought as he struggled to pull her with all his might, thinking about the bear he had watched outside of Keerike. Owen felt the brand on his chest tingle as his skin started to glow red. He let go of Cathay's hand in surprise. As the monster glared at him, Owen watched his arms and hands begin to change shape, shades of red swirling and going down his arms like waves. *The red orb from Orinton?* He thought as he grew larger and his back changed shape. He was not in pain but felt strange like he was surrounded by blankets or water. The monster continued to charge at him. Its eyes locked on Owen as he grew much bigger. The red faded, leaving his arms covered in thick fur and his hands with long claws on the ends. He looked to see Cathay and Pennelope watching as Owen himself turned into a large brown bear.

Sepher jumped between the monster and Owen, firing another arrow at the monster's face, aiming for the eye, but the arrow bounced off the hard frill again. As it charged Owen, its long talon lashed out at Sepher, slashing through his armor and into the flesh of his bicep as it knocked him out of the way.

Owen turned the moment before the monster lowered its head and rammed into his body. The impact knocked him to the ground. He quickly moved his legs to get up, but they did not work like he was used to, and they slid out from under him as the monster advanced. Its jaws were wide open, and it bit into the back of Owen's neck, shaking him by his furry scruff. Owen felt the pain of its many teeth serrating his skin. He moaned in pain as he struggled to move under the force of the monster, wanting to get up and fight back, but he found the new form hard to move correctly.

Sepher struggled to get up and saw the monster shaking the bear that was Owen. He quickly drew his sword and ran at the lizard-like monster. Sepher slashed his sword deep into the neck of the monster, causing it to let go of Owen and turn back towards him. Its yellow eyes looked straight at him while blood dripped from its jaw. Sepher took a step back, struggling with the pain in his arm. He waited for the monster to attack. Its head lowered, and its jaws opened like a snake before it struck. Sepher held his sword up to defend himself as the beast surged towards him. Quickly, he swung the sword, slashing at the monster's gaping mouth as it tried to take him. The blade sliced deep into the side of the monster's jaw, knocking its head sideways enough so that it did not bite him.

The monster recovered quickly and turned back towards Sepher. He tried to swing again. But the blade hit the thick-boned frill as its arm talon swung at him from the side. Its sharp point went straight into Sepher's ribs, breaking the bones and puncturing a lung. He fell to the ground, gasping for air as the monster raised its arm again to drive it into Sepher another time. Just as the arm was raised, Owen lunged back into the fray. His strong bear jaw grasped the monster's forearm, biting down with all its might. His sharp teeth penetrated the scaly skin and crushed the bone within. He swung his arm wide, his thick paw bashing into the left side of the monster's face as the claws slid down, cutting its skin while one sliced deep into its eye. The beast pulled away from Owen, its arm ripping apart in his tightened jaw as it screeched in pain. Owen spit out the arm, letting the forearm and talon fall to the ground, and then he lunged toward the monster again.

As Owen moved his back legs, he felt off balance and went sideways, missing the monster with his clawed paw. The monster reared back and bit at Owen, grabbing his shoulder and neck in its jaws. It began to shake its head, ripping Owen's skin and muscles. He cried in pain as his head flailed around, hitting the ground repeatedly. His eyes struggled to open, seeing Arminiul running towards the monster with his sword.

Arminiul jumped at the monster, sending his body weight through the tip of his sword as he drove it into the monster's right eye. He pushed the blade hard as he felt the monster's skull inside the eye socket, yelling as he felt the blade slide in deeper, through the bone, and into the brain.

The monster's body fell to the ground. Its jaws on Owen relaxed. Its labored breathing rapidly grew shallower and shallower as it died.

"Sepher!" Arminiul yelled as he spotted him lying on the ground, struggling to breathe, with blood coming out of his mouth. Arminiul quickly got to Sepher's side and pressed his hand against the large wound to try and keep it from bleeding. "You're going to be okay," Arminiul said in a panic as he looked at the puddle of blood he was now kneeling in. He hurried to take off Sepher's armor to try and get a better look at the wound while still keeping pressure on it.

"Arminiul," Sepher struggled to say as he turned his head towards Owen. They watched as the bear became a glowing red mass and then shrank back to Owen's normal body. The red glow dissipated in moments, leaving Owen exactly how he was before he changed, with no wounds. Yet the boy was sound asleep. "Arminiul…That is Owen," he said quietly in Elvish, coughing up some blood as he talked.

"Just be quiet, Sepher. Save your strength," Arminiul said in Elvish as he opened the side section of his armor to see the extent of the wound. Looking down at the large hole in his ribs, Arminiul grasped at Sepher's cloak and tried to hold it against the injury to slow the bleeding. Arminiul knew Sepher was dying, and there was nothing he could do about it, but he still tried.

"Protect him," Sepher whispered. "Swear you will protect him. Galadin wants him for a reason."

"I will," Arminiul answered as Sepher coughed up more blood while he held the bundle of cloth to his side.

"Swear it, Arminiul," Sepher slowly whispered as he looked him in the eyes. "Swear it so Hyllo can hear… and hope the gods forgive us for our actions."

"I swear it," Arminiul responded as he could feel tears forming as he watched his friend struggle.

Slowly, Sepher turned his head and looked at Owen. "He can turn into a bear," Sepher quietly said as he laughed and started coughing.

Arminiul smiled as he looked down at Sepher. "Yep, the kid can turn into a bear."

"He's special," Sepher whispered. "Protect…" Sepher trailed into silence.

Arminiul looked down at Sepher as his breathing stopped and blood slowed. He could not help but cry as he bent down, resting his forehead on Sepher's motionless chest, wishing it was him dying instead of his dear friend.

CHAPTER 21

The waves came up the shore at a calm, steady pace. Its waters cascaded over the sand, washing away the thousands of footprints from the funeral the night before. Ulrick sat on the beach closest to his house, about fifteen paces away. He watched as the dark sky began to turn blue. He slept horribly during the night, tossing and turning until he woke up much earlier than anyone else. He lay on his bed for some time as his mind would not quiet down, thinking of his future and what to do. Now, he sat with Huntress on the beach, the wolf being the only one who woke up as he walked out of the house. He did not mind Huntress sitting with him and even spoke to her a few times for her opinion. However, the wolf was not much for answering.

What Cortay said about his path calling his name and it being Cinda behind him made Ulrick question if he should leave. *Is this why Cortay told me about my future? Did she see what happens if I stay in Tolneer and challenge Trent to be Earl?* These questions and many more plagued his mind. "What do you think I should do, Huntress?" he asked the wolf pup. Her head turned to the side, looking at him as she lay beside him. Ulrick shook his head out of habit as if the answer would become clear.

A large splash sounded from down the shore. Ulrick saw a few orcs taking their boats off the racks and placing them in the water since the ice had thawed enough to go out. He sat and watched as the fishermen prepared to leave. It was a race among the many fishing boats. They knew the first one out would always have full nets of fish. *How simple their lives are. Not concerned about being a leader. Just living their life for themselves.* Ulrick thought as the crews pressed on, gathering their nets and other equipment into their boats.

Huntress's ears perked, and she quickly turned towards the house. She ran back with her tail wagging so fast her hips moved from side to side.

"Good morning, Huntress," Cinda said as she petted her on the cheeks.

Ulrick turned and saw Cinda. She wore thick pants and a shirt and carried a large fur blanket over her shoulders to keep her warm on the cold morning. "Good... morn, Cinda," Ulrick said in Terrish as she approached him.

"Good Morning... Why are you up so early?" Cinda asked Ulrick as she wiped the sleep from her eyes, sitting beside him. Huntress quickly attacked her to play, wanting to lick and nip her face. She promptly diverted the wolf into her arms, petting her vigorously to calm her down.

"Bad sleep," Ulrick replied as he looked back over the water, watching the fishermen again.

"Are you worried about fighting Trent?" Cinda asked in a sympathetic tone. Ulrick only nodded his head in response. "I'm scared too," Cinda said as she looked out at the fishermen.

Ulrick turned and faced Cinda, wanting to tell her what he had been thinking, but his Terrish was not good enough to explain, and her Orcish was far from good enough to understand. "Cinda want home?" he quietly asked after a minute of silence.

"Yes," Cinda responded kindly. "I want to go home."

Ulrick nodded again. "Home nice. Tolneer bad for

Cinda?" he asked kindly.

Cinda turned and smiled at Ulrick. "Tolneer is not bad, just different. Not a place for me, I think." Her eyes began to look worried. "Will you be taking me home still?" she asked, nervous about staying in Tolneer longer.

Ulrick nodded in agreement, looking away from Cinda as he did, not wanting to look her in the eyes as he lied about not knowing if he would be taking her home.

The light of the sun began to peak over the mountains. Its rays felt warm on Cinda's face as she closed her eyes and enjoyed the feeling. Ulrick watched the fishermen's boats floating by in the water. The boat crews yelled joking insults as they goaded each other onward. Ulrick then stood up and walked over to the fire pit outside, starting a fire to cook breakfast as Cinda began to play with Huntress.

"Are we training today?" Cinda asked Ulrick as he stoked the fire to get the coals hot enough to cook.

"No," Ulrick answered, his eyes never leaving the dancing flame, thinking if the path were to follow Cinda, then that meant he would follow her to Miterra and Orinton, places he knew orcs were seen as monsters.

The cold response from Ulrick made Cinda think she had done something wrong. Her mind thought Ulrick taking her home would be too hard to do when he becomes Earl, or even worse, dies. She slowly stepped away from Ulrick and walked into the house, seeing Lars waking up from his deep slumber.

"Good morning, Lars," Cinda said as she walked to her section of the one-room house, sitting on her pile of furs for a bed as Huntress came and laid down next to her.

"What's wrong?" Lars asked Cinda as he finished a giant, long yawn. His eyes still blinked rapidly from the bright light of the sun coming through a window.

"Will Ulrick become Earl?" Cinda asked quietly.

Lars moved his head from side to side as if debating with himself. "With all the houses that said they would back him last night, there is a strong chance."

Cinda looked through the window, seeing Ulrick standing by the fire outside. "Will he be a good Earl?"

"He will be good at being an Earl, but being an Earl will feel like a prison for him," Lars said with a hint of sorrow. "Ulrick is too free-spirited to be stuck taking care of Tolneer."

"Then why does he want to be Earl?" Cinda asked, confused.

"That's the thing. Ulrick doesn't want to be Earl," Lars said, and Cinda quickly turned towards him in shock at his words. "But, he doesn't want Thrane's death to be unavenged or his father's dream for Tolneer to be lost. If Thrane had died differently and Trent was a better orc, Ulrick would not have even considered becoming Earl. He would much rather take you home and continue on to the next adventure."

"But that makes no sense," Cinda pleaded.

"Orc and family honor," Lars said simply. "These two things are foundations that Ulrick was raised with. To turn away from them would be like Ulrick turning away from himself."

Cinda sat silently, thinking about how her grandfather was an honorable man who had his throat cut by dishonorable elves. How honor was nice to have but seemed to cost so much to the person that stuck to it. Her thoughts lasted a few moments until they were interrupted as Lars and Cinda both looked out the window, hearing some orcs yelling in Orcish outside. Lars quickly got up and grabbed his sword and axe.

"What's wrong?" Cinda asked in a fearful voice.

"Just stay here," Lars answered and then headed outside. Cinda quickly moved to the window.

Three orcs had come and were talking to Ulrick. Their tone made Cinda feel afraid as Lars walked over to join them. Ulrick turned to Lars with a stern face and nodded his head while Lars looked at him, his face growing sad as if the news he was hearing was not pleasant. As Lars returned to the house, Ulrick started talking to the other three orcs again.

"What is going on?" Cinda asked before Lars could even walk through the doorway.

"Trent knows about Ulrick gathering forces to oppose him," Lars said as he swiftly moved through the house, grabbing pieces of armor, weapons, and shields. "You need to put this armor on," Lars said as he handed Cinda a thick leather torso armor and some metal braces.

"Will we be fighting?" Cinda asked, worried as she looked down at the armor pieces in her hands.

"Hopefully, you won't be, but just to be safe," Lars answered as he got out the last weapons. "What weapons do you feel the most comfortable with?" Cinda stood still, her eyes still looking at the armor in her hands, not moving at all. "Cinda!" Lars yelled, seeing the young girl freeze from fear and hoping to snap her out of it. Cinda looked up at Lars after hearing him scream her name. Her face showed she was about to start crying. Lars quickly moved closer to her and placed his hands on her cheeks, looking into her eyes sternly. "You are Cinda Tand Rycker," Lars said sternly. "The little girl that pulled an orc warrior to the ground by his tooth." Cinda's eyes began scrunching up as tears fell from them, running down her cheeks. "It is okay to be afraid, but you must not freeze from fear. Run or fight, but never freeze," he said calmly.

"I can't do this," Cinda struggled to say. "I can't fight."

Ulrick slammed the door open, and his heavy feet stomped on the wooden floor as he walked through the room. His eyes glanced at Cinda and then at Lars. "I told you to get her ready for battle," he yelled at him in Orcish.

"Cinda is still a child," Lars yelled back.

Cinda shrank away from Ulrick, not knowing what was being said but knowing by the tone Ulrick was angry and on the verge of violence.

"She must be dressed for combat. Get the armor on her," Ulrick yelled as he grabbed his thick leather armor and began putting it on.

Lars looked at Cinda and took the armor from her hands. Then he slid the leather armor over her head so it rested on her shoulders. The armor was large for her, pieces that Lars once wore, so it did not form around her hips well and pressed hard against her breasts.

"Is Ulrick mad at me?" Cinda whispered to Lars as she stood still, letting Lars connect the side straps below her arms.

"Ulrick is frightened and trying to move fast," Lars answered quietly. "When he gets stressed like this, he lashes out at people around him." As he finished clamping Cinda's armor, Ulrick walked towards her.

"Cinda, best fight," Ulrick said sternly as he picked up a human longsword and shield, handing them to Lars quickly before picking up two axes and putting them in his belt.

"I guess Ulrick thinks you should use these," Lars said

to Cinda as he wrapped the sword belt around her waist and handed her the large wooden shield. The weight was heavy in her hand, yet she had grown stronger over the weeks of training, and the shield was not as heavy as the training shield she used. "Just stay in the back, and if things go wrong, run to Cortay," Lars whispered as he picked up his leather armor and put it on, quickly securing the latches on the sides. He then put on his weapon belt with a hatchet, two daggers, and his elven longsword.

A loud horn was heard throughout Tolneer. The deep sound reverberated off the mountains and hills, making it sound like the horn was all around. The long single note of it lasted for a few moments. Lars looked at Ulrick, his lips pressed together in an unhappy scowl. "So, Trent is issuing the challenge," he said to Ulrick in Orcish. The horn was rarely used except for when a fight was to be witnessed by many.

"Then we best not keep him waiting," Ulrick responded in Orcish. He walked out the door to the house, gripping his shield and Orcish longsword. Lars and Cinda walked a distance behind him, with Huntress being held by a leash just in case Cinda needed to run away in an instant.

Ulrick walked purposefully as he headed to the large section of beach where many were already gathering. He could see the new personal guard, two holding banners displaying Thrane's colors. The sight infuriated him, seeing those who killed his brother now raising their banners.

As the three approached the mass of people, Lars pointed to a stack of large wooden boxes. "I want you and Huntress to go and stand on those crates. From there, you can watch, and it should not be hard for you to run away if things go badly," he told Cinda.

"How will I know to run away?" Cinda asked, confused and not sure entirely what was going on.

"If Ulrick dies and they attack those that support him, then you run," Lars said with haste as he started to outpace Cinda.

Ulrick walked through the crowd as they parted for his and Lars's approach until they reached the center. They formed a large circle for the fight, ensuring they were not in the way. As Ulrick walked into the large circle, he spotted Trent, standing with pride, looking Ulrick in the eyes with a stoic face. But his shaking hands revealed his fear.

Beside Trent was his mother, Vools. Her eyes judged Ulrick as he walked before them. Her eyebrows scrunched together, and her lip slightly flared from anger. She was also wearing armor and carried her sword on her hip, looking like she was prepared to fight Ulrick herself in place of Trent.

Trent separated from the group behind him, his hands fidgeting as he walked steadily to Ulrick, a look of concern on his face. He then stopped a few steps from Ulrick. "Are you really planning to challenge me to be Earl, Uncle Ulrick?" Trent quietly asked.

Ulrick looked at Trent with a confused face. "You are the one that blew the horn," he said.

Trent pressed his lips together. A hesitant look flashed across his face, and he momentarily glanced back at his mother. "But were you planning to challenge me?" he asked nervously.

"I had not decided yet," Ulrick answered truthfully.

"But I'm your nephew," Trent said. "Do you not think I am worthy to be Earl?"

"A challenge has been issued," a loud voice interrupted.

Everyone turned to see Beotolt standing near Vools, his hands resting on the handle of his sizeable two-handed axe with the head in the sand at his feet. "Let us see your worth to oppose Earl Trent."

Trent then returned to his mother to gather his sword and shield. His head hung low as he walked while Ulrick looked at Beotolt and Vools, neither seeming upset by the situation. Trent stopped and whispered into Vools' ear, her expression becoming angrier.

Vools then took a step forward while Trent turned around to face Ulrick. "Ulrick Ironhide," she said in a commanding voice. "My son Trent, son of Thrane and your nephew, will grant you this one chance to save your life." She slowly looked over the crowd that was gathered. "Drop your weapons, kneel, and swear fealty to your Earl."

Ulrick's hand gripped the handle of his sword harder, his knuckles turning lighter from the strain. He looked at Trent, unsure of what to do. Trent did not seem like someone who wanted to fight Ulrick, even appearing confused by the situation. Ulrick looked at the ground before him as he thought in his head. *If Trent had nothing to do with the poisoning, then it must have been someone else, someone to gain from the death of Thrane.* Ulrick looked up at Vools and Beotolt, seeing the look of confidence on both faces as they stood next to each other. *Could I be wrong about Beotolt? Would he use poison? Or has it been Vools who has been orchestrating this?* Ulrick then looked around at the people around them. Many had weapons, and the crowd almost seemed split between those supporting Ulrick and Trent. He then spotted Cinda sitting on the wooden crates a short distance away.

Ulrick thought about Cinda as he looked at her. Thinking

about what had happened to her in Orinton, how she was laying on the river bank just as his boat came, how weak and helpless she was then compared to now, dressed as a warrior, watching him, watching him with her eyes that were so similar to Tallus'. "She shows me my path," Ulrick mumbled, thinking all of it added to this moment.

"What was that, Ulrick?" Vools asked sharply, seeing him mumble but not hearing what he said. "Will you swear fealty to Trent, Earl of Tolneer?" she questioned angrily.

Ulrick turned to Trent, seeing his face. The look of his brother was strong with him, the same nose and eyes, how he stood and walked. Ulrick then remembered the times he spent with Trent as a child, teaching him how to throw an axe and catch a chicken with his bare hands. These fond memories surfaced in Ulrick's mind as he looked at the son of his own brother. Slowly, the grip on his sword loosened as he finally made his decision. "No," he yelled clearly. "I will not swear fealty to Trent." Vools and Trent looked in shock at hearing his answer. Ulrick then slid his sword back into its sheath. "But I will also not fight my nephew."

Trent took a breath of relief hearing Ulrick say he did not want to fight. Vools, however, took another step towards Ulrick and began to speak. "You will not swear fealty to your Earl?" She asked, her words filled with spite. She then turned to Trent and spoke quietly as Ulrick stood where he was. His eyes shifted towards Beotolt, who looked at him with an arrogant expression.

Trent stepped forward, looking conflicted. "Ulrick Ironhide," he said in a commanding voice so most in the crowd could hear. "For denying the challenge of an Earl," he looked at Ulrick with a sad expression. "I banish you from Tolneer and its allied territories." Ulrick felt his heart sink as Trent, his own nephew, spoke the words, though he knew they were not his alone since Vools stood behind him, smiling as if she had won. "You are my uncle, however, so I will grant you time to gather your things and find a ship to carry you away from here," Trent said while Vools looked at him with shock.

Ulrick bowed his head respectfully and turned from Trent and the others. He walked through the silent crowd that parted for him again. Hearing other orcs, particularly those there to support him, whispering or quietly calling him a traitor, coward, and much worse insults to his honor. The words cut deep into Ulrick as he walked in shame, turning his head away from his family and his people, hoping, in his heart, he was doing the right thing.

"Why didn't you fight him?" Lars asked as he ran behind Ulrick as they neared the crowd's edge.

"I can't hurt my nephew," Ulrick quietly said with regret as he walked. The idea of challenging Trent weighed heavily on him, but he knew he could not face him in combat once he saw Trent's face.

"You couldn't have figured that out before you made it seem like you would try?" Lars said in a slightly joking manner.

Ulrick turned quickly to Lars after the comment, looking at him earnestly, letting him know that it was not something to joke about. "Cortay told me about my future," he mumbled quietly.

Lars looked at him in shock, knowing Cortay and Ulrick had an agreement about never sharing such information. "What did she say?" he asked in confused anticipation.

"She said for me to pick a path," Ulrick said. He then turned to Cinda, a distance away, who was walking quickly with Huntress to meet up with them. "A path that is led by Cinda, I think."

"Taking her home?" Lars asked.

Ulrick shook his head slightly, "I think I am supposed to watch over her or protect her. I am not sure. Just that she is the path Cortay told me to take."

"Just because Cortay told you to, you are willing to throw everything you have here away?" Lars asked with confusion and dread while they walked.

"Cortay seemed different when she told me. Like she was worried about something she could not say," Ulrick said as he turned and looked at the ground, deep in thought. Ulrick then let out a long breath and whispered to himself. "I hope I am doing the right thing."

"You would have hated being Earl anyway," Lars said with a smile.

Ulrick looked at Lars. "I can't ask you to come. You can stay here in Tolneer if you would like."

"You, in Miterra without me?" Lars said, looking up at Ulrick. "You'd end up scaring a village so much they would chase you down with torches and any weapons they could find," Lars remarked, laughing as he spoke.

"What happened?" Cinda asked in Terrish as she finally got close enough to Ulrick and Lars to whisper since many people still watched Ulrick.

"We are taking you home. That is what happened," Lars answered.

Cinda looked at them, confused. "What about Ulrick challenging Trent to be Earl?" she asked.

"Right now, let's just focus on getting out of here," Lars answered. He then looked at Ulrick. "You find us a boat, and we will get the important things."

Ulrick nodded in agreement, trusting Lars to grab the few things from his house that mattered to him since he was not very sentimental about possessions.

Lars then spotted some of Trent and Beotolt's men watching them. "We should probably hurry," he said, waving Cinda to follow him.

Cinda saw the urgency in Lars and Ulrick's movements as they walked. Even though she did not understand everything that was said between Ulrick, Trent, and Vools, she was unsure what had transpired with the challenge. "What really happened, Lars?" she asked as they approached the house.

"Ulrick was banished from Tolneer, never to return," he said sadly. "We only have a little bit of time to gather our things and leave."

Cinda stopped walking and looked at Lars. "What will you two do now?"

"Guess we will take you home and see where it goes from there," Lars answered with a fake smile as he kept walking, trying to hide how upset he was that they were leaving Tolneer in such a way. He then turned and realized Cinda was a distance behind him. "We need to hurry, though."

* * *

Ulrick opened the door to his home, finding Lars still rummaging around for the last half hour, making sure they were not leaving anything behind that mattered. Cinda sat on her pile of furs that made her bed, holding what was left of the arrow Ulrick had pulled from her leg when they found her. Slowly, she moved it around in her hand, looking at it intently. Her eyes wandered to the braided leather bracelet on her wrist that matched Lars' and Ulrick's. *This is all I have, and now we have to leave here. To go back home, to my home, not theirs. They will have only what they bring from here; their lives are being taken.* Her eyes fixed on the steel arrowhead. *This arrow took me from my home; those elves attacked us, and I was left for dead.* Cinda's hand began to fiddle with the beads woven into her bracelet. *They rescued me, Ulrick, and Lars. Accepted me into their home and treated me well. Now, they are forced to leave their home. Was it all my fault? Am I the reason they have to go?*

"Cinda?" Ulrick said to get her attention. As Cinda looked up at him, she smiled. "Have thing... for... home?"

Cinda's eyes looked around the single-roomed house, seeing the numerous, random things Ulrick and Lars had collected from all their adventures, from weapons to small wooden statues, anything the two of them could carry to remind themselves of where they had been. Yet Lars was not packing most of it. She looked back at Ulrick with sorrowful eyes. "Are you two never coming back?"

Ulrick and Lars both stopped what they were doing and looked at Cinda. Then Ulrick's gaze shifted. His mind was wandering about what he was leaving behind. The history of who he was and what he had seen in the world was in that house. His life was in Tolneer.

"We won't be returning, Cinda," Lars answered.

Cinda quickly stood up and looked at all the training equipment that seemed to be pushed to the side to be left. "Are you not bringing the practice weapons?" she asked.

"Cinda want teach fight?" Ulrick asked as he looked at her. "Cinda home safe."

"I still want to learn to fight," Cinda stated as she looked at Ulrick enthusiastically. "Can we fit them, or will it be too much?"

"Boat big, it fit,"

"You already have a boat waiting for us?" Cinda asked in surprise, seeing that only a few boats had been taken down from the racks and put in the water earlier.

"Grith have boat, leave soon," Ulrick said. He then turned and started to pack things.

"I'll be right back. I need to go get something," Cinda said in a hurry as she ran to the door, carrying the elven arrow and one of the hide blankets from her bed with Huntress following.

"Where are you going?" Lars yelled after Cinda, but she was outside before he could catch her. He quickly moved to the door to stop her, but as he looked, he did not see her anywhere. "Where do you think she ran off to?" he asked Ulrick.

"I don't know. Let's finish packing everything. Hopefully, she will be back shortly," Ulrick responded.

"You don't think she is going to talk to Trent about your banishment, do you?" Lars said as he looked out the door, worrying about Cinda's safety.

"If she did, Trent would not harm her and escort her back," Ulrick said as he walked over and grabbed the training swords to start packing them up.

"And if Beotolt sees her first?" Lars asked as he looked at Ulrick with his right eyebrow raised.

Ulrick looked at Lars's things and saw that he was already packed to leave. "Go find her. I'll finish packing and meet you at Grith's boat at midday." Lars nodded in agreement and ran out the door, leaving Ulrick alone as he continued to pack the training equipment for Cinda.

* * *

Ulrick's hand cart weighed so much that the wooden wheels dug deep into the gravelly sand as he pulled it along the beach. Each stride resisted the movement as he pressed on. Many had gathered to watch Ulrick make his way to Grith's boat, wishing him good fortune and telling him he would be missed. Ulrick's eyes were busy looking for Lars and Cinda as they spoke, hoping to glimpse them while the sun rested in the middle of the sky, telling him it was midday.

"I couldn't find her," Lars said, out of breath as he passed through a group of orcs coming into Ulrick's view.

"What do you mean you couldn't find her? You have had two hours to find her!" Ulrick said in a panic. *How is she to be my path if she runs off like she did. All of this will be for nothing if we can't find her.*

"I ran all around Tolneer checking the places she knew, but no one had seen her," Lars explained as he also started to look around. His view was hindered since he was shorter than the orcs around him. "Do you think Beotolt found her?"

Ulrick looked past the orcs around him. "Beotolt and Trent are right there," he said, pointing his chin toward them. "We must get these things on Grith's boat and then look for her." Ulrick then noticed that Beotolt was not even looking in his direction but seemed to be looking at other places among the crowd and spotted a few of Beotolt's men wandering around as if searching for someone. *He knows Cinda is not with us. They must be looking for her.* He thought as his heart began to beat harder in a panic, thinking about what Beotolt would do if he got ahold of Cinda. He began to pull the cart faster through the sand, determined in each step as he waded through the crowd to the dock. He wanted to say goodbye to everyone properly but could not, knowing he had to act quickly while Lars pushed the cart behind him.

"I was about to ship off without you," Grith, a short human wearing leather armor and a sword, yelled to Ulrick as he finally reached the dock. Grith stood with three of his human crew, all dressed as if they expected a fight, yet almost afraid to stand there.

"We need to go back for Cinda," Ulrick told Grith as he wheeled the hand cart onto the wooden dock. Grith's crew quickly took over and pulled it to the boat to load it, leaving Lars and him standing with Grith.

"We don't have time for that," Grith said, looking Ulrick in the eyes. His face looked paler than usual and full of fear. "We need to leave."

Ulrick looked at Grith questionably, not understanding the rush to depart or why they were all armed. "What happened?"

"Beotolt is what happened," Grith said sternly.

Huntress then lept onto the dock, her tail wagging in excitement as she looked up at Lars.

"Huntress?" Lars said as he bent over and petted the young wolf. "What are you doing here?" Lars and Ulrick then scanned the crowd that was on the beach to see Ulrick and him off. They did not see Cinda among them.

"We have to leave. I fear for my crew's safety," Grith said to Ulrick as Beotolt's men formed a circle in the crowd, all with grips on their weapons. "Ever since you left, his men have been closely monitoring my ship and crew, even roughed up one of my men a little while ago."

"Cinda won't be able to get past them," Lars said as he looked at Beotolt's men. "What should we do, Ulrick?" Lars' hand slowly gripped the elven sword handle on his belt, anticipating Ulrick giving the order to fight.

Ulrick looked over the crowd, seeing those who wished to harm him only a short distance from the dock steps but were hindered by the masses. He glanced back at the boat, seeing the crew signal they were all packed and removing the moorings.

"You forgot this," a voice pierced through the crowd. Lars and Ulrick quickly turned to see Palton smiling at them as he lifted something heavy covered in a large brown bear hide. Huntress ran to the hide and started sniffing, then quickly pulled it open, revealing Cinda curled up inside. She looked up at Lars and Ulrick with a smile.

"About damn time," Lars yelled as he reached down and pulled Cinda to her feet by the hand. Her other arm wrapped around something long and wrapped in a hide blanket. "What happened?" Lars asked in alarm at the sight of her blood smeared on the fur and shirt

As Cinda opened her mouth to explain, Ulrick interrupted her by leaning between Lars and her. "Get on the boat now," he yelled at them in Orcish as he watched Beotolt's men advance through the crowd when they saw Cinda.

Lars quickly began pulling Cinda down the dock with Huntress at her feet. Cinda looked back, seeing Palton's smiling face behind Ulrick as they hurriedly walked. She waved goodbye to him, wanting to thank him more for sneaking her past everyone, but hoped the wave and smile were enough.

The three of them and Huntress boarded the boat. Beotolt's men climbed onto the dock but stopped where they were, knowing they would not get to them in time since Grith quickly ordered his crew to push off while Ulrick climbed in.

Ulrick turned and looked at Tolneer while the boat drifted farther from the dock. Seeing the only place he had ever called home for the last time, he felt sad. Lars looked down at Cinda as she knelt, petting Huntress.

"So what was so important that you almost got left behind?" Lars asked. He took Cinda's hand and inspected the shallow cut on her palm. The wound looked like it would heal fine once she got it bandaged.

"I..." Cinda began to speak but hesitated, unsure if what she did was okay. Slowly, she handed the wrapped hide to Lars. "I had to go get it for Ulrick," she quietly said.

Ulrick turned and watched Lars begin unwrapping the hide blanket Cinda had taken with her from their house. He slowly lifted the last roll, and the handle of Tallus's sword came into view. Ulrick and Lars looked down at the sword, neither saying a word.

"I just couldn't leave it," Cinda pleaded, growing more anxious each moment they were silent. "With Ulrick leaving, there would be no one to take care of it," she explained, panic growing in her tone with every word.

Ulrick slowly took the sword by the handle, his face full of sorrow as he pulled the blade from the blanket in Lars's hands. He looked the sword up and down, inspecting it. Noticing the blood on the edge near the hilt.

"I cut myself trying to pull it out," Cinda explained, holding up her right hand with a cut palm. "I'm sorry," Cinda muttered as she turned away from Ulrick, thinking she might have offended Ulrick and violated his fallen wife's grave.

Ulrick stepped towards Cinda. The sound of his heavy steps growing closer made Cinda freeze, fearing what would happen next. Then, after a few moments of silence, she looked up and faced Ulrick, seeing him holding the sword handle towards her.

"Cinda have sword," Urlick said in Terrish as he looked at her with pride.

"But that is your wife's sword," Cinda said as she looked back at Ulrick in confusion.

Ulrick turned towards Lars and started talking to him in Orcish. Cinda stood and listened, only picking up on the words "sword", her name, and "Tallus." After Ulrick spoke, Lars then turned towards Cinda.

"Ulrick asks that you take the sword. He thinks Tallus would have wanted you to have it instead of it rusting away on the ridge of a cliff," Lars said with a smile.

"Doesn't Ulrick want to keep it?"

"He thinks it would be better served in your hands," Lars said as he raised his shoulders. He then started to laugh as he spoke. "Besides, you are the one that pulled it, so now Tallus will be haunting you and not him."

Cinda slightly shook her head at Lars' remark and looked Ulrick in the eyes. "Thank you," she said with genuine kindness as she reached up and gripped the sword handle. She lifted the sword from Ulrick. It was far lighter than the training swords she was used to. She looked at the blade. How the Allurian steel reflected the sun's light, the sun in the southern sky, the direction of home.

THE END

PRONUNCIATION

Aerlene (air-lean)

Admus (add-mus)

Agmit (ag-mit)

Allure (a-lure)

Allurian (a-lure-ian)

Arminiul (are-min-ee-ul)

Balthis (bal-this)

Beotolt (bay-oh-toll-t)

Blastin (blast-in)

Chalin (cha-lin)

Cinda (sin-da)

Cortay (core-tay)

Dernum (der-numb)

Dewart (de-wart)

Eldis (el-dis)

Eldron (el-der-on)

Ellious (el-ee-oh-s)

Esterra (es-tare-a)

Faylend (fay-lend)

Feirdren (fear-der-en)

Fernil (fur-nill)

Forus (for-us)

Galadin (gala-din)

Glathbern (gla-th-burn)

Grith (gr-ith)

Grumlish (gr-um-lish)

Gromneer (grom-near)

Gustoll (gus-toll)

Gwenil (gwen-ill)

Helflin (hell-flin)

Hendric (hen-dri-k)

Herif (hair-if)

Herrah (hair-a)

Hyllo (hi-low)

Kalrin (call-rin)

Keerike (k-ear-rike)

Kelterra (kel-tare-a)

Kenet (ke-net)

Kilven Lustil (kill-ven lust-ill)

Lars (l-are-s)

Maltius (mal-tea-us)

Miterra (meh-tare-a)

Orinton (or-in-ton)

Owen (owe-in)

Perclin (perk-lin)

Ramous (ray-mows)

Revnar Formil (rev-nar for-mil)

Romagus (rome-a-gus)

Rustal (rust-all)

Sindel (sin-dell)

Stanlin (stan-lin)

Talizeem (tal-eh-zeem)

Tallus (tal-us)

Tand Ryker (tan-d rike-er)

Tavia (tay-vee-a)

Terrasin (tare-a-sin)

Thalson (th-al-son)

Theris (there-is)

Thrane (th-rain)

Tresil (tre-sil)

Ulrick (ool-rick)

Vallous (vall-us)

Veraslen (ver-a-slen)

Vistem (vi-stem)

Vools (voo-ls)

Warrel (war el)

Willhelm (will-helm)

ABOUT THE AUTHOR

Lance Robert Kreutzinger's eyes were opened to the world of fantasy at a young age by his eldest brother, who introduced him to the game Dungeons & Dragons, where his love for fantasy only grew. From there, he learned tales of the heroes of Ancient Greece, loving the battle between Achilles and Hector in The Iliad. His entire family were also fans of JRR Tolkien and Star Wars, with his father often quoting lines from The Hobbit and his two older brothers quoting Star Wars, making such stories a norm in his household. When Lance was still a small child, his life changed when the author Jeffery Deaver stayed at his home for a few days, making him want to be a writer from that point on. From there, he wrote a plethora of stories, most for the fantasy game Dungeons & Dragons, which he played with many friends and still plays. Not until Lance found himself with a family and a stable career could he finally fulfill his dream of becoming a published author and sharing his stories with the world.

ABOOKS

ALIVE Book Publishing and ALIVE Publishing Group
are imprints of Advanced Publishing LLC,
3200 A Danville Blvd., Suite 204, Alamo, California 94507

Telephone: 925.837.7303
alivebookpublishing.com

www.ingramcontent.com/pod-product-compliance
Lightning Source LLC
Chambersburg PA
CBHW021952050726
47495CB00023B/1590